JOURNEY THROUGH THE WILDERNESS

Also by the Author

The Pleasure of your Death (Constable)

The Last of Days (The Bodley Head)

Children of the Rainbow (Saqi Books)

MORIS FARHI

JOURNEY
THROUGH THE WILDERNESS

Saqi Books

British Library Cataloguing-in-Publication Data
A catalogue record for this book is available from the
British Library

ISBN 0 86356 372 4 (pb)

First published by Macmillan, 1989
This edition published 2002

Saqi Books
26 Westbourne Grove
London W2 5RH
www.saqibooks.com

For NINA
who shared the journey

Acknowledgements

To my father, Hayim Daniel Farhi, whose ever-loving spirit remains my guide – my homage.

To: Palomba Farhi; Ceki and Viviane Farhi; Daniele and Eric Gould; Helen and Philip Gould; Jennifer Kavanagh; Anthony Masters; Paul Preston; Nicholas Rankin; Maureen Rissik; Bernice Rubens; Anthony Rudolf; Rachel Sievers; John Swanson; Edward Whittemore; Jeanne Williams – my gratitude for their unflinching support.

To: Patricia Alien; Fanny Blake; Nigel Glendinning; Philippa Harrison; Kate Jones; Victoria Pryor – my gratitude for their help, criticisms and suggestions.

To: Selim Baruh; lan, Anthea and Clemency Davidson; James and Midge Cartwright; Bensiyon and Denise Eskenazi; Nadia Friedman; Jessica Gould; Leah Gould; Julian Lewis; Roy Harley Lewis; Ziv Lewis; Cassandra Marks; Asher Mayer; Richard and Ceinwen Morgan; Gabriele Preston; Hazel Robinson; Elizabeth Rosen; Brenda Rudolf; Bonnie and Mort Sinelnikoff; Irene and Norman Way – my gratitude for their friendship and solidarity.

To the children: Grace and Hannah Davidson; Deborah and Yael Farhi; Emmanuel, Nathaniel, Rebecca and Sarah Gould; Joshua and Samuel Gould; James Preston; and my god-daughter, Rosa – my gratitude for their inspiration.

Foreword

My reason for setting this novel in an unnamed country in South America is quite simple. This work is a protest against the injustices that have become common practice in that continent: injustices that, particularly with regard to the indigenous people, have been known to escalate to ethnocide. Much has been written on the gradual extinction of the Amazonian Indians, less on their Andean brothers, the descendants of the Incas. This novel concerns the latter. Had I placed the novel, say, in Peru, I would have exculpated, by omission, the other countries where the peoples of the highlands have been equally persecuted, i.e. Chile, Colombia, Bolivia, Ecuador and Argentina. An unnamed country embraces them all.

Even so, those readers familiar with South America will not fail to spot the use I have made of some real locations. They will notice that La Merced, the capital of my unnamed country, is a blend of Santiago, La Paz, Lima, Bogotá and Quito, that Monte Rico is Potosi, that Huaca is Machu Picchu, etc.

BOOK ONE

PROLOGUE

He who returns never left

Once there lived a man. His name was Manku Yupanqui, meaning 'rich in all virtues'. It was a fitting name. For Manku Yupanqui devoted his life to finding that ray of the sun which God had misplaced whilst creating the night.

He travelled far and wide. He crossed rivers and oceans, deserts and plains. He climbed to the roofs of the world and he burrowed into its bowels.

When he was forty times forty years old, he came upon a mountain in the Andes.

The snow-garlanded crater of this mountain shed a light that nourished more than mother's milk, exalted more than coupling, repaired the soul more than wisdom.

Manku Yupanqui climbed to the summit and went down into the crater to pluck the light.

At that moment, three giant Judges, each armed with an immense sword, erupted from the stones. 'What are you doing here?' they asked.

'I have come to claim the sun's missing ray,' replied Manku Yupanqui.

The Judges moaned. The oldest stroked Manku Yupanqui's hair. 'Be wise, my son. Go back. The ray cannot be taken by man. Not until he can be ruled by it.'

'He will be ruled by it now,' replied Manku Yupanqui.

The Judges chafed. The youngest held Manku Yupanqui's hand. 'Brave heart, only one person can reclaim the light. He is awaited. But he is not yet born.'

'I am he,' retorted Manku Yupanqui.

The Judges lamented. The middle-aged Judge, much wiser for being halfway through his life, put his arm around Manku Yupanqui's shoulders. 'You are a hero. But that does not mean you will be a saviour. If you try to take the light, you will die.'

'Death is a lie,' declared Manku Yupanqui, and strode towards the ray.

The three Judges, expanding to even greater bulk, blocked his path. 'Know this then. To claim the light you have to answer our questions. If you fail, your questioner will cut off your head.'

Manku Yupanqui smiled. 'I am good at answering questions. Proceed.'

'What is love?' asked the youngest Judge.

'That which is contained in the missing ray,' answered Manku Yupangui without hesitation.

'Correct,' shouted the young Judge, and lowered his upraised sword.

'What is hate?' asked the middle-aged Judge.

'That which will be healed by the missing ray,' replied Manku Yupanqui, again without hesitation.

'Bravo!' shouted the middle-aged Judge, and he, too, lowered his upraised sword.

The oldest Judge spoke in agitation. 'My question is the most difficult. Spare me asking it. Go – with your head on your shoulders.'

'Ask!' thundered Manku Yupanqui.

The oldest Judge steadied his sword mournfully. 'What is fear?'

Manku Yupanqui was perplexed. 'I need to think about that,' he said.

And he meditated for forty years. The Judges waited patiently, served him food and refreshment.

In the forty-first year, Manku Yupanqui sadly declared, 'I have to guess. Fear is a blindfold.'

'Wrong!' wailed the oldest Judge, and swung his sword.

'Before you cut off my head,' shouted Manku Yupanqui, 'tell me what fear is. That is the one thing I have never known.'

The young and middle-aged Judges ran to the other Judge. 'That's the answer! Don't strike. He is the awaited one!'

But the third Judge, being very old, could not act speedily and failed to pull away his sword. He severed Manku Yupanqui's head from its body.

The date of that event, the sages say, was that day when man turned towards the Fallen Angel.

But the winds carry rumours.

One declares that the people do not believe in Manku Yupanqui's death, for the condors, sent to scour the Andean peaks, have failed to spot his clay.

Another asserts that the three Judges are carrying Manku Yupanqui's remains from one village to another in the hope that a healer can render him whole again.

A third – the most recent – proclaims that Manku Yupanqui has miraculously grown another head, and that he has been seen by those whose *eyes can see.*

PART ONE

1
There are wings which cut the silence

Daniel Brac caressed the girl's cheek.

She held on to his hand. She was fascinated by his hands, particularly by their colour: purple-bronze, like the high altitude complexion of the Indians, her own complexion – but, splashed on to his fair skin, odd. When he had told her he bathed them in rainbows, she had almost believed him. What she could not conceive was that he was a painter, or rather, that he did nothing else but paint, and that after so many years immersed in pigments, his hands had evolved their own sheen and odour. *Naturales* painted, too, but they also worked the land, herded llamas; they had the tint of the elements and smelled of earth and animals. How could he, when he had such strong hands, such a powerful body, give life to life without touching life? He had not told her he was not, strictly speaking, a painter, but a restorer.

'We sex more! I like you very much. You my Manku.'

He ran his tongue over her nipples. She had liked him readily, and had proved it by undressing completely. Moreover, wanting him to like her also, she had washed in front of him to show him she was as clean as the whitest *misti*. Pretending he was like Manku Yupanqui had come later, after she had discovered that he was a gentle lover – a consideration she had ceased to expect.

Her amiability gratified him. Women put breath into him – more so now, as he accelerated towards his fifties. Women made him an artist, original. Each new world he created with them provided a glimpse of wholeness.

Tica stretched out, opened her legs. 'Come, my Manku.'

Daniel kissed her navel. 'I must go.'

Conditioned to obey, she jumped out of the bed, rushed into the bathroom, came back with a bucket of water and began to wash him.

He stroked her back, proud of having given her some tenderness. Pillpe, who had procured her, had told him her story. She had been sold into service – an Inca custom that still persisted among destitute campesinos. A Creole lawyer, Miguel, had bought her – not as a slave, but to save her family from starvation. Miguel had been an *indigenista*, one of those few *mistis* trying to alleviate the plight of the *naturales*. Two years earlier, when the local landowner, expanding his hacienda, had seized some communal land, Miguel had started proceedings on behalf of the campesinos. The landowner had appealed to friends in the government. Troops had been sent. Within days, scores of people had disappeared, Miguel among them. Thereafter, prostitution had been Tica's only means of survival.

She dried him slowly, her fingers admiring his powerful shoulders, arms and thighs, his massive chest and muscular stomach; then, nodding approval at his penis which was still alert, she gave it a military salute. I light candles you remember me.'

He caressed her neck. 'I'll remember you.'

He put on his jeans and sweater and watched her sort out meticulously her patched underwear, blouse and the several skirts the Andean women wore, one on top of the other. Then, as she dressed, he moved to the window and gazed at Pintoyaku.

The mountains appeared to have moved closer, and now held the colourful town as if it were a palette and they the gnarled talons of a frenzied bird-god forever repainting a primal landscape. The clouds were rolling down the peaks, devouring rocks, overhangs, ravines and the spumed streams of snow-water. The sleet and the wind danced wildly as if celebrating their first resurrection. It was easy to understand why the Incas had worshipped the sun and built altars to keep it tied down. On a day like this, it seemed natural to fear the sun might die or fall prisoner to other deities and never light the skies or warm the earth again.

There was still no sign of the trucks. Except for campesinos materialising from the terraced fields, the roads winding up from the valleys stood empty. The low clouds would slow the trucks even more – assuming that they were coming and that they would be able to negotiate corniches barely wider than snakepaths. There would be no buses for days; the first wave of pilgrims had hired them all.

Tica had dressed. He pressed some money into her hands and opened the door. Delighted with the large tip, she ran out, waving. 'Adios, Manku.'

He picked up his rucksack and left the room.

The boy, Pillpe, was waiting in the foyer. Beaming his cherubic smile, he waved a carton of Dunhills at Daniel. 'English cigarrillos!'

'Where did you find them?'

'From a smuggler. Five thousand *reales*.'

Daniel paid him. 'You're a miracle-worker.'

Pillpe pointed in the direction of the mountain pool which had given Pintoyaku its name – 'mottled water'. 'We collect more lichens! Plenty time before trucks arrive.'

Daniel tapped his rucksack. 'I've got enough.'

Pillpe, disappointed, kicked an imaginary ball. He was a man of nine, but, occasionally, still a child.

Daniel ruffled the boy's hair. 'Wouldn't have missed it for anything, though.'

That was true. The last week had been idyllic. Days of immersion in the wilderness, of riding that mixture of tension and tranquillity that primed him for lengthy labour. And days of playing at fatherhood with Pillpe.

To think he might never have come to Pintoyaku.

He had started work, five weeks before, the day after his arrival from England, with his usual ritual: shutting himself in with the painting – actually, four separate paintings stitched on to a vast canvas as a polyptych – in order to commune with its creator. After looking at it endlessly for two weeks, he had become possessed by it, succumbing to the intimation that, though each composition interpreted a conventional theme, the ensemble disclosed a hidden destination where God would be unveiled.

Such a whimsical reaction, he had thought at first, was understandable. The polyptych was an incomparable masterpiece. Discovered in the Indian countryside, it had instantly found its rightful status, despite Creole prejudice, as the country's greatest national treasure. No prominent restorer would have been immune to its power. Moreover, the painting was the sole work of an unknown artist. Though the restoration of such a rarity was a challenge most professionals dreamed about, the task itself was purgatory: in the absence of another work which could serve as a guide for colour, style and conception, even the simplest retouch became a matter of intuition.

But the intimation of a mystical dimension had persisted. Eventually, he had realised that it was emanating from the polyptych's predominant colour: a blue he had never seen and which, despite microscopical and chemical analysis, he could not identify with any known pigment or compound. A divine hue imparted to the painter by revelation.

So he had set out in search of it. At the very least, he had thought, he would enter into the spirit of the work by getting the feel of the land and its people.

It had been an inspired move. Gradually making his way to the highlands and thus acclimatising himself to the altitude, he had ingested the majesty of the subtropical valleys and the colossal, serrated ranges of the Andes. He had been dazzled by the incredible array of geological features and their ecology. He had marvelled at the astonishing civilisation of the Incas which dominated the landscape with roads, aqueducts and buildings that, in many instances, were still in use. Finally, having paid the obligatory visit to Huaca, the Incas' mysterious holy city in the Sacred Valley, he had reached Pintoyaku where, in an abandoned Franciscan mission, the polyptych had been found.

And, after an extensive search of the countryside with Pillpe, he had finally located a number of thallophytic plants, one of which, an uncommon moss, had yielded that unearthly blue. He would never forget how Pillpe and he had celebrated the discovery by flinging the treated moss at each other in childlike delight, then dancing round the hotel room like pagans at a rite.

'What you want do now, *amarillo*?'

Daniel had given up objecting to the 'amarillo'. In Spanish idiom 'yellow' had the same connotation of cowardice as in English, and when Pillpe had first addressed him so, Daniel had thought that the boy had instinctively sensed the decay inhabiting him. Later, he had realised the 'yellow' was a literal reference to the colour of his hair which, combined with his azure eyes, gave him, in macabre irony, the classic Aryan look.

'Let me pay the hotel, Pillpe. Then we'll have breakfast. All right with you?'

'Very all right.'

Whilst Daniel settled his account, Pillpe lit a domestic cigarette. When Daniel had first hired him, Pillpe was selling cigarettes individually. The fact that he could now treat himself to one meant he had made a hefty profit on the Dunhills. Daniel approved.

They took the main street to Plaza de Armas, the colonial drilling square which the Spaniards had replicated all over South America.

Campesinos milled around. Hundreds of them – and more were coming. Most, Pillpe had said, were leaving their region for the first time; all had set out to join Manku Yupanqui.

Daniel had been much stirred by the Manku Yupanqui cult.

Initially, he had seen it as the resurgence of the Inkarri myth, a legend born out of the tragic history of the Inca Empire, and so called from the Spanish word 'Inca-Rey', meaning 'Inca-King'.

When the Conquistadores had come – one hundred and sixty-seven men led by Pizarro and equipped with sixty-two horses – Atahualpa, the last Inca king, had thought they were the retinue of Viracocha, the white Creator. When he had gone to meet them, he had been ambushed and captured. To secure his release, he had offered a vast ransom of gold and silver. In 1533, after the ransom had been collected, Pizarro had garrotted him.

After that, the Conquistadores had thought it prudent to set up puppet kings. The second to be so crowned, Manku Inca, Atahualpa's brother, had rebelled at the first opportunity. Setting up a state in the jungle, he had fought the Spaniards for nine years. He had been killed, predictably treacherously, by some Spanish renegades whose lives he had spared.

His sons had continued the struggle. But by then more Spaniards had arrived. Eventually, in 1572, the revolt had been crushed and the then leader, Tupac Amaru, captured. As a warning to all rebels, the Spaniards had executed him in the main square of the capital. Then they had cut off his head and put it on display. The people had come in droves – not to be cowed, but to worship Tupac Amaru's head. The Spaniards had been forced to bury it hastily. The people had then spread the belief that the severed head would grow a new body under the ground and return as Inkarri, their saviour-king.

The myth had gained further credibility two hundred years later, in 1781, as history was repeated in the person of José Gabriel Condorcanqui, a direct descendant of the one daughter who had survived Tupac Amaru. Taking the name of his ancestor, he, too, had launched a rebellion. Though he had come close to defeating the Spaniards, he, also, had eventually been captured. He had been executed in the same square as the first Tupac Amaru. His arms and legs had been tied to four horses. The horses then had been sent charging in four directions. Incredibly, the second Tupac Amaru had pulled them back. The Spaniards had remedied matters by disembowelling and quartering him whilst he was still alive; finally, they had cut off his head.

Thus, both the Inkarri myth and the Manku Yupanqui legend prophesied the advent of a redeemer who had been decapitated. But, as Daniel himself had witnessed everywhere in the highlands, Manku Yupanqui had superseded Inkarri. Historical aspirations had been transmuted into messianic belief. When history fails, Daniel had heard people say, faith takes over; the unreal becomes real. What could be more real than the unreality of a man who has never known fear?

So, as far as the people were concerned, Manku Yupanqui was roaming the wilderness, flesh and blood and whole. Though no one had actually met him, everybody claimed to have felt his presence. To Daniel's amazement, there was even the growing conviction that the 'Pintoyaku canvas' – that priceless painting he had come to restore – was the pictorialisation of Manku Yupanqui's prophesied advent.

The ability to conquer doubt with blind faith – that was what, Daniel had decided, stirred him. That was the way to survive extinction. Like all ancient peoples, the Indians knew how to project their psyche into the future so that if the present pulverised the flesh, the soul remained intact until it found another body, new and unbroken. If only he could imagine a man who had never known fear.

Pillpe was trying to guide him round the potholes. 'Sorry for mud, *amarillo.*'

'I love it.'

Pillpe shook his head in disbelief.

'You obviously don't. Here, I'll help you.' Daniel, scooping up Pillpe, started carrying him.

Pillpe laughed and struggled. 'Hey, *amarillo*, stop. People will say Pillpe become baby.'

Daniel swung him down. 'Sorry. Didn't think of that.'

They laughed; and purposefully, they walked where the mud was thickest.

So good to be feeling so good; enjoying the cold, the sabre wind and sleet burning like cinders; breathing the thin air as casually as a native. Enjoying the bustle of Pintoyaku. Here, on the highest pass in the Eastern Cordilleras, met the roads from the coastal plain to the west, the highland Sierra to the north, the tropical Yungas to the east and the desert stretches to the south. Yet the town had escaped much of the ravages of the colonial presence. Irrespective of the monumental churches, the variety of Spanish churrigueresque architecture, it had remained basically Inca. The narrow streets were still walled by the flawless jigsaw of massive porphyry blocks – immovable even by earthquakes – as were the foundations and ground levels of most buildings, including the cathedral. It was still enclosed, five terraces deep, by the monolithic stone ramparts which had made it a formidable fortress.

And the people did not seem to have changed at all.

Men dressed in ponchos, homespun breeches, sandals, bonnets with ear flaps, and equipped with the ubiquitous coca pouches; women in shawls, multiple skirts and straw or bowler hats. You could name their village, Pillpe had told him, from the way they embroidered their clothes and hats, the colours and designs they used. Children in mantas; babes slung on their mothers' backs or carried in cardboard boxes.

Weathered people, caked with mud and serfdom, dour from a subsistence diet, but as dignified as any victim and, on the evidence of the musical instruments most of them carried, ready to pluck life from the strains in the air.

They reminded Daniel of the Gypsies in his native Yugoslavia.

He smiled at the people, wanting them to smile back, stop him, talk to him, accept him as Pillpe and Tica had accepted him. They avoided him carefully; eyes muted with distrust, animated only when they bargained with the coca-leaf vendors, and fiery when they talked to each other in Quechua, the language of the Incas.

The name, Manku Yupanqui, warbled from every group.

Short people. Daniel, over six feet and bull-like, coveted their smallness. They looked as if they could withstand more pain because they had less flesh that could be hurt.

'Sinchis!' Pillpe was nodding towards a group of soldiers patrolling the corner of the Plaza de Armas. 'I see you in café, *amarillo*.' He disappeared at once up one of the alleyways.

Daniel scrutinised the Sinchis. They were a paramilitary force set up to implement the Junta's 'pacification programme', a euphemism for stamping out discontent, for effecting the disappearances of undesirables like Tica's Miguel.

Yizkor had warned him about the Sinchis. Don't be careless. Don't think that just because you'll only be called to identify Kempin, you're safe. Don't be complacent. We're facing SS-Standartenführer Heinrich Kempin! The Nazis' supreme torch-bearer. For all we know, it was Kempin who framed Ian Campbell for pushing drugs. They could have killed Campbell. The fact that they didn't suggests they're checking up on him – Kempin knows we won't stop hunting. They won't break Campbell, but they'll remain vigilant. So, keep out of trouble. You're not a Yizkor agent – not trained. You may think you're entitled to have your revenge, but you're an outsider, a witness, that's all. Don't do anything rash. Get on with your work. That was God-sent, your work – right where Kempin is hiding. Saved us from having to smuggle you in. Just wait until Campbell gets out of prison. Then you can identify Kempin and forget the rest. We'll take care of the rest.

Daniel walked past the Sinchis' lines. Officers in smart uniforms, not dissimilar to those of the Wehrmacht, steel helmets included; the men in battle-fatigues. The gaze before which everyone stood suspect; the carriage of arbitrary power. Some kept their sub-machine-guns trained on him. He wanted to plough into them. He could break a few bones. He had the strength. And, in his youth, he had had the anger.

The anger was returning.

A lieutenant spat in his path. The same man who had been quartered in his hotel. They had bought each other drinks, yesterday evening. The lieutenant had talked about his wife and children. He had been out of uniform then.

Daniel went into the café. Pillpe had not come yet. He sat at the counter. The old man was still there, sleeping, head resting on his long staff. The staff indicated he was the *varayok* of an *ayllu*, head of a community. He could speak Spanish and had not shied away from Daniel.

As Daniel lit a cigarette, the *varayok* woke up. Daniel offered him a Dunhill. 'Can I invite you to breakfast, *tayta*?'

The *varayok* took the cigarette then nodded at the proprietor. 'The man fed me. But a coffee is pleasure.'

Daniel ordered the coffees, deciding to leave a large tip. The proprietor had treated the *varayok* kindly, giving him and his wife free food and shelter.

The *varayok* lit his cigarette and inhaled deeply. 'How you feel, *hijo*?'

Hijo, in Spanish, meant 'son'; *tayta* was 'father' in Quechua. That was how they should address each other, the old man had decreed.

'Fine, *tayta*.'

'Only fine? Then you did not have enough coca. Like a mountain spirit you should be – high head, cloud hidden.'

Daniel smiled. Last night, the *varayok* had initiated him into coca chewing, showing him how to start with no more than twenty-five leaves, how to roll them in the mouth and soak them with saliva, how to add *llipta* – charred banana leaves – to catalyse the coca's alkaloids, and how to relax for full surrender. In the event, according to the *varayok*, he had chewed better than most gringos. But he had still champed instead of masticating lightly. Consequently, the *llipta* had been hard on his teeth, the leaves had tasted like sore gums and swallowing too much or too little of the juices had numbed his cheeks bluntly as opposed to lulling them, as the *varayok* had put it, like children falling asleep. Even so, the effect, after a couple of hours, had been extraordinary. A pleasant vibration, creating the feeling that his veins were humming, had soothed his limbs; his mind had appeared to ride the wind and expand as an endless horizon; fireflies had burst out of his eyes, sprouting flowers in the shape of snow crystals; a warmth, as if the sun had risen inside him, had possessed his body. The warmth was still there. And his energy seemed boundless.

The proprietor served the coffees and some maize biscuits. 'Have you decided about the desert, *hijo*?'

Daniel dunked a biscuit into his coffee. 'Back to the capital for me, I regret to say.'

'I wish you good road.'

Daniel noted the disappointment in the *varayok*'s eyes. During the coca chewing, they had talked about the people's exodus to the desert. The *varayok* had urged him to go with them. Daniel had declined, joking that not having brought a parachute with him the less he risked the mountain roads the better. The old man had taken umbrage. There was nothing wrong with the roads, he had declared; they had been hewn by the Incas and though no one had bothered to improve them since, they still served because the Incas had built for eternity. Those who perished on the roads served tithes to the mountains and abysses who were *apus*, godly spirits, and, naturally, entitled to receive sacrifices. But this time, this journey, the *apus* would waive all tributes. This time, this journey, they wanted the people to reach the desert safely. This time, this journey, there would be no selection for life or death.

He had actually said selection. That word for ever contaminated by Auschwitz.

'I must get back to work, *tayta*.'

'It is not wise not fighting fear.'

'What makes you think that's what I'm doing?'

'Age, *hijo*. It harvests most mysteries.'

'Fear is not a mystery to me.'

'That is why you should go. Why you should meet Manku Yupanqui. Why we *naturales* go. And mestizos. Even *mistis*. All people sick with fear, but with God in their hearts.'

'But no one has seen him. How do you know he'll be there?'

'We see many ways – not always with eyes. We also hear many ways. He will be there on night of full moon. How so many people can be wrong?'

'It happens...'

'It happened once – when our fathers welcomed the bearded people as gods. It cannot happen again. Our fathers said Inti, the Sun, was killed because he did not know how to defeat men who have the sickness to eat gold. But our fathers lost vision, they did not understand Inti cannot die, was only wounded. Now, there is Manku Yupanqui come to heal him with missing ray. When Inti returns, he will know how to defeat gold-eaters. Touch your faith, *hijo*. Manku Yupanqui will be in desert. And it will be like in Bible. There will be miracles for all men.'

A people's fantasy. A despairing people's fantasy. Translated to its essence: the New Man, the Second Coming, the Kingdom of God, the long awaited victory over Evil.

Daniel was tempted to embrace the fantasy. That was another sign that his soul had turned rebel. The defences that had tamed the hysterical Jew-child, that had then scraped every splash of colour from the violent youth, and that had finally lime-washed the man that had remained, were eroding. The fears that had provided refuge, silence, inaction and peace in Jesus' bosom were being challenged by an irresistible demand for life. Now, there were times when he lost sight of Jesus, when he wondered which god laid claim to him, whether he really preferred the Crucified Son of Christianity he had adopted to the Inconceivable One of Judaism he had abandoned, or whether, in fact, he could believe in any god at all.

So here he was, in a scourged country where Heinrich Kempin had come to wear his sins like medals. Here he was, maintaining that the commission which had brought him here, which had been bitterly contested by the doyens of his feuding, envy-ridden, insular profession, and which he had secured on his record of sustained integrity and skill, was divinely ordained; that by throwing him, quite unceremoniously, into Yizkor's lap, it had forced him, at long last, to open his ears to the relentless clamour of father, mother, sisters – and the countless others – slaughtered by Kempin. Here he was, a Christian, a pacifist, kicking the dust of history like those manic, righteous Jews who cluttered his ancestry.

The Kempin imperative was enough. The Manku Yupanqui craze was none of his business.

Pillpe arrived. 'Hey, *amarillo*. Trucks coming. Sit. They have long climb. We eat.'

Daniel signalled the proprietor for two breakfasts. He turned to the *varayok* to ask him if he would like another coffee but the old man was standing up, nodding at his wife who was summoning him from outside the café. 'I go, *hijo*. Maybe see you in desert.'

With a twinge of sadness, Daniel watched him shuffle out. 'Adios, *tayta*.'

Pillpe pulled on Daniel's sleeve. 'You go to desert?'

'No.'

'You can – if you no get off at Tinge Santa Rosa to take bus. The trucks go all way to desert.'

'I know. But I have to get back.'

'I sorry you go, *amarillo*.'

'So am I, Pillpe.'

'I want go with you, but no can. Have little brother.'

'Have you! You didn't tell me.'

'You no ask.'

'Where is he?'

'Selling cigarrillos.'

'What about the rest of your family!'

'Only brother. Parents dead.'

'I'm sorry. Misery that. Poor you.'

Pillpe laughed. 'Like you know!'

'I lost my parents, too – and my sisters – when I was little.'

'Hunger!'

'Something just as bad. War.'

'I sorry. Misery that. Poor you.'

Daniel stroked Pillpe's head.

The proprietor served them omelettes.

Pillpe attacked his plate. 'You adopt me, *amarillo*.'

Daniel ate with appetite. 'What!'

'If you have wife, children, I sure they no mind. I be good son, good brother.'

'I'm not married.'

'Then definitely – you adopt me.'

'What about your brother?'

'Him, too, sure.'

'I'm sorry. I can't. I wish I could.'

Pillpe shrugged: sadness coated in nonchalance. 'I understand.' 'No, you don't.'

'Sure. Indio boy. No good. Who wants?'

Daniel stopped eating. 'I'm not one of your *mistis*!'

Pillpe ate faster. 'So adopt me.'

'How? I have no home to speak of. Just a small place – in London.'

'My brother and I live in street.'

'Much of the time I'm not there, Pillpe. I work all over the world. Like here – for about a year. Then off somewhere else.'

'I go where you go. No problem.'

Daniel wished he could explain his mission to Pillpe. Because mission it was – no matter how peripherally Yizkor had cast him into it. To be clear about it: Yizkor was an official outfit; Kempin was just one of their assignments. Whereas for him... he had to avenge father, mother, sisters. Which was why, now that he was in this country, he was inclined to defy Yizkor, to disregard all their directives on caution, to stop wasting time waiting for Campbell. Irrespective of the dangers. 'All sorts of problems, Pillpe.'

'Better my problems. Hunger. Sickness. *Mistis*. Sinchis.'

Daniel looked away. He could take the boy with him now – and his brother. He could put them somewhere safe before he made a single move.

'You teach me. Read and write. I learn quick. Find work. I be saved, *amarillo*. And my brother.'

Look back. Back to that time when the Nazis and the Ustashi were running amok in Yugoslavia. There had been another orphan desperate to be saved. The monks who had found him had not rejected him. Risking their lives, they had soothed his nightmares, given him, in their crumbling, island monastery, physical and spiritual salvation.

'I can't, Pillpe. I wish I could. I wish I could.'

Pillpe gobbled up the rest of his omelette, then jumped off the stool. I go find you place in truck, gringo.'

Daniel lit a Dunhill. The *gringo* had felt like a slap.

2

The needle of death looking for a thread

General Oseas Fuego studied the prisoner strapped to the *panilla*, the iron bed-frame euphemistically called 'the grill'.

Ian Campbell, he decided, was a man very much like himself: same compact but solid build; same stoic defiance despite the paralysis of fear. There was similarity even in the racial difference. Campbell had greasy hair, smooth but mottled skin like dried bone and the prototypal Jewish nose. He himself had the equally classic features of the Indio: high cheekbones, eyelids with epicanthic folds, straight hair, heliotropic coloration. Thus they were specimens of two collateral breeds chosen, by virtue of their ancient roots, to be subhumans. The all-important variation was that Campbell had not cut off his malign roots; presumably he had refused to accept the world as the abomination it was.

Campbell, struggling to contain his panic, tried to focus on his inquisitors. After the days of darkness in his cell, the sun in the yard had nearly blinded him; his pupils were still smarting from the sea-spray in the air – the only comfort of this island prison.

He began to discern the uniforms: one creased and unbuttoned, the other, immaculate and bedecked with the armband of the Bridegrooms of Death: respectively, General Fuego and Colonel Angelito. Campbell's terror surged.

Colonel Angelito smiled like a benefactor. 'Ian Campbell? What sort of a name is that!' Soft spoken like a dear friend.

Campbell tried to look ingenuous. 'Scottish.'

Colonel Angelito chuckled: a warm, liquid sound. 'You are as Scottish as

I am Latin.' He ruffled Campbell's hair affectionately. 'We soldiers have a sense of humour, too, you know. I am really Ukrainian. Angelito is only a nickname.'

Campbell knew about the epithet. According to rumours, it had been coined, originally, as an endearment by the Colonel's wife. After Angelito had established himself in the Security Services, it had changed its connotation to that of 'little angel' of death.

Campbell affected confusion. 'Ukrainian!'

Fuego smiled faintly. Angelito, he had long ago decided, was one of those maggots that materialised, like mushrooms, after the heavy rains of history, then assumed substance by wearing several coats of armour, then seized status by living off a flag and then, unable to produce warm blood, either stole it or alchemised it. One of those creatures the Creoles called conquistadores; gold-eaters, in Indio terms. Thus, whenever Angelito admitted to being Ukrainian, Fuego saw the claim as another of Angelito's attempts to pass himself off as human – like the handsome face he had moulded from a statue; the powerful body he had sucked out of an athlete; the cherub-red cheeks he had embezzled from the Russian muzhik and the lacquered charm he had pillaged from all over Europe.

Angelito tenderly wiped the perspiration from Campbell's forehead with a rag. 'When you think about it, those who come to this room – whichever side of the fence they happen to be – are never who they really are. Who are you really?'

'You know who I am.' Campbell twisted his head towards Fuego. 'General, *you* know...'

Fuego approached the iron bed. 'I know you push drugs. But jackals don't always eat carrion. They also hunt and kill. Tell us what you have been hunting.'

Campbell feigned a wail. 'I'm a tramp. A drifter. A wreck of a man...'

Fuego ran his hand over Campbell's naked body. 'How old are you?'

'Forty-one.'

'You are in excellent shape.' Fuego punched Campbell's stomach viciously. Campbell yelled, but his body had absorbed the blow with little protest. Fuego felt Campbell's abdominal muscles. 'Tough like bunch grass. Not at all ravaged – either by age or drugs. A trained body, I would say.' He pulled at Campbell's penis. 'And you are circumcised.' He let go of Campbell's penis with distaste. 'You have been pushing drugs for old Germans. Very unusual for a circumcised man to work for old Germans...'

'I – look, I've been bumming around the world. I ran out of money. I was stranded – destitute. I got roped in. And before I had a whiff of the good life, I got caught. Can't change your luck, can you? But I've done my time – well, another month to go. And soon as I'm out, I'll get the consulate to ship me home. You won't see me for dust.'

'We think you are a foreign agent, Campbell.'

'*Me?*'

'We checked your bumming around the world. Intriguing.'

'You got me mixed up with someone else.'

'Why aren't you crying?'

'What?'

'You are spreadeagled for torture. You look prepared – resigned. Most people would have been calling on their gods by now.'

'I'm innocent!'

'Come now. Only dolphins and savages have faith in innocence. You think *you* can hold out.'

Campbell twisted his head round and registered Fuego's powerful presence. Fuck it! He was a veteran, yet here he was admiring his persecutor like any other victim. 'No, General, look...'

'We have four questions. Whose agent are you? What is your mission? How many of you? Their names and covers?'

'General, you've got to believe me...'

Fuego moved to the bottom corner of the iron bed and unhooked an electric cattle prod. 'I wonder if you are familiar with this, Campbell – known as the *picana electrica...*'

Campbell flinched.

Behind him, Colonel Angelito sighed squeamishly.

Fuego held the prod over Campbell's face. 'No mistaking what it is – but let me tell you what it does besides giving electric shocks. It slithers all over you. Inside and out. Mouth, eyes, ears, nose, arse and genitals. It empties your bowels at every touch. Boils all your liquids – even tears. Never knows when to stop.'

Campbell, coated in cold sweat, had clenched his teeth. There was resolve on his face which Fuego recognised as that of a martyr.

'Of course, it is possible to hold out. There are ways... The one people try first is an erotic obsession. You are heterosexual – so, a woman, in your case. A loved one or an anonymous one or a fantasy goddess. You fix your mind on her cunt and tits, her skin, mouth, eyes, the many ways you want to fuck her. That is a strong defence, but you can't think about sex for long when you are shitting uncontrollably and your cock is being fried. So you shift emphasis. You are desperate for sympathy, tenderness, compassion. You think of your mother – or, if like me, you have never known your mother, of *a* mother, of big, milk-heavy breasts, cradling your head, rocking you sweetly to make you better. But the pain is getting unbearable. And you are still abandoned – the tortured are the loneliest on earth. So you try something else. You exhume – or invent – happy memories, dream places: childhood episodes with father, brothers, sisters; a mountain retreat. Except by now your brain is cooked – it can't hang on to images. You make a superhuman effort and try yet another approach. One that does not involve emotions. Perhaps some facts you have learned. Or the multiplication tables. Meaningless stuff which only heightens despair. Because you know you will be tortured until you answer the questions. Then, maybe – *maybe* – you reach the end of the day unbroken. You feel proud of yourself. But before you can repair mind and body, you find the night has flown away. And there is a new day with the *picana*. And after the new day, another – a whole eternity.'

Fuego paused. Campbell had turned away and was muttering prayers in order not to listen.

'I have seen many men die under torture, Campbell – often for the pleasure of their torturers. Those who survived always talked. *If* you survive, there will be nothing left in your body except pain; nothing in your mind except a slimy soup with some incomprehensible words floating in it.'

Campbell had started shaking. He managed to face Fuego. He tried to smile; instead he began to weep. 'I have... nothing... to say...'

Fuego nodded courteously. Campbell was like him and that was how an enemy should be. But such equality was also an impertinence. He switched the current on and rammed the prod against Campbell's testicles.

Campbell's scream ran like a river, twisting and turning.

Fuego pulled back the prod and handed it to Angelito.

Angelito held it as if it were a sacred sword.

Fuego wondered whether Angelito's wife, Concepción, a vain, maudlin, idle-rich flower of one of the country's oldest families, had ever seen her conquistador so possessed. Perhaps on the three occasions when he had impregnated her with their sons! A woman, some Indio midwives claimed, always sees the brutality in her man when his sperm batters through into her egg. Unlikely. Concepción was not a woman who conceived in the usual, liquid way; whenever she needed an egg, she had an exclusive one tailored by a famous couturière. In any case, Angelito did not indulge in torture for sexual gratification; torture was another of his ways of concocting a heroic identity.

Fuego moved to the door.

'Won't you stay, General?'

'I have to attend to that Manku Yupanqui nonsense.' Fuego walked out. Whereas torture for him was something he had learned from the Creole. And though he excelled at it because it made his skin whiter than theirs, he was indifferent to it.

3
Body of skin, of moss, of eager and firm milk

Santa Rosa, the priest had informed him, was the first person in the Americas to be canonised; she had loved and cared for the persecuted Indians. Tingo was a Quechua word meaning 'confluence of rivers'. The rivers around which Tingo Santa Rosa had haphazardly scattered its mud and corrugated-iron dwellings were two streams that had crawled in exhaustion into a single bed after having hurled themselves frenziedly from the Western Cordilleras. They would stagger on, supporting each other, for countless kilometres – for this was the Altiplano – until they reached the eastern range where, galvanised again, they would leap into the Amazon basin.

Daniel could not respond to the Altiplano. Though these plains, ringed by distant snow-capped peaks and chequered with red earth and rippling *ichu* grass, were dramatic enough, they lacked colour. Rather, either because the rarefied air exaggerated the mountains' contempt for lesser creations, or because the sun, even when it scorched, seemed to belong to an ice age, the colours appeared congealed. Thus every sign of life, including man and his herds of llamas, stood as petrified as the igneous rocks surrounding them.

Father Quintana returned with his canteens. An ancient wraith with a white mane, windsurfing in an oversize black soutane, he punctuated the desolation. 'Alas, no transport, my son.' He also stammered.

Daniel, sprawled on the passenger seat of the priest's dilapidated pick-up, cast an angry look at Tingo Santa Rosa – a large village by Andean standards. 'But there's supposed to be a daily bus to La Merced.'

'Suspended. The transporters are a private company.' He pointed at the mass of people camped on the fields. 'The campesinos hired all the buses.'

'What about a taxi? A *colectivo*?'

Father Quintana sat on the running board at Daniel's side. 'Everything has been hired.' He held out one of the canteens. 'I managed to find some soup – with *chunu*.'

Daniel winced: *chunu* was the dehydrated potato that tasted like turf. But he was hungry and the afternoon was yielding to the cold. 'Thanks. What do I owe you?'

Father Quintana waved his bony hand. 'Ah – you gave me so much for petrol.'

Daniel started drinking the soup. He was having a frustrating time getting back to La Merced. Pillpe, spitefully, had not secured him a place on the trucks. Fortunately, Father Quintana had appeared in his jalopy and offered him a lift. The priest was also smitten by the Manku Yupanqui hysteria and was trekking all the way from the Yungas to the desert. Now, with no transport available in Tingo Santa Rosa, Daniel was forced to continue with him down to San Martin, a fair-sized town at the other end of the Altiplano that had bus services to the coast. His best bet would be to make for the port of Miranda which had sea, rail and air links with the capital. In effect, he would be detouring to the southernmost corner of the country in order to get to the north; but that, the priest had quipped, was one of the joys of travelling in the Andes.

He could be on the road for days. True, he wasn't pressed for time – not pressed, that is, if he was going to wait for Campbell's release. But there was that budding creature inside him yelling for action – and yelling much louder than the fearful colossus that held his heart and brain captive. More to the point, should he wait for Campbell's release? It was all very well for Yizkor to say Campbell wouldn't break. But he had never met Campbell. God only knew what they did to prisoners in this country. What if they did break Campbell, shouldn't he have done something before that? There were ways of finding Kempin. Yizkor had provided a list of his possible whereabouts.

'It's good – the soup.'

Daniel forced a smile. 'Wonderful.'

The priest nodded wistfully. 'One of God's first inventions, the soup was. That's what my mother used to say. She knew about these things.'

At least Father Eusebio Quintana was a splendid old-timer. Bent heavy from carrying countless crosses, he stubbornly nursed the remaining embers in his wizened black eyes. He had a childish interest in meeting people and conferring with their souls. Daniel had been very tempted to confess his life to him; however, that would have necessitated unfurling truths, having to reveal, for instance, that his over-precise Spanish was not the product of his apprenticeship in the Prado in Madrid, but was, in fact, the Ladino of the Balkan Jews which had been his mother-tongue and which, in the early post-war years, he had perfected, in symbolic defiance, to demonstrate that even the Holocaust had failed to destroy the Jew. So many of the early truths had been abandoned in fugues. And so many new truths, real as well as spurious, clung to him, fearing other fugues.

In contrast, Father Quintana had talked about himself quite freely. He was a mestizo – to his regret, with more Creole in him than Indian. A secular priest, hence not a member of a religious community but ordained for the service of a diocese, he had committed himself to the ideals of Liberation Theology.

This was a movement, he had explained, which had officially started in 1968 when an extraordinary conference of Latin American bishops had decided to sever the Church's traditional alliance with the Establishment and to cease supporting those regimes where the military and the privileged élite, on the pretext of fighting communism, ruled with total disregard of human rights and social welfare.

Pastorally interpreted, Liberation Theology demanded that men of the cloth should aid, protect and care for the hungry, the poor, the oppressed and those facing extinction as the Lord Jesus had done at the time of His ministry. Such an inspiring ideal had been difficult to put into practice: many priests, unable to endure the hardships, had abandoned the movement; countless others had been bought off by the Establishment; more had simply disappeared or had been massacred with their flocks; and a few, having taken up arms, had perished in the bush.

Today, Liberation Theology was on the defensive. The First World, the real masters of Latin America, headed by the United States, saw the movement both as a political and an economic threat and, consequently, condoned and supported even the most tyrannical dictatorships. The Vatican itself, ostensibly the originator of the movement, had now become unnerved by the possibility that it might embrace armed revolution and thus create a serious schism. To cap it all, new-fangled evangelists, pursuing a most un-Christian Kingdom of God where Mammon ruled, were undermining the work of the Catholic priests. In this last instance, Moral Crusade, a US fundamentalist sect, had become alarmingly successful in this part of the world: the Indian, forever seeking hope against hope, was finding the blend of gifts of food and medicine, of ostentatious liturgy and of an authoritarian paternalism that was suggestive of Inca times, very attractive.

For himself personally, Father Quintana had explained, the future was bleak. Liberation Theology having virtually collapsed in this country he – and the few like him – had neither sanction nor support for their work. They had to resign themselves to carry on, full of doubts, floundering constantly for lack of guidance and at the mercy of the authorities. Was it surprising then that he should seek out Manku Yupanqui, sceptic though he was that such a paragon actually existed? Sad old man.

They had finished their soup. Father Quintana was storing his canteen. Daniel handed him his. 'Back on the road, Padre?'

'It will be dark soon. Given my driving, I think it would be prudent to spend the night here.' He breathed deeply, as if he were by the sea. 'This is a good place.'

Daniel teased him. 'Plenty to do, is there?'

'What did you have in mind?'

A woman, Daniel wanted to say. 'Some local entertainment?'

'There's a *chicha* house.' He pointed at a hut flying a white cloth. 'The flag – that's the sign.'

Daniel pulled a face. At high altitude the maize spirit wreaked havoc on the uninitiated. When he had sampled it in Pintoyaku, he had lost track of a full day.

Father Quintana pointed at the people camped on the fields. 'How about there – you'll get plenty of music there. Real *huaynos* and *yarawis*. That's where I'm going.'

Daniel tried to look interested. Father Quintana had a weakness for Indian music. *Huayno*, he had told him, was a highland song that expressed the sweet sadness of love; *yarawi* was epic in style and lamented the people's perennial suffering.

'And if my eyes haven't deceived me, Beatriz Santillan is there. She's our greatest songwriter. Want to come along?'

'Why not? I've heard of her.'

Dragged away by the forces of darkness, the sun was bleeding on the summits. A raw shadow had spread over the plains. Rocks now grazed where llamas had been.

It was a desolate landscape. But Beatriz Santillan saw it as a seedbed. The people and the music had put marrow into the earth's brittle bones.

The people numbered thousands. Most had come from the Sierra, some from the coastal strip – people whom both the sea and the land had forsaken, others from the tropical Yungas; and yet others from the slums of the cities.

They had formed a large circle around a mount on top of which stood a smooth slab of rock carved with the figure of Amaru, the Serpent of the lower world. The mound was a *huaca*, a sacred site. It had been Amaru, young legends had begun to declare, that had preserved Manku Yupanqui's head as it was preserving those of its namesakes, the two Inkarris.

Whenever the people looked at the image of the Serpent they had to raise their heads; thus, they experienced a sense of pride. Pride became them, Beatriz observed.

Like any congregation of Indians, they indulged in trading. Those from the Sierra ranged their meagre supplies: potatoes, maize, red onions and quinoa – pigweed that could be ground into flour. Those from the Yungas peddled fruits and coca leaves. Those from the coast and the cities sold confectionery and plastic wares. A contingent from the Altiplano, recently evangelised by Moral Crusade, struck the best bargains: they bartered pills which they had received as free gifts.

The music came from Beatriz herself. Or rather, she orchestrated it as she walked round the mound, playing her guitar and eliciting accompaniments from sicus, quenas and charangos. There was at least one person in every family who chronicled life with melody.

Beatriz revelled in the people's surrender to her music. After years of international engagements, she had learned to gauge the pulse of her audience. There were the rich who adored her because she sang about carnal love and about how orgasm, too, could be learned. There were the intellectuals who sought to include her in their cabals because she also sang about the ordeals of the downtrodden. And there were the complacent of the West who claimed to be the guardians of the world and who saw in her beauty and sensuality the spirit of Latin America – whatever that meant.

But the people here were different. They knew nothing of her fame. Fame belonged to the *misti*'s world; it was a spoon designed to scoop up more gold. However, the people had gathered her songs. Songs belonged to all mankind. Songs travelled on the wind, fell with the rain or snow, streamed up and down the rivers, sprouted from the earth and through the rocks. Thus the people responded to her as they responded to their land: as a presence invested with supernatural breath, hence entirely natural. They made her feel in a state of grace.

She had composed a song for this journey. A new song. The first, in over a year. One that could be dedicated to an ancestor without misgiving. One that was not as seedless as her womb. The people had learned it by heart.

They began singing it again. She joined them.

He is
the water that quenches the gods
the fire that cleanses the past
He is
the earth where the spirit grows
the sky which shepherds the stars
He is
the eagle who husbands the sun
the puma which hurls rainbows
He is
the pure milk of a man's eruption
the kiss that opens a woman's legs
He is
the hope born today
the stone that will build tomorrow

And then they proclaimed: 'Manku Yupanqui! Manku Yupanqui! Manku Yupanqui!'

It was such a fiery summons, Beatriz felt, that it should unlock any door, stir even the sternest prophet.

A campesina with one child on her back, a baby at her breast and another swelling her belly, brushed past, trilling her delight. Her husband, covered in mud, smelling of sweat and llama, played a salutation on his quena.

People nurtured by the earth, carved by the elements, forged by sorrow. Indomitable because their wombs were always ready to germinate, their penises always bursting with seed. Here was meaning, simple and eternal.

Was it likely she could regenerate here, in the wilderness? Had she been wise to surrender to impulse, to give up engagements and adulation, to ignore the voice of reason which insisted that saviours belonged either to a fabled past or a fabled future, never to the present? Did she really expect to mend herself by touching Manku Yupanqui as the woman who had bled for twelve years had been healed by touching Jesus' hem?

She could hope even as she doubted. For there had been signs of reawakening.

She could almost say she had never been happier. Insomnia, delicate stomach, migraines – that brew of lassitude had vanished. Lassitude, if you please, in a sturdy mestizo woman born to accommodate two potent bloods, to toil simultaneously in the cities and the mountain slopes, to preserve innocent cultures which the white man wished to devour because innocent cultures constituted the little spirituality that remained in this world. Lassitude, indeed!

Here she was back at the source she had slighted. After an era of dissipation, of sleepwalking through meaningless white pursuits – wealth, intellectual onanism, good food and fashionable sex – here she was back with her mother's people, reacquainting herself with their sole objective: how to survive the day.

She had sat in the shade of the countless branches of their culture; she had touched its magnificent trunk, Quechua – no, Runasimi, as the *naturales* called it, 'the mouth of the people'. Runasimi, which her mother and father had taught indefatigably at day and night schools during those few years it had been tolerated as the country's other official language. Runasimi, the tongue of the earth, sky, fire and water. Banning that language, after her parents had been killed, had been Aunt Luisa's only failing as godmother. The song to Manku Yupanqui was in Runasimi, composed in the style of a *taquirari*, a summons to a lover far away.

And so she was beginning to disrobe life; seeking in its nakedness what most of humanity craved: the roundness that showed it had been impregnated with the perfect world they had come to sire.

Of course, she knew: eventually, she would discard the Indian clothes she had put on and don the silks of the white man's seductive world. But perhaps she would do all that with her soul yoked to its source. She had a premonition: whether or not she met Manku Yupanqui on the night of the full moon, a week hence, whether he proved a luminary or a charlatan, she would turn off from the middle road – aptly, midway in her life, at the ripe age of thirty-five – and seek one that led towards light.

She started another song. She imagined a man, the man she had always imagined, sowing her womb. Her breasts felt heavy as if suddenly full of milk.

Daniel hooked his sweater and jeans on to the cone of the tent; frozen solid, they looked like a scarecrow. Outside the glacial rain fell, unabated, in metallic monotone. He should have bought a poncho from the campesinos; made of fatty llama wool, the poncho was relatively waterproof.

Father Quintana had fallen asleep, barely managing to mutter good-night. Daniel pulled the priest's sleeping-bag closer to the paraffin heater. He hoped the old man was as hardy as he claimed to be. He always camped out when he travelled, he had said; out in the elements, closer to God. Whilst Daniel had fought the gale, the downpour and the quagmire earth to put up the tent, Father Quintana had clucked and chuckled as if such extremes of weather were merely God's affectionate little pranks. Childlike old man. A Herculean task, my son. Well done. May God give more strength to your arms. A fairyland grandfather.

Daniel lit a cigarette by way of a nightcap, then squeezed into the spare sleeping-bag. He relished the cold with the anticipation of the warmth to come.

Yes, strength was another way of feeling alive; strength, when not tested by danger, produced the fantasy that courage was available in equal proportions.

But this time, I'm not running away; I'm facing up to danger; even believing that in punishing Kempin, I'll be doing God's work.

Father Quintana began to snore: a soft descant. A smile – the smile that made people gather around him – settled on his face.

Daniel drew on his cigarette. He, too, had enjoyed mingling with the people. People clinging to the concept of a future in order to live in the present that was the past continuum. So like Jews. They had fuelled his desire to go to the desert, to embrace the idea of a saviour.

If he did join them, he might also get to know Beatriz Santillan. She had captivated him – as much by her singing as by her mixture of earthiness and delicacy; solidly built but shapely. He should have approached her; it might have led to something – why not! She lived in La Merced and was not married – that much he had found out. Father Quintana would have been only too willing to contrive an introduction.

He had felt intimidated. She had struck him as the sort of woman who would insist on giving as much as she received, on deprecating any dependency; the sort of woman who, when finally abandoning him, would tell him that his devotion was suffocating, that his need to make her happy, particularly in bed, amounted to persecution.

He was getting carried away. Right now, goaded as he felt into getting started on Kempin, the last thing he could consider was a relationship – and with a woman on whom he had set eyes once!

He stubbed out his cigarette.

The sicu players had been magical, playing straight into God's ear. Like the Gypsies with their pan-pipes. The instruments were similar, varying with the type of reed used and the length of the tubes. The sicu sang, in breathy, haunting tones, of lands that climbed closest to the Sun-god and of His children, still uncontaminated by the material world. The pan-pipes, rippling with the liquidity of the Balkan air, did much the same, changing only the names of the protagonists to Great Gardener and His errant flower. Stuff that pleaded for the soul's immortality.

Sleep loomed.

When would he stop doubting? Souls survived come what may. Millions had been demolished, bone by fragile bone, yet they lived on.

I will only be convinced when – *if* – I conquer the terror of physical pain, when – *if* – I corner Heinrich Kempin, when – *if* – I am finally born.

And perhaps, after that, I can create something, something that will fill me with life, lift me above the barrier I am, survive me. Perhaps I can create a child. When Tica was looking at my hands, I was shocked: veins in harsh relief, the thumb and some of the fingers gnarled, a hint of mould on the patina. Like a stillborn man. Time is running out. I have to reach a destination. Achieve substance so that when I look at the world, I can see it looking back at me.

I am very tempted to go after Manku Yupanqui.

4

A branch of secret waters and of submerged truths

Gaspar Huaman turned to his wife. 'The new Trotsky – I am the new Trotsky! But look what happens!'

Kollur may have looked up. He could not see her. He could barely see himself. It was one of those blackest of nights, cloud-ridden and soggy, when the world disappeared down a cosmic gullet. One of those nights that brought him close to recanting his ideals, made him yearn to be back in the hubbub of the capital, back at the family estate by the sea. It never got as dark there; La Merced, neon-lit like any other First World city, glowed; and if there were power cuts, the surf compensated by frothing phosphorescently.

Kollur had probably nodded agreement. She always did; then she carried on with whatever she was doing. At the moment, she was feeding the baby – he could hear it slurping greedily; the twins would be watching her, and she would be smiling at them. All that mystery about suckling; the twins, barely six, were already planning their own motherhood. His family had no time for him.

Well, what could he expect! True, his half of the children's blood was white; true also, after all these years of marriage, Kollur had acquired some of his sophistication. But beneath the gloss, they were as Indio as the *huaynos* they interminably sang.

That sounded like prejudice and he felt guilty. He loved them, of course. But they were worlds apart. He was an intellectual, a revolutionary, the country's political hope. It was all very well having children at one with Nature; all very well having a wife who tilled the earth alongside him, served him meals and *chicha*, laid down her doughy flesh day after stagnant day. All very well, but not enough. He also needed a family that communicated with him, shared his vision, lined up behind him for the struggles ahead. How could they be so passive when he was fighting for them? But they were. Most Indios were.

A Gorgonian roar smote the night.

'*Ech*!'

The sound reverberated like a cannonade.

'*Ech*! *Ech*! *Ech*!'

Behind him, Kollur and the children rushed into the adobe. They would assume it was a thunderbolt, or something as powerful. For the *ech* represented a great magical force striking at a human adversary. And they would sit in the dark, hiding inside their ponchos, as if the Devil was about.

He should go and comfort them. Except that his rationality would be as incomprehensible to them as their belief in magic was to him.

He peered up at the overhang which, sticking out of the mountain like a balcony, shielded the village from the bitter winds.

Tello, the shaman, had chosen the overhang as his altar. He had lit a fire, a small one, in order to welcome the roaming spirits who shunned strong light – which was also the reason why the stupid ritual was taking place on this black hole of a night. He had sat there, since sunset, like a hermetic fisherman manning invisible nets, waiting to catch the *ech*.

Now, the *ech* had struck. And the little light the fire had provided was being tossed by the wind.

Huaman could not see whether the shaman had been petrified into mangled rock or whether he was shaking in the throes of an agonising death, and whether the men witnessing the ritual were also under the *ech*'s attack.

He ran towards the overhang, muttering angrily. 'Would you believe it! The new Trotsky!'

He did not give a damn about Tello. But the men exposed to witchcraft were his guerrilleros, all fifteen of them. If they were in danger...

It was impossible not to despair. How could the revolution succeed with people forever escaping into paganism? He had harangued them, time and time again. The Indios were treated as subhumans because of the primitivism of their culture, because of their reluctance to embrace civilisation. They never understood. How then could they understand the science of politics, the logistics of permanent revolution, the upheavals required to establish a family of man liberated from the evils of race, class and religion?

He was being patronising again. Not all the fault lay with the Indios. He could have forbidden this divination ritual. The men would have obeyed – not happily, but obeyed.

He was not wielding the stick, that was the problem. His objections had lacked passion. They were static from the brain, not the angry roar of the heart.

Passion had been so available once – like sperm. Great passion when he had lived dissolutely to scandalise his august-white, wealth-heavy, Europe-besotted family. Great passion, too, at university when he had discovered philosophy and excelled even his tutors. Greater passion when disavowing the very concept of *limpieza de sangre*, purity of blood, he had embraced *indigenismo* and moved to the Cordilleras to live the life of the campesinos. Inviolate Passion throughout those years in this remote village, sacrificing his heritage – and what a heritage: the scion of de Villasante y Córdoba, not just the country's noblest family, but also of Spain's Golden Age – brandishing the Quechua name he had adopted – Huaman, meaning 'hawk' – taking an Indio wife, siring Indio children, starving or half starving according to the yield of his small patch on this mountain slope. And boundless Passion that had made him the single force to politicise the campesinos.

He had to rediscover that passion. Or greatness would pass him by. He deserved greatness. Though he had emerged at a time when every geopolitical reality conspired to abort him, though he had been forced to pick as his arena a place which even history had forgotten, he had started shaking the world. Already the capital, normally deaf to the groans from the Sierra, had taken notice of him. It did not matter that not having literally taken up arms, he had not yet featured in the 'wanted' lists. It did not matter that the government, anxious to attract foreign investment, appeared to respect freedom of speech and had not yet moved to silence him. All that would change.

He reached the overhang.

His men were sitting immobile, entranced eyes fixed on Tello.

The shaman, seated in the middle of the clearing which he had purified by placing on each corner offerings of coca, llama fat, herbs and *aguardiente*, cane-liquor, was twitching his face muscles.

The *ech* had not killed him. Maybe he was truly indestructible. According to the people, he had been struck by lightning – the definitive sign of the God-chosen – not once, but twice; and, in countless engagements with the *ech*, he had lived through several defeats. In the Indio's perverse logic, his defeats had greater importance than his numerous victories, for survival meant that he could navigate Nature's chaotic half: only Her children were capable of such a feat.

Tello was concentrating on his wand which he had thrust into the ground. Occasionally his eyes darted between a deep hole next to the wand and a gourd of *aguardiente* on the opposite side of the hole. He looked like a wild animal stalking its prey.

The *ech*, Huaman realised, was still present. Tello was preparing to pounce on it.

And when he pounced and captured the *ech* – if he did – it would still not be over. The elimination of the *ech* would only remove the negative elements from the ritual. Then the divination proper would start. Tello would chew coca, spit out the juice and interpret the way the spit spread out. After that, he would chew coca again, this time a single perfect leaf, mash it into a bolus, and determine whether the stalk or the tip of the leaf stuck out. Finally, he would throw a handful of coca leaves on to a piece of cloth and count how many of them had landed on their top sides. Then, at last, he would pronounce how to proceed into the future: whether the men should seek out Manku Yupanqui, or whether they should decide, irrevocably, to mobilise the campesinos, to commence Huaman's revolution and to persevere, irrespective of duration or hardship, until final victory.

It would go on and on until dawn.

Huaman thought he should go back, go to bed. But he could not face the prospect of Kollur sidling up to him with her pappy tits, elephant thighs and big cunt gurgling. That was another thing with the Indios. They took the mystery out of sex, made it as enjoyable as shitting and eating, and just as functional.

He sat down on the edge of the ring of men.

He dozed off.

'*Ech*! *Ech*! *Ech*! *Ech*! *Ech*!'

He woke up with a start.

'*Ech*! *Ech*! *Ech*! *Ech*! *Ech*!'

Tello was on his feet, shouting dementedly. He had seized his wand and was beating the air with it.

'*Ech*! *Ech*! *Ech*! *Ech*! *Ech*!'

Tello stopped whirling. He was holding his wand with difficulty, as if he had hooked something monstrous. The wand, to Huaman's amazement, bent and shook like a rope bridge in a storm.

Tello staggered towards the hole; then, swiftly, but with an effort that seemed superhuman, rammed the wand into the hole. He grabbed a bag of coca and a bag of herbs, and sprinkled their contents along the sides of the wand. He repeated the procedure with the *aguardiente*. He then twisted the wand ferociously, backwards and forwards, to shake off the heavy load. When the wand felt light in his hands, he roared, as if he himself contained thunder, and pulled the wand out of the hole. Swiftly, with an agility that belied his age, he filled the hole with earth, levelled the mound by jumping on it, and sealed the edges with more coca leaves, herbs, *aguardiente* and llama fat.

Then he sat down and, calmly, regulated his breath. '*Ech* is captive. Now, we start.'

The men, who had witnessed Tello's struggle in abject fear, broke into smiles.

Chauca handed Tello a fresh bag of coca leaves.

Huaman spat: an impotent, degutted spit. Chauca was the perfect example of what he had to contend with. A stalwart Indio, on the run, good with gun and knife, perfect at blending with the land, authoritative with the men, hence nominated lieutenant. Yet a throwback to Inca times. It had been Chauca who had asked for this divination. Since the *naturales* were co-creators with God, he had said, the men must consult God. Chauca would fight like a demon, stand loyal to his leader even if he faced a thousand guns, show neither pain nor fatigue on his impassive face, but what sort of an ideologue would he be, with that parched land behind his eyes, when the revolution succeeded?

Tello prepared to chew.

Huaman wrapped himself tightly in his poncho and closed his eyes. He fell asleep almost immediately.

He woke up, feeling Chauca standing over him.

Dawn had broken. The men had dispersed. Tello was down in the valley, wading through the low mist, like the avatar of a water-god, towards his next port of call.

'Is it finished? What happened?'

Chauca squatted down, leaning on his rifle. 'Very strange, *Comandante*. First go – Tello spat out coca juice evenly. Second go – coca ball showed both stalk and tip of leaf. Third go – coca leaves fall eleven top, eleven bottom. Three times, the future looks equal.'

'What's that supposed to mean?'

'It means maybe we find Manku Yupanqui or maybe we start revolution. Tello say Fate leaves decision to us.'

Huaman pulled himself up. 'All that charade for nothing! Right. We'll forget about Manku Yupanqui! We'll start recruiting immediately!'

'Not yet. We not happy yet.'

'You've had your divination! That's it!'

'We want someone to meet Manku Yupanqui. To judge if he is the one who will teach us how to crush skulls of our enemies.'

'And who will judge him – you?'

'I no wise. We ask you, *Comandante*.'

'Me!'

'You we trust. If Manku Yupanqui is he who we await, you will tell us, you will join.'

'And if he is not?'

'No more thoughts. We start your revolution.'

5

In your eyes of mourning the land of dreams begins

'Take you with me, child? Why?'

Teresa Ayala replied shyly, but the sound of the rapids drowned her words.

Father Quintana stepped closer to her, mesmerised by the river which thundered over the boulders, its spray drifting like mist over the verdant banks. The Indians called it 'The God Who Speaks', and disbelieved anyone who told them it ploughed its way to the tropics, there to feed an even greater river called the Amazon. This torrent, they claimed, which could feed a man and kill another at the same time, was subservient to no other; it simply climbed to a peak and lived by the side of the Sun.

'Speak up, child...'

Teresa glanced at Daniel self-consciously.

Daniel, sensitive to the girl's shyness, moved from the convent door to the bus shelter. He paused in front of the timetable, but did not bother to read it: the convent, situated at a stretch where the river began dropping to the lowlands, was on the San Martin road. They had briefly stopped off there that morning to be informed that, until further notice, all the buses had been allocated to those travelling to the desert. Manku Yupanqui, Father Quintana had gleefully remarked, had already achieved one miracle: he had unhitched the Indian countryside from the white man's coastal lands.

Teresa raised her voice. 'My husband will be there.'

A smile of surprise creased Father Quintana's face. She could not have been more than sixteen. He remembered the first time he had seen her. Some dozen years back – when he had stopped at this convent during an equally venturous journey, travelling from the port of Miranda to his new church in the Yungas. A sick toddler. Thrust upon the Mother Superior by emaciated parents who could no longer feed her. She had never gone hungry since. Yet her young face betrayed shades of rust, that particular decay of immutable hardship. Her body had no more flesh than when she was that child of skin and bone. Her hands and feet were already old. The wonder was that she still stood erect, that her spine had not yet buckled. But she would crumble soon, if not from having to slave for the nuns, then for lack of a future.

'I didn't know you had married, Teresa...'

She smiled, adjusting her faded dress. 'Not yet.'

'You said your husband...'

'Will be there, Papacha. In the desert.'

'Is this something the Sisters arranged?'

Teresa, as if afraid that the nuns' hearing could penetrate even the roar of the waters, became agitated. 'The Sisters do not know, Papacha...'

Father Quintana peered at her sternly. 'What have you been up to, Teresa?'

Daniel walked over to the pick-up, barely concealing his impatience. His hopes of finding transport now lay in Salinas, a village on the edge of the desert which had a large saltworks and daily deliveries to the port of Miranda. Father Quintana had promised to get him there before sundown.

'I – I have a little money, Papacha. You won't have to feed me.'

'This man you plan to marry – who is he? Where did you meet him?'

Teresa detected Daniel's impatience as he got into the pick-up. Agitated, she looked in the direction of the convent. The grounds were still empty. The Sisters had not finished their prayers. But they would soon. If she did not leave now, she would never leave. How could she explain her dreams to a priest? Dreams, the Mother Superior had told her, were the Devil's whispers; they diverted the soul from catechism, robbed it of the keys to God's Kingdom.

Holding her case carefully by the strings that held it secure, she ran to the pick-up. 'I will tell you as we go, Papacha.'

Father Quintana shuffled after her. 'You will tell me now, Teresa. Or you're not coming.'

Teresa flashed an apologetic smile at Daniel, placed her case on the back seat, made the sign of the cross, then faced Father Quintana. He was a saint – that was why he was addressed as Papacha, 'Great Father' – even if he had a vehicle like the rich. But the vehicle was old, and it was not a car but a pick-up. And he used it to help the people – carried campesinos, their produce, used it as a school, taught children how to read and write, often got into trouble with the authorities – so the Sisters had said. Which was what saints did.

'I – I have had dreams, Papacha. One dream. But many times. With angels. Not devils. I was chosen his bride. I was called Cura Occlo. Occlo means pure.'

'What are you talking about, child?'

'Manku Inca. He was killed by the Spanish. Before that, his wife, Cura Occlo, was martyred. Scourged with rods, shot with arrows, thrown into the river. It is going to be like that, Papacha. Only this time, Manku will win.'

Father Quintana held Teresa's calloused hands. 'Let me get this right, Teresa. You want to go to the desert because you want to marry Manku Yupanqui?'

'Yes, Papacha.'

Father Quintana forced a smile. 'What do you know about Manku Yupanqui?'

'Everything.' She moved to get into the pick-up.

Father Quintana held her back. 'Teresa! In all probability…' His stammer became more pronounced. '…Manku Yupanqui is a rumour. You know how people love such stories. You can't trust a rumour…'

Teresa looked into his eyes – piercingly, as if her pupils held the sun. 'But *you* trust it, Papacha. I heard you tell the Sisters when they were feeding you and your friend. You came all this way – from the Yungas…'

'I am not running away.'

'Nor I. I will be his bride. I will be a good wife.'

Father Quintana patted her on the cheek to show her he believed she would make a good wife to any man. Then he took her suitcase out of the pick-up, handed it to her and, gently, turned her towards the convent.

Tears welling up in her eyes, she spun round again. 'Why won't you take me?'

'I can't let you leave your life here for a rumour.'

Agonised, she looked to Daniel for help.

Embarrassed, Daniel lowered his gaze.

Teresa threw herself at Father Quintana's feet. 'I must go, Papacha. Please… My dreams – like annunciation. Pure dreams – pure like what makes you go…'

Father Quintana pulled her up. If only his motives were as pure as her dreams. He stroked her hair, wanting to confess that his journey was not one of faith but of doubt; that though he worshipped the Son because he saw His face every day on every campesino, he had never seen the Father or the Holy Spirit lending a hand, alleviating poverty, healing disease, confronting ruthless landowners; that, therefore, he was losing his faith, seeking, in despicable apostasy, either the completion of the self or its destruction. How could he tell her all that, this confused, heretical, lost Eusebio Quintana? 'I can't take you, Teresa.'

'You think I am unworthy.'

'You are pure. Very pure.' Unable to engage her eyes, he mumbled a blessing, then climbed into the pick-up.

As he turned the ignition, she clutched his hand. 'Papacha, in my dreams, the angels tell me Manku Yupanqui has come to do great things. It will be hard work. He will need someone by his side. Who will wash his clothes. Cook for him. Take away the tiredness in his limbs. Serve him *chicha* and coca. Lie with him. Give him breast. Take his seed. Only a wife can do all that. And the angels chose me.'

Father Quintana felt that rush of emotion with which he had witnessed, in days gone by, the presence of Jesus.

Who was he to deny the girl her dreams, to dismiss her passion? Uncontaminated by doubt, she possessed the very faith he so desperately sought. She *knew* that God would come down again and restore man in His image. Challenging what was or was not ordained – was that not an even greater apostasy?

Impulsively, knowing that in days to come he would regret the deed, but knowing also that he was surrendering to Divine Will, he rasped, 'Come.'

She jumped into the back like an angel flying. 'Quickly, Papacha. Before the Sisters finish prayers.'

Father Quintana drove off, glancing at Daniel. The latter offered him an equivocal smile.

The road ran parallel to the river. The waters roared on. At least one god, Father Quintana thought, wished them well.

6
They all believed that having teeth, having feet and hands and alphabet, life was only a matter of honour

Chauca, listening to the earth for sounds of soldiers, indicated that the land was calm.

Gaspar Huaman climbed on to the rubbish heap to survey the salt plains. A good general, he had declared, must check his minions' reports.

At the other end of the forecourt, Father Quintana was still testing Teresa's literacy.

Daniel kept his eyes on the sky. He had never seen the stars so clearly, so close. It was as if the Milky Way was overrunning its banks and splashing on to the earth. For the rest, Salinas was like an abandoned lunar colony: a saltworks ringed by two rows of tin huts for the employees; and an inn, at present shuttered, by the roadside. Its people, including the innkeeper, had gone to meet Manku Yupanqui.

And that had put paid to Daniel's hopes of hitching a lift to the coast from one of the works-trucks. Now, his last chance of transport lay in Illariy, further south, a small town close to the Tapestry of the Gods, that vast stretch of desert etched with endless lines, geometric shapes and animal figures by a mysterious civilisation for a mysterious purpose. Illariy, according to Huaman, had some air-taxi operators. Though these mainly catered for tourists for

aerial excursions over the sights, Daniel should be able to charter a plane –
all the way to La Merced.

Daniel began pacing again. The chill of the night had changed its character:
not ancestral as in the highlands, but the bitter spite of baked earth suddenly
cooling.

Chauca had put coffee on to boil. That man did not move; he simply
vanished and reappeared. He had first appeared soon after their arrival, late
afternoon. Squatted at the edge of the darkness across the courtyard, the
barrel of his rifle sticking out of his poncho, he had watched them, with
menacingly impassive eyes, search for the innkeeper. He had been sniffing
them out, making sure they were not missionaries, government agents,
informers or CIA, Huaman had told them after Chauca had fetched him out
of the darkness. Sniffing them out – despite the fact that, as Daniel had soon
discovered, Huaman and Father Quintana, in pursuit of their respective
vocations, had crossed paths on a number of occasions.

Huaman was a revolutionary. According to Father Quintana, but for his
atheism, he had the potential of a good leader.

Daniel was not keen on consorting with revolutionaries. The imperative,
in terms of the Kempin mission, was to steer clear of subversives. Moreover,
he had little tolerance of any extremist ideology; extremism invariably
produced Kempins, erected Third Reichs.

Nor had Huaman impressed him. A dessicated man seeking moisture as a
political prophet. The way he was scanning the land, for instance. There
were no soldiers stalking him. Since Che Guevara, soldiers had adopted
wholesale solutions; now, they simply laid the land waste and denuded maps
of mankind.

And yet, Daniel had to admit, he was fascinated by Huaman and Chauca.
His reckless half wished to be in their shoes, to grapple with adventure, taste
revolt, surrender to an act of commitment.

'Warm your bones, gringo.'

Chauca had appeared at his side, offering him coffee, smiling with mauve
gums. Malnutrition, he had boasted, had only succeeded in plundering his
teeth and that because he had broken them biting the hand that kept stealing
his food.

Daniel took the tin cup. 'Thank you.' He sat on a crate that served as one
of the inn's outdoor chairs.

In contrast to Huaman, Chauca was impressive. Of stocky build and hewn
Indian features; in his thirties but looking ageless. He was escorting Huaman
as near to the desert as it would be safe for him. For, as the posters of *Servicio
Especial de Seguridad*, which he had proudly exhibited, declared, he was a

bandido. He had sought higher wages for peons like himself, fought for his patch of land seized by a latifundista and killed a Sinchi in the shoot-out.

'Eat, my beauties. God wants you to be strong. He is watching over you.' Chauca, having handed coffees to Father Quintana and Teresa, was now feeding the horses. His speed of movement was startling.

'Hey, Chauca! If what you say is true – show us a sign. A footprint. A corner where He had a crap.' Huaman was pissing; and grinning; and winking at Daniel.

Irritated by the obligatory Marxist blasphemy, Daniel ignored him.

Huaman came down from the rubbish heap and helped himself to some coffee; medium height, narrow shoulders, sallow complexion, a fleshless frame supporting an oversize head; about forty, but still baby-faced.

Chauca stayed with the horses.

Huaman squatted by Daniel, tucking his poncho beneath his haunches. 'I think I've offended him.'

Daniel sipped his coffee. Chauca's smell lay over it.

'That's the Indio for you – can't take irreverence. If they could, there would be no stopping them.' Huaman turned round and yelled, 'Hey, Chauca! *Venceremos!*'

Chauca's face burst into a toothless smile. '*Venceremos, Comandante! Venceremos*, gringo! *Patria o Muerte!*'

Daniel found himself raising a clenched fist. Somehow Che Guevara's old war-cries did not seem anachronistic. The moonscape made them timeless.

Huaman broke into one of his rare smiles. 'But, as you can see, all heart. Give him the right pole and he can shift the earth.'

Daniel ran his fingers over the bullet grazes on the tin cup. They were testimonies to the previous owners – all killed by the Sinchis. Chauca prized the cup as a record of his people's history.

'It's not the earth that needs shifting. It's the evil in man.' Father Quintana strode over to them.

'We will shift that, too, Padre.'

'With slogans and guns!'

'We will drain it like a swamp. By planting on it the good in man.'

Huaman's answer surprised Daniel. He had been expecting some hackneyed polemic, not a pastoral conviction. Maybe the hollowness he saw in Huaman was fear. Maybe Huaman was like him, seeking the self that would wade into life.

Father Quintana sat on the ground. 'In that case, I pray to God you will succeed.'

'Please, Padre. Let's leave God out of it.'

'How can we?'

Daniel's uneasiness increased. Huaman and Father Quintana had been spoiling for an argument. Throughout supper – or what had passed as supper: a stale corn-cake Teresa had shared out – only Chauca's anecdotes had prevented them from launching into it.

He fumbled for his cigarettes. He should not get involved. The political realities of this country and what God did here had nothing to do with him.

Perversely, he found himself joining in. 'That's the crucial question, Gaspar. How can you leave God out of it?'

Huaman twisted round, eager for fresh blood. 'Easily. We don't know Him. He is not from these parts. Judging by the way He deals in Mammon and might, we suspect He's a gringo.'

Daniel's antipathy forestalled Father Quintana. 'We? Chauca didn't sound as if he agrees with that.'

'Chauca still clings to his narcotics – God and coca. But even the Indio can be taught to kick a habit.'

Father Quintana growled. 'The Indio, as you call him, knows better than the *misti*. He will prove you wrong.'

Huaman became contemptuous. 'Look at what God has given him. Yesterday, he was a *flagelado*, the whipped one. Before that, he was an *olvidado*, the forgotten one. Today, he is an *abandonado*. Past erased. No future written. Human detritus clinging to a land where dignity has become a distant memory. You can see his despair from the way he prefers to sit with the horses. His passage through life marked only by the caked shit on his trousers' seat. But come tomorrow, he should have a reason to live. Tomorrow, he will walk in the footsteps of Marx and Lenin, Trotsky and Mao, Castro and Guevara. Tomorrow, at last, he will believe in man!'

Chauca, Daniel observed, was rubbing one of the horse's legs and humming to himself. That was not despair, but the natural harmony between man and his world.

Father Quintana filched one of Daniel's cigarettes. 'The good in man – that is God-given. Chauca knows that. He wants others to know it also. For that, he might need a revolution. But what sort of revolution? What will Marxist ideology do for him except feed his anger, pamper his resentment, provide him with a gun?'

'And a crusade, Padre. It will provide him with a crusade. Tie him to the family of man.'

'He is not alienated. He has his people. His people are part of the family. God is the Father. What good is a crusade that forces people to turn their backs on the Father?'

Huaman sniggered. 'If Chauca had found his crusade sooner, he would still have had his teeth – and that, for here, is unheard of.' His snigger rose to a snarl. 'The first thing he would have done would have been to abandon faith in saviours like Manku Yupanqui. He would have known that the only hope lay in a permanent revolution because only a permanent revolution guarantees the continuous equal sharing of the wealth.'

Daniel tried to imagine the dream that ruled Huaman's doctrines. A revolution welding the working classes and the campesinos, even the enlightened bourgeoisie, to produce a new society of new men in Guevara's image. *In perpetua.* But could the new men breathe life, acquire souls, without the touch of the Divine? 'Equal sharing of the wealth! That's a fantasy. Even if it were not, what good is politics if it only boils down to wealth?'

Huaman addressed him as if he were an imbecile. 'Man's needs are material. Struggling to satisfy them is what he does from birth to death. Therefore, politics can have one aim only: to make wealth his birthright.'

Father Quintana hooted. 'Back to the worship of the golden calf! What of morality then?'

'There is more morality in Marxism than in the whole of Christianity, Padre.'

'You're talking nonsense, Gaspar. All ideologies are ruled by economics. All are variations on capitalism. You can't sanctify material wealth. You need a different foundation for a revolution if you really want to establish a just society.'

Huaman appeared to be distracted by Teresa who had quietly approached to listen to them. Daniel recognised the vulnerability in Huaman's face: the chronic fear of something moving, of even the most innocent thing moving, that afflicted a man stuck in an unending night.

Abruptly, Huaman faced Father Quintana and rasped, 'What sort of foundation?'

'What you keep denying: God's breath.'

Daniel looked up sharply. God's breath! Was that what he had said? Or was he imagining it?

Huaman's voice grated. 'God's breath, Padre? What's that? What does it mean?'

God's breath – no mistake. Daniel felt he was shrinking, losing substance and adulthood, falling into childhood, landing on a chair too big for him, listening to his father, alone, because his mother was in the other room supervising his sisters' music practice. *Wholeness*, Daniel – that's God's breath.

Somewhere above that child, Father Quintana was echoing Papa. 'Chauca would call it the sun's missing ray, Gaspar.'

Wholeness. Duality fused into One. Where hope, intimacy and salvation would not yield to despair, terror and damnation. Where fear would be contained by courage. *Wholeness* – where Evil is defied and, therefore, deprived of its dominion. That's God's breath, *preciado*.

Preciado, meaning 'precious' in Ladino. That's what Papa used to call me.

Daniel's eyes misted. Papa, pure soul, bravest dolphin in the malign sea. You always had God's breath. I've lagged behind. Fear kept coming between God and me. Maybe that's why I ceased being a Jew, why I embraced Jesus. I wanted a God who would replace the malign sea with a clement one; I wanted a God who would germinate the seeds of sanctity we all carry. Failing that, I wanted a God who would take my sins on His shoulders and redeem me.

Huaman was shouting as if addressing a congress. 'The Universalist view. Holiness, happiness and God's kingdom on earth! What the world should be and will be! Dreams of Utopia!'

I'm changing now, Papa. I may never achieve wholeness. But I won't be as fragmented as I have been. I'm repairing myself. If need be, I'll kill. I've never admitted this: I want to kill Kempin; I think I can.

Huaman was still shouting. 'Dreams of Utopia, Padre – what remedy is that?'

Daniel stared at Huaman. The child on the big chair burst into growth, filled up with resolve and sinew, became the man he would be tomorrow. Sternly, he faced Huaman. 'Not a remedy as yet. But a powerful protest. Gathering momentum. Being heard more and more. Most of man's efforts are murderous. Even his best effort at a free and democratic society is imperfect. Hence, it is time to breathe God's breath!'

Huaman met Daniel's anger with contempt. 'You sound like a desperate man, *amigo*. Like you need God, but can't have Him. Or like you are trying to create Him.'

Daniel saw Father Quintana watching him. Pityingly? 'I don't need to create Him. I have Him.'

They were all watching him. Waiting for him to be cornered? And recant?

Huaman smirked. 'No doubts?'

Stand firm! Stifle that inner voice which has been telling you the Second Coming has already occurred in the days of the Third Reich and that it was not Jesus who came but Satan with his single commandment: *thou shalt not consider life sacred*.

'I have Him.'

Smugly, Huaman raised his eyebrows. 'Not even a shadow of a doubt?'

Tell him if you must: you have betrayed. But stand firm: you're seeking absolution. And swear, swear, you'll never be a worm again; this time, when the battle gets hot, you won't desert!

Father Quintana leaned across Daniel and shook Huaman by his shoulders. 'Doubts – and living with them – are part of every man's faith, Gaspar.'

Huaman snorted, then tapped Daniel on the chest. 'You know what, *amigo*? You should go and take a look at Manku Yupanqui. Then decide about God.'

Daniel rose abruptly. 'I should get some sleep – that's what I should do.' He hurried over to the pick-up.

7

A life of stone after so many lives

Daniel sipped the Inca-Cola. It was the only comfort offered by the hut that served as Illariy airfield's all-purpose building. It was sickly-sweet, but it kept dehydration at bay. The parched wind raged from every direction.

The town, next to the airfield, slept in a placenta of dust in the shade of the oasis; its Quechua name meant 'the light of dawn'. Most of its people had gone to the desert.

On the airstrip stood five air-taxi monoplanes and the helicopter gunship; the former had been grounded on General Fuego's orders; the latter was being refuelled by her crew.

The pilots of the air-taxis had gone home.

The Sinchis who had piled out of the helicopter, a company of forty men, sat on the pockmarked, melting tarmac, smoking and joking. Jerry Rice, the American reporter, was pirouetting around them, firing questions. He was getting no response.

Sinchi, Rice had told him, was an Inca title meaning 'warlord'. The corps had been created by General Fuego and was now the most ferocious commando force in the continent. This present unit, distinguished by its armband and sinister nickname, Los Novios de la Muerte – the Bridegrooms of Death – was even more special. Comprising mostly foreign mercenaries and ex-terrorists, and led by Colonel Angelito, it was the SES's storm troops, accountable only to General Fuego.

An amiable depressive, Rice. Mid-sixties, starchy, overweight. A journalist of some repute. One of that breed, he had described himself, who fucked with hang-ups, lived on booze, adrenalin and insomnia, drifted on an unreliable second wind, and ran on severely calloused eyes.

General Fuego's jeep, sent from the Illariy garrison, was parked outside the hut. Dr Luke Williston, the other American, was exhorting the driver with a bilingual Bible. The Word was available now, both in Spanish and Quechua – grab it!

Williston, as he had proudly disclosed, was Moral Crusade's overseer on 'Project Legion', a missionary network commissioned to drive out the unclean spirits from Latin America as Jesus had driven out the devils from the man called Legion. A Doctor of Divinity, his real talents lay in baptism and preaching – activities, he had bewailed, somewhat curtailed by his posting to these lands. But in the past, in the States, he had baptised whole congregations into born-again Christianity, exhorted millions, through his preaching on television specials, to surrender to such Bible-blessed truths as purity, glory, patriotism and capitalism. With the Lord's help, he would sow the same truths here in this country plagued by communism, paganism and Liberation Theology. With the Lord's help, he would lead her poor souls to the Kingdom of God which was the kingdom the Lord wanted established on earth and which, indeed, had already been established in those regions of the United States where Moral Crusade's commandments ruled absolutely.

Daniel had come to detest him. Fundamentalism was a regression to the Dark Ages. Autocratic and obscurantist, it exploited, in the soulless age of materialism, people's desperate need for spiritual values and brainwashed them with zealotry. Williston, he had decided, was one of those *arrivistes* the movement inevitably attracted. Hawking remissions with shammed sincerity; bombast and geniality concealing shit.

Daniel bought another Inca-Cola from the machine.

At the far end of the tarmac, staring at the distant hills which had long expired, was the marmoreal figure of Colonel Angelito, immaculate in battle fatigues. Handsome like a film star. But, as Yizkor had warned Daniel, Fuego's disciple.

Fuego himself, decked with a revolver on each hip, stood on the porch, holding up to the sun the piece of canvas bearing Daniel's tests of the Pintoyaku moss.

Daniel sat down on the bench, gazed yet again at the Tapestry of the Gods poster on the far wall.

This trip had overrun absurdity. Father Quintana had dropped him at the airfield at daybreak, the best time to fly over the Tapestry of the Gods, and, therefore, the time when all the pilots would be available for business. Rice and Williston, having arrived earlier – both investigating the Manku Yupanqui phenomenon in the line of their respective professions – had each hired a plane to fly to the desert. The remaining three pilots had almost fought each other to take Daniel to La Merced. At that juncture, the radio had relayed Fuego's orders stopping all flights. The reason, gleaned later from Colonel Angelito's vague explanations, had surprised everybody; some guerrillas, trapped in the area, had hired a smuggler plane to airlift them under the cover of the people's influx; by grounding all aircraft, the SES expected to track the smuggler plane to its rendezvous for a decisive strike. This operation had been deemed so important that General Fuego had undertaken to oversee it personally.

Daniel lit a cigarette. Damned country. He should have made for a hotel the moment he had heard Fuego's name. This was the Security Chief himself; by all accounts, Satan incarnate; the man who, Yizkor had contended, was very likely hand-in-glove with Kempin.

Instead, he had hung around, telling himself that he might persuade Fuego to permit him to fly to La Merced, that, indeed, with Fuego out of the capital, here was his chance to do something about Kempin immediately – to start checking that list of Kempin's possible whereabouts, at least.

Fuego had duly arrived and, to Daniel's surprise, revealing considerable familiarity with the polyptych, had appeared only too pleased to meet the man who was going to restore it. But he had firmly refused to let him go.

Defying fate by disdaining to run away from Fuego – was that courage?

Sometimes, these days, he could not recognise himself. The urge to disregard Yizkor's directives and pursue Kempin alone, for instance; and the sanguine way he thought he was capable of that. Equally irrational: indulging the whim to chase after Manku Yupanqui, to go and see whether, tomorrow, under the full moon, the desert would be biblical, whether there would be miracles for all men.

His need to know if there could be a saviour had acquired the same intensity as his need to bring Kempin to justice. Perhaps the two needs were the two halves of Wholeness.

Had he really begun to change? Was there hope, at last?

Fuego returned from the porch, sat opposite him and handed back the piece of canvas. 'It *is* an incredible blue, Mr Brac. If there were life after death, its blood would have this colour.'

Basically an ordinary-looking man: a heavily weathered face; sharp, angular features of the highland Indian; medium height. Yet immensely striking; powerfully built with sure-footed gait and luminous eyes, he looked like Ezekiel's Lucifer, the princely creature who walked proudly among stones that flashed with fire. Were Fuego a woman, Daniel might have desired him.

Daniel put the canvas into his rucksack. 'Sad, don't you think – this blue should have been a basic colour for all your painters – not unique to one work.'

'Colonialism, Mr Brac. It always blights indigenous art. What could our old masters do except follow Spanish traditions? Critics say the moderns are at long last ethnic. I disagree. The Indio spoors you find in them are merely acts of reparation to the culture their ancestors almost destroyed. Fashionable apologia, you understand – lacking in spirit.'

Daniel nodded, impressed. How could such a perceptive man be a monster? Yet, the way Fuego had spat out the word 'Indio' had given him a glimpse of a dark, limitless contempt.

Like on that fateful journey in the SS-truck which had ended in a mass grave in a forest clearing shrouded by snow. Pig-dog Jews! And when Joseph Perera had held his son close for the last time, whispering that the men would rush at their captors so that his son, Daniel, his *preciado*, could escape into the forest and hide, hide, then run, run. Pig-dog Jews! Vermin!

'What will you call the blue? As its discoverer, the honour must be yours.'

Disarming. Maybe they had exaggerated about him. 'Inca blue – I thought…'

'Don't be humble, Mr Brac. The virtuous don't get any potatoes in this world. Call it Brac's blue. Stamp your name on history.'

Daniel stubbed out his cigarette. 'It would be a footnote, at the most.'

'Good enough for the likes of us.'

'I'm only a restorer, General.'

'You are being modest again. Or choosing to misunderstand.'

Daniel faced him warily. 'I'm sorry, I don't follow you.'

'I am talking about journeys and destinations.'

Daniel forced a laugh. 'I've always let the wind take me places.'

'Is that because you trust the world or because you believe in predestiny?'

'Neither.'

'Then you must believe in yourself. That is admirable.'

Daniel, disconcerted by Fuego's scrutiny, shrugged.

Fuego beamed another charming smile. 'An Indio sage once told me we all start from the same place – from the altiplano. Most of us run around in circles and end up roughly where we started. The rest find a way out. Half climb the mountains; the other half descend to the coast. Assuming we are among those who escape the altiplano, which is best for us: the mountains or the coast?'

Daniel lit another cigarette. 'Both are equally attractive, I'd say.'

'Attractive, yes. But only one has breasts: the coast. The sea always feeds.

On the mountains, there are only rocks – and not even scorpions under them.'

Daniel drew deeply on his cigarette. 'There is also God. He hangs around a lot on mountains.'

Fuego nodded solemnly. 'Strange. That is exactly what the Indio sage said. But that is not much good if you can't see Him. If you can't find Him. If you cease believing in Him.'

Daniel met Fuego's eyes. Now definitely the eyes of the Prince of Darkness.

He should tell him. There's one place you're sure to find God, in the hearts of those who defy death. You should have seen my father the day he joined Tito's partisans. When Joseph Perera kissed his wife and family goodnight that Friday, when he drove away, contravening the Sabbath for the first time in his life, that provincial Jewish merchant with the fashionable, thin moustache and the perennial smile of the Talmudic scholar, spine and pot-belly curving towards a soft question mark and hands turned to white gloves from successfully dealing with banknotes and ledgers – he had God in his heart. So much God that when you next saw him, he seemed to have erupted straight out of the Book of Judges – a Samson, Nazirite hair and beard complete, who could pull down rock pillars!

Daniel decided it would be prudent to yield to Fuego. 'God can be elusive, yes.' He drank the rest of his Inca-Cola; it tasted bitter.

'He never is! He's always right by our side!' Williston had invaded the hut with his massive frame. 'I know the General is beyond redemption, but you, Mr Brac, surely, you know better!'

Rice shuffled in. 'Hey, look…'

Williston raised an imperious hand. 'Hush a moment, Jerry. We're talking about the Lord. The Lord, Mr Brac, He is your only destination. I'd be mighty happy to show you the way.'

'I can find it myself.'

'He is elusive, you say. You'll get lost.'

Fuego, Daniel noticed, was listening with great interest. But he did not seem inclined to challenge Williston. 'All paths lead to Rome.'

Williston extracted a cologne-wipe from his wrist-bag and refreshed his sweating face. 'That sounds Popish. Are you Roman?'

Daniel ignored the taunt. Smiling disdainfully, he watched Williston grooming himself. Unlike the others, he did not have to raise his head to face Williston; his height matched the evangelist's. As for Williston's greater girth, that was solid rather than supple. Much as Williston had boasted that his size was a gift from the Lord so that he would be a rock, like Peter, he was a man, Daniel felt, who was uncomfortable with his body, his beautifully cut fawn suit, for instance, like fancy wrapping covering up red meat. Not a body, as Daniel thought of his own, which could make love joyfully, relish its fluids as well as those of another.

Williston gushed good cheer. 'Never mind. My communion doesn't differentiate between the misguided. The offer stands. Come and be saved.'

Pointedly, Daniel turned to Rice. 'I apologise. You have something to say...'

Rice, winking at Daniel in sympathy, turned to Fuego. 'The chopper's refuelled, General. They could give us a ride.'

Fuego rose. 'Sorry, Mr Rice.' He held out his hand to Daniel. 'We might meet again.'

Daniel responded to Fuego's grip equally strongly. 'Yes.' Then he watched the Bridegrooms of Death as they trotted towards the helicopter through the billowing dust. Like ghouls from a nether world.

As Fuego strode out, Rice pursued him.

Williston sniffed at his armpits; satisfied that the sweat had not come through, he readjusted the sleeves of his jacket, then sauntered after them.

Daniel zipped up his rucksack. He found the smell of pine-oil Williston had left behind offensive.

Colonel Angelito boarded the helicopter in the wake of his men.

Rice turned argumentative. 'Come on, General. They could easily drop me where the people are!'

Fuego signalled the helicopter pilot to take off. 'My men are going to hunt bandits, Mr Rice. High up on the mountains. They are not running a bus service for people who have nothing better to do than chase myths.'

As the helicopter lifted off, Rice caught a face at a window: Colonel Angelito, grinning. He took a swig from his hip-flask and muttered to himself. 'Fuck you, too, General.'

Fuego moved to his jeep. Williston, pushing past the driver, swooped on him. 'General, I aim to get to that desert – walk, if need be. Now, you wouldn't want to put a good friend of this country to so much trouble, would you?'

Fuego shook his head impatiently. 'Dr Williston. Forget about Manku Yupanqui. He is a figment of the people's imagination. A fairy-tale to rock the children to sleep.'

The formality between Fuego and Williston, Rice felt, was play-acting. There was a special relationship between them. Some sort of pact that dated back to Williston's arrival from the States within days of Fuego's appointment as Chief of the SES. Discernible only in Fuego's tolerance of Williston, like keeping to the background when Williston and Brac were sparring. Fuego never suffered fools, least of all sanctimonious ones. What made him suffer Williston?

Rice took another swig. The trouble was he was having difficulty reading

Williston. Beneath that born-again razzmatazz, Williston had wires and components; not a heart that nurtured dreams or buried ideals. But what else? Some sort of a power-broker? And important enough to make Fuego uneasy! Not CIA, no. Something more clandestine? Given all that fundamentalist drivel, a cabal far to the right? One of the hidden hands that formulated those asinine American policies which drove the Third World to despair and communism?

Rice winced as his mind skittered on the whisky. A few years back, he could have identified a shadow master with his eyes closed. Now, he had to deduce – and not all that confidently.

So he was fading, so what? He still had a few assignments in him. He took one more swig, then propelled himself towards Fuego. He spoke with the careful speech of a man who had conquered the slurring of heavy drinking. 'General, myth or no myth, there is a man out there called Manku Yupanqui – and people gathered to meet him. I insist I'm allowed to report it!'

Fuego shrugged his shoulders. 'If there is a man out there, he is a charlatan. Or a crazed hermit. Or a practical joker. Take my word for it!'

'I'd rather see for myself.'

Williston activated his preacher's voice. 'And I repeat, General, I aim to see him. We've put in a lot of work, spent a lot of money, to bring salvation to this country. It's imperative I check out with my own eyes what sort of adversary Satan has sent against us.'

Fuego scrutinised his driver, then, exasperated, nodded. 'Very well. I will send Luis back with my jeep.'

Williston applied another cologne-wipe to his forehead. 'Good man, General. Moral Crusade is obliged to you.'

Daniel, who had been standing on the porch indecisively, now approached them. 'Would you mind if I tagged along?'

Rice nodded amicably. 'Glad of the company.'

'You, too, Mr Brac?'

Daniel glanced uncertainly at Fuego. 'Well, I've heard rumours that the polyptych has some connection with Manku Yupanqui – I'm intrigued.'

Williston guffawed. 'The things one hears in Babylon – and believes. Sure thing, pal. Come along.'

Fuego smiled blandly. 'I must say, you people amaze me. I tell you, if I had not been chasing bandits, I would have been tempted to go with you!' Suddenly losing interest in them, he jumped into the jeep. 'If you will excuse me, I have wasted enough time!'

8

A spent moon, a moon from hand to hand, from bell to bell

The six *varayoks* and their respective wives, the *mamaconas*, kept their eyes on the full moon.

The children slept.

The mummified remains of the ancestors sat, as they had sat for centuries, waiting for time to give them new breath.

A wingless condor of iron scratched the moon's retina, then swooped down, blades whirring.

The *varayoks* recognised it as a helicopter. They nodded at each other in anticipation; they lifted their long staffs, symbols of their authority, ceremoniously; they smiled. It augured well that Manku Yupanqui had acquired one of those machines of the Sinchis. Had the Incas possessed horses, like the Conquistadores, the Children of the Sun would not have been enslaved.

The helicopter landed. Its doors opened, releasing the rousing cadence of a *jaylli*, a song of victory.

A youth jumped out, gilded in aura like maize, lofty like *apu*, sculpted in the sweat of the sun and the tears of the moon.

The *varayoks* and *mamaconas* moved forward to greet him.

They were leaders and mothers of communities most renowned for justice and love of the land. They had trekked to this ancient burial site as the people's petitioners. They had a simple message to convey. The people had been reluctant to enter the necropolis for fear of disturbing ancestral spirits all of whom, they assumed, Manku Yupanqui would raise from death. They were waiting in the desert in multitudes – every *ayllu* in the land; good *ayllus*; the members of which toiled for the welfare of the community and not for any given individual, worked the land collectively, performed the requisite rituals to ensure fertility, struggled jointly to safeguard the plots, produce, livestock, culture and their very existence. *Ayllus*, therefore, that were still endowed with good shoots. As proof of this claim, the *varayoks* and *mamaconas* had brought some children, chosen at random, for Manku Yupanqui to assess.

The *varayoks* and *mamaconas* had long practice in expressing the words of the heart. But, on this occasion, in Manku Yupanqui's presence, they felt tongue-tied.

They were not given the chance to find their words.

Death-reapers spilled out from the bowels of the helicopters; their cries, full of blood-lust, eclipsed the heavens.

Some of the *varayoks* and *mamaconas* managed to shout a warning to the golden youth. 'Manku Yupanqui! Save yourself!'

The paragon unleashed his fiery hair and roared like a thousand pumas.

The earth tipped over into the pit of the night.

9

For the dead there is land!

They stood close to each other in the pre-Inca necropolis.

Daniel Brac.

Jerry Rice.

Father Eusebio Quintana.

Beatriz Santillan.

Gaspar Huaman.

Teresa Ayala.

Dr Luke Williston.

General Oseas Fuego.

Most of the eyes had turned to salt; most of the minds were shrivelled; most of the hands hung limp.

Daniel felt he was standing at time's window, staring at the past and the present; the future, as ever, was under fog. The past had been scored by Kempin's machine-gun. Today's corpses bore the same angry expression as yesterday's; they, too, had been left to wolves and vultures.

In the past, on the snow, his father's blood had turned into rubies to beseech God's averted eyes. Now, those same rubies sparkled in the dust, still indicting the sky. A brave man, Joseph Perera. Since his execution, he had never failed to lie down with the massacred.

No Sinchis. Just troops from Illariy garrison, raw recruits and still unmilitary. They waited by their trucks. One attended to Fuego's horse; another kept watch on the children huddled near the corpses.

A ring of some fifty families squatted silently at a distance, wary of the soldiers, yet defiant. They were the remnants of the multitude that had gathered in the desert to lay eyes on Manku Yupanqui. Beatriz identified them as highlanders. The coastal dwellers and those from the Yungas had fled.

Most of the hearts cursed the setting sun for having provided light for this abomination.

Disinterred skulls and bones of the necropolis lay strewn on the ground. The wind preached the cult of the spirits by twirling strands of cotton and hair it had prised loose from the mummies. Only a line of algarroba trees on the horizon hinted at a world of life.

Silence ruled. The silence of the dead: the old dead, the new dead, and the living dead.

The mummies, sitting under heavy clothing, skulls blanched, arms across the chest, exhumed by the elements, but still in the position they had been buried in long before the Spanish conquest, appeared to be sniggering into their jawbones. Only Teresa, with that pure wisdom of youth, understood that they were wailing. The old dead, because they knew what death was, always mourned the new dead.

Most of the stomachs pleaded to vomit.

The new dead were the *varayoks* and *mamaconas* who had acted as the people's delegates. When they had failed to return, their sons had searched for them. One of those killed was the old *varayok* from Pintoyaku. This time, this journey, there would be no selection for life or death, he had said.

They had been laid on the ground, in pairs, and face down – a configuration denoting devilry. They had been stripped naked. Their clothes and possessions had been burned in a purification ritual. To prevent them from denouncing their executioners in the afterlife, their tongues had been torn out and their eyes gouged. Their ankles had been broken to stop them from seeking revenge on the living. The women had had their vaginas stuffed with stones to render them barren for eternity. Portraits of Manku Yupanqui which they had carried had been nailed to the ground above each head to specify, like the inscription on the Cross, the charges against them.

Most of the legs strained to flee.

The children had been spared. Not for humanitarian reasons, Gaspar Huaman had told them, but to persuade the people to go on enduring the unendurable.

The children had been unable to provide a lucid account of the killings. They had described the assailants as demons in masks and barely clothed. Maybe riding an iron chariot – but they could have imagined that, or dreamed it; they had been sleeping at the time. Nor could they relate, in their confusion and shock, whether any of the *varayoks* or *mamaconas* had seen or talked to Manku Yupanqui, or whether the saviour had appeared at all – though one child had sworn that he had glimpsed a man who had braided the stars on his head.

On the last issue, the people had drawn their own conclusions. It was inconceivable that Manku Yupanqui had broken his word. He had appeared. And, since no trace of the demons had been found, he had avenged the murdered by obliterating the killers. Such a feat was well within his capabilities. An earthshaker, armed with the sun's missing ray, he had emerged to do just that: to dematerialise evil. And on the strength of that belief, the people could reassure themselves. Manku Yupanqui would reappear. Sometime. Soon. Word would reach them as to where.

Most of the throats swelled with the screams they had stifled.

General Fuego broke the vigil. Clapping his hands and barking orders, he directed the troops to load the dead into the trucks.

Huaman, Rice and Beatriz moved about uncertainly. Father Quintana hurried towards the corpses muttering more prayers. Teresa, slinking behind him, squatted by the nearest body and watched the soldiers prepare the plastic bags that would serve as shrouds. Dr Williston paused by one of the mummies.

Daniel stood still. There was the reflex snapping at him to take to his heels, back to work, to libertinism, to drifting safely where the waters were calm. Against that, there was the newly found intrepidity, the lemming-urge for the dark – the real side – of life, impelling him to stay. A third force, Beatriz Santillan, was lending support to the second.

Since seeing her at Tingo Santa Rosa, he had often thought about her – a great deal, during the long hours of driving. Now that their paths had crossed again, he wanted to fall in love with her, seize her as a constant centre, envelop her, roam over her, enter her and be enthroned in her. Such a hunger in the presence of brutal death was depraved, he knew. But it was also auspicious: seeking life in death was how a person took on substance.

But she had paid little attention to him. They had not even met – not really, not as man and woman, not shook hands, declared who they were, implied who they could be. How then could she consider that this chance encounter might contain a spark?

Strange how they had all gathered together.

Rice, Williston and he, travelling in Fuego's jeep, had duly joined the multitude in the desert. Given Father Quintana's mania for mingling with people, they had, inevitably, come across him. Teresa, otherworldly like all cloistered virgins, had been sticking close to the priest. Huaman, vulnerable without Chauca's protection, had been seeking safe company and, eventually, had sniffed them out. Beatriz, glowing like a lodestar, had proved an irresistible magnet with her singing. Only the presence of Fuego had been unexpected. He had arrived, just before sunset, riding a horse. The guerrillas he had been chasing, he had brusquely informed them, had managed to escape.

Thus, they had spent the night waiting for Manku Yupanqui; like invalids at Lourdes, exchanging few words, keeping a distance. They had separated, this morning, after news of the massacre, during the people's exodus. They had met again here – surprised that they had not been alone in their compulsion to see what had happened.

Rice approached and offered his hip-flask. 'Who the fuck could have done this?'

The smell of the whisky compounded Daniel's nausea. He shook his head, then, as the American moved towards Beatriz, followed him.

Huaman, hearing Rice, joined them. 'These days when the campesinos talk of demons they don't mean spirits. They mean death-squads in helicopters – the Bridegrooms of Death.'

It took courage to accuse the Bridegrooms of Death within earshot of Fuego. And Daniel admired Huaman for that. 'Not so loud, Gaspar…'

Rice mused as Williston sauntered over. 'We saw Fuego send a unit in a helicopter. But he said they were after guerrillas.'

Huaman laughed sardonically. 'What guerrillas? There are no guerrillas in this country. *Not yet!*'

Williston intejected. 'Are you suggesting Fuego's men did this? Why should they massacre ordinary people?'

'To terrorise the campesinos. To destroy their hopes, aspirations…'

'Propaganda!' Fuego had come upon them unobserved. 'What do you expect – from a Marxist?' He spoke quietly, his hands resting on his revolvers. 'I have been speaking to the people, too. I am one of them. They do not say it is soldiers. Bandits, they say. Guerrillas.'

Daniel, seeing that Beatriz was staring at Fuego in disbelief, seized the chance to impress her. 'Why should guerrillas kill the very people who could shelter them?'

Fuego's eyes, changing hue like litmus milk, reappraised Daniel. 'I detect Maoist theory. Guerrillas must blend with the people like fish in water. Right, Mr Brac?'

Daniel, aware that Beatriz was looking at him, became all the more challenging. 'Basic revolutionary principle.'

'Basic nonsense. Fish eat fish. Some fish, like the shark, will eat all the fish it can. Nature's law – stronger than revolutionary doctrine.'

'Nature's laws can be changed – given the right revolution.'

'That's the dream of the blind, Mr Brac.'

Beatriz had stepped nearer; and her hostility towards Fuego had increased.

'I might have a speck of sawdust in my eyes, General. But you seem to have a plank in yours.'

With disarming bonhomie, Fuego patted Daniel's shoulder. 'You are quoting Jesus. My mistake – you are religious.'

'I have faith – yes.'

Fuego nodded consolingly. 'I was religious, too, once. I used to quote Jesus, too – all the time. I still can.' He turned to the children and beckoned them. '*Tamitha cum!*'

As the children approached hesitantly, Fuego took Daniel's arm. He spoke confidingly. 'But I learned. Like these children will. Faith is a blindfold. It is surrender. Not the basis for revolution.'

Daniel's eyes met Beatriz's eyes. 'It's the basis for a just society.' He extricated himself from Fuego's grip.

Father Quintana had followed the children to offer them a protective presence. His white hair flowing in the wind, he waved his arms in the same painfull rhythm as his stammer. 'Jesus was a revolutionary, General. *I have come to set fire to the earth* – that's what he said.'

Fuego smiled dismissively. 'Go away, Padre. The Vatican has ears in the dust. Go – before they damn you as schismatic.'

Williston veered towards Father Quintana like a juggernaut. 'Shame on you, Padre – inciting people with apostasy!'

Father Quintana faced him defiantly, furiously pointing at the corpses. 'This – this is apostasy!'

Williston assumed his preacher's voice. 'This is what happens when there is revolution – anarchy! Which is why obedience is the Christian imperative. That's what Saint Paul said. Any challenge to the state, to the social order, is treason against the Lord since it is the Lord Himself who put them there in the first place.'

'Saint Paul was ruled by fear. Jesus rebelled for us, died for us and saved us with His Blood!'

Williston's voice boomed. 'You should be unfrocked, old man!'

Daniel stepped in between Williston and Quintana. 'Leave him alone!'

Williston rasped, 'I won't stand by and listen to profanity!'

Daniel stood his ground. 'Move off, then. Stop bullying him.'

Fuego intervened. Steering himself between Daniel and the enraged Williston, he prodded Father Quintana amiably. 'Go, Padre. Attend to the dead. They are waiting to enter the Kingdom of God.'

Father Quintana blinked, disoriented by Fuego's gentleness. 'Yes. They are. Yes.' He shuffled back towards the corpses, still waving his arms. 'But remember Jesus. *I have not come to bring peace, but a sword...*'

Fuego shouted after him. 'Don't you see? That was the greatest confidence trick of all! He gave you a toy. A crucifix! A piece of wood that looks like a sword. Blunt on both sides! And sharp at the hilt so that he who holds it cuts his own wrists!'

Father Quintana paused, stared at Fuego pitifully, then resumed the prayers for the dead.

Fuego sighed. 'There you see it. The face of perennial defeat. Even his eyes clang with chains.'

'Chains can be broken.'

Fuego turned to the speaker. 'How, Beatriz?'

'By a people united!'

Fuego's voice dropped to a caress. 'Only in your songs, *querida*. That is why we love you so much.'

Daniel could not mistake the eddies of an old intimacy. He was stunned. How could Cain have known Shulamit of the Song of Songs? He felt searingly jealous.

'I echo the people's sentiments, Oseas.'

'You were wiser before you met the people, *querida*. But, I am told, you are wilder now.'

Beatriz looked embarrassed. 'I am still searching, if that's what you mean?'

'For what is not there? And panicking – more and more?'

'I am not panicking. That's the difference.'

Fuego pursed his lips dubiously. For a moment he watched the soldiers, now loading the corpses into the trucks; then he scrutinised those around him. All, except Williston, were confused creatures because death had crossed their precious little paths.

'Where were we? Oh, yes. Guerrillas. Revolutionaries.' Fuego clasped two of the children nearest to him. 'You imagine them as enlightened men. Fighting to make good the injustices that occur inadvertently in a society seeking to safeguard its integralism, its love of Religion, Morality, Fatherland and Family. You imagine they want to clear the warts of order and tradition so that we can all live a little better. You are wrong. All they want is power. Why? Because they lust after the campesinos' possessions – their lands, their women. How can they seize power? By terror. With killings like you see here.'

Huaman mocked him. 'Disinformation, General! Who will believe it? The people? They know there are no guerrillas!'

Fuego's response was equally mocking. 'They know *you* have no guerrillas. That you, our great agitator, lack either the courage or the charisma to recruit any. That is not the case with your rivals.'

Huaman bellowed. 'They know who the enemy is – the government! They know these people were killed because they thought a saviour had come!'

Fuego laughed. 'A saviour? There is no such thing!'

'I happen to agree with you! But you were worried all the same. You realised how desperate they had become. Let me tell you, your troubles have only just begun. Now, these people won't be chasing shadows! They will seek out a real leader!' He stopped, raked by a coughing fit.

Fuego chuckled. 'You? Gaspar?'

Daniel, concerned for Huaman's safety, broke in. 'What if Manku Yupanqui does exist? And appears – as the people say he will! You can crush guerrillas with superior power. What can you do against a messiah? Crucify him again?'

Fuego smiled at him. He had noted Daniel's attraction for Beatriz; and he had enjoyed watching him squirm while he was talking to her. Daniel, if he was not mistaken, was one of those romantics destined to flirt with heaven and hell. A tailor-made victim. 'Why should I, Mr Brac? I love messiahs. They are useful. They dispense great comfort from shrines and medallions and... *paintings*.'

Daniel matched Fuego's scorn. 'Yet you seem to be afraid, General.'

'Afraid!'

'Of what Manku Yupanqui represents.' It was Rice, swigging whisky, who had come to support Daniel.

'Or that he might still prove himself a saviour.' Beatriz, too.

Daniel smiled at her gratefully.

Fuego, contempt suffocating his tenderness, grinned. 'I hope he does not, *querida*. For his sake. Myths have a way of repeating themselves.' Then, abruptly, he turned to the children and prodded them. 'Your duty is to survive. Go – to your villages!'

As the children edged away, Teresa snatched one of Manku Yupanqui's portraits lying on the ground. Daniel saw her.

The children headed for the hills. Heavy-footed; forlorn; a few daring to look at the trucks for a final sight of the dead.

Fuego signalled the soldiers to set off. Then he mounted his horse. As he spurred the animal, he looked back at Daniel.

Daniel noted the anger. He should not have tangled with Fuego. Still, he had shown mettle, and not entirely because he had wanted to impress Beatriz. He was filling that large frame of his with sinew, taking on responsibility as a man takes on work.

A column of sand, twisting like a dust devil, was all that could be seen of

Fuego. Strange, the tricks the desert played. Fuego now seemed as erasable as himself.

The trucks drove off.

Father Quintana addressed them. 'I have my pick-up. I can take you to Illariy.'

Beatriz and Huaman nodded acceptance. Teresa, clutching Manku Yupanqui's portrait to her chest, followed.

Daniel, anxious to stay in Beatriz's orbit, turned to Rice and Williston. 'Do you mind if I go with them?'

Williston, ignoring him, started off in the direction of the algarroba trees where the jeep was waiting. Rice, giving Daniel an understanding look, followed Williston.

In the distance, the families that had ringed the necropolis swayed. Then they began to walk – slowly, so that the children could catch up with them.

Father Quintana drove slowly. Much of the time they remained silent. Occasionally, they exchanged survivors' smiles, like weary soldiers pulled back from the trenches. Beatriz's smile, Daniel felt, had an additional quality: should they meet again, it seemed to say, she would remember him. They also communed, Daniel thought, whenever they gazed at Manku Yupanqui's portrait which Teresa had placed on the dashboard.

There was no frame to it. The paper was rough, probably from a school sketch pad. Torn at the edges. Mildewed here and there.

The work of a village artisan. Or several. Or the collective brushstrokes of every campesino in the land.

A handsome head, youthful with straight black hair. Gaunt cheeks bearing the purple stigmata of the highlands. Partly an Indian Jesus in the style of Holguin – a human landscape of desolation. And partly the face of Che Guevara from the popular poster of the seventies – the New Man as an armed prophet.

So arresting a man, Daniel decided, could not exist. Yet he hoped that he did.

PART TWO

10
I want to jump into the water in order to fall into the sky

LA MERCED

According to a Ministry of Tourism pamphlet, La Merced extends to 63 square kilometres, is an important commercial and industrial capital and incorporates all the breathtaking wonders of South America. She rises from a natural harbour on the coast, climbs up two mountains serving as portals to the Andes, and descends through tropical dells and rivulets into moonscaped craters. She has a population of 1,247,095 souls of diverse ethnic groups. It is said – sometimes with pride – that this racial mixture makes the people of La Merced as temperamental as '*El Joven* – The Youth', the volcano that stands as a guiding star on the distant horizon.

Other tourist pamphlets record one cathedral, 83 churches of various denominations, one opera house, one national theatre, two commercial theatres, one classical ballet company, five museums (one entirely devoted to the Inca heritage, though little has survived the gold craze of the Conquistadores), 42 cinemas, one university, two technical colleges, three hospitals, 104 hotels, eight beaches, one public swimming pool, one polo ground, two stadiums, five country clubs, 14 night clubs with Parisian cabaret, one casino, one railway station (for a network that barely stretches to the interior), one international airport and 118 banks of which 78 are foreign branches.

To date there has been a total of 711 songs composed in praise of La

Merced. The moods of these songs range from the romantic to fiesta-gay, from the way she seduces lovers to how she provides hope and dispenses salvation. Without exception the songs have a subtle texture which conjures for the listener a luxurious damask. For instance, when a lover contemplates suicide because his beloved has abandoned him, one sympathises only to the extent that it must be distressing to lose the favours of a wide-hipped, passionate mistress; thereafter, one dismisses the death-wish as romantic licence and assumes that since the lover's pockets are lined with money and since he is so handsome, so melancholic, he will most certainly find a new conquest at the next elegant café – a madonna who will be wider-hipped and more passionate than her predecessor.

But there is another side to La Merced, other songs that few ever hear.

Three-quarters of the capital's inhabitants are destitute. Of the 63 square kilometres, only 12 are fit for habitation. These are reserved for the temples of the multinationals, the corrals of superpower agencies, the pleasure gardens of the predominantly Creole establishment. In the barrio-belt which constitutes the rest, the pervasive sound is the chant of tin and mud huts, open sewers and the last sacrament.

That is not all.

La Merced has six jails, each aspiring to be a region in Dante's 'Inferno'; 14 Sinchi barracks where countless *desaparecidos* – disappeared ones – begin their march to the great darkness; one picturesquely dramatic ravine, the *barranco* – once a popular picnic site, now known as 'the place where the cadavers appear' – which serves as the dumping ground for the victims of the sporadic *matanzas*, killings. The stench of the *barranco* varies according to the discretion of the wind.

Last, but not least, La Merced has 883 brothels, as renowned as those of pre-1959 Havana or present-day Seoul. These joy palaces provide one vital service: they feed lotus to those who might otherwise cure this city dying on the Andean scrap-heap.

Daniel put the newspaper aside. Jerry Rice's article. Acerbic, with a tendency to hyperbole, but committed.

He recalled his last encounter with Rice, the day after the massacre at the necropolis – three weeks before. When Father Quintana had dropped them at Illariy, Daniel's old wound – the wound of old killings – had been suppurating. Father Quintana, perceptive, had urged him to return to the desert and this time to look at its deathless side, at the Tapestry of the Gods. He had taken the advice, expecting, at best, a phenomenon that would interest him professionally.

But the desert, true to form, had been revelatory.

Those lines, pathways, spirals and figures etched on a giant scale by mysterious ancients in a perspective that no one had as yet deciphered had struck him like God's squiggles.

He was still captivated by the vision.

God who was a child as opposed to the Jewish God who judged or the Christian God who redeemed, offered a more attractive meaning to life and to its aspired sequel, immortality. A meaning which asserted that God was innocent, full of joy, laughter and love; but that, having conceived His own Self by restructuring chaos, He was, poor He, an orphan, therefore, in need of affection, care, holding and protection. That being so, it befell mankind, as God's very own creation, to act as God's mother and father. When mankind undertook this task, the universe would be transformed into a glebe where they and God could play together. In the process, they could produce the New Man who would be child, mother, father and God all in one.

A naive epiphany, admittedly. But what else from a man seeking a new spirit? From a man who had been unable to resist chasing after a mythic saviour?

Nevertheless, it had bound him more together.

For a start, he had banished fear out of his head and pushed it back into his bowels, its designated place. Fear would still threaten, of course. But only in the way it had been commissioned to threaten. As an instinct. Not as a succubus.

Secondly, he had re-evaluated the Kempin mission – this time, dispassionately. He had strengthened his resolve to bring him to justice. But he would do so methodically: by following Yizkor's instructions, trusting their expertise and curbing his impatience.

He turned towards the telephone, willing it to ring.

Wait. Wait. It'll ring. Soon. Maybe tomorrow.

Afterwards... when they found Kempin, he would decide. He could let Yizkor deal with the damned Nazi, as originally agreed. Or he could take matters into his own hand and keep his long overdue promise to the dead. Either way, he would have done his share to protect God, the child.

He rose from his seat, glanced once more at the newspaper, put it in the rubbish bin and lit a cigarette.

He wondered about Jerry Rice. On his return from the Tapestry of the Gods, he had found Rice roaming Illariy with that ethereal girl, Teresa. The others had left. Teresa had stayed behind, to continue her search for Manku Yupanqui. Rice, frustrated by the fact that any coverage of the massacre had been prohibited by General Fuego, had stayed on to see if he, too, could trace the sage. In the event, both had found the straggling pilgrims silent and distrustful. Teresa, undaunted, had set out for the highlands. Rice had dragged himself to the hotel bar, there to quarry, in a succession of pisco bottles, for those words that could best indict this terrible country.

The article on La Merced was the result. Commendably angry, but tangential to the people's messianic yearnings. Perhaps Rice was not the crusader Daniel had thought he was, but merely a drunk.

Still, he would keep in touch with him. After Kempin, he might have need of Rice's pen.

He cast another look at the telephone.

He should get down to some work.

He put the kettle to boil and laid out some biscuits.

He stared at the atelier. It was a huge room, the size of a courtyard, with high ceilings and a skylight; a coach-house in the days when the museum had been the palatial residence of some dignitary. Though a six-paned window overlooking a peaceful square had replaced half of the rear wall, it had not affected the atmosphere of sprawling austerity. Its private entrance was also on that side, with a guard-hut separating it from the square.

He had infused some life and colour into the atelier. There was the hammock he had slung opposite the platform, ideal for looking at the painting, thinking and relaxing; a monk's seat which he had salvaged from the rejects room; a vitrine, also salvaged, large enough to accommodate his reference books and the dozen or so novels he was determined to read. Jars of coffee and biscuits, some earthenware mugs and plates strewn over the kitchenette, in the far corner. By the windows, a colourful rug depicting the Inca calendar. And the most comforting of all, the smell – the smell that defined him. Emanating from the tools of his trade, piled in meticulous order on the shelves along two walls and the work-bench: various solutions, turpentine, alcohol, glue, plaster, cotton wool, canvas, tubes of paint, tins of powdered pigments, brushes. A room like the monastery cell of his childhood writ large; a haven compared to the luxury apartment the Museo Nacional de Arte had provided as accommodation.

Daniel stubbed out his cigarette and turned on the spotlights. He adjusted their position around the platform, dimmed and brightened them until satisfied that they provided the Andean radiance that had been the painter's light.

He secured the mobile scaffold, then climbed on to the platform. He examined the stretcher on which he had tacked the canvas. He had had to make the stretcher himself. Carpentry was not his best craft, but he was proud of his effort. He checked that the copper tacks had not come loose.

The kettle had boiled. He jumped down from the platform. He made a cup of coffee, then sat on the monk's chair; dunking a biscuit into the coffee, he immersed himself in the polyptych.

It was a leviathan of a work. Four paintings, stitched on a canvas equidistantly, in the shape of a Greek cross. Eight metres by eight. Belonging to no school; an absolute original; destined to be the precursor of a new wave when eventually exhibited. A uniform blue, the blue of Pintoyaku – Brac's blue, as General Fuego had suggested it should be called – covered the blank spaces in the epicentre and between the arms of the cross.

The top centre was occupied by the Trinity, three identical figures of Christ, seated side by side on top of a globe and surrounded by adoring cherubs and haloed saints.

At the right-hand side stood the Virgin, represented as *Pachamama*, Earth-Mother, in a vast robe shaped as a perfectly triangular mountain.

At the left-hand side, grouped on the heights of a fastness, were the portraits of the fourteen monarchs that constituted the Inca dynasty.

And the bottom centre contained a glorious version of the Tree of Life, depicted as inverted and shown to be attached to the Tree of the Knowledge of Good and Evil. On the Tree of Life, an Inca Adam and Eve climbed towards Heaven. The Tree of Knowledge bore the crucified Jesus.

Daniel helped himself to another biscuit and considered the people's theory that the polyptych was the pictorialisation of Manku Yupanqui's prophesied advent. Having started as a rumour in the highlands, it was now part of the folklore. And it was continuing to gain credibility, despite the government's attempts to curb the Manku Yupanqui craze. In fact, for some days now, groups of campesinos had become permanent fixtures in the small square at the back. Men and women, they stood, watching the atelier, for hours on end, silently but alert. When one group left another took its place. And whenever he went in and out, they scrutinised his face respectfully, as if he were a doctor and they invalids in a hospital.

Yet there was nothing in the polyptych remotely connected with the Manku Yupanqui myth. Nothing unless the configuration of the various personages represented an arcane symbolism. But then, no such theory had been advanced either by the people or by the *indigenistas* investigating the belief.

Leaving all that aside, the polyptych was an extraordinarily compelling work. All four of its themes had been favourite subjects for South American painters. But invariably, they had been treated separately, as single paintings. This was the only work which united them all in one canvas. As if the artist were a physicist and had succeeded in defining the forces of the universe in one formula.

To think that the artist was unknown; that the painting might never have been found, or, judging by the ravages of dampness, found too late, too damaged to be restored effectively.

And to think, indeed, that he had been chosen to restore it. Daniel, the repairer of the past!

He examined the strip-linings. He had taken the canvas out of the presses only that morning, but he wanted to make sure that the epoxy resin had set and the joints were secure.

He inspected the holes and tears. He had had to do a lot of patching and chamfering. Securing pieces of canvas of the same weight and weave had proved difficult. Mercifully, after days of urgent calls to various museums, the Louvre had obliged.

The patches looked fine. No discoloration, the tell-tale sign of excessive use of the warm iron; no problems from the beeswax and resin mixture he had used as adhesive. He was also pleased with the stoppings beneath the cracks. The days of experimentation for the right mixture of plaster of Paris, glue and stand oil to produce a putty suitable for the climate had been justified. Inpainting would pose fewer headaches.

He was, in fact, ready to remove the varnish on the first section. Except that he did not feel like starting on such a delicate task when he was so tense. The latest directive from Yizkor, forwarded by his bank, stated that Ian Campbell's release from prison was imminent and that the agent who would act as both Campbell's and Daniel's controller would be establishing contact this week. The week was three days old and he was still waiting. The varnish had severely deteriorated; there was bloom over much of the canvas. It would be a long and painstaking labour. He would prefer tackling it after the controller's call. When he would be calm. When, advised of his next move, he would know how to organise his work.

The telephone rang.

Damn! I don't mind waiting a few more days! No! I'm ready! He picked up the receiver. 'Daniel Brac.'

'This is Yizkor.' A woman's voice. Solemn. Yizkor was the opening word of the Jewish memorial prayer. It meant 'he will remember...'

He gave the requisite response. 'My father will be remembered.'

'My brother arrives on Saturday. He has to see you immediately. Meet him at the pier – the ferry from El Chulpa. Four p.m.' Click.

The controller was a woman. With a caressing voice. But under strain. Like Beatriz saying goodbye at Illariy. Stop thinking about Beatriz. Ships in the night.

Saturday was four days hence.

Why did Campbell have to see him immediately? So urgently, in fact, that he was asking him to meet the prison ferry. Was that prudent? What about all that caution Yizkor had droned on about?

Calm down. Calm down. Don't jump to stupid conclusions. Yizkor knows what's at stake. They won't make a false move. The pier is a public place. Anyway, you don't know Campbell. He'll approach you. And he's not likely to approach you if he smells danger. You're afraid – and that's the truth! Imagining things! Panicking! Come on, calm down! Keep your courage on the boil!

He had to go out. Walk a while. That would calm him down.

He did not have to account for his movements. He was not on a salary; they were paying him for the job. The Curator had never questioned his erratic schedule. He obviously knew that all picture-restorers, especially one committed to work on a single item for over a year, had to be indulged. Complete independence was one of the perks of the profession, and, in his case, the only freedom he had ever had.

Go out now! Pull yourself together! There's another freedom ahead: freedom from Kempin!

11

Ancestral sources, appointments in a forest from another age, dark wet drums

Father Quintana gazed at his world. Was there a more desolate spot on earth, another such village barely rising from the crumbling clay, its families atomised and cast into dirt and disease? Yet this was a corner of Eden, a place where a man might put a stool and ask God to sit down, have some *chicha*, rest His feet, admire His work. Look at this plateau, jutting like the Cordilleras' priestly hand and sprinkling baptismal waters on the valley below. And look at the river down there, gracefully dancing though chained to its heavy load. And look beyond where the valley and the river disappear into the folds of the 'Shimmering Darkness', where, on the Third Day, You created all the vegetation and where, after the Expulsion, You hid the Tree of Life.

Gaspar Huaman, coveting the shade his shadow had cast in the sun, kicked at a stone. 'What will you have us do, Padre? Turn the other cheek?'

Father Quintana wiped the sweat off his brow with the sleeve of his soutane. 'If we had a cheek left...'

'You agree then. We fight.'

'My faith cries out against bloodshed.'

'There is a season for everything, Padre. Jesus Himself, as I've heard you say, was a revolutionary.'

Dejectedly, Father Quintana moved to the shade of the church. His sanctum: La Iglesia de Sangre de Oro, the Church of the Golden Blood. It was a landmark in the Andes. Built on the ruins of the Inca Empire's outermost storehouse, it rose, with its twin bell-towers, like a border post between the Sierra and the endless jungle of the Shimmering Darkness. It was the last refuge from which a person ventured into that primordial world and the first haven he saw if he ever returned. Thus it had provided shelter for countless misfits, bandits, adventurers, fugitives from justice or injustice, wealth or poverty, life or death. And for those who saw death as deliverance – he did not, not yet – it was the perfect place to die.

Father Quintana's stammer punctuated his gloom. 'Tell me about your revolution, Gaspar.'

'I have started recruiting.'

'How many can you recruit?'

'A few hundred.'

'What can a few hundred do?'

'Fidel Castro started with eighty-two.'

'Cuba is an island, a small place. You can't compare it with this country.'

'The country's size is an advantage. To start with, we'll be fighting in the wilderness. Moving from place to place. Keeping the initiative...'

'Che Guevara had the same illusion. They killed him – not far from here.'

'Guevara came unprepared. I won't be. I'll have good men; fierce Indios; dissidents toughened up in prisons...'

'You will still be too few.'

'We'll grow in numbers. The people will join us.'

'The people are bludgeoned. They won't have the will to fight.'

'The people have had enough, Padre. They are clamouring for a saviour.'

'A saviour, yes.'

'So we'll be their saviour. A group of courageous and dedicated people – that is all it takes to create a revolution. They'll join in droves. We'll become a popular force. There will be no stopping us.'

Father Quintana sat down and imbibed the coolness of the stone porch.

His lovely church. Built in 1883 – the year of Karl Marx's death, Huaman had caustically pointed out – by Father Timothy O'Neill, an Irish priest who had turned his back on the false piety of the Establishment. On the day of consecration, the blessed Father had passed away disgorging molten gold from wounds identical to those on the crucified body of Christ. The miracle, in addition to providing the church with its name, had been interpreted as an act of expiation by Christendom for the sins committed against the Children of the Light. In the expectation that there would be further divine manifestations, Father O'Neill's remains had been kept as holy relics. Though there had been no other miracles since, the people had not lost patience.

Miracles, like volcanic eruptions, they claimed, occurred every hundred years – give or take a few – when gods awakened.

Were miracles now imminent? Father Quintana wondered whether it was that conviction, somehow rooted in him, that kept him confused about his calling. He was, as he often humoured himself in sinful pride, one who like Jesus, had harkened to the cry of the downtrodden and now sang, together with the psalms, songs of liberation. He liked to think, also in sinful pride, that though he feared for his life, and though he had seen other priests disappear from the face of the earth, he was committed to his work. He was a good shepherd to the base communities. He had turned them into effective rural congregations, encouraged them to embrace faith like the early Christians and thus rediscover Christ's true identity. And there had been various occasions when his involvement with them had caused him to suffer threats, harassments, beatings. That he had held out was a miracle in itself. How dared he pray for more?

Yet, the reality of miracles was integral to his faith. That was what had sent him in search of Manku Yupanqui; and, more important, that was still what made him expect the Saviour's arrival.

'I want to believe you, Gaspar. But they say it is impossible to repeat the Cuban revolution in South America.'

'Who says that? The fascists! Why do they say it? To discourage us from fighting!'

'On the other hand, it is very easy to lose sight of the stars which point the way home.'

'My vision is impeccable, Padre. I am going to repair history.'

Father Quintana's eyes wandered over the village. Could that desolation ever be repaired? That vast dustbowl square in front of the church, could it receive blood in its veins? The dying adobes beyond – could they be made to stand firm against the wind? And what about the people?

Most of them were women; except for the old and the toddlers, the men had been crimped into the cocaine trade and were unlikely to return.

All the single women were parading before Huaman's men. They knew no rebel group would endanger its mobility by burdening itself with camp followers. But survival depended upon trying. The young were lifting their skirts to show how well they could be of service; those with children were offering coca leaves from delicately embroidered pouches, hoping that the promise of narcotic calm would compensate for the extra mouths; the rest pleaded with tired looks, already resigned to the fact that passage from one season to another would be all the more hazardous.

'Arms, Gaspar – where will you get them? People don't give arms without strings attached.'

Huaman sat on the porch and massaged his weary legs. Father Quintana had touched a sore subject. Strings were indeed the curse of revolutions.

Procuring arms was easy. Though he was, as yet, an insurrectionist without a military boot, he was, none the less, a name that opened doors. Any door – right or left; ideology did not matter. Power-brokers were like vultures. They could not feed unless the country was dying.

There were hordes of them, dropping words into secret channels, urging him to establish contact. Agitators from rival dictatorships in neighbouring countries; Russians, those despicable capitalists in pseudo-Marxist clothes, and their East European and Cuban lackeys; radicals from Central America, from Europe, from Africa; fundamentalist Arabs seeking sympathisers; covetous Chinese and Indo-Chinese; even Mafiosi trying to move in on the drug trade; and the most surprising, those forgotten communists, the Albanians. Not to mention the wolf in sheep's clothing, the American, Dr Williston, tempting him with the kingdoms of the world.

He had rejected them all. His revolution, though it was Fidelista in spirit, had to be home-grown.

'There will be no strings, Padre. We'll get the arms from the Sinchis. The Bridegrooms of Death. The police. We'll raid border posts. Local barracks.'

'How? With bare hands?'

'Yes.'

Father Quintana stared at Huaman's men. Dour campesinos, they appeared more preoccupied with the lands they had left fallow than with bringing justice to the country. Only their lack of interest in the women showed they would rather die than live as they had.

'In your revolution, Gaspar, will there be room for light? For the Church?'

'The Church will be healthier than it is today. We won't interfere with it. We'll let Jesus shine with the face of the sun.'

Father Quintana squinted at the sky. Jesus was up there, in the realm of the sun – had always been there – and He did not need Gaspar Huaman's sanction to shine. Look at Him beating His chest for an end to suffering.

An end to suffering! A beginning for the true Christian way of life. For the rights of the poor, the weak, the oppressed. The liberation of the spirit which would transform the world, reinvest all men with dignity. That was what Gaspar Huaman wanted to achieve. Whatever the odds against his revolution, he had to be given the chance. And if that meant priests had to pick up the sword which the Son of God had brought – so be it! That, even if the Vatican could not see it, was the mission now.

'If only you were Manku Yupanqui, Gaspar.'

'I will be better. Not a myth – but real.'

Father Quintana stared into the distance. 'How can I help?'

Huaman, surprising himself, kissed Father Quintana's hands. 'We'll need a base. Somewhere forgotten by the government. Where the people will be on our side – won't betray us. Where we can assemble, plan, establish communications, hide. This place is ideal. A bridge to the highlands, but isolated. We will also need somewhere to store food and arms. I thought your church...'

Father Quintana nodded. 'It's big enough. You'll have to clear the vaults.'

'We will do it.' Huaman shouted at his lieutenant. 'Chauca! Clear the vaults!'

Father Quintana watched as Chauca summoned the men and led them into the church. Grave men transformed into children. He wondered whether they would ever smile again. 'I feel like a murderer, Gaspar... They will kill you all before you learn how to use a gun.'

'They will have to catch us first.'

'My church is not a fortress. How long could you hold out here?'

Huaman pointed at the Shimmering Darkness frothing in the heat haze, like a sea spilling over.

'If they track us down to here, we'll go into the jungle. If they follow, we'll pick them off one by one. If they don't, we'll sneak back and pick them off in tens and twenties.'

'You make it sound very simple. You will be facing General Fuego...'

'It's not simple. And Fuego can be defeated.' He smiled, thinking back on his activities in La Merced. He had sneaked into the capital in search of recruits. Fuego, alerted by informers, had been forced to take him seriously, and had scoured relentlessly for his whereabouts. But lacking even such a basic facility as a safe house, he had known how to keep on the move, where to hide. And, to cap it all, he had left with five good men. If he could outmanoeuvre Fuego in Fuego's domain, he should have fewer problems evading him in the countryside. 'The secret, Padre, is to keep a step ahead always.'

Father Quintana leaned against the cyclopean Inca boulder which formed the base of the bell-tower. Its smoothness and size, banishing all thought of mortality, had always comforted him. But his own mortality – was what he also wanted to ask of Huaman. What will happen to me, caught between revolutionaries and death-squads? He stifled the question. How could he expect a miracle if he feared to lay down his life for it?

'When does the fighting start?'

'Soon.'

Father Quintana shut his eyes. He could no longer distinguish what was right or wrong. Confusion belonged to Satan as suffering belonged to man. Conversely, both death and La Iglesia de Sangre de Oro belonged to God. He was not sure what all that meant.

'Are you afraid, my son?'

Huaman rose abruptly and walked into the church. He did not want Father Quintana to see just how afraid he was. The thought that he would finally pick up a gun and, maybe, one day, take a man's life with it, wavered between elation and agony. He, Gaspar de Villasante y Córdoba, who had never picked up anything more dangerous than a book, would he have the courage? Would he be able to treat a gun like his men did – as a bride?

12
I am not just one man but all men

I told them nothing. They smashed me up, but they didn't break me. They flattened my cock and fried my balls, but they didn't break me.

Don't gloat. Keep sharp. Listen to the concert.

Aye. But don't expect me to cheer and sing like this mob. I've no voice left from screaming. What did she call the song?

Manku Yupanqui's song.

No wonder the prisoners have gone wild. Poor sods. Brave of her, though – to sing it here.

She's Beatriz Santillan. Very famous. She can get away with it.

I told them nothing. They pulverised me but they didn't break me.

Your mind's wandering. Pull yourself together!

My name is Ian Campbell. Born David Lewis. Glasgow. Scotland. Scottish Jew, now Israeli. The sea – can you smell the sea? Thousands of inmates in this quadrangle, broiling in the sun, stinking of sweat, piss, shit and a million masturbations, but you can still smell the sea. If you have to go to prison, always choose one on an island.

Stop rambling. You're leaving today. After the concert. Keep the mind working.

Why this concert? Is it Christmas or something? We don't often get treats like this.

Beatriz Santillan decided to entertain the prisoners. They couldn't refuse her.

The smell of the sea. I love it. And the spray in the air. It's like medicine. My insides burn less. They're still like lava, but they're cooling.

She sings well, Beatriz Santillan does. There's Fuego – on the platform. And that Waffen-SS, Angelito. You wouldn't think that angel-face elevated torture to a religious order. Quartering people is now an absolution as available as the confessional. Only the sea, where occasionally some bodies are dumped, refuses the dead and lays them out on the beach. But even he couldn't break me. The mystery is why he didn't kill me. He made a mistake there. One day... when I can breathe without burning, I'll deal with him: blood and frogs, lice and swarms, pestilence and boils, hail, fire and locusts, darkness and his firstborn.

You're rambling again. Get a hold of yourself!

The jock sitting on my right... The one on my left, too... They don't look like prisoners.

Don't be stupid! Except for those on the platform and the guards, we're all prisoners.

Not these two. They smell fresh. They're too healthy.

Probably new prisoners.

I think I saw them talking to Fuego.

Think, did you say? They didn't leave you any brains to think, laddie!

I'm telling you. I don't like the look of these pricks beside me.

Stop thinking about them. The concert will soon be over. Then you'll get your belongings and off to the ferry.

There'll be someone to meet me?

Naomi.

What will I do when I get out?

Like it said in that message Naomi managed to send with the guard, you will meet one of our auxiliaries. You'll give him all the intelligence you have on Kempin. Then you'll fly out. To Miami, Florida. You'll have a good rest. Get yourself patched up. Then you'll be smuggled back – for the kill.

Will I be able to fuck again?

Of course. They'll make a new man of you.

Tell me the truth. They didn't break me but they smashed me to smithereens. Fried my balls, flattened my cock.

Come on, laddie. You're made of iron.

They've melted me down. I'm in such pain it no longer feels like pain.

Don't get hysterical now.

They're applauding. Look at them going wild. That's the end of the concert. I want to get out. I want to get out.

Stay still. The prisoners will leave row by row. If you get disorderly, they'll throw you into the cooler.

This auxiliary. They said he's not a professional. Just someone who wants to bring Kempin to justice because Kempin wiped out his family. I mean, is he any good? We don't want a bungling amateur.

We won't throw him at Kempin. All he'll do is identify him.

They've started moving the prisoners. Won't be long now. I'll be out! I'll be out! Look at these arseholes next to me – sodding me about… 'Hey, stop pushing!' Fucking hell! Mother! He's got a knife! So's the other one! 'Och, you bastards!'

Someone… help me… 'Help me…' You… All these feet around me… 'Help…' … me… I've just been stabbed… Och, too late… '*Schema Israel, Adonai Eloheynu, Adonai Ehad…*'

13

Not just stones but shadow, not just shadow but blood

Bright sun, smelted from Inca gold, sat on a gently rolling ocean.

South of the promontory lay the beaches, the famous cafés and the seafood restaurants that had earned stars in gastronomic guides. They were crammed with the unemployed – not those who failed to find work, but those blessed with family fortunes.

To the north lay the estuary. Haunted by the wildlife which, whenever not feeding or cackling, watched the river stipple the sea with brown semen.

Beyond the estuary lay the docks. As grim as docks anywhere; though, still awaiting modernisation, not yet an eyesore.

The promontory was the spot where the third wave of settlers had landed and where, as a first imperative, they had built a fishing village. Here, the developers had stayed away – not to commemorate the patriarchs, nor lured by more profitable pastures, but because the district accommodated the sacrosanct brothels.

Daniel liked the promontory. And the people. Punters and prostitutes. Petty smugglers and their armies of child peddlers. Low-income workers grabbing a meal in the *picanterias*. Courting couples from the barrios. Prisoners' relatives.

The last came to cast wistful looks at the island penitentiary known as El Chulpa, 'The Tomb', lying two miles across the water, or to meet the ferry that serviced it for a released prisoner, or to seek a guard, a cleaner, a caterer whom they could bribe for some news of their man.

Daniel, too, was mesmerised by El Chulpa. It disinterred memories of other island prisons. His own: the island of Brač, off the city of his birth, Split. And that of his mother and sisters: the island of Pag, also in the Adriatic.

Brač, which had furnished him with his Christianised surname, had been benevolent. Certainly it had provided him with a sense of freedom – normally illusory under the Third Reich. True, he was still a child then. True, also, he was being sheltered by Dominican monks who saw in the children they hid the new generation that would repair, with the teachings of Christ, the world Hitler had shattered. But primarily it had been the sea that had saved him. Not only by keeping the Nazis at bay, but by making him grow, hour by hour for four years, with the promise that on the day his mother and sisters returned to Split, he could run to them – swim across, so easily.

But his mother and sisters had been taken to Pag. There, Christian humanity had had little influence. There, the Nazis and their collaborators from the Croat Ustashi movement had run a labour-extermination camp for Jews, Gypsies and Serbs. There, as he had found out from the Nazis' meticulously kept records, one sister had been hacked to death by axes; the other two had been dumped into the sea, bound together, back to back. There, those who had survived such sport – like his mother – had returned to the mainland only to be transported to Auschwitz.

Was El Chulpa haunted by his mother? By his sisters? By those millions who had lost flesh, spirit and identity in island prisons all over the world?

The ferry from El Chulpa was manoeuvring to dock.

Daniel began to tremble. He looked about furtively. Nobody seemed interested in him. If he was being followed, it was done expertly. Despite all the years of outflanking officialdom, breezing through post-war Europe without identity or substance, any challenge to authority still felt like a crime – and seemed to be branded on his face for all to see.

Determinedly, he sauntered cowards the landing stage. Courage was still with him.

He watched the ferry disgorge.

A jeep first, bearing a flag and a number plate with two stars. Empty, except for the Sergeant driving it.

Then a police van, washed and polished, sparkling like a family-size coffin. And a few trucks, purveyors of the sundry goods a prison needed.

Finally, the passengers. A shift of guards, some labourers, a few mechanics, a civil servant. No visitors; visiting was allowed only on the first day of the month.

And no released prisoners.

What about lan Campbell?

Cold sweat invaded Daniel. There was General Fuego, coming off the ferry, smoothing his uniform. Accompanied by Colonel Angelito, spick and span and strapped with the Bridegrooms of Death armband.

And Beatriz Santillan – included in their company but keeping a distance. Looking funereal.

Daniel wanted to run.

But Fuego had seen him and was scrutinising him quizzically. Daniel looked away as if he had not recognised him.

The prisoners' relatives had besieged the other passengers. Most walked on, ignoring the tendered packets of cigarettes, corn cobs, bags of shrimps and eggs. A few deigned to stop, tempted by better things on offer: cassettes, lighters, live chickens, a woman with her hand suggestively on her breast.

Fuego strode up to him, good-humouredly, 'Mr Brac...'

Daniel smiled blandly as if vaguely recognising him. 'General.' There was nothing to be afraid of.

'What brings you here?'

'The sights.'

Beatriz and Colonel Angelito had paused in the background. Daniel waved a greeting at her. She nodded at him – cordially, sadly, but not without warmth.

'You don't mean the brothels?'

Daniel kept his eyes on Beatriz, hoping she would come across. 'No.'

Nearby, a mother, numb with misery, was listening to a prison guard. The latter, examining the chicken she had offered him, was terse. Her son's health was deteriorating.

'You certainly choose your sights, Mr Brac. For a moment I thought you were meeting someone.'

Beatriz was coming over. Daniel smiled and braved Fuego's eyes. 'What a bizarre idea, General. Nice to see you again, Beatriz.' Her eyes were puffed; she had been crying.

'Are you well, Daniel?'

Had Fuego upset her? Molested her? 'Thank you. And you?'

Fuego answered for her. 'Lovely as ever, as you can see. But very upset. She was giving a concert – at the prison.' He shook his head at Beatriz. 'I should have forbidden it. It was a mad idea – more of this Manku Yupanqui nonsense.' He turned to Daniel. 'There was an incident. It disturbed her.'

Beatriz barely stifled her rage. 'They killed a prisoner!'

'You make it sound as if we killed him.' He sighed, officiously regretful. 'Someone from your part of the world, Mr Brac. Man called Ian Campbell.'

Daniel lost the feel of his limbs.

Fuego put his arm through Daniel's. 'I am giving Beatriz a lift. If you have had enough of sightseeing, let me drop you home.'

'Home?'

'The museum, I should say. You prefer it to the apartment.'

'I do. How do you know?'

'It's my job to know. Then I can tell who is friend, who is foe.'

'I see. No, I don't... I mean, I'm working for the Ministry for the Arts. Surely, that makes me a friend.'

Fuego smiled expansively. 'I haven't decided yet.' Engaging Beatriz with his other arm, he pulled Daniel towards the jeep. 'Come along. You might cheer up Beatriz.' He glanced at Angelito; the latter moved to Daniel's other flank. 'You remember Colonel Angelito. He was at Illariy.'

Daniel nodded a greeting.

Angelito smiled genially. 'Honoured, sir.'

Daniel shook the proffered hand. A strong grip. A pleasant accent: mid-European. Full of charm, but for his uniform.

They reached the jeep. Fuego pointed at the back seat. 'It will be a squeeze – but that always adds salt to friendship.'

Daniel helped Beatriz to climb in, then followed. Fuego sat between them.

Angelito and the Sergeant clambered into the front. Angelito turned to face them, presenting an unlined face and pleasant, interested eyes. The Sergeant drove off.

Fuego breathed in the sea air contentedly. 'I have been hoping we would meet again, Daniel.'

Daniel lit a cigarette. 'Any special reason?'

'Yes. I wasn't sure before. I am now. There is something in you I recognise.'

'What's that?'

'A reflection.'

Daniel caught Beatriz's troubled look. He dragged on his cigarette. Miraculously, no fear. Just a strange levity.

The conversation during the drive had been restricted to small talk, as if Fuego, like Daniel, had wished to defer the important issues until later. Beatriz had remained silent.

At the museum, Fuego had insisted that he and Beatriz should see the polyptych. Angelito, having promised to take his sons to the circus, had excused himself and departed.

They had settled in the atelier: Fuego, half slung on the hammock; Beatriz, in the monk's seat; Daniel, at the foot of the scaffold. A bottle of Armagnac, swiftly procured by Fuego's Sergeant, had steamed off the outside world.

The polyptych had captivated Fuego, stimulating him to discourse knowledgeably on its colours, technical brilliance and vision. Daniel had had to admit that Fuego looked at art as if it were matter brought to life by the touch of God's finger – as he himself believed it was. What else but devilry could produce such an attitude in a man whose hands were as chapped as those of Pontius Pilate?

By contrast, Beatriz had remained subdued. But whenever she had talked to him, there had been goodwill in her eyes and warmth in her voice. On the two occasions we met, in the necropolis and today, Daniel imagined her saying, death stood between us; but if we ever meet in a world of life, I will liberate your soul.

Fuego, there could be no mistake, was interested in Beatriz. God only knew what he would do if he decided Daniel was a rival. Maybe he had already decided. He had steered the conversation to love.

'... And some say it's chemical. Musky smell attracting musky smell.'

Daniel listened distractedly. What was he to do about Kempin? Did the Controller know about Campbell's death? He could not ring her; he did not have a number; the arrangement was that she would ring him always. But what if she did not ring for days, weeks? What should he do then? Write to the address in Miami Yizkor had given him?

A frightening thought gripped him. What if she rang now, while Fuego and Beatriz were still here? Fuego would immediately smell something. You look worried, Daniel, who was that? A friend? A *lady* friend?

Daniel glanced at Beatriz. If she thought he had a lady friend...

Still withdrawn, she was staring at his work-bench. To his disappointment, she had not been overwhelmed by the polyptych. Naturally, she had recognised it as a work that contained divine breath; but painting for her, she had confessed, was not an art form that could lay hands on a person, pull her by the hair, shake her body until she wept. On the other hand, gratifyingly, she had been fascinated by the atelier's spartan atmosphere; as awed by the pigments and the tools of work as he would have been in a composer's study. And with the delicacy of the true artist, she had treated him as one whose gifts were never in doubt.

'I suppose you creative people would define it as something like the Manku Yupanqui nonsense. *Love is that which is contained in the missing ray.*' He waved his glass at them. 'Very poetic. But contradictory. If it is in the missing ray, how do we know about it? If we know about it, how can it be in the missing ray?'

Beatriz sighed in irritation. 'How did we get on to this subject?'

'I'll tell you what love is: immolation.'

Beatriz snapped caustically. 'You're being a bore, Oseas!' Daniel smiled at her.

Fuego unbuttoned his jacket and stretched out on the hammock. 'I am making myself at home, Daniel.'

Daniel helped himself to more brandy.

'Everywhere is home to me. Power, you see. Like death: all-conquering.' As if prompted by his remark, Fuego pointed at the polyptych. 'Will you finish it – the restoration?'

Daniel looked at him warily. 'Why shouldn't I?'

'I have the feeling it has a rival.'

'I've no other work at hand – if that's what you mean.'

'An attachment, then. A woman, perhaps – a wife?'

Daniel glanced at Beatriz. She was staring at her feet. Interested in his answer? He prayed the Controller would not ring. 'No attachment.'

'Never?'

'I am not a eunuch.'

'Still an active volcano, eh? That's good.'

Daniel toyed with his glass. No doubt about it. This was not banter. Fuego was suspicious and was testing him. He relaxed. He was doing well.

'Rapture – sharing a bed is. Like having the sun all to yourself. Ask Beatriz. We were lovers, you know.'

Jealousy tore through Daniel. 'I didn't.'

Beatriz retorted trenchantly. 'A long time ago.'

Fuego lay back and stared at the skylight. 'Time – what does it mean? I have never forgotten what it was like.'

'I have.' Beatriz proffered her glass to Daniel. 'May I have some more?' She had noticed his jealousy and felt sorry for him. She knew about jealousy – the full spectrum: from professional envy to coveting friends' husbands to staking a claim on a man, even one who meant little. Like envying those who had living parents, only more acute and of much longer duration.

Daniel refilled her glass. Quivering cordiality; trying to control his jealousy.

She smiled at him. 'Thank you.' She was also pleased. He was attracted to her. She liked him, too. A manly man. Well-built and strong. Athletic in his movements. Sweet when he smiled. Gentle manners. Fair skin, tantalising like clean sheets. And that European poise that suggested culture, class, sensitivity all at once. There was something of her father about him: the temperance of a good white man. Though, she had to say, he had not impressed her at first. That day at the necropolis. When she had shuttled between sanity and madness amidst those corpses, she had desperately wanted – though any such act would have outraged her – a man to hold her and avert her eyes. She had taken a good look at him. He had had the decency to defend Father Quintana against Dr Williston, but had been too composed; then when he had challenged Fuego, she had thought him a poseur, regurgitating liberal tracts. Later, on the journey to Illariy, in Father Quintana's pick-up, she had seen him in a better light. Staring at Manku Yupanqui's portrait, listening to the Padre's doleful account of the misery of the Indians, he had taken on features, character, form, like the moon coming out of an eclipse. So, she had occasionally thought about him. She had been glad to see him at the pier.

'Do you ever scream, Daniel?'

She looked up with a jolt. Fuego was staring at Daniel through his brandy.

Daniel was caught off guard. 'Scream?'

'Like this.' Fuego demonstrated with a piercing wail. 'But from deep inside. Like an eagle who has broken his wing.'

Another thing about jealousy, she thought: anybody could see it. Fuego, whose antennae were sharper than most people's, had also seen it. And Fuego was a predator. Unless, maybe Fuego, too, was jealous. No, such an emotion was unimaginable in the man he had become. More likely he felt threatened by Daniel; anybody with any integrity threatened him. She should intervene. She laughed harshly. 'You've become banal, Oseas. Everybody screams.'

Daniel looked at her gratefully but saw the caution in her sad eyes. And the promise of support? And, if need be, protection? Behind her skirts? On her bosom? Between her thighs?

Fuego sat up. 'I met a man who didn't. Campbell – the man who was killed.' His tone had become mordant. 'Aren't you interested, Daniel?'

'I'm not a ghoul.'

'It is educational. One of those long-haired, globe-trotting middle-aged bums. But that was a cover. He was Jewish, in fact.'

'With a name like Campbell?'

'I had occasion to see his cock. Circumcised.'

'A lot of men are.'

'Are you?'

'Yes.'

'Lucky you. I am told women prefer it like that.'

'I wouldn't know.'

'Now you are being modest. But we have an authority. You know, *querida*, don't you? You have sampled enough men...'

How do you speak to this creature? Was he like this when we were lovers? Yes and no. Eight years now. He was a colonel then. Just appointed to form the Sinchis. Not as powerful, not as secure. Prepared to do anything to bulldoze his way to the top. I was on the cusp. Suddenly an international star.

Disoriented by success. I saw his violence immediately. I was attracted to it. I also wanted to change it because the world saw me as soft and healing. Disaster. Yet there were moments of tenderness. I used to think I had almost changed him. I might have – if the Sinchis had not made his name.

'*Querida*, you are keeping us in suspense.'

Beatriz smiled icily. 'Whatever its features, a cock is a cock, Oseas. What makes it special is its soul.'

Daniel looked at her in embarrassment.

'I never knew that. Does your cock have a soul, Daniel?'

Daniel retorted angrily. But the answer, he knew, was a declaration to Beatriz. 'Yes.'

'Evidently mine does not.' Fuego laughed heartily. 'What was I saying? Oh, yes. Campbell – definitely Jewish. Recited prayers as he lay dying. *Shema* something. Are you Jewish, Daniel?'

'No.'

'Sometimes the unlikeliest people turn out to be Jews.'

Daniel defied his discomfort. 'Why was he in prison?'

'Running cocaine.'

Beatriz was enraged. 'That's hardly a crime here.' Why was Fuego hounding Daniel about the prisoner? Did he think they had had dealings?

'He was small fish. We have to catch a few to impress the American senators.' Fuego turned to Daniel. 'The irony is, he was going to be released today.'

Daniel could not control the tremor in his voice. 'How did he die?'

Beatriz rasped. 'He was murdered.'

Fuego nodded sadly. 'Stabbed. It was a wild concert. Beatriz had got them all singing and clapping...'

'Who killed him?'

'We have some five thousand suspects – that's roughly the number of prisoners in El Chulpa. Why he was killed is more pertinent: he was an undercover agent. The cocaine barons hate undercover agents.'

Beatriz resisted the thought that Daniel might be involved in some clandestine work. An eminent restorer who was also an agent?

'The Junta are the cocaine barons. So *you* killed him.'

Fuego smiled, keeping his eyes on Daniel. 'There are others – great white kings who run the Junta – and me.'

Daniel met Fuego's eyes. 'You don't strike me as the servant type.'

'We all are.'

'Then we should choose our masters carefully.'

'Who would *you* choose, Daniel?'

'Not the devil.'

'Nor God – surely!'

Daniel did not bother to reply.

'Do you really believe in God, Daniel?'

'Yes.'

'I don't.' Fuego chuckled. 'I should qualify that. Officially, God, of course, exists. He is everywhere – just, compassionate, omniscient. He provides us with religion, Fatherland and family. His wisdom is such that He has appointed me Chief of the SES – to serve directly under His Immaculate Mother who is the Commander-in-Chief of the Army.' Fuego guffawed as Daniel and Beatriz exchanged looks. 'Don't laugh, it's true.' He stopped laughing suddenly. He looked grim. 'But, off the record... If there is a God, how could I be the Chief of the SES?'

Daniel was sardonic. 'There can't be good without evil.'

'And day without night. I have heard the sermon.' Fuego slid off the hammock acrobatically. 'To satisfy my curiosity, Daniel – did you know Ian Campbell?'

'No.'

'He was going to meet a contact. Not you, was it?'

'No.'

'You were there spicing the day, eh?'

'Right.'

'Some friendly advice. Get yourself a woman. You spice the day better with a woman. Why not Beatriz? She has redeemed many men.'

Beatriz hissed at him. 'You're an abomination!'

'I think he is shy, *querida*. I think you should take the initiative –jump on him.'

'That's enough, Oseas!'

Fuego, grinning, buttoned up his jacket. 'I will leave you to it.' Walking past Daniel, he patted him on the shoulder. 'I enjoyed this interlude.'

Fuego's hand, Daniel felt, was like a cupping glass, its warmth – and vacuum – drawing blood to the surface, turning flesh into lumps.

As in winter 1944. He had made a snowman in the grounds of the monastery, had caught a severe chill and had been treated with cuppings. The swellings on his chest had terrified him, and Father Gracijan had pacified him by encouraging him to paint them. He had drawn absurd caricatures of the monks and they had laughed a lot.

Today the swelling had the quality of an augury. It pulsed the conviction that he and Fuego had been destined to meet. He had had the same intimation in the desert necropolis, after his absurd journey, but had ignored it. Enemies, chosen by fate, until the spirit of one succumbed. Don't believe it. Paranoia!

On his way to the door, Fuego paused by the window. He contemplated the group of Indians in the square, keeping their strange vigil for signs of Manku Yupanqui's advent which the polyptych would allegedly reveal. He turned to Daniel abruptly. 'You must finish the restoration.' Then he walked out.

For some time after Fuego's departure, as if waiting for the air to dispel any shadows he might have left behind, Daniel and Beatriz remained silent.

Finally, Daniel found his anger. 'I'm sorry. He offended you. I couldn't prevent it. I never know how to handle such situations.'

He looked so battered, so desirous of her. She got up, collected the empty glasses and went over to the sink. 'Much of what he said is true. I have been promiscuous. I enjoy sex.'

'You don't have to explain.' He followed her. 'I'll do those.'

'I like housework.' She started washing the glasses. He stood shyly, next to her – almost like a child. But in suspended heat, arms forcibly crossed over his chest, ready to burst out as a man. What engaged her most, however, was the domesticity of the situation. Like a couple clearing up after receiving guests. She could not remember a similar scene with any of her past men – except, ironically, Fuego. 'I won't jump on you.' Having finished washing up, she dried her hands. 'I don't see you as a casual affair.'

'How – do you see me?'

She touched his cheek. 'More human than most. And somewhat lost.'

He held her hand. 'That's good.'

'Good for you. Is it good for me?'

'Isn't it?'

'It wasn't good for my mother. My father had something of you. He was white, too.'

'Oh.'

'They had a wonderful relationship. And they had a crusade: keeping Runasimi – Quechua – alive. Do you have a crusade?'

He pointed at the polyptych, trying to look truthful. 'I have my work.'

She was not entirely convinced, but chose to believe him. 'Good. Crusades become obsessions. Then dangerous. Then they kill. That's how my parents were killed.'

'I'm sorry.'

She walked away from the sink, picked up her handbag and moved towards the door.

He strode after her. 'Will I see you again?'

'Can you fill a vast emptiness?'

'I'd like to try.'

She kissed him on the mouth. 'I'll consult the stars.' She licked her lips. 'Nice.'

And she was gone.

14

Let us converse with roots and with discontent waves

The maize had been garnered. It was a good crop, but there could still be shortages in winter. The big landowners had bribed the province's overseers to reduce the campesinos' shares.

Hope lay in potatoes, ready to be sown.

Thus, on this festive day of ritual battle, the people were circumspect. They had agreed there would be no quarter given. The majority, Chauca suspected, prayed for at least one death even though he would be a husband, son or brother. His life would serve as an offering to the earth.

The *communeros* had formed two groups: those belonging to the *ayllus* on the northern and eastern shores of the lake against those from the southern and western shores. Both groups would field thirty men each. In accordance with tradition, there would be two meetings. Ten youths from each group – the initiates at coca chewing, ready to take on wives and responsibilities – would contest the morning trial. The men would fight in the afternoon.

They had prepared for weeks. They had reminisced about ancient disputes over land, water and chattels. They had primed their weapons: *huaracas* – slings – and polished rocks for these; *bolas* – clusters of honed stones in leather thongs; and *macanas*, clubs. Both groups, boasting blind courage, had tried to intimidate the other with accusations of cowardice; the combatants' doors had been despoiled with dead frogs and donkey skulls – normally a feature of another festival, when men made fun of women.

Teresa Ayala and Chauca, both outsiders, stood on the heights overlooking the designated battleground, the narrow valley that rippled down to the lake. They had been permitted to watch the proceedings on the understanding that they would neither favour a group, nor partake of the midday feast. No alien element was to influence the course of the day.

The young combatants, their slings wrapped round their heads, set off on their horses.

The women, dressed in their best attire – girandoles of embroidered skirts, bright shawls, bowler hats and quilted bonnets garlanded with flowers – followed on foot. Mothers and wives carried the spare weapons. The unwed, animatedly chattering, reassured each other they would all be captured by brave youths for trial marriages.

The children and the musicians, also festively arrayed, followed next – the latter already in good voice and tune.

The elders, in ceremonial raiment, came last. The *varayoks* carried the conch-shell horns with which they would trumpet the beginning and the ending of the hostilities. They walked solemnly, imbued with timeless authority. The shamans, equally solemn, displayed their wands and their bags of herbs and llama fat. The rest, the ageing men, brought the pouches of tobacco, chayuts and coca leaves, the gourds of *aguardiente*.

They progressed slowly, through the blur of the low clouds, visible in shards of colour, like a giant centipede pursuing a leaf in the sky.

Chauca had come well supplied with coca and had started chewing early. Mama Coca had become a treat, rationed to special occasions – a discipline imposed by Huaman who, like all *mistis*, considered indigenous habits insidious. Now, his mouth full and numb, his body anaesthetised, Chauca could relax, think back on his life, remember how the plant had mainly served to suppress hunger and fatigue, and consider himself a new man, a man of mission.

Languidly, he observed Teresa. He wished he could show his generosity and offer her a few leaves. But she was young. She still had to bear children. When her monthly bleeding stopped, she could join the men, chew as much as she liked.

They had remembered each other from Salinas. She had matured since then – like all girls, between sunrise and noon.

She had a nice face. If thickened considerably round the chest and haunches, she could even look beautiful. And she seemed a tranquil person. Had he not been a guerrillero, he would have been interested in her. 'Pity you're also a stranger here...'

She looked at him, bright as water from the moon. 'Why?'

He pointed at the young horsemen. 'After the game, those eaglets will be looking for wives. One of them could have chosen you.'

She smiled shyly. 'Oh, but I am spoken for.'

He nodded approvingly. 'From around here – is he?'

She looked towards the snowy summits. White-haired *apus* carrying the sky. 'No.'

'From up there! Does anybody live up there? What could they farm?'

She shrugged, unable to think of an answer.

'Make sure he is not a city fellow. They are hymen thieves. They lie as easily as the south wind.'

She protested angrily. 'My man is important. He travels a lot.'

Chauca preened himself. 'So do I.'

'You are not him.' Regretting her harsh tone, she moved closer to him. 'But you know of him.' From inside her blouse, she took out Manku Yupanqui's portrait. 'I have his picture...'

Chauca glared at her, thinking she was mocking him.

Teresa put the portrait back close to her bosom. 'If you see him, tell him his bride is looking for him. Teresa Ayala.'

Chauca contemplated her. She looked as honest as a sunflower.

'His bride? You mean, he is real?'

'Of course he is real.'

'You've been with him, touched him, heard him talk?'

'Many times. In my dreams.'

Chauca, disappointed, nodded, humouring her.

Teresa gazed at the mountains again. 'Now, he wants me to join him. I thought he might be here.'

'Why here?'

She made a vague gesture towards the procession. 'To stop the games. People will get hurt. Die.'

'They'll get hurt or die for a good reason. It's rare they get hurt or die for a good reason.'

'The earth is our mother. How can she ask her children to die?'

Chauca pondered a moment. 'Too big a question.'

She dropped her gaze, sensitive to his uncertainty.

The procession reached the valley.

Chauca scrutinised the combatants. He liked the look of them. He had a good eye for men – and these carried thunder.

The twenty youths contesting the morning bout spurred their horses to give them a feel of the terrain.

The shamans hung coca bags from their necks; their chests and stomachs thus shielded, they were ready to provide magical support. With the men in attendance, they circled the valley, beating the ground with their wands to establish the boundaries of the battlefield. Here and there, they directed the *varayoks* to bury sprigs of chayuts as barricades against malign spirits. At points east, west, north and south, representing the Inca domain of the four quarters of the world, they spread perfectly formed coca leaves to sanctify the terrain.

The combatants spurred their horses to the centre of the field. Still guided by the shamans, the men presented further offerings: burnt balls of llama fat to solicit a good harvest; libations of *aguardiente* for Pachamama, Earth Mother.

The horsemen were given coca to chew.

The women, laying the spare weapons inside the boundary, moved to the heights. The shamans and the musicians followed, leading the rest of the villagers. When they had taken position on the heights, the men, too, began to chew coca.

In the valley, the contestants broke rank and rode off to seek attacking positions. They tested their *bolas*, swinging them above their heads, unleashing susurrations that both rivalled the wind and counterpointed it.

The *varayoks*, when satisfied that the *communeros* had reached the desired transcendental state, blew on their horns for battle to commence.

The young combatants attacked. Their war-cries, as old and harsh as the land itself, echoed from the spines of the mountains.

'*Wanuchiy*! *Wanuchiy*! Kill! Kill!'

The women joined hands and intoned an Inca chant – a three-noted, haunting refrain. They would continue chanting throughout the engagement to voice concern for the wounded and valediction to the dead.

Few clashes occurred in the first hour. The warriors, anxious not to waste their missiles, manoeuvred around each other, seeking territorial advantage or a striking position with the wind or the sun behind or for signs of weakness in an opponent or his horse. They impressed with their tactical skills and horsemanship.

The next and last hour, all caution was abandoned. Slings and bolas were fired on glimmers of chance. This reckless strategy, too, impressed the families. It provided proof that the new generation had the haughtiness of the forefathers. They would be capable of sacrifice when called upon.

The climax, true to tradition, came in the last fifteen minutes. By this time, the youths had all been unseated from their horses, and in the frenzy of time running out, they fought hand-to-hand, first with clubs, then, in an ever-shrinking radius, with bare fists. Those wounded and still conscious dragged themselves through barriers of pain; the unscathed struggled equally hard to surmount exhaustion. One youth, a lanky fellow, exemplified the spirit of the day: bathed in blood from a gash on his chest, he chased and clubbed down three opponents before he himself was knocked senseless.

At midday, the *varayoks* brought the battle to a close by blowing on their horns.

The combatants collapsed; they writhed until they could catch their breath. When they discovered there had been no deaths, they laughed, shook hands, slapped each other on the back.

The families ran down the heights to join them. The women nursed the gashes with poultices; the shamans tended the broken bones with herbs and splints; the children rounded up the horses; the men served drinks and coca leaves.

Then the women laid out the food.

The youngsters, including the injured, sought out the maidens. When a girl had more than one claimant, the *varayoks* drew lots.

Then they feasted – the youths, separately, with their intendeds. Shyly, they ignored them at first, and boasted of moments of prowess or danger during the fighting; but gradually, they succumbed to feminine attention. Soon it was impossible to tell whether their bodies steamed because of their exertions or from desire.

Up on the heights, Chauca and Teresa kept to their word and did not eat.

Chauca was pleased. 'They shook the earth – and the best is yet to come.'

Teresa forced a smile; it burst forth in tears.

That bothered Chauca. She had not watched the fighting. She had just sat, her face buried in her skirts, her arms looped around her head to ward off the sounds of battle. 'Look – these games are important! They are necessary.'

She mumbled. 'The Sisters – the Church – they say not.'

'That's because they don't understand.'

'The government, too. They want it stopped.'

Chauca smirked. The government would. Not to prevent deaths. The government hated every Indian tradition. Because if the people stuck to their customs, held on to their songs and dances, the government couldn't do with them as it liked. That's why it pushed the *naturales* out of sight, up on to the mountains. Which would have been all right if they could grow foodstuff on the peaks. It was important to stay a *naturale*. Traditions were like rivers inside the earth. Sources to reincarnate souls, to invest a man with dignity, to tell him who he is and who his fathers were. 'Never trust the government, girl!'

She wiped her tears but kept her face down, like a child who had been scolded.

Chauca spat out a ball of coca, frustrated that he could not explain things like those campesinos who made up songs. 'Listen, girl. Pumas don't change. He'll tell you the same – Manku Yupanqui. If you ever find him.'

That reanimated her. She stared, once again, at the mountains. Could he be there, resting on a seat carved for the Morning Star? 'I will find him!'

Chauca suddenly believed her. And he was bewildered. Maybe the coca, like the *mistis* claimed, had clouded his mind. Impossible. Anything the *mistis* said about coca was envy. On the other hand, it could only have been the coca. The divine plant of the forebears. Which the Inca had offered the Conquistadores for perfect union. The grace the white man, poisoned by the Old World and blind to the New, had rejected. Mama Coca. She who exposed Creation, revealed the eternal conflict between the good and the bad spirits, communed with the deities of fire, earth, water and sky. Mama Coca who laid out the *naturale* like a poncho on the loom, with all his glorious colours.

Chauca felt the Light of Nature rise inside him. It projected on to the pool of his soul reflections of this pure girl and Manku Yupanqui, he with the new head, with the sun's missing ray in his hands, with the wind in his hair, and with eyes that damned the slave-makers. Walking side by side over the four corners of the world. Where there were no abodes, they built houses; where there were no crops, they impregnated the earth; they melted ice into water, transformed dungeons into temples; they calmed the seas and put the Sun, the Moon and the stars back into their old places. And, as could be expected from his seed and her womb, they produced golden children.

He smiled reverently, elevated by the workings of mysteries. 'Sure, you will find him. If you walk far enough you can meet the whole world. And when you find him, tell him we need him. Tell him, my *Comandante* is not waiting for the *mistis* to grow a heart. Tell him, we're preparing to fight.'

'Fight?'

'That's why I'm here. To recruit men.'

'But – there will be no need to fight. He has the missing ray.'

'We've already picked our first target. Monte Rico. To liberate the miners. If he comes before that, all the better. If not, we'll fight until he comes. Tell him that.'

Teresa nodded uncertainly.

Chauca resumed chewing coca. In respectful silence, they waited for the afternoon's engagement.

The battle of the men was fought with greater panache. Both the spectators and the combatants had eaten and drunk their fill, and had chewed large quantities of coca. So replete, they felt like giants, freshly moulded by Viracocha, the Inca's Creator.

Unlike the youths, the men wasted no time in tactical manoeuvres. They were all expert slingmen, all capable of wrapping a *bola* round a chinchilla in full flight; and as their sobriquet, *macaneros*, indicated, they were masters with the club. Moreover, they had fought each other in previous years and knew their opponents' strengths. Much as they were goaded by old rivalries, they knew no one would end the day inferior to the other.

And so they fought. Swooping like eagles, charging like jaguars. Forty men on horseback who could have saved Atahualpa and his horseless legions from the gold-eaters. The people witnessed the valour, exalted before the nobility, felt reclaimed by the pure blood. And they blessed Nature for providing such gifts.

The battle ended at dusk. Three men lay dead – one with his skull smashed by a club; one, his chest crushed by a missile; and one strangled by a *bola*. Eleven had been injured. The potato harvest would be bountiful.

Finally, the *communeros* set out for home.

There, the dead would be attended to. That part of their souls which would remain as counselling spirits would be identified; food and drink which they had particularly liked would be eaten; songs that had entranced them would be sung; their names would be inscribed in memory as forebears. Tomorrow, they would be buried far from home so that their ghosts would not disturb the living.

Chauca lingered to search for Teresa. She had walked off in tears when the games had finished. He had assumed she had gone to piss. She had not returned.

He searched the length and breadth of the valley. Distraught, he climbed to the crest of the highest hill and scanned the plains.

He spotted a spark, far on the horizon. Brief at first, like a firefly; then glowing, like a corona. Seemingly drawing light from the moon, fire from a distant volcano. A star travelling across the face of the earth. He assumed it was she. Or perhaps really a star – sent by Manku Yupanqui to guide her.

It was she. For he could sense her slim shadow standing out from the other shadows of the night.

He shouted joyously. '*Vaya con Dios*, Manku's bride! Don't forget – when you find him, tell him about us!'

As his voice echoed from the mountains, the star and her shadow paused, turned, waved and moved on again.

When the moon stood high in the sky, he set out to recruit. He danced over the stones. There had been great fighters amongst the youths and the *macaneros*.

114

15
Stained with forgotten blood

'Jeees-us – this place...'

Jerry Rice was staring at the mural which dominated the bierkeller from the back wall.

Styled crudely after Dürer, the painting depicted a skeleton, garbed in bridal dress, carrying a posy of weapons, standing next to a rugged young officer in ceremonial uniform. In the background, a devastated city expired in streams of smoke.

Daniel sipped his beer.

The mural, like a natural successor to the swastika, had inspired the insignia which the Bridegrooms of Death wore as armbands. It had been painted in the 1950s when the bierkeller, the *Berliner Luft*, had opened up as a corner of *heimat* for German émigrés. No one knew, or was prepared to reveal, the identity of the artist.

Rice gulped down the remains of his whisky and signalled the waitress for another round. Daniel lit a cigarette and studied the patrons.

The Germans dominated, both by their numbers and vociferousness. Some dozen old men, wheezing the last of their military bearing, formed the nucleus. They sat at a long table next to the piano. A coterie of Europeans of various ages pirouetted around them. Younger groups of Germans, judging by their deference, scions of the old men, sat near by, acting as intermediaries. An outer ring of tables harboured the local thugs and the odd Bridegroom. This phalanx of muscle also functioned as errand-runners; coming in and going out as directed, they seemed interchangeable.

That ensemble occupied one half of the bierkeller. The other half, where Daniel and Rice sat, catered for passing trade and tourists. Since the regulars consumed little in proportion to the time they spent sitting, it was the latter who kept the establishment solvent. Even so, they received no special treatment save for exorbitant prices. The attractions, such as the good beer, the pneumatic waitresses – local girls – in low-cut, mini Bavarian dresses and blonde wigs, and the Aryan pianist – imported – were strictly for the pleasure of the old men and their minions.

'Probably war criminals, Dan – every one of them.'

'Small fry.'

'Like hell they are! Let me tell you. Collectively, they launder all the cocaine money. Run the black market currency racket. And control most of the import-export licences, the Defence Ministry sub-contracts and government appointments – particularly those of the Ministry of Foreign Affairs.'

'They're still small fry.'

The waitress arrived with the drinks. Rice waited until she had served. 'What's big fry, then?'

'The ones you don't see.'

'Maybe. But I've seen this lot in their heyday, too. The way they swaggered…'

'That was the uniform. Does a lot, a uniform…'

Daniel drew on his cigarette. Uniforms, any uniform, transformed a person. He had seen timid young men turn into hyenas as they put on army grey. He had seen doughty men shrink into mice when draped in prisoners' rags. Bully boys shine with the light of cherubs in the gowns of church choristers. And if those were illusions, he had seen himself. When Heinrich Kempin had mown down his father and the partisans, it had not been just outrage and grief that he had felt. There had also been the secret desire – unfocused then, unmentionable since – to be vested with Kempin's dazzling uniform; the acknowledgement of the power a uniform held over life and death; the perception that a uniform elevated the underprivileged, put him above the law, above the first commandment, made him god; and the revelation that every man could be a Kempin given the right uniform.

Or the obverse of that revelation: that a godless man can find God simply by putting on a priest's soutane. Because he, Daniel Brac, Christian, born Daniel Perera, Jew, had certainly glimpsed Jesus that time when he had secretly donned Father Drago's cassock. Only his uncompromising sex-drive had stopped him from entering a sacerdotal order. Not, as he had often pretended, his confusion, as a displaced person, in post-war Europe. Nor, as he sometimes agonised, because he could not surrender to God.

Rice gulped down a mouthful.

'Quite an authority, aren't you, Dan? Well, so am I. I fought the motherfuckers! Right across Europe. From D-Day to the end.'

'You were a soldier? Not a correspondent?'

'Ordinary GI. But I saw plenty. That's what hitched me to the typewriter. A platform to shout from. How did you get mixed up with them?'

'I was born in Yugoslavia.'

'Must have been rough.'

'Not for me. I escaped the concentration camps.'

Rice's tone softened in condolence. 'I should have guessed. The name – Brac. Jewish!'

'Not my original name. I was hiding on the island of Brač.'

'Old Jewish tradition – adopting the name of a place.'

'Not consciously. I had ceased to be a Jew.'

'I thought you never ceased to be a Jew.'

'I was saved by Dominican monks. I embraced their faith.'

Rice stared into his whisky. 'I was there at the graveside. Buchenwald, Dachau, Mauthausen – my unit liberated them. I was also at the rebirth – covered Israel's War of Independence. Ended up a Judaeophile.'

Rice's attitude to him was like a Jew's towards a turncoat. Sweet-sorrow, his father had once called it, when he had instructed Daniel on the lost tribes of Israel, the *dönmes* and the *marranos*. An attitude that combined all the pains: the condemnation of apostasy; the assurance that the Chosen People cared even for its errant members; the guilt and apology for the proselyte who had been persecuted into conversion; the disputation that Judaism was still the mother of religions; and the plea for the prodigal son to return to the fold.

'I've only converted, Jerry – not turned into an anti-Semite.'

'Glad to hear it. Can't say I understand you, though. Maybe because I'm low church – wary of religious mania. I mean, I can see a guy giving up orthodoxy. But giving up the ethos... like cutting off your head.'

'It's not fatal – providing you can grow another one.'

'Like Manku Yupanqui?'

Daniel smiled. 'Speaking of him, how are you getting on with your investigation?'

'Not very far. But I believe there is a sage about. Or one in the process of being forged by the mass unconscious. That's how each generation gets its saint. Manku Yupanqui will come – and I'll be there to see him.'

Daniel nodded. The silence anointed their friendship.

Rice pushed his drink aside and leaned over. 'OK, Dan – what's with this creepy joint?'

Daniel stubbed out his cigarette. 'I thought it might stir your bile. I need your help. I'm looking for someone, too. One of these creeps' big boys.'

'You're kidding me.'

'SS-Standartenführer Heinrich Kempin.'

'You're not kidding!'

'Ran riot in Yugoslavia.'

Rice conjured up the names – household names – of those Nazi war criminals who had escaped to South America. Bormann. Mengele. Eichmann. Barbie. Kempin. Some had been hunted. Mystery surrounded the others. 'Is he alive?'

'In this country. Calls himself Joseph Perera – sorry, José Perera.' 'That's like John Smith in Spanish.'

Daniel lit another cigarette. 'Actually, my father's name. He was one of Kempin's victims.'

'You don't mean it…'

'I see it as a tribute. My father so branded his name on Kempin that when the bastard had to choose an alias, that was the only name he could think of. That's my theory, anyway.'

Rice's imprecation was drowned by hearty applause.

Daniel scrutinised the newcomer: the pianist. Girth like the archetypal Bavarian farmer, eyes projecting towards superior horizons. An image from a Leni Riefenstahl film.

'Why come to me?'

'You're famous. Well connected. A good ferret.'

'Any ideas where Kempin is?'

'I have a list of his possible whereabouts.' Daniel nodded towards the old Germans. 'They should know. Some of them, certainly.'

'Let me get this straight. Are you with an organisation? Yugoslav or Israeli – wanting him for trial? Or are you hunting alone?'

Daniel, hesitating a moment, watched the pianist sit at the piano and flex his fingers. Bloody ham! 'As things stand now, I'm hunting alone… I'd better explain…'

Predictably, the pianist started playing the *Deutschlandlied*. Equally predictably, the old Germans burst out singing. Loud and lachrymose.

Daniel moved his chair closer to Rice and told him the facts: about Yizkor, an organisation he presumed was Israeli; about his minor role in the hunt: identifying Kempin; about his own injunctions to do more than that; about Ian Campbell; about his encounter with Fuego and Angelito after Campbell's death; and about the Controller, damned woman who, six weeks after Campbell's murder, still had not rung.

Deutschlandlied came to an end.

As if timing its entrance to the rapturous applause, an amber procession walked in. Beaming, swanking, flaxen hair shining, eyes haloed. The prototype hero and three boys, aged between five and eight. Colonel Angelito, in combat fatigues and his sons, in cub uniforms.

The patrons greeted the children as tomorrow's light and Angelito as one echelon lower than God.

'Speak of the Devil. Did you know he'd be here, Dan?'

'No. I didn't even know he was German.'

'He's not. He's Ukrainian. Well, well, well. Peas in a pod.'

Angelito sat down with the old men, drawing vigorous laughter with his cajolery. His sons, displaying the discipline expected of them, sat at a nearby table. The waitresses tripped over themselves to serve Angelito with beer and food and the children with ice-creams and cakes.

Rice took a swig of his whisky. 'All right, let's look at the score. From what you told me, I'd say they've nabbed your controller woman. Let's believe Fuego that Campbell did not scream. But it'd be too much to expect the same from her.'

'I agree. That means I'm exposed. Another reason why I came to you cap in hand.'

'Let me ask you something. If you found Kempin, what would you do? Kill him?'

Daniel stubbed out his cigarette and snatched another one. When they had been bundled out of the truck, at the forest clearing, Joseph Perera and his men had attacked Kempin's squad so that Daniel could run away. They had put up quite a fight. From his hiding place, not far away, Daniel had seen them collapse under rifle butts. Then he had watched them dig, with broken bodies, their mass grave. And, as the SS squad had set up the machine-gun, he had listened to his father singing eerily. About joy. About children without whom there could be no joy. About women, who, by bearing children, put topsoil on the earth and new shoots on the branch. It had been that song which had saved Daniel Perera. It had so amused Kempin that he had forgotten about him. Robust laughter had accompanied the burst of machine-gun fire.

'I don't know, Jerry. I often imagine that when I confront him, he breaks down and repents – and I prevail on Yizkor to spare him. But, in the main, I believe, I should kill him. And I pray that I'll have the will.'

'I could expose him…'

Daniel looked up anxiously. 'You mustn't write about him. Not yet. He'd instantly take to his heels. Then nobody would ever find him.'

'I'll have no truck with killing, Dan.'

'It would be justice! You believe in justice! Everything you write pleads for justice!'

'Justice – for me – excludes capital punishment. Pompous as it sounds, I adhere to the commandment. *Thou shalt not kill.*'

'Is that how you fought your war!'

Rice looked away, remembering. Europe. Africa. Indo-China. Middle East. Shouting as he waded through blood-soaked earth. Stop it! Stop it! Stop it! Had anyone heard him? Would anyone hear him now? Did anyone *want* to hear him? 'I've seen other wars since. Learned the hard way.'

'What do you want me to say, Jerry? How can I make sense! The way I'm talking about my *mission* – that's a different me. Someone who's changing – has changed. Someone trying to be what I want to be. But someone I hardly recognise. God knows how many times I've asked myself why Yizkor approached me. I mean, an outfit that has a success rate as long as your arm. You'd think I was a seasoned hit-man. The truth is they approached me because I'm the only person they could find who can identify Kempin. So here I am, stranded in no-man's-land. Panic barely under control. Wishing I wasn't involved. This thing has been hanging over me most of my life – and I've always found an excuse to run away. I'd run away now, if I could. I can't. There's a revolt going on inside me. I want to change. I want to be strong. Not just physically strong. But also in spirit. Above all, in spirit. Because my fears are endless, Jerry. And the worst is: I fear that when the moment comes, I'll turn coward – as I've always done. Maybe before you decide, you'd better think about that, too...'

Rice nodded, moved by Daniel's sincerity. 'The same goes for me, Dan. Anybody with a nose can tell you – my bladder stinks with fear. OK, from where I'm standing, I think we could outmanoeuvre Fuego. You're a celebrity of sorts. I can write about your work here and make you more so. The sonofabitch would think twice before he touched you.'

'Even celebrities can have accidents.'

'I'd say you're more at risk with the Bridegrooms.'

'What's the difference? They're Fuego's death-squads.'

'They're more than that. Your ordinary death-squads are made up of Sinchis. You've seen the Bridegrooms. More sophisticated. Murderers. Ex-terrorists. Sewer rats from Europe – like these guys here.'

Daniel contemplated the patrons. Still dreamy with *Deutschlandlied*. Still licking Angelito's arse. 'Are you saying the Bridegrooms control Fuego?'

'Can't you smell it, Dan – there's an alliance here. Fuego uses the Bridegrooms as his private army. Keeping his position secure, taking a share of the cocaine racket. In return, he gives them legitimacy and some autonomy.

And if, as you say, Kempin is here, he must be part of the equation – for all I know, grooming the Bridegrooms for the Fourth Reich.'

Daniel pondered a moment, blowing smoke rings. 'Fuego more or less admitted there were figures behind the scene. I can understand cocaine, organised crime. But old Nazis – preparing a comeback?'

'Why not? Fascism is in vogue again.'

Daniel stared at the Germans. 'They're a spent force.'

'The old men are. Not the ideology. Now, that's a reason to go hunting for Kempin.'

'But that makes things all the more dangerous, Jerry.'

Colonel Angelito, Rice noted, had spotted them. 'We're in it now, Dan. Siegfried over there has seen us together.'

As if to punctuate Rice's statement, the pianist started playing the *Horst Wessel Lied*.

Gooseflesh crept up Rice's skin. Angelito, singing and pumping his arms fervently to the rhythm of the song, was smiling – no, leering – at them.

Then, to Rice's astonishment, Daniel, simpering either dementedly or desperately, also joined in the singing.

16
I sing for those who did not have a voice

The guests, in between stops at the buffet, milled around the Olympic-size pool; the water, reflecting on their faces, highlighted their expressions, fixed, according to status and concern for survival. Their preoccupations were evident in the way they circled General Fuego who was occupying centre stage in the vast patio.

Daniel descended the grand staircase. Fuego, who had arranged the invitation, had specified that the *soirée* was the major event of the year and Daniel, on the possibility that the gathering might include Heinrich Kempin, had accepted.

It was a reckless move in view of the fact that Fuego, in all probability, knew about his involvement in the Kempin hunt. But he relished it. It confirmed that he had reactivated the former Daniel, that ancient, intrepid youth. And it felt as if God had taken a step towards him.

There was, of course, another reason that had compelled him to brave this party. Fuego had let him know that Beatriz, too, would attend – not as a guest, though she had been formally invited, but to provide a brief cabaret, one song, in fact, for which she had exacted an exorbitant fee. Even the fearful Daniel could not have resisted that.

Fuego appeared to have been waiting for him. No sooner had Daniel reached the patio than he was by his side, guiding him through the guests. 'Let me brief you, Daniel, on our grandees... First, our host: Don Xavier Vargas. Emperor of the mines. And his wife, Doña Eugenia.'

Daniel observed Vargas. Upright. Early sixties. Immaculate in white.

Manicured. Delicately gnarled – like dead coral. Wearing a smile as his wife – a fleshless, parchment-skinned woman at least ten years his senior and, perhaps, therefore, the source of his wealth – talked to Dr Williston.

'Dr Luke Williston of Moral Crusade, you've met...'

Daniel cast a cursory look at the massive man, encased in silky dinner jacket.

Fuego pointed at a group of men and women, miscellaneously aged and as anonymous as fashion models. 'Don Xavier has sons, daughters and grandchildren waiting to inherit his empire...' He indicated a number of foreigners, strewn in the gathering. 'Above all, he has his vultures, the paladins of the multinationals. A lot of souls to provide for.'

Daniel, who had always imagined that the shadowy figures of the multinationals were, by their very greyness, imperceptible, scrutinised the last with interest. Short or tall, lean or obese, faces ruddy with alcohol or sallow from boardrooms, they certainly looked like creatures of one species. Not vultures. Indisputably inferior: slugs.

'But, lately, Don Xavier has been having problems from the base communities – the groups run by revolutionary priests like that Father Quintana. So he has washed his hands of Rome and become a born-again Christian.' Fuego indicated the women around Vargas. 'With a special dispensation to maintain his herd of mistresses.'

Daniel observed the colony of women, like hungry damsel-fish floating near Vargas, waiting for Doña Eugenia to dematerialise. But Doña Eugenia appeared to be as durable as the curtain of jewels which shielded her from life.

'There are another thirty-two like Don Xavier. Together, in a hierarchical order, they own ninety per cent of the country. You will spot them easily. The rich, like the poor, look alike.'

Daniel did not bother to spot them.

'Don Xavier has been chasing me hard. He wants me to help the Moral Crusade missionaries in the mining areas. He thinks if his serfs are evangelised, they will forget Liberation Theology and go back to being slaves. I will help – if he pays my price.'

Daniel glanced at him, suspicious of the direction the conversation was taking.

Fuego smiled, self-mockingly. 'Nothing exorbitant. A symbolic gift. This hacienda. With all its contents and acres.' As Daniel looked away, seemingly uninterested, he held him by the arm. 'You don't believe me?'

Daniel pulled his arm away. 'Why tell me?'

'Everybody needs a confessor. I don't go to priests. So I choose an admirable person.'

'It's none of my business.'

'Make it your business. Information is the best defence. Knowing things about me more so.'

'That sounds like a warning.'

'Provocation.'

'Why?'

'That reflection I see in you. It goads me. Now, ask me why this hacienda?'

Daniel hesitated a moment then smiled defiantly. 'Why?'

'I have coveted it since I was ten. Since when I was slowly dying in Vargas's mines. I swore: one day, I would take from Vargas what he represented: this capital within the capital. I am what I am because of that promise. I will keep my word – I always do. After that, every brick can sink into the sea – with my blessing.'

'Will Vargas give it to you?'

'Sooner than he expects. There will be a strike at his richest mine. Not the work of base communities as it happens. But post-Manku Yupanqui tango. With another would-be saint, Gaspar Huaman, as the conductor. Remember him?'

Brave, pathetic Huaman. Daniel wished him luck then locked him in a drawer of his mind. To each his own fight.

Fuego grinned. 'Losing the family seat to an upstart – an Indio, to boot – that will turn Vargas's wine into water. It will be a good lesson.'

'Lesson?'

'Even if the times, as they change, remain the same, there will always be a defiant man.'

'Strikes me that's a lesson you should be the first to learn.'

Fuego chuckled, then winked. 'I would – were I not that man.' He led Daniel towards the pool, indicating a group. 'Some of our parliamentarians and civil servants. All the more pompous for being the catamites of the military.'

Adipose men in penguin suits and distinguished from the waiters only by the presence of wives with ample Spanish shapes and gaudy formal dress. Daniel looked past them, searching for Beatriz. Perhaps she had changed her mind.

No Kempin either, though there were a number of Germans, regulars of the bierkeller. They were trading good humour with Colonel Angelito. A chestless, anorexic woman in a *grande toilette* stood next to him, smoking through a gold cigarette-holder.

'Angelito you know. His wife, Concepción. Superior to the Mother of God with *three* virgin births.' Fuego pointed at the military. 'The

Generalisimo, the Admiral and the Air Marshal – our Junta. Attended to by the top brass – all waiting in the wings. Their adjutants and protégés...'

Daniel glanced at them. They seemed grateful that the party had specified formal attire. Otherwise where would they have put their unearned medals and ribbons, the sashes which matched the size of their bellies and ranks? And their wives: in unfashionable dresses – as if under orders not to outshine their husbands – yet, looking livelier than the rest of the women.

Fuego nudged him. 'You like the women? You have a good eye. If you have to choose between civilian or brass wives, always go for the latter. You have nothing to fear from the husbands. They are busy playing musical chairs in the palaces. It is a game that withers their cocks. So they are grateful to whoever tends to their wives' orchards.'

Daniel felt briefly aroused. He had often indulged in fantasies of cuckolding the armoured men. The Pyrrhic victory of the proles.

'The diplomatic corps...'

Daniel cast his eyes at the foreign contingent. Ambassadors, consuls, attachés, strutting like peacocks. Wives with gin-and-hysterectomy looks.

'...Like gringos everywhere. Blessedly equal. Some, depending on the flag stuffed up their arses – and the multinational that provides the Vaseline – more equal than others. But all superior to the natives.'

'You sound like Gaspar Huaman.'

'All Latin Americans do. But I am more pragmatic.'

'By sucking up to them!'

'No. By *sucking* them.'

'What's the difference!'

'When you suck someone, you have their pants down. I don't like boasting, Daniel, but I can bite off every nut and cherry here. That includes the Junta. I would hardly be where I am – if I could not.'

'But for how long? There will always be men who will challenge such power.'

'In theory, yes. In practice, they turn out to be like Manku Yupanqui. Imaginary beings.'

'Some are flesh and blood. You can see them standing on God's side. I certainly have.'

'*Have*? If they are dead, they have failed.'

'They always leave their courage behind. So that others can succeed.'

'Do you have that courage, Daniel?'

'I should do.'

'You sound like a penitent.'

Trust him to see that. That day when I could have finished with Kempin, there was a strong wind wailing through the poplars. A sibilation impeaching my treachery. 'Betrayers often are, General.'

I was weak. And afraid, Papa. It was me who buried you and your men. Kempin had left you to the wolves. Me who buried you. May there always be good earth over your grave.

'Now you are confessing to me. Why?'

'Everybody needs a confessor.' See, Papa, I'm defying fear. Today, I'm sane enough to think the past will be redeemed. *I* will be redeemed.

And he saw Beatriz. Lighting up the throng like dawn. Her head held high. In rags. Guitar slung across her shoulders.

Fuego smiled. 'At last! Someone who offers flowers to our eyes.'

At the pool, Beatriz began climbing up to the diving platform.

Daniel savoured the sudden effervescence of his spirits. Bounteous woman; dark Indian hair cascading down her back. Oh, to clothe her with his body.

Insidiously, Fuego observed the hunger in Daniel's eyes.

Beatriz reached the diving platform and moved to the edge.

'She sure knows how to grab an audience.' Dr Williston, his plate piled high with caviare, had sidled up to Daniel and Fuego. 'How goes it, Mr Brac?'

Angelito was lurking behind Williston, delicately sniffing a brandy balloon. Daniel smiled. 'Fine.'

'The restoration?'

'The usual snail's pace.'

'Haven't seen Jerry Rice by any chance, have you?'

Ingenuously, Daniel scanned the guests. 'No. Is he here?'

Angelito shook his head. 'He declined. He is working on his Manku Yupanqui story. Travelling around.'

Williston winked at Daniel. 'Dedicated, Jerry is.'

Beatriz strummed some chords and bleakly contemplated the guests. Then she began to sing.

Believe me
there were
days
when
the grass smelled like sea-sand
and the earth shuffled
softly, sweetly...

Fuego imagined that he was fighting the Angel of God; it was the only way he could listen to Beatriz without crying. He was musical enough to know that her voice, despite its power and range, was not exceptional – nasal, in fact. What made it sublime was the immediacy she put into a song, the way she fused melody and lyrics so that her singing became a natural sound. Like clouds crossing electric swords over the Andes; or birds reporting the mood of the jungle; or water recounting creation's mysteries. For him Beatriz *did* represent the very spirit of South America – not the contaminated cities and stagnating backlands, but the paradise man had rightly assumed it was but had lacked the eyes to see.

It had been that spirit that had forced him to abandon her. Had they stayed together, Oseas Fuego, the wise boy from the Cordilleras, would have succumbed to perceiving the world as he had perceived it before wisdom: simple and correctable. He would have striven, like a shaman, his chest full of thunder, to heal it. Inevitably, he would have turned rebel. He would have been hunted down by whoever occupied his present office. Or, he would have been seeking, stubborn with hope and defiance like the contemptible Daniel – for God. Or, at the very least, for a messiah, a Manku Yupanqui. And he would have perished – taking Beatriz with him.

No, he need not regret the loss of love. Yes, he could cope with the lamentation in his heart. It was in the nature of even the strongest man, to pine occasionally for mythic food.

...there were
days
months
maybe years
when
people hummed
made love...

Daniel slipped away from Fuego. And absorbed Beatriz's voice. It had a tone that painted pictures. It conjured images: mother cuddling, father praising, sisters playing games; it made them deathless by investing them with light and colour.

...believe me
there were such days
I almost saw them...

The last phrase reverberated like an angry sky. Beatriz, out of breath, glared at her audience. They burst into applause. Some shouted, 'bravo', 'bis', 'encore'. Some even burst into tears, happy that they stood accused.

Fuego remembered another occasion – in Washington, USA. He had been on a course with the CIA. They had taken him to a show. Political satirists indicting capitalism and the American dream. Why be subjugated to a system devised by greed and, consequently, miss life, leisure and happiness – that sort of thing. The audience, as élite as the present one, had given a thunderous ovation. His CIA instructors had stressed the moral. People craved to be rebuked. Mass catharsis – a great need. So cleansed, people could regress to self-righteousness, slipstream behind any policy that promised further riches and ignore whoever or whatever was destroyed in the process.

The applause continued.

With a desolate sweep of the arm, Beatriz threw her guitar into the pool. Then, clutching at her breast as if shot, she catapulted from the platform. She dropped, spinning in the air, arms and legs dangling lifelessly, and hit the water like a dead bird.

The guests, thrilled by the spectacle, clamoured wildly.

Daniel, pushing people out of the way, ran to the poolside.

Beatriz surfaced, swam to the edge of the pool and hauled herself up. Her effort to stand upright indicated how painful the stunt had been.

Daniel reached her. 'Can I do something?'

She stared at him as if trying to refocus; then she stroked his face. 'Let me go. Please.'

Daniel stepped aside.

A waiter fished out her guitar. Another offered her a bathrobe. She refused both with a shake of the head and walked towards the changing rooms. The guests made way for her, still applauding. Except when she parried the arms that desired to touch her, she ignored them.

Fuego, relishing Daniel's misery, moved forward.

'Hang on, Oseas...' Williston, taking a last mouthful, handed his plate to a waiter. 'A little talk.'

Angelito moved to his other flank, at half attention with an earnest face. 'Somewhere quiet.'

Fuego cast a disappointed look in Daniel's direction, then whispered. 'I know a deaf tree in the garden.'

They stopped beneath an apple tree in the orchard. Fuego leaned against the trunk. Angelito drifted from one shadow to another. Shadows, Fuego mused, gave Angelito substance.

Williston placed himself opposite and stared at the orchard. The apples, glinting in the moonlight like stars, made him feel like crying – and rejoicing. Apples were part of his life. They'd been everywhere, in every corner of his childhood house and in his bed and under his pillow. Even now, he could not sleep in a place if there were no apples in it. They weren't for eating, but to remind how easily a man could fall, how naturally a woman turned harlot. For years, every time a bus stopped on the highway, his mother would run to the front porch to see if her husband had returned. He never did. So, she would take Luke to where the apples were, out to the orchard or into the house, wag her finger at those fruits of sin that were everywhere, whip him twenty lashes and ten hard slaps on the face for good measure so that he would never forget what they stood for. And his sister, older by two years, would watch, bawling, because Ma's husband was her father whereas Luke's father had been an itinerant farmhand who had pushed Ma to sin, who had then decamped forcing Pa to go chasing him with his shotgun, and Pa was still chasing him for all anybody knew. Well, Ma, I'm saved. Not so Sis. She died soon after you. Whoring and drugs. She couldn't renounce the flesh like I could. Oh, sure, Ma, I'm always straying into Onan's ways, but that's just my father's sin visiting me. But I make sure I'm purified afterwards. I wash and beat the hell out of myself.

'Well, Luke?'

Williston faced Fuego sombrely. 'Right. This miners' strike... I want to give Vargas my word as a Christian that it'll be nipped in the bud.'

Fuego nodded brusquely. 'You know it will be.'

'I hear Huaman will be involved. He's pushing himself right out of the Lord's light, I'm told, since that Manku Yupanqui business. That's bad news.'

'You can't be taking Huaman seriously!'

'I take everything seriously, Oseas. I thought you understood that when I insisted on going to the desert. I have to account both to the Lord and to Caesar.'

Fuego waved a conciliatory hand to stop Williston launching into his favourite speech. The Lord, Oseas, means Moral Crusade. A pan-evangelical movement with a four-point programme: the translation of the Good Book into every living language; the deployment of a vast army of missionaries; holy war against all left-wing ideologies; zealous intolerance of secular humanism, by which I mean all liberal and social policies, all the fields of science, like the theory of evolution, that challenge the Bible, and all art which, by inciting such excesses as promiscuity, homosexuality and radicalism, infects the living body of Christ.

But quite brief on Caesar. A constellation so bright, Oseas, you can't look at it without burning your eyes. Each star formidable. Suffice it to say they all sit on the right-hand side of the White House.

Fuego had not taken Williston's word on trust; he had found out for himself.

The constellation comprised a plethora of ultraconservative, racist and fascist institutions, both in the US and abroad, that either underwrote Moral Crusade's fundamentalism or paid lip service to it to further their own particular ambitions. Their collective stature was never fully seen, but given their members' influence on the US administration, Fuego had no doubt that it was one of the richest and most powerful alliances in the world.

Angelito emerged from the shadows, eyes mischievously wide open. 'We have plans for Huaman. We'll sprinkle the mountains with his ashes.'

Fuego stiffened. He had no scruples about killing. Life was worthless – his own included. But those who killed with sophistication, or, as was the case with Angelito, fastidiously, like a child dismembering an insect, invariably disgusted him. But then, Angelito was a European, imbued, as the white man incessantly claimed, with a superior civilisation.

The breeze had ruffled Williston's wispy hair. He took out a comb from his wrist-bag and began to groom himself. 'This story about Jerry Rice investigating Manku Yupanqui. Not altogether pure as the driven snow, I hear. He's ferreting after José Perera.'

Angelito raised his brandy balloon to Williston, then turned to Fuego. 'We should stop Rice, General.'

All things to all men, Angelito was. Williston must be lapping up all that deference. 'Rice is an old man – what can he do?'

Angelito smiled haughtily. 'Kempin is an old man, too. Look at all he has achieved.'

'Rice has the power of the pen, Oseas.'

'And you have the power to stop him publishing, Luke.'

Williston finished combing his hair. 'What about Daniel Brac?'

Fuego remained inscrutable. After tonight's sparring. Daniel, he had decided, was his prey – no one else's. 'Brac is a picture-restorer. He is harmless.'

Angelito rasped. 'He's after Kempin. Now, he's teamed up with Rice!'

A new component had crept into Angelito. Fuego could smell it. Fear – reeking like the clap. This was the man who had danced whilst mutilating the *varayoks* and the *mamaconas*. 'What are you afraid of, Angelito? Do you think he is after you, too?'

Angelito glared at him. 'I wish he were. Unfortunately, he knows nothing about me.'

'Which proves he is not a hunter. Hunters know that dogs always piss where other dogs have pissed.'

Angelito burst out laughing. 'Shall I repeat that to the *kamaradenschaft*?'

'Don't waste your time. Your *kamaradenschaft* have hidden in sheep's clothing for so long they have forgotten what proud wolves they were. Or how good it must have been to be a wolf.'

Angelito moved to Fuego's elbow, his smile all the more threatening. 'You know my record, General. In Europe – and here.'

Williston moved in between Angelito and Fuego. 'Gentlemen! Gentlemen!' He waited for Fuego to lean back against the tree and for Angelito to withdraw into the shadows. 'The problem, as I see it... any indication this country is sheltering old Nazis...'

Fuego snorted. 'Or the new...'

'...Would be adverse propaganda. The last thing you need.'

'Rice and Brac are not campesinos, Luke! They are gringos – not expendable.'

'Even gringos are not immortal.'

'Shut up, Angelito!' Williston, putting on a deferential face, turned to Fuego. 'What do you have in mind, Oseas?'

'Rice, I will let chase his tail. Brac is a fly; I will be the spider.'

Angelito became petulant. 'Why all this Andean folderol, General? There is a simple course. Direct action. Eliminate them.'

Fuego unleashed his scorn. 'Watch out, Angelito – before this Andean kicks you back to your precious Europe. There are many authorities there just waiting to give you direct action.'

Angelito, momentarily betraying his fear, grinned. 'You would never do that, General. I am your sword. *And* your shield.'

'Swords and shields you can buy by the dozen – remember that.' Fuego turned to Williston. 'Everything agreed?'

'Sure thing. Even if we hadn't, you call the shots. I'm only here to advise.' Williston had one hand in his pocket and was playing with his coins.

Fuego started walking off.

Williston held him with his other hand. 'Out of interest, Oseas. This painting Brac is restoring. Does it have any connection with Manku Yupanqui – as the people are whispering?'

'Why? Would you destroy it if it did?'

'Does it?'

Fuego looked at him grimly. 'I am surprised at you, Luke. That's Indio nonsense. Beneath you.' He strode away.

Daniel had picked a chair in the penumbra of the large bungalow that served as changing rooms. He was sweating profusely and trembling. Normal state of affairs for a man chasing a woman, he wanted to think, particularly for a man who had chased so many so compulsively. But this tension had an intensity he had never experienced.

In the past, he had shied away from women who saw love as an eventful –

emotional – journey on a never-ending sea. He had wanted only physical joy and carefree companionship. Hence, he had never breathed a woman deeply enough to want her for herself – and for the children they could have had.

Now, suddenly, unexpectedly, as if courage had brought with it the gift of maturity, he did not want to chase. Now, he wanted to be in love. He was in love. And ready for love. Now, he was petitioning love. Now, as he waited for Beatriz, he believed that if she rejected him, it would be the end of hope.

Yet reason prayed that when she came out, she would fail to see him – otherwise, why sit in the dark – or, if she saw him, nod a greeting and move out of his orbit. Reason doubted he had anything to offer her. And if he had, reason mocked, he would not give it. He was not capable of giving. Above all, reason said, he had his work, not to mention his mission. She would disorient him. Bearing in mind her past association with Fuego, she would be a source of trouble. If it was a question of sex, reason reminded, he could get it anywhere, he had the knack; if need be, he could buy it.

But, fortunately – miraculously – reason was floundering. His flesh and soul sought to revert to the particle of a woman that a man was.

Beatriz came out of the bungalow – in shirt and jeans.

Daniel rose from the chair.

Fuego materialised by her side.

Daniel stood still. Had Fuego been watching him?

Benignly, Fuego shook his head. 'Was it worth, it, *querida* – your stunt?'

Beatriz glared at him. 'Not a stunt. A declaration.'

'That you despise the Establishment?'

'That, given the chance, I'll fight it.'

Daniel stepped out of the shadows. See how brave I am. How I resist reason. I want light. I want life.

Fuego gave him a cursory glance, then ignored him. 'It was a beautiful song.'

'Did you listen to the words?'

'Yes.'

'Did they mean anything?'

'Yes. The mountain yearns to be a valley, but it is not in its nature.' He saluted her, nodded at Daniel, and walked away.

Beatriz turned to Daniel and studied him for a long time. ' Trees – can we become like trees?'

'I love you.'

'Join our roots? Turn green? Flower? Live through winters? Green and flower again?'

'You are light. Life.'

'Don't say that. It's unfair. I am a childless woman. I need to be wise.'
'I want to be born.'
She clutched his hand. 'Take me home.'

PART THREE

17
What spring does with the cherry trees

'I want to sleep with your cock in my mouth.'

'You'd suffocate.'

She laughed, then settled between his legs.

He stroked her hair. 'You're arousing me.'

'Good. We can continue.'

He closed his eyes. They blended so spectacularly. Like two colours creating a new chroma. This was life – real life. Not just a taste of it. Was it also salvation? Had he ridden to that oasis, which his father had assured him he would, where the traveller could hitch his horse – for ever, if he was lucky?

Papa, his tenderness glowing like wheatland, promising an endless time, his hands running through his wife's hair. *Sapphira, Sapphira, you present me to God every day.*

'Are you with me?' She was looking up at him in mock anger.

He tapped her nose with his erection. 'What's it look like?'

'Oh, *he* is with me. But you...'

'Come...Ride me.'

She straddled him immediately.

This time she had pretended to sleep. And lying in the crook of his arm, she had seen him stare through the night into that inner darkness he had tried to hide from her. Now dawn was entering the room and she felt frightened. The new day might not be indulgent.

She turned, giving him her back and cradling her buttocks against his thighs. She felt it was a safe position for talking. 'Don't you ever sleep, Daniel?'

He took a long time to reply. 'I don't need much sleep.'

She imagined his eyes. Less threatening than when he avoided hers. His thighs enjoyed her buttocks, but without commitment. 'Why is that?'

'A quirk in the mechanism.'

'The mechanism is great. Don't mock it.'

'Go back to sleep.'

He caressed her back and let his eyes wander around the room. Her bedroom. She called it unfeminine, a *wagon-lit* in a train. He loved it. Loved the house, too. Originally, it had been the stables of a riding school. Having to rebuild it completely and unable to give it soft curves, she had compartmentalised it, starting with an entrance hall at the centre and progressing east and west, room after room, all of them interconnecting and all with doors leading to the front and back gardens.

Now, the west side was used for her business; offices for her secretary and manager, a rehearsal room, her own recording studio, guest rooms for musicians and visiting artists. The east side was home: a whole room converted into a music centre; recreation chamber complete with swimming pool; salon; dining room; kitchen; sitting room; bedroom; bathroom. Haphazardly furnished. Records and tapes everywhere; speakers the size of wardrobes standing at every wall. A grand piano and musical instruments from all over the world; shelves of books. Strewn with what she called clutter: statues and sculptures; *objets d'art* and souvenirs from her concert tours. And for someone not very interested in painting, a large collection of pictures and drawings, mostly nudes – male and female. Armchairs in which a person melted like sugar; antiques, mostly indigenous.

But the bedroom was Shangri-La. A king-size futon which she called her wrestling mat; dimmer lights; a vast mirror as a headpiece where they could see each other making love; Inca carpets hanging on the walls and covering the ceiling; an array of Turkish cushions – no chairs; incense sticks to deodorise the stench of the death-pit that hung over the city; a dressing alcove bursting with clothes and shoes. And an effigy, as tall as Daniel, of Ekeko, the god of good fortune and prosperity, in the shape of a jovial man in modern clothes with banknotes, bottles, food tins and every other symbol of wealth pinned on him.

'Daniel, I want to talk.'

His hands stopped caressing.

'I want to talk about tomorrow.'

'I might be dead tomorrow.'

'Don't say that!' She whirled round, kissed him, biting his lips. 'Don't say that!'

He withdrew behind his smile. I want to be with you for ever – why could he not say that? And then abandon the Kempin mission!

'Can you tell me, Daniel… How long will the restoration take? What will you do afterwards? Where will you go?'

'I'm here for about a year. After that…?'

I'll tell you why you're withdrawing. Nothing to do with Kempin. You're feeling guilty, ashamed, disappointed. You deluded yourself into thinking you could be as giving as her. You can't be. She wants you to fathom her. You won't fathom her in any way except sexually. And when she tries to fathom you, you run away. You're afraid of what she'll find – or rather, what she won't find.

'After that, what, Daniel?'

'We'll see what's on offer. We'll decide.'

The suggestion that they would weigh up love, like vendors, offended her. But she refused to be perturbed. '*We* being you and I? Or just you?'

'You and I.'

She kissed him again, deeply; then snuggled up. He stroked her forehead. 'Come on – sleep…'

She nodded, pushed her breasts against him. He did not exploit the physical contact. Undiscouraged, she held his penis. That, at least, pulsated immediately.

Why – how – had she fallen in love with him?

She thought back to the necropolis: it had been on the flight back to La Merced, gazing at the vertebrae of the Andes and thinking about the massacre, thinking how she had decided to change – had already changed – thinking about seizing life – above all, producing life, that she had first wondered about him as a lover, imagined the texture of his skin – strong and velvety – and the power of his athletic body.

Then, meeting him again, immediately after El Chulpa, after another brutal death, he had struck her as a man uncontaminated by the evils of her blighted continent. Hence a man of solidity, integrity, compassion, sanity – of that rare Europeanness that had summed up her father.

And she had seen her vision of his purity confirmed in his artless stance against Fuego. Like a child, she had thought. Which was acceptable – lovers were often like one's children; flesh of one's flesh.

Of course, since then, she had had many glimpses of his troubled soul, of its impenetrable walls. But what was love if not the constant flow of water that eventually cracked the stone? For years, she had looked for a man who would be capable of permanence. Now, here he was, needing only her help to release all his rays. She could make him her own Manku Yupanqui. And she had known, the moment he had first entered her, that he had the thrust to give her the child she wanted.

She squeezed his penis. 'I love you. I have never said that to any man.'

She had told him everything about her past. Belief in promiscuity – like a prospector sifting endless earth for gold dust. Thus the countless men – including Fuego, surprisingly a gentle lover. And Daniel had seethed because he could find no signs of them on her body and saw them standing beyond reach, like everything else in his life.

She kissed his arms. 'I have never been able to love before. The body can be abused – it's strong. Not the spirit. You can entrust that to only one person.'

That was the difference between them. She had the capacity to dissolve into him. He was entombed by his defences. 'The spirit is strong, too, Beatriz. Must be.'

She was looking up at him. 'But all this suffering...'

Daniel gazed at her eyes. Her secret garden started there, in her pupils. 'It's unavoidable.'

'Is it – always?'

'You know about suffering...'

'I don't.'

'Your songs...'

'My songs say what I should feel.' She held him tightly. 'But – I have been running away from suffering. I see it around me. I sing about it. But I avoid it. I am ashamed to be such a coward. That's one reason why I went to the desert: to remember how to face it, how to fight it. I came back a better person. Ready to fight. That stunt at the party – that was my declaration of war. But now that I love you... When life is sweet, it is beautifully sweet. I want to run off with it and hide.'

He felt afraid for her. He caressed her mouth.

'Am I despicable, Daniel? Is it necessary to suffer?'

'I can't answer that. I've also taken to my heels all my life. But I do know this: cowardice kills the spirit. Whereas suffering creates consciousness. Makes you question God.'

'You still end up with no answers.'

He teased her nose. 'He always answers. If we don't understand what He says, it's because we choose not to understand.'

She held the hand teasing her nose. 'Are you still running away?'

'Not just now.'

'Might you – tomorrow?'

Her eyes had opened wider, making her all the more beautiful. Daniel looked away. For a man whose life had begun to change only recently, tomorrow was such a new concept. Tomorrow meant Kempin and forbade any procrastination. And if God was vindicated, if Good triumphed over Evil, tomorrow also meant a sort of life left to live, a portion of time to resurrect the soul.

'Not if I can help it.'

'What could make you run?'

'Obligations.'

Warmth drained away from her body. 'A woman?'

'No.'

She held his face, relieved. 'What then?'

'It's a long story. I'll tell you one day.'

'Are you in danger?'

'Why should I be?'

'Is it something to do with Fuego? I mean, he is always baiting you…'

'Nothing to do with Fuego.'

She chose to believe him; but she remained uneasy. 'Be careful of Fuego.' Then, eager to lighten the mood, she rubbed her hair over his face and whispered in his ear. 'Let me tell you my hopes for tomorrow. To be with you. To have children. I don't mind where we go, what we do. I want you to know that.'

'I'll pray for that.' He cupped her breasts. 'I love you.'

18
I listen to my tiger and weep for my absent one

Valdepeñas, the regional capital of the Yungas, was the furthermost city from La Merced – about a thousand kilometres east from the Pacific as the condor flew. But for the earthling going overland, the distance trebled in endless detours over two Andean ranges, the Altiplano in between, and a great expanse of the Amazon basin.

Jerry Rice had trekked to Valdepeñas once before, in late 1967, whilst reporting Che Guevara's last campaign. In those days, Valdepeñas had been a quiet frontier town with simple, whitewashed Spanish houses linked by roofed-over sidewalks – like something out of a Hollywood western.

He had been an old hippie then – as Debbie used to tease him. And Debbie had been a whirlwind, receptive to his love, ambitious to be a good wife much as she debunked marriage, ecstatic that they could work together, albeit as rival correspondents, and fanatically committed to life – as if she had known that the cancer which was to devour her five years later was already eyeing her body.

They had loved Valdepeñas; its balmy, tropical lushness and its people: stolid Spanish pioneers, serene Mennonites, ascetic Japanese, all toiling on God's acres.

That Valdepeñas had disappeared. The rot had set in, Rice chose to believe, after Che's execution. It had quickly spread, feeding on the collective curses of the waning flower-people who had sought his grave and who had discovered that he had not been permitted one; that precisely in order to deprive the people of a cult and a shrine, the ashes of his cremated body had been scattered in the wilderness. After that, with the dead flower-people reborn as nihilistic corporation-men, a plague had ruled.

Valdepeñas was a boom town now, its entrails bloated with oil and cocaine. The Spanish pioneers, the Mennonites, the Japanese had been pushed deep into the outback. Exclusive suburbs, exhibiting psychedelic blends of Grecian, Romanesque, Gothic and modern architecture, rippled away from the old commune like ground blast. The historic centre itself creaked under the sport, vomit and commerce of brothels, bars and luxury shops. The narrow streets, furrowed for horses and carts, now subsided under the weight of Cadillacs, Porsches, Ferraris and Rolls-Royces.

Walther Dyck pointed out a concrete-and-glass building. 'And that is the José Perera Clinic.'

Rice glanced at it. A fair size and busy.

Valdepeñas had been the last entry in Daniel's list of Kempin's probable whereabouts. It had had an asterisk indicating that all the evidence had singled it out as the likeliest place, but that it should be investigated after all the other places had been eliminated with certainty. This method, though perverse, would enable Yizkor to deploy slowly but surely, tightening the ring all the time, so that when, finally, the target was unreservedly confirmed, they could move in and out swiftly, safe from a possible counter-attack on their flanks or rear.

No doubt, such a strategy was sound and well tested. But Rice was of the opinion that Yizkor should have ignored the rule book and beelined here straight away. For, in Valdepeñas, José Perera's name was everywhere. Admittedly, no one had met him or seen him, but there were some good people, not least, dear old Walther, who were never fooled by evil and who, consequently, shied away from everything that carried his stamp.

'Quite a philanthropist, then. A school, a park, a hospital.'

Walther squinted at the blanket of clouds. 'It is going to rain.'

Rice craned to take another look at the four skyscrapers, rising like prison watch-towers, from the corners of the town. They bore José Perera's name, too. As did the companies that occupied them. As did every *cambio-wechsel-change* office. 'Small price to pay, I guess – in order to own the town. Then again, it's insurance. What's a few million dollars to a billionaire if he can get the people beholden to him?'

Walther concentrated on the heavy traffic and made no comment. Rice patted his friend's shoulder. Walther, a Mennonite, would not perjure his faith by passing judgement on any person. Scrupulous in word and deed, he would merely state facts.

'That's all the empire, is it, Walther?'

'That is all there is here.'

Rice stared at the flagpole outside the clinic. Like those of the skyscrapers, it was flying the emblem of a castle, pseudo-Bavarian in style, which, Walther had said, had been built, irrespective of countless obstacles, in the remotest part of the Yungas, as the headquarters of José Perera Enterprises. 'How do I get to the castle, Walther?'

'You need to be invited.'

The clouds burst; rain cloaked the town.

'What if I drove there now and knocked on the gate?'

A semblance of a smile streaked across Walther's face. 'Not in this truck. There are no roads to speak of.'

'I could hire a four-wheel drive.'

'The castle has a moat. The moat is surrounded by an electric fence. There are many sentries and guard dogs. You cannot get in.'

'Those invited – how do they get in?'

'They fly in. There is an airstrip.'

'So I charter a plane.'

'You would not be permitted to land.'

'What would they do? Shoot me down?'

Walther wrestled with the steering-wheel to keep the truck afloat. The street was turning into a quagmire.

'I could pretend an emergency. Surely they'd give me the benefit of the doubt!'

'Do you have to go there, Jerry?'

'How do you expect me to write an article without meeting the man? Also, I'll need some pictures.'

'Choose another subject. This one is outside the perfection of Christ.'

Rice stifled a gasp. *Outside the perfection of Christ.* The first time he had heard Walther utter that phrase, Debbie had been by his side. And she had wondered, for the rest of her short life, whether the world, in the nuclear generation, could ever move inside the perfection of Christ.

Details, crystal-clear, surfaced in a rush.

One of those anarchic days in the aftermath of Che's execution. Valdepeñas had been full of troops: some back from the wilderness where they had been hunting, unsuccessfully, for Che's companions; others, mobilised to take up the chase – all angry and resentful. Walther, his family and other members of his community, had been buying provisions at the general store. Serene as ever in their traditional costumes – men in overalls and broad-brimmed hats, women in nineteenth-century long dresses and bonnets. They had drawn the wrath of a group of drunken soldiers. They had been attacked – first verbally, as revolutionaries in fey disguise, then physically, as enemies of the state. The men, barely managing to shepherd their wives and children into the safety of the general store, had offered no resistance – true to the Mennonite confession of faith which stipulated the way of the Cross as the only response to evil. The beating had been brutal. But unlike most such incidents, the townspeople had not stood by indifferently. Led by some Japanese, they had rushed to help the Mennonites. So had Debbie. And always afraid for Debbie, so had he. The soldiers, now facing an angry crowd instead of the children of God, had drawn their guns. There would have been many dead but for Walther's voice, creaking through broken ribs, pleading with the people. *Do not fight! Do not fight! Do not put yourselves outside the perfection of Christ!* And the crowd had dispersed. Soldiers first – back to their senses, ashamed. Then the others – when satisfied that the Mennonite women and children could take charge of their injured men. But not Debbie. And, because of Debbie, not he. They had stayed with the Mennonites, helped them home, fetched doctors, nursed them. And they had found themselves – imperfect Christians – embraced as friends.

Now, with that same tenet that declared all man's politicking as incompatible with the promise and fulfilment of morality, Walther was warning him. Proof enough that Perera was Kempin.

Rice resorted to his hip-flask. He would heed the warning. But would Daniel? 'OK, Walther. I know where Perera drinks his soup. To hell with the rest.'

Walther's face lit up. The rain had stopped – as suddenly as it had begun. But the road remained a muddy creek. 'Take you to the farm now? Marianne would be very happy.'

Marianne, Walther's wife, was the universal sister. She would insist on washing his feet, a rite which Mennonites, emulating Jesus' homage to His disciples, practised. It would embarrass him. But he would also feel honoured. He would absorb a sense of humility. Then there would be a feast. Sons and daughters and their respective consorts and children. They would talk about Debbie. Marianne would cry. He would, too. It was time for a good cry. 'I would be very happy, too, Walther.'

Walther broke into a smile and a whistle.

Rice took another sip from his hip-flask.

They were driving past the Plaza de Armas. There was the splendid cathedral, dominating it – full of treasures in hand-wrought colonial silver. And the grand steps where Debbie and he had sat in the evenings and watched the courting couples.

The steps seemed unusually crowded. People, obviously having disdained the rain, were steaming under the sun.

'Hold it, Walther! Can you stop?'

Walther braked and manoeuvred towards the kerb. 'What is it?'

The people were clustered around a young girl...

'That girl!'

Walther turned to say something, but Rice had jumped out of the truck. Walther grimaced and parked.

Rice bustled across the Plaza.

Teresa Ayala. She was sitting, cross-legged, by the entrance to the cathedral. All in white. And though drenched by the rain, she looked immaculate. She held on her lap, in the manner of a bouquet, an icon.

There were a lot of people around her. Some were hostile, leering at her. Others seemed uncertain or troubled. Most were reverential, even supplicatory. These last also carried icons, and held them up, like sacred symbols, whenever they caught her eye. And they offered her presents: fruit, vegetables, items of clothing, talismans, even money. She accepted some food and refused the rest graciously.

Rice approached her. He could now discern her icon: Manku Yupanqui's portrait. The icons carried by the others – the same.

She saw him. Smiling beatifically, she beckoned him with a slight move of the head. The crowd made way.

'Teresa... What are you doing here?'

'This is where Manku's footsteps brought me.'

Rice studied her. When he had last seen her, in Illariy, she had been a strange adolescent – childlike, but possessed. Now she had the poise and the features of a mature campesina. The eyes still bore the fire of the obsessed, but framed by a weary, weather-beaten face, they looked as if they had abandoned the present. A sibyl might have such eyes.

'Have you been travelling all this time? You must have covered most of the country.'

'He wanted me to see the four corners. To know the people. It is my duty as his bride. Did you follow his footsteps, too?'

'No. I – I'm just passing through.'

'They are easy to follow. At night – under the stars – they shine.'

Rice became aware of an elderly woman tugging at his sleeve. She was carrying a whole set of clothes – a skirt, a shirt, a shawl, a pair of socks and sandals. All in white and brand new. 'Please, señor. Maybe she listen to you. She is all wet. Tell her to change clothes. Or she is ill.'

Rice looked quizzically at Teresa. Teresa smiled, then addressed the woman gently. 'Thank you, *mamacita*. I do not feel the wet. Also my clothes have dried.'

The woman withdrew, walking backwards, bowing, but still concerned.

Rice dropped his voice to a whisper. 'Who are these people, Teresa?'

She gazed at them as if she were their mother. 'They believe in Manku Yupanqui. They believe me.'

Rice, shaking his head, scanned the crowd again.

'Some say Manku is at the castle.' Teresa pointed at the José Perera Enterprises flag on a skyscraper. 'That one.'

Rice used his gentlest tone. 'No, Teresa. He wouldn't be there.'

Teresa smiled equivocally.

A middle-aged couple approached. They were carrying a young man on a stretcher. Placing the stretcher before Teresa, they knelt down. Rice noted that the young man, emaciated, appeared to be in a coma.

Teresa, touching the young man, whispered. 'Manku Yupanqui loves you.' The young man's parents rose. Teresa touched their hands. They crossed themselves, then, picking up the stretcher, withdrew.

Rice fidgeted. 'I – I'd better be going...'

'*Vaya con Dios*, Mr Rice.'

Rice edged away. 'And you, Teresa.'

He hurried back to the truck.

Walther had got out and had been watching him, intrigued. 'You know that girl?'

'Yes. She's... she's still searching for... it's crazy.'

'Why crazy? She has faith. Any faith that reflects the perfection of Christ is a blessing. Except for my Marianne, I have not met a person in a greater state of grace.'

They got into the truck. Walther drove off. Rice looked back as they branched off the Plaza de Armas. Teresa was submerged by the people. He only caught a glimpse of her white dress.

19
A spider who spins the sky and leaves

'When it comes to faith, there are three kinds of people. Those born blind. Those who put on a blindfold. And those who dare retain their eyes and see the world as it is. Which one are you, Daniel?'

'Blind, I suppose, General.'

'That is better than being blindfolded. Blindfold, the Manku Yupanqui legend says, is fear. Call me Oseas.'

'Blind or blindfolded. We can see things which the sighted can't.'

'Propaganda. Be careful. The eyes of the sighted have blades. Especially here.'

Daniel, having mixed a measure of alcohol with ten measures of turpentine for a fresh cup of solvent, looked up. '*Yet you shall be brought down to Sheol, to the depths of the abyss.*'

Fuego chuckled and shifted on the hammock. 'Isaiah excoriating Satan. You flatter me.' He raised his bottle of *aguardiente* to toast Daniel.

Daniel took a sip from his bottle. Stupid bravura. But he was not going to be intimidated. Fuego had brought a full case, declaring that this was going to be a very special occasion. Fine.

He took the solvent and climbed the scaffold. He moved on to the platform. Coffee and biscuits – that's what I need. Just stay sober.

'You never told me who you betrayed, Daniel. Confessions lack merit unless they are full.'

Daniel hesitated a moment. 'A hero.'

'Tell me about him.'

Daniel ignored him and resumed work. He wiped his hands on his dungarees, then made a swab by twisting some cotton wool on a matchstick. He dipped the swab into the solvent. Choosing a spot, he carefully rubbed the varnish. He examined the swab to see whether it had drawn any of the impasto. He found no trace of colour on the cotton wool – just the dirty brown of the decayed resin.

'You have a beautiful face, Daniel...'

Daniel threw away the dirty swab. 'Are you propositioning me?'

'Like a crater lake. A miracle of nature. But useless to fish or fowl.'

Daniel fixed another swab. He was working on the section depicting the Trinity. And with each swab, the three Jesuses appeared more incarnate – as if projecting themselves to stand by his side.

Fuego drank some more. 'Where is Beatriz?'

'Recording. The song she sang at Vargas's place.'

'Good. The people need to cry. In love yet – you two?'

'We think so.'

'Sounds very non-committal.'

'It's not, I can assure you.'

'I am jealous.'

Daniel grinned. Let Fuego see: Beatriz's flesh was imprinted – was being reprinted daily – all over him.

'Are you jealous of me, Daniel?'

Damn the man!

'I was always jealous of her previous lovers.' Fuego smiled and stared at the ceiling. 'I have spent many nights outside her house watching her bedroom, knowing you were there... Though that's not jealousy. But the urge to protect.'

'She'll come to no harm with me.'

Fuego snorted dubiously, then drank a mouthful.

Daniel turned again to the polyptych. Depicting the Trinity as three identical figures of Jesus – as opposed to the more prosaic European convention where the Son, the Father and the Holy Spirit bore features that defined their different personages – had been a popular tradition among South American painters. Those of the Cuzco school, in particular, had painted many variations, ranging from the classical stylisation where the three Jesuses sat side by side on a vast single throne to the surrealism of portraying them as a single head by joining the right and left profiles to the full frontal face. Daniel had come to espouse the South American tradition; for those seeking spiritual fare, the triple presence provided more bountiful nourishment.

'Does Beatriz know about your hero?'

'No.'

'Keeping your betrayals secret, eh?'

The Trinity were sitting on simple wooden thrones perched on a vast globe. Their bare feet were strong for having walked the lands and the seas. There were no geographical details on the globe; it simply glowed in a paradisaical emerald green.

'Was it love that pushed you to betrayal? It often does.'

The Jesus on the right represented the Son. Except for a broadcloth covering his loins, He was naked. With his left hand He held an upright cross. A newborn lamb sat on his lap, on the broadcloth. Myriad hues of white counterpointed the Lamb with the Son's skin. The cross, in melanin black, and the broadcloth, in iodine scarlet – a pigment seldom seen after the nineteenth century – further highlighted both the Lamb's and the Son's purity.

'Which reminds me, Daniel. Have you had a taste of our brothels yet?'

The Jesus in the middle represented the Father. He was dressed in a long robe coloured with the earthiest sepia, like an atavistic memory of a teacher of righteousness who had roamed the desert. Over his robe, He wore a cape, Roman in design but embroidered with Inca motifs. The cape was in purple of Cassius, a very costly and rare pigment. It was held together, on the chest, by a buckle, round and golden and portraying the sun as a child would draw it: a fat, circular, smiling face casting rays in spirals and arrows. Painted in the warmest of Indian yellows, it identified Inti, the Inca Sun-God, with the Father.

'Let me take you to one, Daniel. You'll fuck like no other place on earth.'

The Jesus on the left represented the Holy Ghost. He was dressed in a sleeveless immaculate length of cloth. A pointillistic application of blue and Naples yellow gave the cloth the rippling luminosity of an expanse of sun-blessed water. Thus, the Holy Ghost also personified Viracocha, the Inca Creator whose name signified 'foam of the sea'. The blue was the one Daniel had discovered in Pintoyaku: dreamy, yet robust, blending the Andean skies with the Andean stones. *Inca blue*, as he had decided to name it, resisting Fuego's suggestion of 'Brac's blue'.

'Every kink known to man, Daniel. Plus a few others.'

The Trinity wore velvet crowns in kermes scarlet with simple mountings painted in silver. The cherubs and saints which surrounded them on all sides had been underworked: a few impressionistic brush-strokes to convey adoration and skins the colour of amaranth to indicate that these were indigenous cherubs and South American saints.

'You switched off!'

'I'm working.'

'Well, you can stop. I want to talk.'

'About brothels?'

'About God and the Devil.'

The replicated face, except for the overall expression that might have been influenced by Melcher Perez Holguin, was Semitic. Straight, dark, lustrous hair. Assyrian-style beard. Hands, powerful harbours of sinewy arms, standing raised, dispensing both benediction and the assurance that they could ward off any assault, protect every soul. Nose that sniffed all the evils. Ears that heard each plea. Mouth smiling welcome to the Kingdom or God. Eyes cascading love.

Enlivened by their truth, Daniel put away his swab, jumped down from the platform, picked up his bottle of *aguardiente* and faced Fuego. 'All right.'

Fuego swung off the hammock, very fast for a man who had been drinking steadily. Daniel was reminded of a television sketch that had deferentially poked fun at the General. That his corpular dexterity was as much inherited from the puma as from the tin mines of his early youth; that muscles trained in evading live burials never got flabby.

'You are right, Daniel. I *am* propositioning you. I want to see what you look like naked.'

Daniel, momentarily taken aback, stared anxiously at Fuego. The uniform, rumpled, but a good fit. The animality. The full male eroticism. Though not sexual. Contentious – like a buck flaunting its horns. He smiled. 'Your mother or your sister, Oseas. I've never fancied men.'

Fuego whooped with delight. 'If I had a mother or a sister, *hombre*, I myself would open their legs for you. But my mother died giving birth to me. No sisters. I was the first.'

'I'm sorry. Stupid of me. I was trying to imitate you. I'm not good at being coarse.'

'Don't apologise. Mothers and sisters – they have *chicha*, too. And a nice fire like everybody else. Someone must drink them and keep that fire going. What about your mother and sister?'

'Leave them out of this!'

'Ah. An old sickness... Vomit it – much better.'

Daniel strode towards Fuego, determined to match bulk with bulk. 'Look, this is between you and me! Designs, you said...'

They stared at each other. Two ageing mastodons.

'Very well, Daniel. The crux... The reflection I see in you... It's my face. You are not the godly man you think you are. Time to test it.' Fuego clinked his bottle with Daniel's. 'Drunk yet?'

'On the way.'

Fuego grinned, then began pacing the room. 'You're looking for José Perera, I hear...'

'Yes.' Daniel froze, shocked by his impulsive answer. Then he felt relieved. He could dispense with subterfuge now. And recklessness felt good. No fear.

'Do you know who he is?'

'I know who he was.'

'Forget Perera.'

'Heinrich Kempin – call him by his real name.'

'What's in a name?'

'Honour...among other things. Joseph Perera was my father.' 'That I did not know.'

'Murderer taking the name of the hero he killed – nothing new...'

'Your father? *He* was the hero?'

Daniel raised his bottle to Fuego and drank.

Fuego paused by the work-bench. 'Come here. And your mother and sisters? Also Kempin's victims? Come, come.'

Daniel moved to the work-bench. 'Three sisters.'

'Let's arm-wrestle.'

'If I win – what would you do?'

'I'd hate it!'

Daniel smiled and walked away.

Fuego started pacing again. 'So you came to kill Kempin?'

'To find him. I don't know if I'll kill him.'

'You don't *know*? I would – a hundred times.'

Daniel drank again. 'He may have repented...'

'If he has – would you forgive him?'

'I might.'

'Because you're godly?'

'Penitence merits mercy. Mercy overrules justice.'

'Church shit!' Fuego guffawed. 'Why should he repent?'

Daniel leaned against the scaffold. 'Sinners do.'

'I never have.'

'That's why you are so tormented.'

'Am I?' Fuego, chuckling, shook his head in self-reproach. 'I sometimes dream I am a fawn.' He drank some more. 'Let me warn you. About Perera. A colossus. Controls... almost everything. Cocaine. Multinationals. Politicians. But that's only the tip. Underneath... he is a dung beetle. Recycling Hitler's droppings. And underneath that... a tape-worm. Fucks every shit-hole. Including Williston's people.'

'Come on...'

'But then... Who would fuck a fundamentalist except a fascist! Or vice versa.' He stopped by Daniel, placed a hand on his shoulder and chortled.

'Those campesinos in the necropolis – you know why they were massacred?'

Daniel, swaying as he supported Fuego's weight, shook his head.

'Two reasons. One: fascists don't want their subhumans chasing myths. Two: Manku Yupanqui smells of Jesus and the Second Coming. Anathema for fundamentalists, an Indio Jesus – particularly as they are the only ones who know how, when, where the Second Coming will be. I am drunk. Are you?'

Daniel took another drink. 'Yes.'

Fuego trundled back to the work-bench. 'How about the arm-wrestle?'

'Better not.' Daniel massaged his head. He relished his drunkenness. Fear – no longer prowling, fallen off somewhere. That was how he should be – always. 'I've located Kempin.'

Fuego picked up a jar of powdered pigment and inspected it like a short-sighted man. 'Jerry Rice did, you mean.'

'You know about Rice?'

Fuego put the jar back on the work-bench. 'So naive. Why do I bother with you?'

Daniel giggled. 'Reflection.'

Fuego faced him. 'You located him. What now? You know who Kempin's men are? The Bridegrooms…'

'I thought they were *your* assassins…'

'I seconded them.'

'So Kempin controls you, too?'

'No. I do – him. He can never… fuck me.' Fuego waved his bottle. 'Understand, Daniel. Absolute power. Without it… you might as well be powerless…'

Daniel pondered a moment, then grinned mischievously. 'How about me… propositioning you. *You* help *me* get Kempin.'

Fuego burst out laughing.

'Next time you visit his castle. Take me along.'

Fuego hooted. 'Original. I like it. Give me one good reason.'

Daniel, also laughing, tottered over to him. 'If I'm your what's-it – reflection… you're mine…'

'I'm Satan – remember?'

'An angel – before his fall… Let's pull him out of his… pit.'

'Why pit? Why not the lake of El Dorado?'

'Besides, Oseas –'

'You called me Oseas!'

'…Satan was a rebel.'

'Against God.'

'So – let him rebel against the new gods. Kempin... and the rest.'

Fuego took a long drink. 'Not bad, Daniel. Except... I am one of them... one of the gods.'

Daniel leaned over Fuego. 'You're no fascist... Racial, national supremacy... Elitist, superman drivel... You don't believe all that diarrhoea...'

'Survivor. Ruthless. Adaptable. I am. They come and go... I am... always around.'

'Pity.' Daniel drank the rest of his bottle. 'I'll get Kempin – somehow.' He tottered away and picked out a new bottle.

Fuego slumped against the work-bench and stared at him. 'Maybe I am wrong. Maybe you are genuine... and have the thirst of the Cross.'

Suddenly, Daniel felt drained. He flung himself on to the hammock. 'You can go now. You got what you came for. You know what I'll do.'

Fuego rubbed his face briskly to shake off his drunkenness. 'That's not what I came for.'

'What else? Oh, yes – loose ends.' Daniel began swinging on the hammock. 'Campbell. Yes. I was going to meet him.'

Fuego, barely listening, staggered to the window.

'I'll tell you why... So you know, even if I fail... that's not the end of it.'

Fuego stared at the group of Indians keeping vigil in the square. 'Is there something in the painting? About Manku Yupanqui?'

'An outfit called Yizkor. Hunts war criminals. Met them when they were compiling evidence – on the Holocaust in Yugoslavia. That's where I'm from... Born Jew, as you suspected. Christian now...'

Fuego lumbered to the monk's seat, flopped into it and riveted his eyes to the polyptych. 'I can't see it...'

'Anyway, we kept in touch...'

Fuego looked haunted. 'But I feel there is...'

'So when Campbell infiltrated Kempin's gang...'

Fuego, unable to sit still, lurched out of the monk's seat. 'I know about Campbell. Picked up the Controller. Naomi de Taranto. Greek Jewess.'

Daniel remembered her dulcet voice. 'I guessed you had.'

'Not through Campbell. He didn't break. But Kempin smelled him... stinks like a Jew, he kept saying. So we put him under surveillance. Caught him out – a letter drop. Swooped on her, after she bribed a guard from El Chulpa – for a message to Campbell about meeting you. We broke her. When she rang you – it was from prison.'

'You killed her, too?'

Fuego paused by the scaffold and took a closer look at the polyptych. 'She's dead – yes.'

'I wish I'd met her. Campbell, too.' Tears welled in Daniel's eyes. Not just because he was drunk. Outrage. He swung off the hammock. Not afraid. But regretful. And resigned. 'My turn?'

'You're important. Gringo. Restorer of our national treasure. But if you... persist with Kempin...'

Daniel stumbled over to Fuego. Feeling strong. 'I will. Wrote to Yizkor. Told them. And about the castle – nothing doing unless they send paratroopers. Told them, I'll go on my own... Find a way...'

'One step, Daniel...'

Daniel grabbed him by the sleeve. 'Come here... Come...' He pulled Fuego to the work-bench. He cleared some space, then placed his elbow on the work-top. 'Arm-wrestle. Come on!'

Fuego, grinning maliciously, discarded his jacket and took up position opposite him.

They locked hands. They strained. Muscles taut, arms shaking with the effort. Neither arm yielded. Their grimaces became grunts; their faces turned red; they dribbled saliva. The arms stayed locked, as if turned to stone.

Daniel grinned. 'Stalemate, I'd say.' And he let go.

They disengaged, breathing heavily.

Fuego raged. 'Why did you stop? You insult me. I could have won.'

'Or lost. Silly – either way... But I made my point.'

'You backed out!'

'I'm no weed. Wanted you to see that. There was violence in me. I can find it again. I'm the son of a *hero* ... I've touched courage...'

Fuego, livid, seized another bottle. 'I don't believe in heroes.'

Daniel leaned against the door. 'Want me to tell you?... My father?'

Fuego, clucking angrily, stopped by the vitrine and stared at the books.

'We – my mother, sisters and me – went into hiding. My father joined Tito's partisans. Became commander of a crack unit. Came this mission – an ammunition train. They would ambush it, carry all they could, blow up the rest. Listen to this. The station where they loaded the ammunition was also the station where Jews, Gypsies and such were sent to the coast. To be shipped to the island of Pag. To the labour camp there run by the Ustashi. Auschwitz was a treat that would come later. Now. One of those unimaginable coincidences. Of which there had been thousands during the war. My father set up the ambush somewhere south of the station. Whilst his family – us – caught in our hide-out, were to be transported north to Pag. Same day. Same station. As we waited, my mother watched the ammunition train. Across the tracks. Not heavily guarded. Get on that train, she said. Hide. After it leaves, when it gets dark, jump. Join your father. I didn't want to leave – you can imagine. But she made me. I had to fight. Be like my father. My duty as a man. All that… So I crawled under the Pag train. Ran to the other. Climbed. Hid under some tarpaulin. Eventually the train left. Now, the irony. I waited for nightfall. As we approached a tunnel, I jumped – the guards wouldn't be looking then. Before I could run, I heard the train derail – inside the tunnel. Then shooting. Then silence. Then whispers, heavy breathing, people scurrying. I was shocked. Rooted to the spot. Somebody grabbed me – a partisan. Dragged me. Yes – to my father. Imagine. Joseph Perera holding his petrified son. Crying with joy. And crying in despair – wife and daughters taken and nothing he could do. Anyway, he blew up the train and we left. No lorries or pack animals. Men carrying the ammunition on their backs. Me, too. Four days of night-walking ahead. We could have made it – any other time. But SS everywhere – Kempin and his men. Because of the Pag transports. They captured us. Took us to a forest. My father and his men grappled with the SS. To give me the chance to escape. I hid somewhere as Kempin executed them. After they left, I covered up the mass grave. I was five years old.' Daniel paused, and took a long drink.

Fuego, his back turned to Daniel, rasped. 'The betrayal! What about the betrayal?'

'Years passed. I never forgot Kempin. Became violent. Picked fights. Nearly killed a man. I went back to the monks who had saved me. Asked them to save me again. They brought me back to Jesus. Then got me a scholarship. I became a restorer. A good Christian. Then. In the sixties – after Eichmann – Yizkor found me. Told me: after the war, Kempin was recruited by US Army Counter-Intelligence. To spy on communist cells in Germany. Then went on to work for the CIA. Yizkor wanted to kill him. Asked me to help. Identify. I didn't turn up. Fear. Cowardice. Doing well, you see, a good life. I pretended I was ill. The agent went to the rendezvous. He was spotted. And killed. After that, Kempin disappeared.'

Fuego, Daniel noted, had moved to the sink and was washing his face.

Daniel raised his bottle for another drink, but it slid out of his hand and smashed on the floor. 'Now I have to atone. Prove… my father's courage… in me, too. Somewhere. Waiting to erupt.'

Fuego moved away from the sink, water trickling down his face.

Daniel, reduced to stupor, closed his eyes. Tears running down his cheeks, he sank to the floor.

Fuego came up to him and pulled him to his feet. 'Get up! Haven't finished with you!'

Daniel tumbled over Fuego. They fell in a heap. Fuego picked himself off the floor. Daniel, still weeping and using Fuego as support, also stood up.

Fuego held him straight. 'I have a confession, too.'

Daniel mumbled, a giggle escaping through his tears. 'Confess... Confess...'

'You think *you* know. What fear is. I know more. Because... I never ran away...'

Daniel, breathing heavily, put his hands on Fuego's shoulders. 'You're a good man, Oseas – deep down. We all are.'

Fuego disengaged himself in disgust. 'All my life! All my life! Afraid.'

'I understand...'

'A warning to you! Men who are afraid... are dangerous. Who can't run away – deadly.'

Daniel wiped his tears. 'I'm too drunk, Oseas...'

'Listen! All my life... And now... More afraid than ever...'

Daniel pulled himself away and tottered towards the scaffold. Towards the polyptych.

Fuego followed him. 'What of? In the past – I understand. Today? What can I fear? Who? Nothing. No one.'

Daniel slumped against the scaffold and let his eyes rest on the Trinity. 'God? His wrath?'

Fuego leaned against the wall, stretched out his arms as if he were crucified. His eyes burned.

Daniel watched him, mesmerised. Then he reminded himself that Lucifer meant Light-Bearer.

Fuego dropped his arms in disgust. 'No. I don't fear God. No more than... the curses of those... I killed.'

Daniel wondered whether God stood exposed and in danger. 'Curses strike dead.'

Fuego rushed over to him, murderous. 'What does that mean? Something deep? Shit talk! Feel something!'

Daniel outshouted him. 'Near the knuckle, eh?'

'Words! Counterfeit! You're a fake! I know a fake – always! *You* know – nothing! Nothing!'

Daniel pushed past him and picked another bottle. He sniggered and taunted. 'Afraid of God! – you are!'

'God does not exist!'

'Afraid because you crucify Him. Every day. Every day. Instead of accepting His grace.'

'What is grace?'

'The absence of fear.'

Fuego stared at him at length, then shook his head. 'Sounds good. But still shit!'

Daniel felt invincible. That was it. Grace – the absence of fear. 'No. Not this time. God does exist. He's even here in this room, judging you.'

Fuego cast a fearful look at the polyptych, then scrambled to the corner of the atelier. He squatted by the wall, looking very much like an Indian withdrawing from the world. He drank at length.

Daniel ranged his eyes over the Trinity, relishing his triumph. And, as if in celebration, suddenly desperately hungry for Beatriz.

'Shall I prove – God does not exist?'

Daniel shut his eyes. 'Go away, Oseas. Go away.'

'Here I am. The Devil. You – in the wilderness. I'm tempting you. Be honoured. Makes you like Jesus.'

Daniel kept his eyes shut.

'Shall I prove it? Make you fitter to survive. Not a false promise. Not the Kingdom to come. True salvation!'

Daniel growled and moved across to Fuego. He stood above him, holding his bottle like a club. He tried not to slur. 'This is why you came! To destroy my faith!'

Fuego appeared to be on fire. 'Yes.'

'How does my faith threaten you?'

'Used to be... my faith. Also. Then I saw. What it was. Blindness. Blindfold.'

Daniel ran the bottle carefully over Fuego's face. 'I struggled hard for my faith... I'd kill you before I lost it!'

Suddenly, Fuego seemed sober. 'Then you prove to me there is God!'

'I don't have to. Open your eyes...'

'No. No. None of that every moment God creates something from nothing nonsense. Real proof. The One who loves. Turns the other cheek. Heals. Comforts. Saves...' He pointed at the polyptych. 'Him! The One who is Three! Who takes our sins on His shoulders! Prove Him to me!'

Daniel retreated to the monk's seat. He fixed his eyes once again on the Trinity. But this time, he could not see them. This time all he could see was darkness.

Fuego bounded over. 'Better still, *hermano*! We make a bet! See who wins!'

Daniel waved a limp hand to banish him.

With a yelp, Fuego staggered to the door. 'Now, I am going!'

Daniel started retching. And as he heaved, he nodded. A man could train for martyrdom until he was fit for it.

20

What can be done with only anger in the eyebrows, with only fists, poetry, birds, reason, pain?

COME AND SEE GOD ON STRIKE!
MINERS AND REVOLUTIONARIES HAVE UNITED! GIVE US A SONG!

Two telegrams. The first from Fuego to Daniel; the other from Gaspar Huaman to Beatriz. And here they were in Monte Rico.

They should not have come.

Daniel put a poncho over his thick sweater and sat on the bed, opposite the window. He rubbed his hands until they were warm, then slid one under the covers and placed it on Beatriz's rump. She purred in her sleep and parted her legs.

They should not have come.

He gazed out of the window. Light was breaking – a dull, grey sheen refracting through the heavy sleet. There was the hint of the thaw Rice had said had been forecast. It had been one of the severest winters on the Altiplano. And the last week – coldest in decades – had almost scuttled the miners' strike.

He could see, as the day was being born, the perfect triangle of the solitary mountain, Monte Rico – 'Rich Mountain' – reverting from an aesthetic silhouette to megalithic density, rising some 1,500 metres, from the edge of the city named after it.

The city, over 4,000 metres above sea level, was the highest and most inclement in the world; it had come into existence to exploit the mountain's minerals, confident that the deposits would last an eternity.

Old myths about the mountain, counterpointed by the romances of the early Spanish miners, depicted it, by virtue of the vast quantities of silver it had yielded, as a benevolent *apu*. Modern traditions, recriminating over the precious white veins that had been bled dry, contemptuous of the tin and copper that had remained, and mourning the generations who had perished trying to extract such inferior lodes, indicted the same *apu* for having whored with the white man. But, since the reawakening of the Manku Yupanqui legend, some of the locals had designated it as the sacred mountain which had safeguarded the sun's missing ray.

Tiny movements caught Daniel's eye. *Guiñeros*, the independent miners, crawling on the slopes. They were the old men – or rather men in their thirties who looked ancient – who had been miners until silicosis had made them unemployable. In lieu of redundancy pay or sickness benefit, they were allowed to mine the rock-face on the condition that they shared their scant extracts with the Company. Lacking any equipment, they mined with hammer and chisel, cutting holes on the icy ridges just wide enough to accommodate their prone bodies. So meagre were their earnings that the strikers had voted unanimously to exempt them from any form of industrial action.

The throbbing in his head accelerated; his breathing became sluggish. He was finding it difficult to acclimatise.

He unscrewed the Thermos flask for some of the *mate de coca* the hotel receptionist had prescribed for altitude sickness. Williston had mentioned people who had died of soroche. He sipped the coca-leaf tea. It was good medicine.

They should not have come here.

He gazed at the mouldering half of the town – the people's half. Desolate; dwellings collecting shadow and filthy, alley by alley, like gradations on a map.

The miners' district, a maze of tin and mud shacks humping each other on the skirts of the mountain, lay at the very edge of this wasteland. It stood silent – an occult emptiness. No night shift returning; no morning shift setting out. No Moral Crusade missionaries casting nets for souls. Not even street vendors hoping for some business from the sprinkling of labour officials, teachers and university students who had come from various parts of the country in solidarity and were billeted with the miners. What money strikers and supporters had available had run out. Smug anecdotes in the town's colonial district, in the historic streets and majestic churches, in the baroque offices and mansions, told of miners and supporters now sleeping ten together simply to keep warm.

If that was the case, how were Gaspar Huaman and his men faring, camped out as they were in the frozen wastes beyond? Crudely written leaflets proclaimed that Huaman now had a sizeable force, and that the revolution had started. The sizeable force, according to Fuego, was some ninety men.

Except for some foreign correspondents, no one treated Huaman's revolution seriously. For Monte Rico swarmed with Sinchis; in addition, the previous day, a plane-load of Bridegrooms, commanded by Colonel Angelito, had arrived as reinforcements. Fuego, Daniel surmised, had secured his price from Vargas.

Daniel could only assume that Huaman, having run out of patience, had come to seize his place in history, to enact his grand gesture with the few bullets he had scraped together.

Would he ever attain Huaman's quixotic courage?

He had had word from Yizkor. They would have to reorganise; it would take some time; they would contact him when ready. Daniel had wondered whether they ever would; the death of two of their number may have proved too high a price; and Kempin was already an old man, time was not on their side. So he was on his own; and he had decided: if he found a way to get to Kempin, he would confront him. Whether he would engender the will to perform his own grand gesture, he could not say. More and more, life with Beatriz was nurturing the idea of a future.

They should not have come here.

Beatriz murmured dreamily. 'Come inside me.'

'Sleep.'

'I am. But it will be nicer with you inside me.'

He caressed her buttocks.

He so admired her. She had not wanted to come. She had protested that suffering was infectious – a plague she could fight only if it were quarantined.

She had composed a song, as Huaman had requested. She would have preferred to launch it, as an act of solidarity, on radio and television. Instead, she had decided to hand it personally to the miners. She had witnessed the suffering – as if it were her vocation – by attending every strike meeting. She had not been permitted to venture out into the wilderness. But her song, elevated to an anthem by the miners, had reached Huaman. For some nights now, it had soughed over from the glacial plains, in the defiant baritone of the guerrilleros.

Initially, Daniel had thought she had forced herself to come to show him that she could follow him wherever he chose to go. She had not asked why he had responded to Fuego's summons.

He had soon realised that she had come to support him. She had sensed that he himself had not known why he had responded to Fuego's telegram, that his compulsion had borne terror, that he had had need of strength, an aide, an example. What might she say if he told her about Fuego's bet?

The fact was Beatriz was brave. Born brave. She did not have to make herself brave.

'Daniel…' She rolled over to lie on her back. She opened her eyes and threw off the covers.

His eyes imbibed her naked body. 'Cover yourself. It's very cold.'

She spread out her legs. 'Switch on the heater.'

'There's no electricity. And no central heating. The strike.'

'There is you.'

He bent down and rubbed his face on her pubic hair. Fibrous, but fine-spun and soft.

She tried to push his head away. 'No. I am not fresh.'

He resisted her.

She tried to wriggle away. 'Daniel… Please… I need to wash…'

He pinned her down. 'I'll wash you as I drink you.'

She surrendered to pleasure. Raced on.

Her stomach contracted. She ran her hands over her breasts. Her voice stretched in a shrill cry. Beads of sweat collected in her navel. She began to moan.

He held on to her, his tongue deep inside her, his mouth fully enclosing her.

She sang her orgasm. A glorious aubade in the primmest hotel in the staid colonial district.

He lay his head on her vagina, listened to her body ebbing, drew a line with his finger over the beads of sweat on her breasts. 'A new man – who would have thought it…'

She stared at him, suddenly tense. 'What?'

'*The* New Man – I should say.'

'You bastard!'

He looked at her, confused.

She twisted round and buried her head in the pillow.

Perturbed, he sat next to her. 'What's the matter?'

She pushed him away and jumped out of bed. 'I'm getting dressed.'

'Beatriz – what is this?'

Sorting out her clothes, she hissed at him. 'If you're going to throw my past in my face… I won't stand for it! You are not a new man – but *the* man – the, the. Not a fling. Not a change of pillow. *The* man. You've nothing to be jealous of!'

'I wasn't being jealous!'

'You are a jealous man. You have been from the beginning.'

'Not this time. I was...' He looked away in embarrassment. 'I got carried away. Suddenly I saw what I could be... A new man... A second Adam... And you... the goddess who could transform me...'

She stared at him in amazement. 'You felt that... sucking me?'

Gently, he pulled her to him. 'What's strange about that? Who else?' He laid her down on the bed and kissed her vagina. 'Where else except in there – where I am reborn?'

She clutched at his hair, wanting to believe him. 'Do you mean it – really mean it?'

He nuzzled between her breasts. 'With all my heart.'

'Then listen... Maybe not just you... Maybe also another New Man...' She pressed his head hard against her. 'I am... I don't know whether it will please you... My period – I am overdue... So... Maybe...'

'You can't be... What about the pill?'

'I threw it away.'

He stared at her – pleased and troubled.

An explosion shook the room.

Beatriz began to shake and pant like a wounded animal. Daniel rushed to the window, feeling disembodied.

A column of smoke swirled in the miners' district. Tongues of flames rode the wind. Men, women and children stampeded about. Soldiers deployed, inexorably, like the tide moving in.

Beatriz managed to whisper. 'Is it – Gaspar?'

He faced her, quavering. 'The miners...'

She stuffed her hands in her mouth, bit her fingers fiercely. Tears ran out of her tightly shut eyes; her breasts lurched aimlessly.

He staggered to the door.

She screamed, eyes still shut. 'What will you do?'

His voice, as he ran out, was another scream. 'I don't know!'

She keened, still biting her fingers. Then she began to beat her head into the pillow.

The bomb's target had been the union house, where strikers and their supporters had met for the past week to decide strategy.

Panic had been brief. An old miner had had the wisdom to set off the pit-disaster alarm. The shrill braying had activated the community's reflexes. They had swiftly organised to meet the emergency.

The women had rushed to the union house – some, to brave the blazing rubble for whatever could be salvaged; others, to put out the fire before it engulfed their homes.

The children had been delegated to hustle the dazed supporters to the safety of the mountain ridges.

And the men, seizing whatever was at hand – hammers, chisels, knives, clubs, stones and the odd stick of dynamite – had assembled in the small square to make a stand.

The community faced two forces.

The first, the full complement of Sinchis, under Fuego's command, had already been in place. They had taken up positions around the miners' district in the early days of the strike and had moved to tighten the ring within minutes of the explosion.

The second, the Bridegrooms of Death, were in the process of deploying. They had been quartered at the airport, close to their Hercules transporter, expecting a sortie into the wilderness against Gaspar Huaman. They had arrived swiftly and had piled out of their armoured cars like bees swarming.

They formed the spearhead and advanced through the ring of Sinchis, leaving wakes in the thick slush. Sparkling in the stillborn morning, they could have been mistaken for celebrants in a sombre rite. Occasionally, they fired warning shots fractionally above the miners' heads. Angelito rumbled warnings through a loud-hailer.

Fuego watched the proceedings from a jeep blocking the road to the colonial district. Dr Williston and Jerry Rice were with him, picked off the street for their safety. Williston, clothed like a polar explorer, was nervously fiddling with a tape-recorder. Rice, still soggy from the previous day's booze, shivered in his anorak.

The bombing of the union house was a subversive act; it had been perpetrated by communists bent on destroying democracy; the miners should help expose these terrorists; failure to do so would indicate complicity and only serve to absolve the security forces from any action they might have to take – so Angelito had launched his tirade. The miners, accusing the Sinchis of planting the bomb, jeered and heckled.

Williston spoke his version into the tape-recorder. Here was the perfect example of how communism reduced ordinary God-fearing men and women into Satan's legionaries. Henceforth, the priority for Moral Crusade was to wipe out all political dogma. Immerse the people in the Good Book, for it contains *all* the truths.

Rice managed a hungover shout. 'Why the Bridegrooms? Everything was peaceful until now.'

Fuego was watching some other reporters being bundled into jeeps.

'Huaman's men have infiltrated the miners. There could be more bombings.'

'Why should they bomb the union house? They're not *against* the miners.'

'Fanatics, Mr Rice. They would use any means to create chaos.'

The strikers had formed a dour human laager, several men thick. The women, abandoning their efforts at the union house, were running to join them. The jeering continued, now punctuated by declamations urging courage and resolve.

The Bridegrooms were beginning to aim their guns directly at the human wall. Angelito had disposed of his loud-hailer and drawn his pistol. The miners and the Bridegrooms were drenched and mud-spattered. He looked immaculate in his uniform and appeared to be skimming above the quagmire with his shiny boots.

The pit-disaster alarm was still braying.

Fuego tried to shut his ears to it. It hurled him back to his days in the bowels of this very mountain and triggered rustily an old reflex which urged him to lend a hand, to return to the fold, to stand, like those fools, on the wrong side of power.

Lost souls! Deformed by silicosis, cursing the yesterdays that had cruelly prolonged their lives, eager to forfeit the tomorrows. His own father had been one of them.

The hated father; flagbearer, until his death as a *guiñero*, of powerlessness; stoic slave of meekness, submission, impotence. Why had he not run, sought power – or risen in anger, revolted like these poor bastards and demanded, at the very least, a speedy dispatch?

Look at me, Papacito, I am no longer weak. I no longer watch helplessly as my family dies, as my friends and their families die.

Still the pit-disaster alarm brayed.

Miners are like looters of ancient tombs. Like that distant cousin of yours, Papacito, who used to rob the Moche pyramids.

Grave-robbers, Papacito, shackled to a world of death by the *misti* who is himself dead to his very bones which is why he needs gold to stand up.

What would they know of life, Papacito, these inhabitants of a dark realm forbidden even to bats? Eating the rock which eats them back. Eyes hidden in coca leaves. Ears muffled by the rattle of the drills. Muscles melted down by dehydration and heat exhaustion. Feet so bloated they look as if they're walking on water. Hands imprinted with the wagons that carried away their souls.

Born to see meaning only in death, how could they ever choose life? But I did. Milk of defiance, Papacito – some men's spunk have that. Yes, that woman, Jacinta, too.

That time of the rock-fall. Esteban, my yoke-fellow, crushed to death. And I, half buried. Suddenly there she was, like an apparition, Jacinta, Esteban's wife. Inconceivable because women are barred from the mines. They represent life so they are considered unlucky for the death-seekers. She had sneaked in to save her man, reached us ahead of the rescue teams. One disconsolate look at the pile that had buried Esteban; and a wail that had the weight of a lifetime's mourning. Then she came to my side. *How bad are you, Oseas?* I, spitting blood, passing out. *Hold on, Oseas.* Gathering her skirts, squatting over my face as if to piss or to give birth. *Hold on, Oseas.* Carefully placing her cunt over my lips. Musky cunt. The one thing, she believed, a man needed to cling to life. Primeval magic. *Hold on, Oseas.* Dewy cunt – not with her juices but with the condensation of my faltering breath. Giving me the kiss of life. *Hold on, Oseas.* I held on.

And the next day, exodus. Slipping out of the infirmary, dragging broken limbs. Living in the valley, by the river. Eating wild fruit and fish until healed.

Then La Merced. Into the Army. Gaining selection for officers' course. War Academy. Training fanatically. Consuming manuals and books. Licking arses and climbing. Climbing and licking more arses. Until today's power.

Dead now, Jacinta. Banished for desecrating the mine. Her life-giving cunt dried up for lack of food or man.

Does that give the lie to my claim, Papacito – that I never run away? Was that running away?

Deafening silence, like a dream dying. A Sinchi had switched off the pit-disaster alarm.

Fuego realised he had been watching the miners' women. Having joined their men, they were now trying to move to the front. Some were even arming themselves with stones.

Their behaviour solved the riddle that had been nagging him: how the miners had found the will to go on strike; to envisage and want – tomorrows.

Women. Always the first to grab the branch that might break a fall; to seize the idea that offered a future; to be politicised in the heart long before the mind reasoned. Women – carriers of that plague, hope.

The miners' quarters lay on a shelf carved out of the side of the mountain to accommodate heavy-duty vehicles.

Daniel slowed down, barely out of breath, despite the altitude, despite running uphill all the way from the hotel.

He weaved his way through the giant trucks. The Sinchis were just ahead, a tight, grey, coiled mass of Wehrmacht clones. Through chinks in that ring, he could glimpse the miners' bright garments. Defying the cold and the guns with colour.

It was physical pain that was always at the roots of fear; pain which induced loss of face and humiliation. Yet, that had not always been true. He could vouchsafe, with the memory of his violent years, that pain could be borne as if it were a passing sickness.

So, now, if he could just slip past the Sinchis, join the miners, face the guns with them – as his father had faced Kempin. There would be so much to gain. True courage first and foremost. And expiation, equal first. And not least, a shared martyrdom.

He realised he had stopped advancing. Nor could he turn back as logic nagged him to do.

He was not in danger. Fuego was after his faith, not his life. All he risked was a stray bullet. All he was doing was playing vicariously at sainthood; a furtive look from his ivory tower at real life – the one where people suffered, were debased, torn, killed arbitrarily. Had he grown at all from that child who had watched his father's execution, who had burrowed into the snow, not uttering a sound?

And yet... He had run here instinctively. Wanting to help the miners. There had been no ulterior motive, no deliberation. Surely that was not fake!

Move then! Do you think you can be a hero without flexing a muscle? Forward!

He could not.

Suddenly he was running, his feet barely touching the ground, his arms dangling, and iron wedges at his shoulder-pits.

He stared left and right. Two Sinchis, one at each side, were running by his side. He realised they were carrying him. Terror bit into his genitals. 'Let go of me!'

They paid no attention to him. He could not struggle. His muscles had atrophied.

They dumped him on a seat. He looked up, still astigmatic with fear. There was Jerry Rice, coughing. Dr Williston, rubbing gloved hands together to keep warm.

'Daniel...' Fuego's voice, mocking. 'I did not expect you.'

They were in a jeep. Relief.

'Dr Williston and Mr Rice – yes. But not you.'

Safe as safe could be. You can say anything. 'You invited me...'

'I invited God, too.' Fuego pointed at the strikers. 'Is He out there? Did He come with you?'

The miners and their women, arms linked, were swaying, trying to steady each other, seeking better footholds in the slush. Facing them were the Bridegrooms. Submachine-guns at point blank range. And that corn-gold statue, Angelito, standing sideways, arm stretched with a pistol, like a competitor in a small-bore tournament.

Daniel shouted at Fuego. 'What are you going to do? Shoot them all? In cold blood?'

Fuego smiled savagely.

The miners were rasping orders, encouragements, valedictions.

'Can you hear them, Daniel? They are saying God is on their side. So I am waiting to see what He will do!'

Rice staggered out of his seat, as if leaving a bar-stool. 'Like in a western, General – right? You're waiting for them to draw first.' He shuffled to get out of the jeep. 'I'm going to fucking well warn them.'

'Sit down, Mr Rice. They won't listen to reason! They want blood! A ritual cleansing. God is on...'

An explosion in the distance drowned the rest of Fuego's words.

The Hercules burned. Charred frame buckling, blades corkscrewing, windows melting the way eyes melt – a barbarian at the stake. The people's Inquisitor had arrived. Imbued with political, historical and philosophical determinism.

Cursing the cold, Gaspar Huaman looked at his watch. Four minutes since they had blasted the plane. The Bridegrooms should be on their way.

Chauca's platoon had piled up the corpses in the centre of the airfield and was booby-trapping them.

Huaman stared at the dead: six Bridegrooms and the plane's crew. He had crossed the Rubicon – with ease. There would be many more dead, and some whom he would slay personally.

He had feared that each killing would erode his spirit, leave him, eventually, soulless, no less a victim than those he had vanquished. What a misconception. When God was proved absent, man, fatherless, but still a child, turned to the prodigal brother: Cain. Cain, who had indicted God with injustice, who had perceived that only a violent struggle would rescue the Persecuted soul. Cain, the righteous, the New Man.

The guerrilleros were scrambling to positions around the perimeter. Not with the urgency he would have wanted. But he resisted taking them to task. They were still raw. They would soon learn that in a revolutionary struggle, speed was of the essence.

He listened to their whooping. They had acquired new arms – assault rifles and grenades from the Hercules – and were like ploughmen who had been given tractors. Which was another reason not to harry them. They had only had theoretical instruction on the use of such sophisticated weapons. If he rattled them now, all that he had taught them might evaporate from their minds.

He turned towards the Nissen hut that served as the terminal building. No one there. He could see the last of the staff towards the plains. He had let them go, despite Chauca's fears they might divert to the town and alert the Bridegrooms that an ambush awaited them. He knew his petty bourgeoisie: they always ran in the opposite direction from trouble.

He checked his watch again. Time to take up his command post. He signalled Chauca to take cover.

He walked away – slowly. Wanting to linger by the blazing Hercules. His very first blow. Inspired planning – simple like all good plans. A time-bomb, planted by one of his men, in the union house. Unbeknown to the miners so that they would blame Fuego and rise up against him. It had put the miners at risk, but they would be the first to admit it had provided the perfect diversion. The Bridegrooms had rushed to assist the Sinchis, leaving their base and plane vulnerable. And he had moved in with his guerrilleros, silently, on the wings of the driven sleet. Then, the engagement: brief as a spring day in winter. His vanguard, deadly accurate with slings, accounting for the Bridegrooms guarding the Hercules; Chauca's platoon garrotting the crew as they dozed; the rest of the men herding off the airport staff. Finally, the first, the sublime sweet first taste of triumph.

But he must not get complacent. The day had yet to be won. There was still the ambush to come. It would not be easy. He was pitching an inexperienced group of men against seasoned fighters. He, himself, who had learned his strategy by devouring everything written from Clausewitz to Debray, the most inexperienced of all.

They had to win. They had nowhere to retreat. Not the plains: they would be stranded and defenceless there. Nor, as Chauca had suggested, the mountain's countless *guiñero* tunnels. They would be hunted like foxes. Or die of exposure.

They would win. Precisely because they were desperate. Desperation had been a key factor in his planning. That was why he had decided to start his campaign here, on a field of battle, instead of a traditional guerrilla terrain like the jungle. To show his men that they could triumph anywhere. To score a victory that would overawe the people, goad them into support.

Chauca whistled sharply, pointing at an armoured car clearing the bend round the mountain.

Huaman ran to the eastern perimeter. At a stretch where the airfield met the mountain, he took up his position. He flattened himself on the freezing ground and lined up his grenades and spare ammunition. He straightened his M-16, checked the magazine, then looked through the sights. He kept his finger off the trigger. His hand was shaking too much.

Another first: holding a gun in the firing position. It felt good. As if he had been destined for it. It mitigated the abominable cold. Would it mitigate the fear of death also?

Unexpectedly, the attack on the airfield had disrupted the miners' cohesion. Instead of launching them into battle, it had diffused the edge of their anger. Neglecting their tight formation, they had settled to relish, with a growing sense of the miraculous, the confusion that had struck Fuego and his troops.

And abandoning themselves to hosannas, they had burst into song – Beatriz's anthem.

This is where we start
at the bottom of the abyss

we will journey
alone
until
you and they
join us

we will climb
the fires of the sky
we will scale
the darkness of the underworld

we shall not possess
earth to sit on
sea to wade in
there will be
only
the agony of kissing tears
the burnt boats
the beds of stone where we cannot love languidly

we will not stop
until
words can be spoken again
songs find the faith to be born
freedom is raised from its pit of cadavers

we will not stop
until
we reach
the rainbowland we promised our children

And they had indulged in mockery. When Fuego had catapulted out of his jeep, barking orders, they had jeered at him: a worm searching for its testicles. When the Bridegrooms had driven off with Angelito performing macabre mimes, they had taunted them: motherless men, born out of arseholes.

Thus, when the Sinchis had redeployed, they had been caught in disarray. Though they had swiftly regained their defiance, they had been unable to close ranks. And the Sinchis had attacked, bayonets drawn.

Now, the Sinchis were running amok: trampling on the wounded men and women; closing in on those desperately seeking to form a line.

'Where is God now, eh? Where *is* He! Where?'

Fuego had returned to the jeep and had been haranguing incessantly. He smelled evil.

Williston had rushed back to his hotel to find solace in the Good Book.

Rice appeared to have broken down. He had slunk away from the mayhem and was crying.

'Why isn't your God saving them, Daniel, eh?'

Rice's shaking shoulders, more than Fuego's frenzy, unleashed Daniel's rage. 'Shut up!' He wanted to run back – back to Beatriz, deep into her flesh – but he could not summon the courage. The Sinchis might mistake him for a miner.

'My God! It's Beatriz! Daniel!'

He spun round. Rice, a moment ago cataleptic, was heaving himself out of the jeep. Fuego was spitting angrily.

Staring dumbly at Rice's run, Daniel saw her.

Standing rigid. Where the first shacks met the road from the town. Petrified. Daniel bellowed. 'Beatriz! Over here! Over here!'

Then he saw the danger. A miner and his woman, chased by some Sinchis, were running towards Beatriz. The miner had a stick of dynamite.

Daniel propelled himself forward. His legs, quite hollow, buckled under him. He fell out of the jeep. 'Beatriz'.

As he pulled himself up, pasting himself against the vehicle, he saw Fuego aiming a pistol. 'Oseas! No! Not Beatriz!'

Fuego fired. Then he was out of the jeep and running.

Daniel twisted round, dry throat smothering his soul. The miner with the dynamite, shot dead, lay sprawled on the ice. His woman had thrown herself on him. The Sinchis were about to reach them.

The dynamite detonated.

Smoke and blood and pieces of flesh where the miner and his woman had been. And those Sinchis in pursuit – prostrate; one or two writhing. 'Be... aaaa... triz...!'

He saw her through his tears. Still standing. Rice was almost by her side. Fuego not far behind.

Daniel shot forward. Legs, miraculously no longer amputated. Running like a hero because he was safe.

Angelito scanned the airport perimeter with his binoculars. The sleet, the pewter earth, the ashen light severely limited visibility.

Most of the guerrilleros had dug in. But he had spotted a few who had yet to learn – and now would never learn – the skills of the chameleon. Their position had revealed all he needed to know.

Huaman had cast a ring around the airfield. It was an ambush according to the book; but the book probably dated from an era when infantry had faced cavalry and had striven for victory by killing or unsettling the horses with sustained salvos. Doomed strategy unless Huaman and his rabble possessed the magic that would make armoured vehicles buck, rear and run wild.

Angelito planned his attack. He had six armoured personnel carriers: three mounted with mortars; the others with machine-guns. Excluding the mortar and gun crews, there were ten men in each vehicle, manning the lateral firing ports.

He would start by pounding with the mortars to scatter the guerrilleros. Then he would blitz in, all guns firing; one column circling the perimeter clockwise, from inside the guerrillero ring; the other anticlockwise, from the outside. The manoeuvre to be repeated until all the scum were killed.

The deafening noise – that had been the worst. Threatening to go on for ever. The shells pulverising the earth, pulverising reason. Bludgeoning him to run away. An inner voice shouting, shoot back, he answering, shoot at what, where, they are beyond range. Another voice bitterly weeping, it's unfair, they should not have mortars; they should walk into the ambush. Other voices, cursing him, lamenting the humiliation, demanding that he atone for his stupidity by dying.

Then the loudest voice of all, howling, because he was hit, protesting not so much at the pain, but at the certainty that this first battle was also his last. So much for his chosenness.

Now, silence – or just the rumble of the armoured cars, the screams of his wounded men, of those dying, of those already dead.

Gaspar Huaman raised his head from the ground, his shattered arm dangling. Could he fire his gun one-armed?

He scanned the airfield. Smoke copulated with sleet. But nothing could obliterate the armoured columns.

The guerrilleros were doing better than he, redeploying, forming another circle to compensate for the dead. How many dead! How many wounded?

He saw Chauca, scurrying, directing the men to new positions, bolstering their resolve. Exemplary lieutenant.

He yelled as loud as he could. 'Chauca!'

Chauca ran to his side. 'Your arm, *Comandante*!'

'Never mind. The men...'

'Will fight on.'

'It is hopeless. I failed.'

'We will do better next time.'

'There won't be a next time. We can't pull out!'

'Some of us will.'

Huaman felt like crying. He took another look at the armoured cars. Any moment now, they would flank the men and start firing.

'Chauca – finish me off. Tell the men I died fighting. It might inspire them – knowing I held my ground.'

'You will live. I will see to that.'

'With my men, Chauca. That is how I want to die.'

'The men want you to live. To continue.'

'I failed them – don't you understand?'

'They do not think so. They think it would be failure if you die. Because then this revolution will be without a head. They will fight for us to escape.'

'Escape? Where?'

'Anywhere – is good.'

The Bridegrooms opened fire. The guerrilleros responded. Huaman watched with tears in his eyes. They had no chance. A few, trying to throw grenades, were instantly mowed down and then disintegrated from the blast of their grenades. Those firing from cover positions more often than not struck armour.

'We go now, *Comandante*! *Venceremos*!'

Huaman tried to grab his rifle. 'No!'

Chauca punched him, knocking him unconscious. Then he began to drag him away, towards the mountain, seeking the smoke, the thick mud, any boulder, any shell crater, any blind spot.

PART FOUR

21

What does man need? Bread or the mysterious victory?

The day after the day of death, the sun chased away the clouds and shone – much too furiously, the mourners observed; reflecting off the ice, it would dazzle its own eyes, eclipse the sight of its Children crying yet again.

Monte Rico rose quietly and tiptoed into purgatorial silence. Apathy, hope, despair and defiance disputed with each other in whispers. Rivers of mud, disgorged by the thaw, daubed one and all as if they were a new batch of sheep destined for the slaughterhouse.

Daniel, Beatriz and Jerry Rice stayed on.

They had not seen Fuego after the killings; he had been too busy dry-cleaning the blood-soaked day.

Rice had obtained the facts and the figures.

Of the strikers, their families and their supporters, 83 had been killed and 216 wounded, most of them seriously.

Of the Sinchis, three fatalities and two injured – all five, victims of that one detonation which could have killed Beatriz.

Gaspar Huaman's band had been totally wiped out. Their number, Angelito had reported, was approximately 92; it had been impossible to conduct a full body count: little trace had remained of those who had been directly hit by mortars or who had been blown to pieces by their own grenades. Gaspar Huaman's corpse itself had been unidentifiable.

The guerrilleros had been buried in a communal grave outside the city limits.

The Bridegrooms of Death had suffered five more casualties in addition to the crew and guards of the Hercules. All five had been victims of the booby-trapped corpses of their comrades.

The fallen Bridegrooms and Sinchis, flown to the capital in flag-draped coffins, would be buried with full military honours.

Of the surviving strikers, 164 – including some severely injured, and some women and children – had been arrested.

These prisoners had been herded into two Hercules transporters, summoned to evacuate the troops, and taken to the capital for interrogation. Thereafter, they would be dispatched to various detention camps. Rumours that some of them had been thrown off the planes in mid-air were rife.

The end of the day of death had seen the arrival of Don Xavier Vargas, bearing a cornucopia of philanthropy.

First and foremost, he had forgiven the strikers. They had not known what they were doing.

Then, as further proof of his goodwill, he had announced that all mining personnel, irrespective of seniority or grade, would receive a wage increase of 250 *reales* per month – about 45 US cents. This unilateral gesture would stretch his resources to the limit, but, hopefully, it would remind his employees that in him they had a caring patriarch.

Finally, to emphasise his compassion, he had taken charge of the funeral arrangements of the 83 killed. This, despite the fact that some of them had been outsiders – labour officials, students, teachers – and, no doubt, communist agitators.

For the interments, he had purchased a plot of land adjacent to the miners' modest cemetery. Eighty-three emergency graves, he had claimed, would encroach on the resting places allocated to those still alive.

But the people had not been fooled. They had understood that Don Xavier wished to execrate the dead strikers even in the afterlife by excommunicating them from the bones of their ancestors. So, they had sworn that over the years, they would elevate the segregated burial ground into a shrine.

A monumental shrine. Each grave would have set on it a miniature mansion of good stone; adorned with a cross, it would stand as a house of God; painted in benevolent blue, it would depict the dwelling the martyr had merited in life. A shrine that would haunt Don Xavier and his children after him and their children after them. A shrine where every burnt offering would inspire future generations to new strikes, new rebellions until they secured their birthright: freedom from tyranny and hunger.

And perhaps, one day, this shrine would inspire the country to erect a national martyrion over that pit in the wilderness where the guerrilleros lay buried.

Much of the new day had been devoted to the funerals.

Initially, the mourners had comprised relatives and friends. The people, fearing they might provoke another massacre, had kept away. But when reassured that the soldiers had left, they had come in multitudes, from the city and the countryside. Artisans and labourers, farmhands and herdsmen, miners and *guiñeros*, street vendors, stall holders and the unemployed, students and teachers, office workers and factotums, clerics and nuns, beggars, children and the aged, even anchorites and shamans.

The Establishment had made no appearance. No Don Xavier – funerals, he had proclaimed, devastated him. No landowner or businessman. No civil servant or professional. No one of Spanish descent. And not a single missionary from Moral Crusade.

Daniel and Rice had attended from the beginning. At each burial they had paid their respects twice: once for the dead, and once more for Huaman's guerrilleros.

Beatriz had not come. She could see no honour in an act which surrendered noble men, ceremoniously, to worms and maggots. She would lament in her own way.

They were conducting the last funeral.

As they began to lower the coffin, an Indian brushed past Daniel, stopped and faced him.

Daniel stared, incredulous. 'Chauca…'

Chauca nodded, studying Rice.

Daniel registered Chauca's condition: ashen face, eyes fading, forehead and cheeks spattered with mud, arms and hands hidden beneath his poncho, more mud on the breeches, calves, feet and sandals. 'My God, Chauca… Weren't you with Huaman?'

Chauca swayed, but continued gazing at them.

'You're on your last legs, *compañero*. Have some of this.' Rice had edged closer and was offering his hip-flask.

Daniel tried to dispel Chauca's suspicion. 'It's all right. He's a friend.'

Chauca took the hip-flask and drank deeply.

'I think your friend is wounded, Dan.' Rice was pointing at Chauca's leg where lines of crimson had scored the caked mud. As Chauca swayed again, he held him. 'We'd better get him out of here.'

Daniel became agitated. 'What can we do?'

'Find a doctor.'

Chauca rasped. 'Beatriz Santillan – I need see her. You know where she is?'

Daniel hesitated, wary. 'In the hotel.'

'Tell her meet me. In church. Near gate to mines.'

Daniel snapped. 'What for?'

'Is important.'

Rice intervened. 'You could come to the hotel. We can patch you up.'

'Too dangerous, Jerry! An Indian. They'd kick him out! He's also a wanted man'

'Gringo right. I have price on the head.'

The coffin had been lowered. The priest was intoning the last prayer. People were shovelling earth into the grave. Some of the crowd had begun to leave.

Chauca whispered fiercely. 'The church. After dark.'

Daniel responded, equally fiercely. 'I won't let her take risks, Chauca! What do you want – tell me!'

'I have message. From Gaspar Huaman.'

'Huaman is dead!'

Chauca's hands, blood-caked, shot forward and grabbed Daniel's coat. 'Do what I ask! If you betray – if soldiers come – I find you. I kill you.' He released Daniel and turned to Rice. 'Also you!'

And before either could move, he disappeared into the crowd.

There were two unsigned paintings in the church which, portraying miners at their devotions, reminded Daniel of Van Gogh's sketches from Le Borinage. Any other time, they would have electrified him.

They should not have come here. This was none of their business.

He glanced at Rice, sitting on a pew, drinking from his hip-flask. Rice loved churches, or so he had said, and seemed to be at peace. Why was he half cut then?

Beatriz was praying before the statue of the Virgin which stood to one side of the altar like an anxious, protective mother.

She had not hesitated over meeting Chauca. She had not even been surprised that a dead man had sent her a message. She had simply shaken off the shock of the massacre like a saint shakes off life, and had spent much of the early evening buying food and medication.

Was she pregnant? They had not talked any more about that.

Daniel checked his watch. Midnight approaching. They had been waiting almost three hours. The few worshippers, friends and families of the martyrs offering prayers, had left. 'He won't come. It's not safe.'

Rice drawled through his hip-flask. 'We had no trouble getting here. The streets are clear.'

Daniel wished he could smoke. 'Then he collapsed somewhere. Maybe died. He was wounded...'

Beatriz rose from the altar and came up to him. 'He will come.' She took his hand and kissed it. 'Don't worry.'

He nodded. He moved his arms about in frustration. 'It's cold...'

She sat in a pew, beckoned to him to sit next to her.

'... I still say it's crazy. A message from a dead man?'

Rice interjected tipsily, 'I've been thinking about that. Must be something that'll keep the revolution alive. Some vital information Beatriz must pass on.'

'Pass on to whom? All the revolutionaries are dead!'

Rice pulled himself off the pew and moved towards them. 'Maybe there are others. Waiting to decide – waiting for a miracle. Now Huaman's given it to them.'

'A miracle?'

'He struck a blow. Destroyed a plane. Killed fifteen. A great victory, Dan, by guerrilla standards...'

Beatriz interrupted them. 'Why should Huaman have chosen me?'

Rice spoke gently, admiringly. 'He asked for a song – you gave him an anthem.'

Daniel rose impatiently. 'I think we should go! Now!'

'You go! She stay!'

Daniel, Beatriz and Rice, spinning towards Chauca's raucous baritone, stared at the darkness at the back of the church. They could not see Chauca, only the barrel of a gun, pointing at them.

Daniel barked. 'About time! We nearly froze to death!'

'Go now!'

Beatriz edged forward towards the gun. 'You have a message for me?'

'Only for you. I no trust gringos.'

'These two you must.'

The barrel of the gun disappeared into the shadows.

Then, quietly, from behind them, Chauca appeared by the altar. He kept his gun on Daniel and Rice, as if debating whether to kill them. Then, suddenly, he collapsed, falling backwards on to the communion table.

They rushed to him.

Daniel pointed at Chauca's poncho. 'He's bleeding.'

Chauca leaned on them, trying to pull himself up. 'Is nothing. A little wound.'

Beatriz gathered her bag of provisions. 'We will take care of it. Can you eat? Drink something?'

'Later. The message.'

'It can wait.' She signalled Daniel and Rice to take off Chauca's poncho.

'No. Is urgent!' Chauca yelped as they divested him of the poncho.

Beatriz felt nauseated as she peeled off Chauca's vest. There was a deep gash on the chest and Chauca's difficulty in breathing suggested broken ribs.

Chauca grabbed Beatriz's hands. '*Comandante* – he needs help.'

Daniel seized his arm. 'Huaman?'

Rice gaped at him. 'He's alive? Where is he?'

'Bad wound. Arm in bits. I hid him. A *guiñero* hole.' He tightened his grip on Beatriz's hands. 'He must live. Or no revolution.'

Rice had sobered up. 'Is that how you fell – carrying him up the mountain?'

'Yes.' He tried to stop Beatriz attending to him. 'I take you to him.'

Daniel, compulsively, tightened his hold on Chauca. 'And then what?'

'We take him away. To safety. Yungas. Father Quintana.'

'How? How?'

Chauca held on to Beatriz's hands desperately. 'You will think how.'

Beatriz began cleaning Chauca's gash. 'Yes, Chauca. We will get him there – and you.'

Daniel's hands went limp.

The tunnel where Chauca had hidden Huaman was like a prehistoric tomb hewn from the rock. It was halfway up Monte Rico, on the southern flank which, exposed to the bitter winds of the plains and ice-packed much of the year, was the most inclement part of the mountain. Some time in the past, someone must have discovered a rich vein in it, for there were countless other tunnels up and down the escarpment. But either the vein had been exhausted or mining in such an inhospitable terrain had proved impossible even for the desperate *guiñeros*. Consequently, people seldom ventured there.

Entry into the tunnel was possible only in a prone position. For Daniel, wide-shouldered, it was a very tight squeeze. He crawled in on his belly, switching on the pocket-torch strapped to his head like a miner's lamp, grateful for the mask which Beatriz had improvised out of gauze and liberally sprinkled with frangipani.

When hiding Huaman, Chauca had been guided by one imperative: in the event of a chance inspection of the tunnel, either by troops or *guiñeros*, the intruders should not suspect Huaman's presence or hear his moans. To effect this, he had pushed Huaman some thirty metres deep and had sealed him off with a mound of rock, leaving only a small gap to let the air through.

Daniel reckoned it would take him about an hour to clear the mound, reach Huaman and pull him out.

The cold was ineffable. The floor and the walls of the tunnel were covered with a thick layer of ice which, occasionally, when his torch directed some heat on it, glistened briefly with moisture then froze again. Somewhere behind him, he imagined, his breath fell as snow. Worse was the claustrophobia, the sense of crawling through his own grave, of a pot-hole lurking ahead to cast him into the magma core where, in all likelihood, Hell would be.

Yet, incredible as it was, he felt in his element. His fear was under control, his exertions no more arduous than those of a sportsman stretching himself to his limit, almost enjoyable. A total contrast to how he had felt the previous night and much of this day.

He reached the barricade and dismantled some of the rocks. He squinted through the gap. He could not yet spot Huaman. He shouted, 'Gaspar!'

No response. Maybe dead. Gangrene had set in on Huaman's arm and, according to Rice, he would be prey to all sorts of infection. The cold, they had hoped, might save him from the most virulent.

Daniel crawled back, feet first, towards the opening, carrying the loose rocks. He moved well.

The previous night he had almost disintegrated. Fear, already present during the meeting with Chauca, had increased unabated. He still could not remember how he had climbed, effortlessly, the treacherous terrain, or how he had supported both Beatriz and Rice through the worst stretches. His panic had reached its apogee when Chauca, treating his gash and broken ribs as of no account, had pulled Huaman out of the tunnel for some treatment. The sight of that shredded arm! The smell of gangrene!

Fear, at its most persecutory, had urged him to run away, to leave everybody behind, even Beatriz. And he would have done so, if Beatriz had not sensed his panic, had not buried her face in his chest, forced him to comfort her. He would still have run, later, if she had not demanded his presence – his strength, she had said – to hold her steady so that she could dress Huaman's arm without fainting. Later still, when they had pumped Huaman full of antibiotics, wrapped him up in their anoraks, pushed him back into the tunnel, would he not have run if she had not praised his *valour*? She had continued to support him through the rest of the night, as they had discussed how to smuggle Huaman out. *You are my man. I thrive in your strength. I will always need you. Need*, that healing word. How patiently it had forced fear back into its incontinent shithole. Perhaps the cure for fear was simply *need*.

He reached the opening of the tunnel, legs first. Chauca and Rice pulled him out. He dumped the rocks. Beatriz smiled, blew him a kiss.

He nodded and crawled back in. He progressed faster.

That morning, fear had changed places with the conviction that by getting involved with Huaman, he was enmeshing himself in a fatal adventure; that the pity would not be that he would die; but that he would leave behind the unfinished business of Kempin. Consequently, he had punctuated the arrangements with anger and resentment.

Bearing in mind the urgent need to amputate Huaman's arm, they had decided that he could only be smuggled out by plane. The trains would be watched; driving overland in a hired car, even assuming they could avoid the army patrols, would take too long; the river, which snaked to the Yungas, was scored with rapids, and, in any case, lay miles away.

He reached the barricade, collected the remaining rocks, and crawled back again.

Beatriz had come up with the solution: Guillermo, dare-devil pilot – an ex-lover, too – who had an air-charter company. He had taken her all over South America on one tour or another. A man with his heart in the right place. Rice had thought it a great idea. Daniel, fetching excuses from forty sources, had tried to overrule them. But Beatriz, diplomatically interpreting his resistance as a show of jealousy – some truth in that – had placated him with her cajolings.

One telephone call and Guillermo had rushed over. He was waiting at the airfield, his Cessna refuelled.

Daniel reached the cave opening with the rest of the rocks. Beatriz, Rice and Chauca sprang forward to help him. There was awe on their faces, maybe even gratitude. He liked that, though only a fool would be so seduced.

'What's the time?'

Beatriz whispered back. 'Almost ten.'

Rice patted him on the shoulder. 'We're doing well.'

Daniel crawled back in. He progressed even faster now. They had to get to the airfield before daybreak.

Fear still under control. Still feeling heroic. Best of all, that pulsating hope, squeezing out from between his legs, that he was giving birth to a new self, that admirable self who had eluded him all his life.

He was approaching Huaman. He could smell the gangrene even through the frangipani. He slowed down, nauseous, suddenly terrified. He would never get out of this tunnel. The walls would collapse on him. Rodents would eat his eyes and tongue and cock. Vampire bats would suck him dry.

'Chauca...'

The voice, Huaman's, frail, floated over. He could see him now, icicled hair glistening in the light of his torch.

'Not Chauca – Daniel...' He edged forward. Angry with himself. Angry with everybody.

Why do I have to do this? Just because I am big and strong! Just because Chauca is too weak! Why not Rice who had spent the last twenty-four hours prancing about like the redeemer of all revolutions? Rice is old, so what! And when I pull Huaman out, who'll carry him? Not Rice. Not Chauca.

The stench became overpowering.

Daniel stretched his hand, touched pulpy flesh.

Huaman's piercing shriek blasted his eardrum.

'All right, Gaspar! We're taking you out.'

Barely a movement, then screwed-up eyes, trying to avoid the light of his torch. 'Chauca...'

'He's outside.'

Saliva, like pus, colouring delirium. 'No...' Pupils rotating behind slitted eyelids. 'Don't take me... Not alive... let me... die... here...'

Daniel heaved a hand under Huaman's good shoulder.

'I don't want to... be taken alive... Please don't take me alive...'

Daniel put his other hand under Huaman's injured side. Huaman yelped. The pain was a good sign. If Rice's knowledge of gangrene was to be trusted, not all the flesh had died; Huaman stood a chance. 'Gaspar, I'm going to pull you back. You push with your feet.'

Delirious eyes. 'I'll resist... Not taken alive...'

If he does not co-operate, knock him unconscious, Chauca had said. Yes. But how to pull him out?

'Come on, Gaspar. We haven't got much time!'

A snort passing for a laugh. 'Time...? All the time in the world... the other world...'

Daniel hit him hard, angrily.

Huaman passed out, a semblance of a smile still on his face.

Daniel pulled his hands from under Huaman's shoulders. Stuck! After all that! *Why me? Why me?*

He pulled at Huaman's collar. Not too difficult – except he risked strangling him. There was one thing to do. The way they saved a drowning man. Drag him by the chin.

Chauca led the descent. Daniel, carrying Huaman on his shoulders in a fireman's hold, followed. Beatriz and Rice brought up the rear. Huaman remained comatose.

They progressed slowly. With the strike broken, the mountain was active again. Consequently, they avoided the main tracks.

Daniel, anxious to get out of Monte Rico, vetoed any pauses for rest. His prodigious effort inspired them. Their admiration compensated for Huaman's foul dribble washing his neck and the fetid cloud of gangrene which enveloped him.

185

They did have to stop once – when Rice slipped and sprained his ankle. Beatriz managed to patch him up, but had to support him the rest of the way. During the treatment, Daniel kept Huaman on his shoulders.

They reached the airfield just before first light.

'Who did you say?'

'The man of my life.'

Guillermo's broad grin was like a sunflower. He pumped Daniel's hand enthusiastically. 'Wonderful! Such great pleasure! Finally, eh, *bellissima*?'

Beatriz smiled. 'Finally – yes.'

Guillermo kissed her; then, much to Daniel's surprise, kissed him, too. 'Wonderful! I could do somersaults!'

Guillermo had not reacted to their sweaty, begrimed appearance – not even to Huaman's smell which had settled on Daniel, perhaps for life.

Guillermo, Daniel had imagined, would be one of those handsome macho types. He had turned out to be a squat mestizo, past fifty, with a barrel-chest and a fat, grizzled, bearded head. Perpetual motion, even as he stood still, and the large blaring portable radio-cassette, which he carried like a life-support system, appeared to be his major eccentricities. But it was his weather-beaten face, creased by laughter lines, which reinstated faith in patron saints. Daniel was so transported that he could not feel jealous of this ex-lover of Beatriz – even though Guillermo's twinkling eyes constantly undressed her and, no doubt, remembered the miracles of her flesh.

'Can we leave, Guillermo?'

'When you like.' He stroked the fuselage of his Cessna. 'She is ready – like a good woman. And I picked up your cases from the hotel.'

'What about clearances?'

Guillermo guffawed. 'This is South America, *hombre*. You come and go as you please – unless there is an emergency.'

'There was an emergency.'

Guillermo pointed at the dark and empty shadow of the airport terminal shack. 'Seems the airport is back to normal – closed for the night!' He guffawed at his joke.

Beatriz scanned the airfield. 'And the runway? There was some fighting here...'

'If I can land, I can take off.' Guillermo looked puzzled. 'But you said you were five.'

Daniel indicated a point in the darkness. 'We are. I'll get them.'

Guillermo shrugged. 'Crazy.'

'We had to make sure everything was all right.' Daniel glanced at Beatriz. She had assured him Guillermo would collaborate whatever the intrigue.

186

Beatriz's voice trembled. 'I couldn't tell you everything, Guillermo – in case the lines were tapped. One is seriously wounded.'

Guillermo's smile evaporated. 'Who is he?'

'The less you know, the better – in case you're questioned.'

'Let me worry about that, *hombre*. Who is he?'

Beatriz blurted it out. 'Gaspar Huaman.'

'Not – dead?' Guillermo shook his head. 'You amaze me... Bunch of amateurs...'

'Good thing we are, Guillermo. Professionals wouldn't have dared...'

Guillermo broke into his beautiful smile. 'True enough, *bellissima*! God bless you! Time somebody shat on this government!'

They took off five minutes later, at first light.

Huaman remained unconscious.

Chauca sat immobile, chewing coca leaves which Guillermo always carried for medicinal purposes.

Rice sat next to Guillermo, eager to view the terrain from the cockpit.

Beatriz sang softly.

Daniel, pretending to be asleep, enjoyed the tears of pride that periodically surged to his eyes. What he had done could be said to be heroic. The joy of it!

22

Your name is in the petals of the rose that grows in the stone, my name is in the caverns

Happily, Teresa walked towards José Perera's castle.

Everything was dressed in its best spirit: the sun, the earth, the waters, the bush, the birds, the insects, and those shy animals keeping out of sight. A teaming congregation of *apus* in the colours of a carnival.

She had known it would be so. Every day since she had left Valdepeñas, she had propitiated the spirits. She had not neglected a single *apacheta*, those imprecatory cairns at crossroads and mountain passes, nor a single *huaca*, the sacred mounds and fetishes by rivers and fertile valleys, lakes and pastures. She had revered them with prayers, offered them hairs from her eyebrows in thanksgiving.

All the spirits had known about her. Some had taken her to their hearts immediately; others, cautiously and gradually; and she had soon convinced those few who had doubted her immaculate love for Manku Yupanqui that she had the ability to leaven his workload.

She had shown them she needed only to stretch a hand towards the sky or the water, the escarpment or the fissure, the foliage or the dune, to detect a storm or a whirlpool, to sense a chasm or an earthquake, to divine a swamp or a spring. On those occasions when she had lain down to rest, at a spot where Manku's breath had clung like mist, she had shown how eager her body was for him, how the dew between her legs spurted like a fount.

She cast a look behind her.

The people were still by the fence that encircled the castle. They had refused to follow her.

She had explained, when they had warned her that the fence contained electricity, that it was natural for a barrier protecting Manku to be invested with awesome power – though not electricity, not that instrument of the *misti*, more likely a shard of sun or a sheaf of lightning. She had reassured them that since they were her followers, the fence would not harm them, that there would be a passage. And she had demonstrated the fact by walking over a tree which a thunderbolt had felled on to a section of the fence.

Naturally, she had realised, it had not been fear but discretion that had made the people stay behind. They wanted her to meet Manku alone. They knew a man and a woman needed time to memorise each other's features and put dreams into pledges.

Good people. They had followed her untiringly, crossed the plains and the deserts, the bush and the mountains like a poem travels to the four corners of the world.

She directed her attention to the men in uniform and armbands. They were still behind her, still holding their guns as if she might suddenly attack them.

She could not understand who these men were. They had been at the fence when she had crossed it, discussing how to remove the tree, using words like 'short-circuit' which belonged to those who could read or write. Except for their surprise when she had greeted them, their faces had been dour.

She came upon the moat that girdled the castle. Her followers had warned her that it would be hazardous to cross. She gauged the water – stagnant, blanketed with weeds and lilies, but not dangerous.

She waded in. The men in uniform were shouting, but she did not hear what they were saying; she was skimming the water's surface like a fisherbird. She also heard guns firing. Were they celebrating her arrival?

She reached the opposite bank. She cleared the wet hair from her eyes. She ran up the steep slope.

Huge dogs, frothing at the mouth, stifling growls as they ran backwards and forwards, met her at the top of the slope. Strange.

She smiled at them. 'I am Teresa Ayala... Manku's bride...'

The dogs quietened down. When she began stroking them, they jumped over each other, competing for her hand.

'There, there, sweet dogs...'

More men in uniforms appeared. Also holding guns. She was reminded of the story Sister Columba, who was a *naturale* like herself, had told her. In the good times, Viracocha, the Creator, used to turn stones into fully armed

Inca soldiers. Could Manku do the same? But why – when he had the sun's missing ray?

'Good day, *compadres*. I am Teresa Ayala. Manku's bride.'

They did not speak; just stared at the dogs following her meekly. Maybe they were deaf and dumb. She slipped past them; smiled, baffled, when they followed her like those other men on the other side of the moat.

The castle, she noted, was to her left. Ahead, to the right, a magnificent garden, perhaps the size of Eden, stretched like an ancient mirror.

And there, where the grass met the low sun, beneath a tree as majestic as the Tree of Life, stood a man. Tall. Sparkling in rays of light, like the sea at sunset.

It could only be he. Manku Yupanqui.

She stopped to gaze at him. In love. With awe.

He turned and looked at her, flashing the sky in his eyes. Then he beckoned her. 'Come.'

She ran to him.

23
The cat and the scorpion fornicated in the forested country

'*The world is divided between democracy and communism, Senator. These forces, repellent to each other, are in unabating conflict.*'

'*I'm familiar with the polemics, Generalisimo.*'

'*We are on the side of democracy. And since our geographical position puts us on the borders of this divide, we are the vanguard of democracy.*'

The Americans were on another inspection tour of their backyard. They had swooped down – senators, congressmen, officials of various aid agencies, military experts, grandees of multinationals and clergymen – on behalf of one committee or another.

'*National security is imperative, Mr Representative. We cannot protect the free world unless we are strong.*'

'*There is a difference between strength and totalitarianism, Admiral...*'

'*Strength, in terms of Latin America, must be absolute. To the people, a state run by soldiers is like a father: incorruptible, unassailably authoritative, but loving.*'

Fuego had conceived the idea of entertaining them all under one roof. It would be enlightening, he had told the Junta, to observe the dynamics of what amounted to a cross-section of the American Administration. The Generalisimo, the Admiral and the Air Marshal had agreed readily – not because they had thought they needed enlightenment, but because for junior partners any opportunity to dazzle their patrons was most welcome.

'*Why not free elections, Air Marshal?*'

'*Ninety-five per cent of our people are uneducated. They cannot be – nor do they want to be – involved in politics.*'

'*Then education should be your priority.*'

'*We do not have the resources, Mr Secretary.*'

'*You would – if you distributed your wealth evenly.*'

'*Surely – that is communism.*'

'*We, in the States, are also capitalists. Yet we do endeavour to have social justice.*'

'*Your people are different. They want to improve themselves. Our people prefer to live like animals. We have tried reforms – it is like casting pearls at pigs.*'

These Americans – mostly liberals – were easy opponents. Not like their ghoulish counterparts, the Willistons, from whom the Junta had learned their catechism. Certainly not like those old Europeans who had written the catechism.

'*What about individual rights, Generalisimo? Pluralist views?*'

'*In the war against communism, certain rights have to be sacrificed, Your Honour.*'

'*Security should be secondary to human rights.*'

'*Is that how it is in your country, Your Honour?*'

Fuego had his own reasons for assembling the Americans. After the events of Monte Rico, he had found himself stranded in a void, reduced to a state of inertia. Like when he had left the mines. Incarcerated in a present that could contain neither the past nor the future.

'*You persecute dissenters, Admiral.*'

'*We do not. We teach them that happiness comes through order and obedience.*'

'*By torturing them, making them disappear, throwing them into death-pits?*'

'*I admit, there have been abuses. We deplore that. Whenever we catch the culprits, we punish them.*'

Power was what really filled the present. Except that there were times when power became featureless – simply the purveyor of status, privilege and riches. He had to rediscover power as the catholicon it was. Keep faith with it, mystically, absolutely.

'*Each time the people try to negotiate fair employment, fair wages, health care, or try to organise unions, they are brutally persecuted.*'

'*Communist propaganda, Monsignor…*'

'*Even priests are harassed.*'

'*You are talking about bad priests. The Church itself is the State's staunchest supporter.*'

'*No priest who tries to help the poor, the oppressed, the starving can be bad, Air Marshal.*'

'*They turn bad when they meddle in politics, Monsignor. Like those who advocate Liberation Theology. In effect, Marxists, Trotskyites. Their aim is to dismantle the capitalist system. Given the opportunity, they would march against the cream of our society, those who pulled this country out of the Stone Age. And all our civilisation – all we hold sacred – would disintegrate. We would end up rejecting God – just as they did in Russia.*'

So, he listened to the proceedings from the tower of Vargas's hacienda – his hacienda now, lock, stock and barrel. The most salubrious place in the capital – secluded even from the stench of the *barranco*. His prize for ending the miners' strike. But now that it was his, disposable, like all symbols.

He sat like God – if He ever existed – and listened uninterestedly to every disputation. The electronic eavesdropping devices he had installed throughout the mansion worked perfectly.

'*We need more arms, Senator.*'

'*In view of what happened in Monte Rico, Generalisimo, I doubt whether we could process that request.*'

'*You should praise us for what we did in Monte Rico, Senator. Not punish us. We wiped out a revolution.*'

'*Wiping out a lot of innocent people at the same time.*'

'*No innocents. All were part of a fifth column.*'

'*You are losing credibility, sir. Back home, people are asking questions. Like having fought fascism in Europe, why the heck are we helping to establish it in South America?*'

'*Fascism, Senator?*'

'*And we are criticised – often with justification – that it is our support of fascism which pushes the Third World countries towards communism.*'

'*Latin America is not part of the Third World, Senator. The Monroe Doctrine clearly states our special status for the United States.*'

Farcical these good Americans with their lofty ideals. All you needed to silence them instantly was a mere mention of the Monroe Doctrine.

'*Our decision to invest is governed by one factor, Admiral…*'

'*We offer the best terms, Mr Chairman. That is why we are a haven for multinationals.*'

'*Then I'd say we're in business, sir.*'

'*There will be some miscellaneous charges… to be paid in Florida…*'

'*No problem.*'

Brass tacks now. Even less entertaining.

Fuego tried to summon up the desire to get drunk.

The Junta would soon leave to attend to other state matters. The Americans would be left to the servility of the thirty-three 'first' families, with old Vargas at the forefront. The latter, always equating Americans with extra pocket money, had rushed back from his retreat in Spain as if chased by an earthquake. How did he feel being a guest in his old hacienda?

There would be tennis, croquet, swimming, riding, shooting, fishing, hunting and girls for those who cared for such things. For those who preferred gluttony, champagne by the gross and enough to feed the barrios for a month.

He would not be missed.

He could not be bothered to get drunk.

He needed to do something crazy. Like roll down the crater of a volcano to the very edge of the pool of fire. Or lie on the Humboldt Current facing the sky and float out with the tide, then float back on the next.

But volcanoes and the sea belonged to another era.

Why this depression masquerading as boredom?

There was the rumour that Gaspar Huaman had survived the battle of Monte Rico.

Nothing to do with that. He hoped, in fact, the rumour was true. Huaman had been too briefly an opponent, too easily defeated.

Was it Daniel?

He had had reports that Daniel, Beatriz and Rice had stealthily left Monte Rico for an unknown destination in a chartered plane. He could not dismiss the possibility, unlikely as it was, that they were involved with Huaman, that Daniel, as the most able-bodied, might have had a part in Huaman's alleged survival.

No, he was not depressed because of Daniel. Indeed, would that Daniel had saved Huaman. It would prove he had measured him correctly. Not a coward, as Daniel saw himself, but a man whose courage had been condemned to stagnation and now ached to flow.

And the bet would continue... And to win it, he would have to think of something with which to destroy Daniel.

'*We've been re-evaluating Kempin.*'

'*What's there to re-evaluate? He's a legend – God almost.*'

From the gazebo. Quiet. Conspiratorial.

'*Watch your blasphemous tongue, Angelito!*'

'*Sorry, Luke. What about Kempin?*'

'*He's gone and made waves!*'

Fuego, interested at last, poured himself a brandy and settled back into his armchair.

Williston, having dusted the gazebo's balustrade with a handkerchief, leaned against it. 'Let me wise you up, Angelito. The Lord, as Calvin revealed, divided mankind into two: those predestined to wickedness and therefore condemned to eternal damnation, and those selected for salvation. But the latter – we amongst them – must continuously prove we are worthy of this judgement. We do so through duty, purity, humility, asceticism, unworldliness, patriotism. Through obedience to the Lord's Word. What the Bible condemns, what Jesus, Pure and Perfect, brands as degeneracy, we reject as anathema. Kempin has strayed from that path!'

Angelito, overwhelmed by the pine-oil perfume Williston wore, looked puzzled. 'How?'

'He's indulged in some death-camp stuff.'

'He never served in death-camps – just organised deportations.'

'Looks like he's making up for it now.' Williston, whose much publicised hobby was horticulture, gazed in admiration at the flowers on a climber. '*Clematis tangutica*. I love them, don't you?'

'Beautiful. What camps stuff?'

Williston's deep blue eyes trailed into space. If one looked lovingly out there, he had once told Angelito, one could see Jesus, one's Personal Saviour, waving the Good Book. 'A nasty video. One of our auxiliaries – a CIA guy – got hold of it. Features an Israeli agent – female. Kempin put her through hell, then killed her. Taped the whole thing. Sent it to the Jews as a warning. Surely, you know about it...'

'Not in so many details.'

Williston glared to indicate that Angelito had incurred a demerit. 'The Israelis are up in arms. Washington is full of Yids lobbying for US intervention. Unless we act now – this country will have a plague of Jew-boys. What the consequences of that might be, I leave to your imagination...'

Angelito retorted disdainfully. 'We can handle Jew-boys.'

Williston checked the line of his sleeves. 'Talking of boys. I was chewing the rag with your good wife in there. Told me she's expecting again. Congratulations.'

Angelito, familiar with Williston's sudden changes of mood, remained wary. 'Thank you.'

'When's the happy day?'

'In six months.'

'I guess you want a girl this time.'

'Looks like it'll be another boy. Concepción's getting very sick – like the previous pregnancies.'

'I wondered why she left early. I'll get our Assembly to send her something nice. For you, too, of course. Stamps, your passion – right? French Colonies, I seem to recall. Let me know anything you particularly want.'

'Thank you.'

'What were we saying? Oh, yes...' Williston's geniality turned to simmering fury. 'This agent – Campbell's Controller, I presume.'

Angelito nodded.

'Fuego's prank, was it – handing her over to Kempin?'

'No. Fuego lost interest in her. But Kempin wanted to interrogate her. So I obliged.'

'*You* did?'

'I have the authority.'

'You have the authority for local issues – *certain* local issues. For the rest, you consult me!'

Angelito adjusted the armband on his uniform. 'Kempin is not the *rest*.'

'They all are! From Kempin to Fuego to the Junta! That's the understanding between your people and mine!'

'Kempin founded the New Order. He is still our leader. I can even say, he *is* the party!'

Williston looked as if he might launch into a jeremiad. But he spoke with restraint. 'Now, listen to me, Angelito. I'm not just speaking for Moral Crusade. This is official – straight from my associates in Washington. We are all soldiers of our respective factions. And since yours and mine have a common objective – to bring order to this beleaguered continent – we are the soldiers of sanity. That means: no one – not even the Kempins – can be permitted to fail in their duties. That also means you consult me. We take decisions jointly. Is that clear?'

Angelito nodded grudgingly.

Williston, checking his shirt for signs of sweat, walked over to Angelito, towering over him like a patron saint. 'OK, old friend. What's done is done. But the Lord is on our side and we can repair the damage. Kempin has lost his soul – that's the long and the short of it. All he wants is wickedness. There have been other incidents – with Indio women. We managed to hush those up. I suppose, if this abomination had also involved a native, maybe we could have swept it under the carpet, too – maybe even have found some justification because women, Indio or otherwise, are, in the main, slimy temptresses... But we can't. This time Kempin has really sinned!'

'He is an old man. We must make some allowances...'

Williston's voice rumbled like an angry sky. 'You're not listening, Angelito! No allowances! If we did, we might as well surrender the world to Satan's sidekicks! To scientists clamouring that the world was not created by the

Lord but by some cosmic accident! To humanists telling us man evolved from animals and therefore can live like animals! I'm telling you, one moment of weakness, and before we know it, the integralism of God, Temple, Country and Family that brought us into such a formidable alliance would crumble. We would be ruled by liberals, sodomites and libertines! Instead of establishing the racial superiority which is the white man's divine right, we would be slaves of multi-coloured pagans! Instead of upholding the Bible as the repository of *all* truths, we would perish, our paradise lost, through moral leprosy! Do you understand, Angelito?'

'But Kempin – *Heinrich Kempin...*'

Gently, Williston pushed Angelito down on to a bench. 'No buts! Remember him as he was. Think of him as a fallen hero. Uphold your credo: Believe! Obey! Fight!'

Angelito yielded reluctantly. 'What did you have in mind?'

Williston's eyes smouldered. 'We'll get Fuego to arrange something. Let the Junta take the credit. Purging the country of a Nazi war-criminal – it'll show them in a good light. And it'll stop the Jews from hunting.'

So Kempin was expendable. Fuego felt he should be laughing. He had never minded doing the dirty work. On the contrary. The reason why no one ever crossed him, why even Williston – the only person around who could carry two melons under one arm – stood wary of him was precisely because he had always done the dirty work himself. That was the secret of absolute power.

But why was he resentful now? Why did the thought of smashing a totem like Kempin lack joy?

Daniel. He had been thinking of pitching Daniel against Kempin. A dramatic confrontation. With the heavy smell of preordination. With echoes of Solomonic judgement. With a taste of Lucifer's perversity. With the pomp of a God-game.

He could not do that if Kempin had to die. He had to think of something. Turn the proposition on its head.

He needed inspiration. Some violent activity. Like pulling a house down. Crushing a mob. Riding a horse to death. Beating someone to a pulp. He left the tower.

Angelito ran. Long, easy strides; heart purring; lungs indefatigable. Imagining he was on a bayonet charge. Spitting out the miasma Williston had left in his mouth.

He had no objections to Kempin's removal. There was nothing left in that antediluvian that could serve New Order. Nothing – except the name.

What offended was the way they were going to dispose of him. Conquistadores should die without dying. With a ritual that disseminated their names into the very air people breathed. Myths were born from names. And myths created races, countries, flags, anthems, uniforms – all the silver and all the gold.

But what could be expected of functionaries clinging to their high-chairs? Wait until New Order is fully established. Then it will be the Willistons who will be purged.

Williston! That pseudo-janitor of souls speaking in tongues! Did he really believe in all that God-dust he preached! Sleeps in rubber nappies, Fuego had said; never touches woman, man or beast; is revolted by hot skins and bodily fluids; loves illusions because they lack genitals. Yet top brass in the strongest underworld in Washington.

Angelito put on a spurt.

A disturbing thought gripped him. There might be some people – Fuego, for a start – who might think he was of the same mould as Williston. He did not much care for pigging either. Procreating sons – that was its only virtue. And his beliefs were clear-cut, too. Except that they made sense. Nothing illogical like a despotic God witlessly deciding who was saved and who was damned. God was God – to be worshipped in church – dutifully. As for the fascist ideology. Once winnowed from all of its historical dead-wood, it had perfect clarity. Order that would wipe out chaos – on a global scale. Not dissimilar to God creating the world.

Angelito eased back into a jog.

No – nobody could think he was like Williston.

Then there was violence. The godly virtue. It raised him above the rest of mankind. Made him the natural conquistador. The ravisher of the *world*.

Forged, like steel, under the hammer of brutal parents in the anvil of brutal times. Of the most excellent stock: Ukrainian. With the august name: Vassily Maximovich Ignachenko. To be unveiled one day. Survivor of the Jewish conspiracy against humanity. Educated by Teutons and Stalinists. Baptised by every conceivable fire.

Crime, first. A thrill or two. Until the realisation that it was merely the illegal pursuit of bourgeois aspirations.

Then, murder. More thrilling. That wonderful sensation of a body bursting in his hands.

On to, terror. And revelation. He who can kill *all* is God.

No stopping him, thereafter. The world his stage. Terror: the greatest show on earth. Violence: the ultimate sacrament. All over Europe. Transferring from one terrorist organisation to another, like a star footballer. Conquering and killing, killing and conquering.

Finally, transferring here. And the first taste of gold. A uniform and a high rank.

And now... Keeping himself supreme whilst everything around him rotted, whilst mongols like Fuego muddied the water. And breathing, breathing violence.

Violence, the immaculate cleanser. The perpetual catharsis. Violence that healed isolation and doubt. Decontaminated injustice, humiliation, usurpation. Violence that fortified a man with the blood of his victims. That created wholeness out of nothingness. Violence that was rebirth, therefore, salvation, therefore, immortality.

And tomorrow... New Order was filling up with his peers, young strategists with brains like computers. Leadership awaited the super man, the total man, the protean man. The man who intuited what people wanted, who knew how to be all things to all men.

I am he.

The Arab thoroughbred was also possessed with fury – willing to burst its lungs providing Fuego could manage to stay on its bare back. Fuego would have ridden it to death had he not spotted Angelito running up to the copse on the western hillock.

'Angelito!'

Angelito glanced in his direction, but ignored him.

Fuego hammered the stallion with his heels.

They raced, both men aiming to reach the copse first.

Fuego had a lot of ground to cover.

Angelito ran as if he had winged sandals.

They reached the copse at the same time.

Fuego jumped off the stallion and let it trot into the trees.

They faced each other, catching their breath.

'Let's fight, Angelito!'

'How? I can't strike my superior officer.'

'We'll forget rank. Just two men.'

'I'm still at a disadvantage. You can break me afterwards.'

'I won't. You have my word. Besides, you don't have a choice. I want to fight. That makes it an order.'

Angelito stared at him, caution mitigating his hatred. 'No rank involved? Just two men. I have your word?'

'Yes.'

'Very well.'

'Naked – like natives!'

'In uniform. Like duellists.'

Fuego began undressing. 'Keep yours. I won't!'

Meticulously, Angelito beat the dust off his uniform. Fuego undressed completely. They approached each other.

Angelito glanced in revulsion at Fuego's Indian physique. 'Before we start, General – why?'

'No reason. And every reason. Two men wanting to explode. Good enough?'

'It will do.'

They fought. For a while, achieving little impact, like birds fighting in the air. Angelito, as hard and supple as a judo master, twisting, circling, pivoting, blocking, lunging, chopping; Fuego, as agile as a *capoeira* dancer, spinning on his haunches, cartwheeling arms and legs, soaring, kicking, diving, butting.

Then as they tired, their movements became leaden, like bears wrestling. Fists and feet found targets. They washed the landscape crimson. Body entangled with body. They licked each other's spit, sweat and blood. Legs buckled. They ate earth.

Then Fuego, losing all sense of movement and colour, drained into the twilight's grey pool.

When he regained consciousness, night had fallen. The stallion was at his side, waiting patiently. Angelito had gone.

Fuego held on to the horse's reins and pulled himself up. He could stand. He ran his swollen hands around his body, noticing a couple of teeth imbedded between his knuckles. Angelito's. Good. He breathed deeply, flailing at the pain in his diaphragm. No bones broken. Not even his nose. The old rock was still granite-hard.

Slowly, he collected his uniform.

Deadly fighter, Angelito. With youth on his side. He would keep his word and not punish him. But there would be a day of reckoning.

He slung his uniform on to the horse's neck, then, painfully mounted it. He spurred it gently. The stallion ambled forward at a funereal pace.

He began to laugh. It hurt him laughing, but he could not stop.

24
Life goes with me and death is behind us

It was their last night at La Iglesia de Sangre de Oro. A night to commune with the wilderness, Father Quintana had suggested, and because it was full moon, the time when the earth cleansed itself, a night when they should be able to hear God whispering.

Daniel and Beatriz sat, in the silvery glow, on the porch of the golden church. She patched up the trousers he had torn in the tunnel; he watched her and caressed her neck.

The villagers were still about, sitting or standing with their children in the square, admiring the plane perched on the plateau.

Guillermo had returned to pick them up. He was in the plane with a woman who had lost her husband to the cocaine trade. They were guffawing – she perhaps for the first time in months. Guillermo had a way with women – possibly because he was satisfied with what he was.

Chauca had left, carrying his wound and broken ribs, to recruit new guerrilleros. He had kissed Daniel's hand as he had said goodbye.

Huaman would live. Father Quintana, aided by Rice, had amputated the gangrenous arm and cauterised the stump just below the shoulder. Huaman had regained consciousness by the fifth day and, though still very weak, was progressing satisfactorily. The countryside now talked of him as a deliverer and saw Monte Rico as a major victory. It seemed immaterial that he had lost all but one of his men – revolutions were born in the blood of martyrs. What counted was that he had killed fifteen of the enemy and destroyed one giant plane. That was an exploit imaginable only of someone like Manku Yupanqui.

And there were many who thought he was that paragon. Huaman now debated whether he should encourage these rumours or dispel them. The former, he had admitted to Daniel, was tempting; after all, he had come back from death.

Rice had dusted down the religion he had kept on the shelf. Ensconced with Father Timothy O'Neill's sacred relies, he was completing a feature on the history of the church.

Father Quintana appeared to have acquired a new lease on his faith. He had banished all doubts about the revolution. He would nurse Huaman with the devotion of Saint Luke. Thereafter, he would politicise the campesinos through the base communities.

Daniel's faith had also strengthened. God was living and did care for the righteous. Otherwise why should Huaman be saved to resume the struggle against the Sons of Darkness? And why should he, Daniel, have been proved to be brave and given a taste of dignity?

Thus, he could proudly meet Beatriz's gaze which held the moon and the stars, and hum in accompaniment as she sang her new song – another new song.

We are left with
hope
now
perhaps...
some day...
if...
but
hope
is not
a stranger
in our house
we entertain him
royally

She put the patched trousers aside and laid her head against his chest. 'Daniel – there will be a new man.' She placed his hand on her belly. 'I am pregnant – no doubt about it.'

He stared at her, seized by joy as well as fear. Since that day of the miners' massacre, she had refused to talk about her condition. Each time he had tried to broach the subject, she had found an excuse: that they had Huaman on their hands, that she might be imagining it, that she wanted to wait until she knew for certain. 'How can you be sure – I mean, without tests...?'

'I *feel* pregnant.'

'I don't know what to say.'

'Say you're happy.'

'I am.'

'And say you love me.'

'I do.'

'That's enough for the time being.'

They searched each other's faces for meanings beyond the words. She smiled constantly; he, occasionally.

'You don't mind? I mean – your career...'

'It's all I've ever wanted: my man, a child, children. Together you'll make me blossom in many songs.'

'We'll need to get married.'

'Need?'

'Well, we must.'

'Don't be so conservative, Daniel.'

'Don't you want to?'

'Yes. But it's not a need – or a must.'

'Right. As soon as we can.'

'Do you want to get married?'

'What a question...'

'Are you ready for it?'

Daniel tried to joke. 'Who can ever be?'

'I am.'

'Well then – so am I.'

'Let's wait.'

'Why?'

'I want to be sure.'

'Ah – *you*'re not ready!'

'I want to be sure you want to stay with me – and with him – the rest of your life.'

'It might be a her. The New Woman.'

She smiled, then kissed him softly on the lips. 'We'll wait.'

Daniel held her tightly. He should have been elated. Doing somersaults, as Guillermo would say. A child – of his own. From Beatriz. God's gift – crowning his week of grace, his emancipation as a man of free will, granting him absolution for the cowardice of the past.

And yet.

Doubt.

Still the big test ahead: Kempin.

And, inevitably, still the fear.
And yet. And yet.
There would be a New Man.
Maybe two. Both the father and the child.

PART FIVE

25
Even the child without a voice had to be ordained with a new name and the school of torment

So much food. She had never seen so much food in one place. And five times a day. It was not right. Not when the countryside starved. She would tell Manku...

Unless it was not real food. Not grown in the land, that is. But food from the sky. Though it tasted real enough.

Teresa forced herself to eat more. It was her duty to put on flesh and strength, to become fruitful like Pachamama. She had been chosen to be the womb from which her ancestors would be reborn.

The Sisters – all, except Sister Columba who was a *naturale* like herself – had refused to teach her about the Incas. Of course, as Christ's consorts, they had had few interests beside their work and prayers. But on the occasions when they had reminisced about life outside the convent, they had invariably talked about an Old World called Europe, and about the faith and values the *misti* had brought from there to civilise the Indio.

Sister Columba had not been so severe. She had told what she knew. Inti, the Sun, Quilla, the Moon and Pacha, the Earth, were created by an old white deity called Viracocha. This Viracocha put the Earth and the Moon in the Sun's care, then left walking over the water and disappearing beyond the western ocean.

The Sun created two humans. One in his image, Manku Capac, and the other in the image of the Earth, Mama Occlo. To the male, he gave the spirit of the Sea, to the female, that of the Moon. And he showed this couple how to teach mankind languages, rituals, the cultivation of crops, the husbandry of animals, the building of homes and tribes. Then he gave them a golden staff and told them it would lead them to their home.

Manku Capac and Mama Occlo travelled far and wide. At a place where the land was shaped like a puma, the golden staff sank into the earth. There, they founded their kingdom. And there they erected a majestic temple to the Sun and called it Coricancha, the Golden Enclosure.

Many glorious Incas – which is what the kings were called and why their people received that name – ruled after Manku Capac and conquered all the lands. They named this empire Tahuantinsuyo, 'the four regions of the world'.

Then the Spaniards arrived. They murdered the last king, Atahualpa. Mad with gold hunger, they stripped Coricancha of all its treasures.

She finished her food. She rose from the table, feeling bloated. She should walk about. Digest.

Passing by the door, she saw the eye behind the spying hole. She was watched day and night. She did not like it, but she had to accept it. She was not just Teresa Ayala any more. She was Manku's bride. She had to be prepared for wifehood, like coca leaves had to be prepared for rituals.

She paused by the spy hole – still shy: the man had instructed her to remain naked at all times. She pirouetted clumsily so that he could see the fullness of her breasts, the solidity of her buttocks, the strength in her thighs. She had put on weight, even she could see that.

The door did not open. She had to eat more.

Now she knew more about the Incas than Sister Columba. Father Quintana, during that journey to the desert, had told her a great deal about them.

The greatest happiness of the greatest number. That had been the Incas' principal law. The people had been divided into *ayllus*, clans which had survived to this day. They had been apportioned labour according to their age, strength and abilities. Every male had been given a slice of land large enough to feed his family and to pay a tithe. The tithes had been preserved in storehouses for distribution among the people in times of war, drought or deluge. Thus, the Incas had had no need for money. Thus also, there had been no hunger. No head of family had been allowed to abandon his plot; when they had to serve in the army or work on a construction, the family had attended to the land. No man, woman or child had lost life, dignity or name by trudging the roads in search of food or work. No slums had come into existence. No families had splintered. Marriage except for those chosen for duties that demanded chastity – had been compulsory for all men and women.

On their nuptials, couples had been rewarded with additional plots. Similarly, at the birth of each child.

Because their world had been just, there had been little abuse from those in high office. Governors and generals, sun-priests and astrologers, historians and poets had risen to their positions on merit. For, though they were often selected from the nobility, they had to be schooled by an *amauta*, a sage, and become wise before they could be admitted to court.

The Incas had achieved other glories. They had not known about the wheel and yet they had built roads that stretched from the highlands to the seas and to the deserts and the forests. And great temples, fortresses, houses – all erected with giant boulders so that none should move when the earth quaked. And terracings on the hillsides for good farming, irrigation channels from mountains to the valleys, and silos and manure pits. Also worked gold shining with soul – a countryful of it which the Spaniards had gluttonously eaten, having first boiled it like maize cobs.

Such a fine history. Such a blessing to have Inca blood.

A cough interrupted her thoughts. She looked towards the spy hole, alarmed. Was she doing something wrong?

The cough was repeated.

She glanced around the room. So big, she felt lost in it.

She spotted the earphones on the couch. She had been asked to listen to the words pouring out of it. Tales about a people called Jews. She could not be Manku's bride, she had been told, until she knew what Jews were. She did not understand why. But Manku had promised to explain it one day. She wished he had asked for something else. Like weaving a poncho for him. She could thread the rainbow into any garment.

She sat on the couch and put on the earphones. No more coughs. She tried to concentrate. But her mind wandered.

So funny – that first time she had seen Manku. She had thought he was an old man. She had been too excited, hardly believing she had finally found him. Also, there had been the setting sun playing tricks on her eyes.

As it happened, an old man had soon appeared to take charge of her. A strange old man; tittering much of the time. The few times he had spoken, he had talked in riddles. Only from the things he had asked her to do had she guessed who he was: an *amauta*, instructed by Manku to supervise her. His was the eye that watched.

But she had to admit, having an *amauta* was very unusual. She was an *aclla*, a virgin. She should have been in the care of a *mamacona*.

She knew about *acllas* from Father Quintana. Young girls of beauty, true blood and clarity of soul chosen to enter cloisters very similar to convents.

There, the *mamaconas* taught them languages, history and domestic skills. Some became consorts to noblemen and generals; others were appointed *mamaconas* themselves; yet others, chosen to remain chaste for life, were assigned to the Sun-God's service; and a select few were approved as wives for the ruling Inca.

She was like one of the last. Why then did she have an *amauta* supervising her? Was it right that every time she was told to soften the area between her legs with perfume and oil, or to comb the down that crowned the entrance to her womb, the order did not come from a woman? Was it right that the eye which beheld her nakedness – the nakedness which belonged to Manku – was that of a man?

She could not tell. She could only imagine the old man was very special. In fact, she suspected he was the old Judge who had accidentally cut off Manku's head. Though he had since helped him grow a new head, he must still be doing penance by undertaking a woman's task.

Well, she would find out after the wedding.

Until then, she had to do as she was asked. Learn about Jews. Become as plentiful as Pachamama.

And not worry about the old Judge's eyes. She was still a virgin. No woman had lost her maidenhead to an eye.

26

What is important is to be barely discernible, to shout from a hard cordillera and see on the other summit the feet of a woman newly arrived

Of all the women created by the Great Masters, Daniel had been obsessed by four: *The Madonna* by Beltraffio; the goddess Athene in Botticelli's *Pallas and the Centaur*; and the two nudes in Courbet's *Laziness and Sensuality*. Collectively, they had embodied his sexual ideal.

Beltraffio's Madonna represented a beautiful, serene young woman, regally dressed, cradling the infant Jesus and offering Him a lacrimiform breast which, though contoured by her bodice, did not appear integral to her body. Her eyes were modestly cast down, but there was a hint of abandon in her hair: some strands escaped from her fringe, others lay on her shoulders. The passionate man could perceive she had Eve's blood.

In his flights of fancy, Daniel had seen himself initiating this virgin into the pleasures of the flesh. Thereafter, to become his woman and bear his child, she renounces her immortality; offers him paradise and the pain of paradise lost; undertakes to love him more than her child, because having been deprived of his own mother, he needs, above all else, maternal care.

Botticelli's Pallas Athene represented a more erotic figure: a tall, sturdy woman in a diaphanous Grecian robe, garlanded with olive branches. She was depicted consoling a tormented centaur by caressing his hair.

She had been another favourite reverie. A virgin ready for maturity, she chooses him as her man. Her feet are strong and will follow him everywhere; her legs are supple and crave to entwine his body; her vigorous breasts, endowed with large aureoles and visible through her dress, yearn to pummel his face. He is the suffering centaur – misfit, rebel, ostracised. But she knows his virility is her happiness. She affirms, as she plays with his locks, that he will find meaning in life only if he completes her.

Courbet's *Laziness and Sensuality* portrayed two voluptuous women sleeping naked in each other's arms. One had satiation imprinted on her face; the other bore a troubled expression.

These two nymphs, seemingly unneedful of a man, had provided Daniel with his most licentious fantasies. The two have unassuageable carnal desires. They are not, as some would assume, lesbians. They are women who cannot find a man who is their equal. Their sleep betrays their hunger. The one with the troubled expression is dreaming that she is searching for a satyr. The other, keeping her loins parted by resting her right thigh across her companion, waits to be taken even as she sleeps deeply. Enter Daniel. He can match their passion orgasm by orgasm. He is their saviour.

Now, all of them belonged to the past. Or rather, now Beatriz incorporated them all.

'Daniel, I thought you said you would finish.'

He blew her a kiss. She was lying on the sofa, checking through a recording contract. For nesting, she had said, when she had had the sofa delivered. She was wearing a kimono – nothing underneath. 'Almost finished.'

Beatriz twisted her face in mock impatience.

He moved back on the platform and, dunking a biscuit into his coffee, gazed at the Virgin depicted as Pachamama. Cleaned of her old dark varnish and with the inpainting of the stoppings finished, she looked magnificent.

She was dressed in a vast robe of mesmerising red. Whilst endeavouring to identify the primary pigment for this red, he had been reminded of Turner. That association had prompted him to try safflower which the English painter had saved from disuse. Mixed with the yellow-brown of quercitron on a base of alumina, it had provided a perfect match.

The Virgin's robe suggested a wide Indian blanket. It hung down in a perfect triangle in the shape of a mountain. The Virgin's head, illuminated by Her halo, glowed from the angle of the summit. Except for Her hands which blessed the world, palms outward and auroral, no other parts of Her body were visible.

She appeared, however, to be standing with Her legs wide apart. This visual effect was achieved by the presence of a smaller mountain, also perfectly triangular, rising centrally from inside Her robe.

Since the inner mountain was painted in the same red as the outer one, and since its peak reached the level of the Virgin's crotch, the composition suggested that the inner mountain both burrowed into Her and was part of

212

Her flesh. Thus, symbolically, She was represented as receiving the Divine Phallus and, at the same time, preparing to give birth to Her son.

The robe contained various South American motifs: rural paths branching out in various directions and men, women and children – some white, some Indian – travelling on them; coca bushes, trees and flowers; birds, llamas, vicuñas and alpacas; adobes, haciendas and churches; and, prominently in the centre, a giant, in the full regalia of an Inca king, holding a golden spear.

The giant Inca, personified as Pachamama's shoot, Beatriz had suggested, might be the rumoured representation of Manku Yupanqui. Daniel, seduced by the idea, had waited for a telepathic response from the people keeping vigil outside the square. There had been none.

'You are a workaholic, Daniel.'

She had moved to the floor and was doing her pre-natal exercises. She was barely two months pregnant, but she had sworn to present him with the healthiest and sanest new man. Aged thirty-six, she had said, she was aware of the finiteness of her body; the exercises would disperse the anxieties of housing a new person.

He counted the spots he had to retouch. 'Five minutes.'

'I suppose eternal love can wait five minutes.'

The Virgin had affected him deeply. Her stylised face and hands portrayed deathlessness. Seen through his own prism, they soothed the unabating pain he felt about his mother and sisters. Since no photographs had survived their deportation, he could bestow on to them some of the Virgin's features; mourn them as real people. Sisters: young girls with tresses glowing like coronas. Mother: endowed with eyes which understood fear, preached passion and glorified life. In effect, this Virgin was unique because she was the mother everybody needed: spiritual yet earthy. As Beatriz had pointed out, Her earthiness was evident even in the redness that surrounded her – the colour of fresh earth and menstrual blood. Was it surprising that he now saw Beatriz as nature and reason fused, as a soul made in both his mother's and the Virgin's image?

'Five minutes are up.'

'Almost there.'

He applied himself to the retouching. His brush effused mastery. He had never worked so hard and so fast yet felt he was hardly working. Anointed by her creativity. Since their return from the Yungas, they had kept together, spending the days in the atelier and the nights at her villa. Moving in with each other, she had said, after she had brought some of her instruments here and he had taken preparing some of his pigments there.

He finished the retouching. Swiftly disposing brush and palette, he jumped off the platform. 'All yours.'

She stopped her exercises. 'Another minute and you might have missed it.'

'What?'

She rose from the floor, took his hand, led him to the sofa, made him sit down. She sat next to him, bared her belly and put his hand on it. 'Feel.'

He caressed her. 'Beautiful.'

'No. Feel! Feel him kicking!'

'Kicking? Isn't it too soon?'

'Not if you desperately want to feel it. Wait. You'll see. Now!'

He ran his hand on her belly. He did not feel the baby kicking. Just that soft muscularity of her flesh that electrified him.

'Did you feel it?'

He beamed and lied. 'Yes, I did.'

'He is a person now.'

He gathered her in his arms. 'I want you.'

'Thank God far that. I was getting worried.'

He began to undo her kimono.

She jumped up. 'No. This is my go!'

He sat back and let her undress him completely. She blew kisses at his erection. 'I'll make you explode.'

He reached out for her.

She pushed him back. 'Hands off!' She slipped out of her kimono, spun slowly, displaying her body.

He beckoned her. 'Come.'

She moved towards him, then stopped. She smiled mischievously. 'Paint me.'

'What with!'

'Your oils.'

'Not for oral consumption.'

She pretended to pout. 'Eating me – that's all you think about! Very well, I'll get my paints.' She grabbed her handbag, poured its contents on the floor, then, bending down wantonly so that her buttocks were fully exposed to him, started collecting her make-up sticks. 'Are you having an eyeful?'

He laughed bestially. 'Oh, yes.'

'Nice?'

'The fruit of the Tree of Life.'

'Flatterer.' She straightened up and handed him her make-up: lipstick, mascara, eye-liner, highlighter. 'Here you are.'

'What shall I paint?'

She held his penis. 'You're the artist.'

He painted concentric circles on her breasts, like ripples spreading out of her aureoles, using different colours of the make-up sticks.

'They look like targets.'

'They are. My targets.' He drew lines like bullrushes on her belly and thighs. 'Turn round.'

She let go of his penis and turned round.

He drew more bullrushes on her back, buttocks and legs. He stood back. 'This is torture.'

She faced him. 'One last thing.' She took the make-up sticks. 'I'll do it.'

She spread out her legs and daubed lipstick on her labia.

They imbibed each other, able to contain their lust because the tease was so enjoyable.

'Do you still want me?'

'Desperately.'

She flung away the make-up sticks. 'Lie down.'

Daniel lay on the sofa.

She straddled him; slowly lowered herself down; stopped when he had barely penetrated her. 'I love you, my man.' He tried to kiss her aureoles. She pulled her breasts away and pressed them on to his throat, on to his shoulders and arms and chest. 'I am painting you now.'

Daniel glanced at his chest, smudged with make-up. 'Beautiful.' He tried to pull her down and enter her fully.

'Don't be impatient!' She rose from his penis, turned round and straddled his face.

He fixed his eyes on her mount. Deliciously swollen; and so moist that it was glittering. 'Beatriz, I can see God!'

She wrapped her breasts around his penis, sucked its tip.

'In there, my love! Inside you!'

Her breathing accelerated in guttural squeals. 'Kiss me!'

Daniel clasped her buttocks, drank her juices.

She rolled over him. 'Take me! Take me, now!'

He entered her, but did not move inside her, preferring to remain imbedded, to feel the way she gripped him. He squeezed her breasts together and took both nipples into his mouth.

She laughed. 'You're wearing lipstick.'

He felt her climb towards orgasm. He erupted. 'Oh, my beauty!'

The thrill of free fall and the sadness because it had to end. 'Oh, my Beatriz!' A sadness that echoed the expulsion from Eden. But bearable, because it was only an echo. This paradise would always be open to him.

She was panting, laughing, her head thrown back joyously. 'You kill me, my man! You kill me, my heart!'

He laid his head against her head.

She rubbed his back whilst he tried to catch his breath. 'My baby... My man...'

He lay between her legs, his tongue gently teasing her vulva.

She giggled. 'It must be pretty crowded in there... I mean, the New Man – definitely. We felt him kick. But God, too?'

'He's no fool. Best place to be.'

'Crazy idiot.'

'You don't believe me? Well, let's have a look...' He parted her labia and peered in.

She burst out laughing. 'Oh, Daniel...'

'Hmmmm. A veritable Aladdin's cave.'

'Don't tell me Aladdin's in there, too.'

'No. I'm out here.'

'Your legs are out here. Where's your head!'

'Where it should be. Hey, I can see the New Man. He's having coffee with God. You won't believe this, but he takes after his father. He's smoking.'

She laughed all the more.

He looked up, rolling his eyes. 'They've asked me to join them.'

'I love you! You're so greedy!' She pulled him by his hair. 'Go on then. Don't keep them waiting!'

'Hosannah!' He entered her, carolling.

Beatriz dug her nails into his back. Lord of the World, please don't take him away from me...

'Are you still interested in Kempin?'

Fuego's voice – all the more menacing through the crackling line.

'What...? Yes...'

'I'll take you to him. Be at the airport. In one hour.'

The line went dead. Daniel hung up, shaking.

Kempin! He had been trying to forget Kempin; trying to catch hold of life. Now that he had his woman, he had everything he needed, God included.

And simultaneously, wanting to finish the unfinished business quickly, storm the castle, judge Kempin, do what he had to do – forgive him? – and be done with it. Finally consecrate the exhumed names: Joseph and Sapphira Perera; Sarika and Allegra and Clara Perera. He had everything, yes. But as long as those names continued roaming the ether for a proper burial, he did not have the freedom to live. Bury them at last! Now! Now when he had defeated cowardice!

'I'm ravenous, Daniel. Shall we eat out?'

He gazed at her, fighting his fear. Her glorious body hidden beneath a shift. He had dressed, too. He imagined he looked like a figure in an early Picasso: touched by death. 'Beatriz...'

She saw his fear. 'What is it? Who was on the phone?'

'Fuego.'

She stiffened. 'What does he want?'

Daniel fumbled for a cigarette. He had not told her about Kempin. He had wanted to. 'Beatriz... I have to go away...'

Her voice stifled a scream. 'We've got to get home! I've got a gun there! We'll barricade ourselves! He'll have to kill me first before he can touch you!'

Daniel forced a smile. Such a brave woman – born brave. 'Love, you don't understand...'

'He's after you – for saving Huaman!'

'He doesn't know about Huaman.'

'Don't be a fool, Daniel!'

'Listen, my love, listen. He's... going to help me... I have to meet someone. He's arranged it.'

'What someone? Who?'

'It's a long story. I'll tell you one day.'

She calmed down a little. 'You said that once before. Obligations, you said. Tell me!'

'Another time. I have to go.'

She moved away from him as if repulsed.

'Beatriz... Trust me... I swear...'

'This meeting... It's dangerous, isn't it?'

'Not with Fuego around.'

'Fuego is your enemy! Our enemy! Everybody's enemy!'

He held her by the hand and sat her on the sofa. 'Beatriz... I'll be back – tomorrow, all being well. And I'll be free...'

'Free? Of what?'

'Look, go to Jerry Rice. Tell him Fuego is taking me to Kempin. He'll explain everything. Reassure you...'

'Don't go!'

'Trust me, my beauty. I'll be free. Free – to be blessed by you.' He rose sheepishly. 'To the end of my days.'

She let him embrace her. 'Don't go!'

He edged towards the door. 'Trust me.'

'Don't go! Don't go! Don't go!'

He paused by the door. 'I love you.'

As he slipped out, she screamed. 'They'll kill you.'

27
Without earth, without abyss

Guillermo checked his charts again. Two refuelling stops: one at a cocaine refinery in northern Amazon, the other at a trans-shipment centre in the Caribbean. Both airstrips were in the hands of independent *coqueros* who, as rivals to the barons and the government, were unlikely to inform on him. True, he would have to buy their services by smuggling a consignment of cocaine into the US, but that was all right. Even if he got caught, there would still be life, whereas once the Bridegrooms swooped on him...

What are you waiting for then? The Cessna is ready.

He moved to the window and scanned the airport. His office, situated in the small-craft perimeter, offered an excellent view of the other three compounds. The domestic section had closed for the night; the international terminal was quietly awaiting the last flight, an Air France, due at midnight; and the activity at the military precinct had settled down since General Fuego had taken of – in a helicopter with Daniel Brac under custody.

Guillermo checked his watch. Ten minutes since they had left. Towards the east. Fuego was playing safe. Daniel, after all, was an important gringo; his disappearance would spark off investigations from international bodies; and bribery being the profitable industry it was, they would unearth the facts. Not so, if no one knew or saw how Daniel had been hauled into a helicopter.

An hour, and Daniel would confess everything – no one kept quiet whilst dangling over the void. Half an hour after that, the Bridegrooms would seize Guillermo for helping out in Huaman's rescue.

Run then! What are you waiting for?

Guillermo watched an ambulance drive across the tarmac. Somebody in the Air France must have been taken ill.

He picked up the telephone. He would try Jerry Rice once more.

Fuego had not foreseen this. He, Guillermo, was witness to Daniel's abduction. Jerry Rice would act on the tip-off, unleash a storm.

Rice's number was still engaged.

Ring Beatriz!

I can't. I can't hit her with such news.

Then run, *hombre*. They have telephones in the US, too. You can ring tomorrow. It's not as if you can save Daniel. He's dead.

One last try.

He redialled Rice's number. Outside a vehicle screeched. He craned for a look. The ambulance. Medics.

He heard Rice's number ring. Simultaneously, he recognised the first medic. Tall, handsome, golden-haired.

He heard Rice on the line. 'Yeah?'

He dropped the telephone. He remembered, too late, that swooping in ambulances was the Bridegrooms' latest sophistication. It put victims off their guard.

Rice was still on the line. 'Anybody there?'

The Bridegrooms stormed in. They hauled Guillermo on to a stretcher. He could not resist. 'Where are you taking me?'

Colonel Angelito smiled disarmingly and waved a hypodermic syringe. 'We heard you were going to disappear. We came to give you a hand.'

Guillermo lost consciousness with two thoughts in his mind: Daniel must have talked within minutes; Rice was still on the line...

28

To bury those that do not want to die: carnations, water, sky

The dining-room suite was Chippendale. Large table. Two places laid out.

Daniel glanced across at the skeletal man perched on the leather armchair. Heinrich Kempin had started giggling again, dribbling saliva. Was this the man who had stood as tall as the trees on the snow, loading his machine-gun with journeys to heaven whilst Joseph Perera and the partisans dug their common grave? So much of the past had been clouded by the cataract of time. He would not have recognised Kempin under different circumstances. Only the occult gaze of the piercing blue eyes had not changed.

Teresa entered. Dressed in rags. Like those worn in concentration camps. Bearing a yellow Star of David.

Kempin walked in. In SS-Standartenführer uniform. Bemedalled and shimmering. Old man looking young.

He smiled at the camera. Grabbed Teresa's hand. Exposed the inside of her arm. A number had been tattooed. The camera zoomed to a close-up: 12345678.

One, two, three, four, five, six, seven, eight. A joke? Someone learning to count? Or a ledger of extermination continuing endlessly?

Daniel turned to Fuego. 'Do we have to watch this?'

Fuego appeared to be asleep. 'Unless you know which snake bit you, you cannot find the right antidote.'

'I know this snake.'

'Not well enough.'

Kempin dropped Teresa's arm. 'Now, Esther, we make shabbas.'

Teresa offered a coquettish smile. Took his hand. Ran it over her breasts.

He slapped her. 'You don't rush a ritual!'

She bit her lips. 'I apologise. I find being a Jew very difficult, Manku. I am an Inca virgin.'

'No excuses. You must be a Jew first. I took great pains to instruct you. Now perform!'

Ingenuously, she tackled her part. She pointed at the table. 'We are ready to receive the Queen of the Week!'

'Have you performed your ablutions?'

'I am going to the mikvah *now*.'

Kempin burst into spasms of giggling.

Daniel glared at him. 'Bastard!'

Kempin ignored him. He had ignored them since their arrival. He was of sound mind only on video.

The scene dissolved into the interior of a luxurious bathroom. A king-size tub was filled with water.

Teresa and Kempin entered.

Teresa undressed.

When Daniel had first met her, she had been a skinny girl with a definite stoop. Now, she was robust. And her naked figure was attractive, almost opulent.

Teresa got into the bath and began to wash.

The scene was arousing him. Him, Daniel Brac, who hated sadism, who prided himself on his gentleness, who treated a woman's body like a temple.

He tried to think of something else.

Fear. Still absent.

They'll kill you, Beatriz had shouted. It had not frightened him. He had been agitated leaving the Museum, but that had been no more than the anxiety of reaching the airport late, of missing Fuego. He had not paused to think how he would confront Kempin, whether he would dare do anything in Fuego's presence. The behaviour of a somnambulist.

Teresa finished washing. Stood up to get out of the bath.

Kempin stopped her. 'Aren't you forgetting something, Bathsheba?'

She smiled, grateful for the prompt. She picked up a pair of scissors.

'My hair must be shorn. Like a bride's. I must not attract other men.'

'Strictly speaking, not a shabbas *ritual. But there is virtue in zeal.*'

She began cutting her hair.

Very calm when he had met Fuego. Their first meeting since Monte Rico.

Fuego, disdaining to shake hands, had bustled him into the helicopter. One terse remark: he had found out about Huaman's rescue. Even so, no fear.

In close-up: lumps of Teresa's hair blocking the outflow. The camera pulled back. With stubbly hair, she looked like a boy. Somehow still feminine. But more vulnerable.

She stepped out of the bath. Faced Kempin, eyes seeking approval.

Kempin nodded curtly. Took out a wig from a box. 'Your *sheitel, Jezebel.*'

The *sheitel* made Daniel's flesh crawl. A relic of the ghettos; a symbol of the Jews meekness. *Sheitels* had formed mountains in concentration camps; before that, in countless pogroms, they had been transfixed on swords.

Kempin was still giggling. Daniel thought he could kill him.

The dining room again. Teresa, wearing the sheitel, *but still naked. Anxious, as if she had forgotten her lines.* 'What do I wear?'

Kempin pointed at a length of silk draped over a chair.

She unfolded it. The camera tightened to a close-up.

It was a Torah mantle, exquisitely embroidered with gold thread. Looted from a synagogue. In Yugoslavia?

Teresa was trying to wrap the Torah mantle around her body. It was too small.

'Wear it like a shawl, Miriam. That will suffice.'

No fear either during the flight. Just wisely tense as he kept reminding himself that throwing undesirables off planes had become routine procedure with the SES. And confident that with only the pilot and Fuego in the helicopter, he could put up a good fight, at the very least, take them with him.

No fear even when they had landed and he had seen all those Bridegrooms lined up at Kempin's airstrip.

But a sense of journey's end. Without a grain of triumph or disappointment. A feeling of meaninglessness instead. Because though it had been a long journey, the short path he had actually trodden had been too easy.

And a sense of breaking a taboo. As he had walked to that grotesque castle, as Fuego had pointed out Kempin standing at a window in the tower, a sense of violating the past. Churning old dust should only be fantasised, never attempted. Because resurrection was God's métier.

'Perform your duties, Judith.'

Teresa had draped the Torah mantle over her shoulders. The hint of modesty accentuated her nudity.

'May I have some money? Before the advent of the Sabbath, one must set aside something for charity.'

He gave her a few coins.

She placed them under a vase on the mantelpiece.

She emanated such holiness, that girl. No wonder she had spellbound the countryside.

There had been a large crowd along the castle's perimeter. Waiting for her to return with Manku Yupanqui, Fuego had told him, waiting for weeks.

Teresa moved to the sideboard. Picked up two silver candlesticks. Aligned them at the top of the table.

The relief on one candlestick depicted Abraham leading Isaac to sacrifice; on the other, Jacob's dream. Sixteenth century, Daniel thought. From Bosnia. Plundered heirlooms.

Teresa lit the candles. She closed her eyes. Passed her palms over the candles towards herself.

'Why did you light two candles, Lottie?'

'One each for the Lord's commands: "Remember the Sabbath Day", "Observe the Sabbath Day".'

'Why do you close your eyes and pass your palm over the candles?'

'The Talmud says: "The soul is the Lord's candle". The Divine Presence descends upon the Jewish home every Sabbath.'

'You're doing very well, Hettie.'

'I am so pleased, Manku.'

The Perera household had not been an orthodox one. Joseph and his wife, Sapphira, had observed the high holidays, but little else. Daniel could not remember whether there had ever been a Sabbath celebration. Now, he felt deprived of a spiritual dimension.

Teresa was reciting: '"Blessed art thou, O Lord our God, King of Universe, who has sanctified us by thy commandments, and commanded us to kindle the Sabbath light."'

She moved a step back. Appeared to be praying silently.

'What are you doing now, Sadie?'

'I am asking the Father of Mercy to continue bestowing on me and my loved ones His loving kindness. To make me worthy of righteousness, loyal to His law and able to perform good deeds. To protect me from all manner of shame and dishonour. I am asking my God to be a light of peace, to be a light of peace to me for ever.'

Daniel fought back his tears. Stop behaving like a Jew. You're a Christian. All this is alien. Detritus of a faith renounced. Why then do I feel such loss? Because you're thinking of your family. But they were different. They were good Jews! Not like the rest! Aren't the rest like everybody else – mostly good, a few bad? If they were, they wouldn't be hated all these centuries.

Admit it, you hate the Jews, too! You hate their chosenness, their archaic rituals! Why do they have to be different? Let them join us or perish! Oh, sweet Jesus! What am I saying?

Teresa placed two braided leaves by the candles.

'What are they for, Leah?'

'They represent the double portion of manna provided by the Lord for the Sabbath.'

She covered the bread with embroidered napkins.

'And that, Havvaleh?'

'Bread is the staff of life. Whilst we bless the wine, we must not slight the bread.'

She put a bottle of kosher wine and the Kiddush cup next to the hollas. 'We can welcome the Sabbath.'

'Good shabbas, *Sheineh.*'

'Shabbath shalom, *Manku.*'

The *shalom* did it. A word that had been evergreen for the Pereras. Peace. The father who had attained heroism, the mother who had died in a tangle of bodies and excreta, the sisters drowned and hacked – they had all loved peace.

Daniel burst into tears. 'Oh, God, Oseas. I'll kill him!'

Fuego smiled.

Kempin was reciting the Kiddush over the wine. '"Blessed art thou, O Lord our God... who createst... holy Sabbath as an inheritance... a memorial of the creation... For with thee is the fountain of life... in thy light do we see light..."'

Daniel's mind began to retreat.

Kempin and Teresa started singing the hymns.

Daniel's mind retreated further.

But there was no relief in this fugue. He could hear what he did not want to see; see what he did not want to hear.

Why should an old Nazi, in SS uniform, enact a Jewish ritual? Because, for evil men, there is pleasure in desecration. Also, every torturer secretly desires to take his victim's place.

'Wrong! This is a demonstration. This is to show vermin for what they are. All vermin must be exterminated. The Jew is the most virulent so he must be destroyed first. With this film you will recognise the Jew. When we have finished with them, we will tackle the rest: commies, Gypsies, Indians, Blacks, Arabs, Chinks, Japs, mixed bloods...'

That was Kempin speaking. In person? Or on video?

Fuego was chuckling. 'Does that answer your question, Daniel?'

'What question? Did I ask a question?'

Fuego kept on laughing.

'And Teresa, desperately trying...'

'Vermin are interchangeable.'

'...Trying to substitute for a Jewess – occasionally succeeding, often grotesque, but always preserving her inner self which is Indian and and pure, but alas, mad... what does she see in this charade?'

The voice echoed in the room. Daniel was surprised that it was his own voice.

'She sees redemption through suffering.'

Through a veil of tears, Daniel tried to focus on Fuego. 'Does she know she is suffering?'

'She knows she is being tested.'

'By a maniac!'

'By man. Kempin is in our image. Therefore, she is also being tested by God, the original image.'

Kempin discarded his trousers. Kept on his boots and bemedalled jacket.

'The Crucified One, Daniel. That's who she hopes to find at the end of the road.'

Teresa served the Sabbath meal.

Gefilte fish, *knaydel* soup, roast chicken, *tsimmes*, apple crumble. Traditional.

'Traditional to the Ashkenazi, North European Jews. Not traditional in Yugoslavia. We are mostly Sephardi.'

'What difference does it make, Daniel?'

Teresa ate the gefilte *fish off Kempin's rump.*

Daniel's mind, unable to retreat any further, fragmented.

Kempin drank the knaydel *soup off Teresa's vagina.*

Fragments like broken pieces of mirror; each piece reflecting a different vista.

Teresa climbed on to the table and ate her chicken on all fours. Bare buttocks facing Kempin.

Kempin inserted his chicken bones into her anus.

Don't get aroused!

Teresa licked the apple crumble off Kempin's penis.

Peter, the Fisherman, though he thrice denied his Master, found the courage to embrace martyrdom. The moral of that is: we are allowed to be human – confused – three times. Not for ever – as you choose to be. You know what you have to do. Bring this temple down! But you won't. Because you are enjoying this. Fuego is right. You are in Kempin's image.

They finished eating.

'Now, Rizpah. The apogee.'

Teresa smiled. Divested herself of the Torah mantle. Spread it out on the floor. Lay on it. Opened her legs.

Daniel's mind restructured itself. Voyeur! Pervert!

'The speech first, Yentl.'

'I am a sewer. Do not be misled by my unblemished skin. Like a carpet of flowers on a battlefield, it covers a graveyard. I have beautiful breasts. Moon shaped. With rosy aureoles and thick, protruding teats. Do not imagine they feed honeyed milk. They spurt venom. I have a wine-bowl belly. Watermelon buttocks. Palm-tree legs. A cunt like a lagoon. Labia like hyacinths. Do not be seduced by them. My arsehole is a whirlpool. My mouth – the guillotine. My snatch – the valley of death.'

Kempin shouted. 'Why offer yourself to me then?'

'Because I want to destroy you. Kill your seed in my diseased wells. Exterminate your race.'

'Why?'

'Because I am the Jew. We are vermin. Cloven-footed demons. Perpetrators of genocide. Murderers of prophets.'

'But you are not invincible!'

'Of course, we are.' She lifted her legs and parted them. 'Come, embrace death.'

Kempin stood over her, his penis erect, masturbating.

'Come, I offer you the abomination of desolation.'

Kempin ejaculated.

As his sperm spluttered on her body, Teresa strayed from her role. She cooed a young girl in love. 'Come, Manku. Come, my beloved. Come, to your bride.'

Kempin, giggling, picked up the candlesticks.

He rammed one of them into her vagina.

With the other, he set fire to her pubic hair.

Daniel, retching violently, passed out.

When he regained consciousness, his head was hanging out of the window. He registered the Bridegrooms in the castle grounds; also some by the helicopter. Not on duty, but smoking, talking, laughing. And, in the distance, behind the electrified fence, Teresa's followers. Still waiting.

Fuego pulled him up.

Daniel smelled the vomit on his clothes and heaved.

Fuego handed him a glass of water.

Daniel drank it gratefully.

He saw Kempin, still sitting perched on his armchair, still giggling. He had rewound the video and was watching it all over again.

Daniel threw his glass at him, hitting him on the shoulder.

Kempin did not react, kept on giggling.

Daniel turned to Fuego. 'Teresa – is she...?'

'She is alive. She was lucky he used candles. He normally douses them with petrol. That was how Campbell's Controller was killed.'

'Dear God... How many others?'

Fuego pulled out his revolver and offered it to Daniel. 'Kill him.'

Daniel fought his nausea. 'What?'

Fuego thrust the revolver into Daniel's hand. 'Kill him.'

Daniel stared at the revolver. 'He's... mad!'

'Not mad. Senile. Or rather, selectively senile. He has forgotten the world, but not the Jews. The video where he immolates Campbell's Controller – he sent that to the Israelis. But mainly, he withdraws to the past. Particularly, the war. Even more particularly, Yugoslavia.'

Daniel tightened his grip on the gun. 'Yugoslavia?'

'He relives those days. Kill him and let's go.'

Daniel raised the gun. He caught a glimpse of Teresa, on the screen, shearing her hair. He edged forward. Trembling, he looked at Fuego. 'In cold blood?'

'Cold blood! After what you have seen? He used to do the same in Yugoslavia – on film, they did not have video in those days! Entertained his troops with them! Killed hundreds of Jewesses like that! For all you know, your mother and sister died like that!'

Daniel spun round, the revolver pointed at Fuego. 'No! I know how they died. Not like this...'

Fuego sniggered. 'A better death, was it! Like your father's?'

Daniel wailed. 'No.'

'What is the matter with your blood? You are here to avenge them! So avenge them!'

Daniel stumbled to Kempin's side. Pointed the revolver at Kempin's head. Kempin remained blind to his presence. On the screen, Teresa was draping the Torah mantle around her shoulders. Daniel closed his eyes, urged his hatred to pull the trigger... He whirled round. 'Why do you want me to kill him?'

Fuego smiled. 'I believe in justice.'

'Answer me!'

'Then there is God...'

'Keep God out of this!'

'How can we?'

'The bet, is it? Makes no sense.'

'Makes sense to me. If there is God, you must kill Kempin. Because God wants him punished and has chosen you as His instrument. If you kill Kempin there is no God. Where is His mercy then, His forgiveness? I win – either way.'

'You're insane, you know that?'

'Incidentally, if you are worried about yourself, you have my word. Nothing will happen to you if you kill him.'

Daniel had not even considered that. But it spurred him to face Kempin again. He stared at Kempin's head, listened to his infernal giggling. The hair – or what was left of it – still blond, but lustreless, extinguished. The scalp, thinning, wrinkled, blemished with large patches of purpura. This monster was old, near death. When its soul left its body, it would not rise. It would crawl with its burden of innocents to Judgement. There the blood it had spilled would give testimony. *For with thee is the fountain of life; in thy light do we see light.* And it would receive its eternal sentence.

Daniel dropped the revolver and moved away from Kempin. 'I can't – I won't.' He faced Fuego. 'Your stupid bet. Meaningless. Claim victory. But remember. The commandment – thou shalt not kill – overrides all others. Even if only one person obeys it, he proves God's existence.'

Furiously, Fuego drew his other revolver.

Daniel felt life drain away from his legs. 'Can you tell me where Teresa is? She must need help.'

Fuego fired.

Daniel sank to the floor, surprised that he was not hurting. Easy death? After an easy life?

The sound of furniture falling.

He turned round.

Kempin's armchair had toppled over. Kempin himself lay twisted. Like Joseph Perera in that big hole in the woods. The disintegrated half of Kempin's head had sprayed the wall with large carbuncles.

Fuego was shouting. 'I have done your dirty work, Daniel! Isn't that what you always expect from your God?'

BOOK TWO

PART SIX

29

Will you bring us the algae of the moon, the mysterious stone from Aldebaran and a guitar from Ursa Major?

'His shoulders – can they carry the earth and the sky, water and fire?'

'His hands – can they forge our dreams?'

'Does he breathe our songs and laughter, our tears and ancestors?'

Teresa clasped her hands and pressed them against her groin. The pain was an endless earthquake.

The people were running towards her, shouting joyously. She had not been aware of their number as they had travelled; had only sensed a comforting presence behind her. Now, seeing them cascade over the castle fence, she was gratified.

'Tell us about his smile!'

'And his voice and eyes!'

How pure they were for housing Manku in their hearts. It was their pain she was carrying in her womb because they were her children.

'And tell us about his stride, his strength!'

Could she describe Manku to them? 'If you look at him from afar, you see an arch of light. If you stand close to him, it is like seeing a God. You have to close your eyes.' She pointed at Daniel and Fuego, standing by the gate. 'You can ask these Judges. They are my witnesses.'

'And when you lie down with him?'

Teresa smiled. 'It is like embracing the sun. When he entered me, he scorched me. I still burn.'

The women nodded stoically. Pain, they knew well; they drew their glow from it as the moon draws hers from her dark side.

'Are you with child, Teresa?'

She looked at the sun for the answer. 'I must be.'

Her followers shrieked with delight. They had predicted she would be.

Proudly, Teresa turned to the two Judges. Why did they never smile? Distrust was the tool of their trade, she understood that, but could they not see how these people worshipped Manku? Strange men, the Judges. The old one had disappeared. Then these two had come to escort her out of her chamber. She had immediately recognised them as the young and middle-aged Judges. Strange, too, the way they treated her. Like a child or a sick person. Stranger still: there were times when they did not look like Judges, but familiar, like two men she had met at the time of the massacre in the desert.

'When shall we meet Manku?'

'When will he bless us?'

'When will he place his words, his hands on us?'

Teresa was surprised. 'Did you not see him – when he left?'

They shouted in anguish. 'Left? Has he left?'

'Last night. How did you miss him? He sparkled!'

They whispered animatedly to each other.

'We saw a star run across the sky.'

'That was him.'

They reassured each other. 'Then we did see him.'

'But he did not speak to us.'

'Nor touch us.'

Teresa walked amongst them. She held their hands, stroked their faces. 'Oh, I am sorry. He went to prepare our wedding. He was in such a hurry. I am sorry.'

Happiness infused them. 'Where will the wedding be?'

'On the highest mountain. Where we will build our home – close to the sun. You are all invited.'

'We will live in your light.'

'You will both be branded on our eyes.'

'Come then.' She began to walk, riding the pain, smiling like all suffering servants.

They lined up behind her.

Daniel ran to her. 'Teresa! Wait! Don't...'

She waved at him. 'Come to the wedding.'

Daniel turned to her followers. 'Listen, she's not well! She mustn't go! She needs looking after...'

They appeared not to hear him.

Daniel picked out an old woman. 'Don't you see... This Manku Yupanqui – it's her delusion...'

The old woman was in a trance. 'Come to the wedding.'

Daniel appealed to the others. 'Look, Manku Yupanqui doesn't exist! She didn't see him! There was no joy here! What happened here was abomination! She was raped! Ritually! By a madman! It's affected her mind! Don't you see? She needs care!'

His words flew past them. They smiled in their enchantment. Some offered food, drinks and coca leaves; others gesticulated that he should join them.

Fuego started walking towards the airstrip. There were a number of Bridegrooms on guard duty around the perimeter, watching the procession contemptuously. The helicopter was ready for take-off.

Daniel ran to Fuego. 'Oseas! Stop her! She's hurt!'

'She will be all right. She is an Indio.'

'She needs help, for God's sake!'

'I spit on your God!'

'All right – what about this Manku Yupanqui madness? You've done all you could to stamp it out! Are you now going to let it get out of hand?'

Fuego turned on him. 'If I stop her – will you look after her? Take her home to Beatriz?'

'I'll see she gets some treatment!'

'Your treatment would kill her! There is poison in your goodness!'

30
This blood was falling deeper, was falling towards the roots, was falling towards the dead, towards those who would be born

The Shimmering Darkness, refracting in the heat haze, appeared to be moving. Pushing up valley, river and knolls like a primeval anaconda, it had almost scaled to the edge of La Iglesia de Sangre de Oro's plateau.

Gaspar Huaman upbraided himself for having assumed, before the return from death, that the jungle was a protector, a mother that would hide him beneath her skirts whilst destroying all those who threatened him. The jungle was hostile. It even had hills big enough to be mountains that he had not noticed before.

He moved away from the window and burned the letter from Jerry Rice's Mennonite friend.

He tried to raise his spirits. Deploying to the Shimmering Darkness would offer safety from Fuego and eventually open up the road to the capital. Remember that and just watch out for snakes, vampire-bats, pumas and those clouds of mosquitoes which cluster round the mouth to bite the gullet.

At least he felt fit now. There was still the dull ache of the amputation – and his stump still searched for the severed arm – but he welcomed that. Pain put steel in a man.

He walked out of the adobe. The humidity assaulted him. Across the square, the church glowed. But nothing would redeem its ugliness. A savage heap of monolithic rocks – like all Inca relics.

He began exercising his single arm. He was determined to make it as strong as two. To compensate for his ineffectiveness with a gun, he would excel at hurling grenades. That should silence the voice that urged him to give up the cause, to go back home and infiltrate the government through his family contacts.

He paused to watch the men. They were packing their gear. They snapped to attention and saluted.

They were in awe of him. *They* understood about death and the return from it. It was a journey they suffered daily. What they could not imagine was that a white man, softened by indulgence, was also capable of such a journey. Hence their readiness to believe he was Manku Yupanqui, and their impatience to crown him with the red-tasselled fringe of the Inca Emperor.

He had embraced the idea, at the time of his amputation, as an excellent ruse for raising an army. But now he had reservations. He did not want to undermine his place in history by impersonating a mythical Indio. There was a point where even expediency became dishonourable.

He watched Chauca helping the newest recruit, the campesino from Valdepeñas. Huaman had his doubts about him. The man had had close dealings with the Mennonites – which was why Rice's friends had entrusted him with the message about Guillermo – and was bound to have been proselytised to pacifism. Chauca, arguing that any good man would proudly yoke himself to a just cause, had disagreed. They would see.

Loyal Chauca. Twice the man now, having saved his *Comandante*'s life. No one could think, watching him carry out his duties, that his broken ribs had not yet fully mended. More to the point, it had been Chauca who had brought this new force into being – recruiting all one hundred and seven men, training and indoctrinating them – with more on their way.

Huaman walked towards the church.

Weapons – that was the next step. The new men had brought what they could. Medieval stuff: machetes, slings, clubs and the odd revolver they had managed to steal. Also they must get some uniforms, throw away those stupid Indio rags. Once they had adapted themselves to the jungle, they would have to mount raids. There were a number of Sinchi outposts with bulging arsenals that should prove ideal targets. Blood would be the currency of the future.

Blood. It had been blood, swearing vengeance for his suffering, that had spat at the face of death. Blood, his new diet, as irresistible as freshly baked bread.

He went into the church.

A travesty of holy ground. None of the exquisite rococo that dazzled the eyes in La Merced's cathedral or in the numerous Spanish churches up and down the country. No side altars. A small crypt, at the back, housing Father Timothy O'Neill's reliquary. Not a vestige of any precious metal, let alone the gold that had allegedly poured out of the Irish priest's veins. Not even a sanctuary for the Virgin. And, of course, no organ. Just the basic needs: some ten rows of pews, a crude Communion Table, the Stations of the Cross along the aisles, and a wooden statue of Jesus on the Cross. The last, painted in garish colours, at least depicted blood as it should be depicted – running in streams. The Indio knew how cleansing blood was.

Father Quintana and the six Delegates of the Word – preposterous title – were sitting, huddled, in the front pews. They smiled, as if illuminated by that inner light they constantly prayed for, and waited for him to join them.

Father Quintana had reclaimed his belief in his Sweet Jesus. Well, good luck to him. He had been tested severely, first, when he had amputated Huaman's arm, and then, when he had nursed him untiringly all these weeks. Such devotion deserved recognition and what better than the delusion that Christ, having shown him how to heal, was within him.

The Delegates of the Word would have been a laughing stock had they not been pitiable. They were Indios. In tatters. Emaciated. Anger was what they should have been manifesting – not piety. Their title had more physical weight than the six of them combined. What it denoted was just as preposterous: lay leaders of communities striving to become the foundation stones of a revitalised church. Their aim was to live like the first Christians; to love mankind by learning first to love their neighbours, then to teach them what the spirit of Christ meant, how, in practice, this enabled them to share not only their scant material resources, but also their misfortunes, and how, by doing so, they could improve their standard of living, organise education and health facilities, and, in due course, take their rightful place in the family of man. Father Quintana was their mentor and organiser.

He sat with them. Father Quintana was wearing a new soutane, a gift from the Delegates: a heavily embroidered, outlandish concoction that was both a cassock and a poncho. The old priest had fallen in love with it. It symbolised Liberation Theology, he had said: the man of God marked by the people. Gone native, in reality. Pathetic.

'Well?'

Father Quintana shook his head gently, as if a halo restricted his movements. 'I'm not going with you, Gaspar.'

'You've read Rice's message, Padre. The Bridegrooms have taken Guillermo. They'll find out about this place and they will come down like maddened dogs.'

'We could do much until they come.'

'They might come today. Why do you think we're moving out?'

'We've agreed, have we not, that my presence here won't be a danger to you – that whatever I tell them, they'll soon know you're in the Shimmering Darkness?'

'Yes.'

'Then I'll carry on with my work.'

'The gun – that's the work now!'

'Alas, I agree. But I'm incapable of touching a gun. And I am of more use to you here than in the jungle.' He pointed at the Delegates of the Word. 'We will fan the fires. The more we open the people's minds, the more recruits you'll have. We want your revolution to succeed, Gaspar.'

Tears unexpectedly pricked Huaman's eyes. 'At the risk of your life?'

'You mean, my *earthly* life.' Father Quintana smiled faintly. 'I can live without it. In fact, I believe I *shall* live without it – and much better.'

Huaman stared at the Delegates of the Word. They were shaking devout heads. 'I don't know what to say…'

'Just promise me you'll keep faith with your men.'

Huaman nodded curtly and rose. 'Good luck, Padre.'

'I'll see you off.'

Huaman allowed ten minutes for valedictory rituals.

Those guerrilleros who made burnt offerings rushed through the rites.

Father Quintana, too, was brief with his prayers. He could not decide how best to commend a band of combatants into God's care. So he prayed as if he were praying for himself. He glorified God, sought forgiveness in His Son, and pleaded that He should reveal His purpose to those He had created.

When Huaman's band disappeared down the plateau, Father Quintana moved to the shade of the church, sat on the porch and leaned against the timeless stone.

His mind, as it had been doing more and more recently, wandered to Saint Paul. He had always questioned the little tent-maker's humility, tenderness and forbearance, that self-portrait of 'less than the least of all saints'. He had always felt that the apostle, having worshipped a stern deity before turning to Jesus, had failed to see with his new eyes the truth of a gentle God, the truth of the boundlessness of His love; that a good portion of the ethos that had alienated Jesus from those to whom He belonged, the righteous, the poor, the oppressed, had come from Pauline stringencies.

And yet, it had been none other than Saint Paul who, with his glorious plea to the Romans, had directed him to his calling. *I implore you by God's mercy to offer your very selves to Him: a living sacrifice, dedicated and fit for His acceptance.*

That Good Friday – coincidentally his ninth birthday – when he had first understood those words, was still imprinted in his mind: the irrevocable decision to offer himself as a living sacrifice by becoming a priest; the joyous tears of his mother, hunchbacked from washing other people's clothes; the jubilant shouts from his father, a street cleaner, that this was predestined: what else for a boy christened Eusebio after the early Church father, what else for the third son among ten children – three being the number of the Trinity; ten, the Pentecostal days between Jesus' ascension and the descent of the Holy Spirit upon the apostles? What else, indeed?

But much of his life since then had lacked challenge. School had been a hibernation; ordination a long tedium like a rainy season. And he had wasted a whole manhood in undemanding parishes, abandoning the countryside, like most Latin American clergy, to foreign priests. Only when reawakened by old age some fifteen years ago had he finally pursued his calling and ended up here.

Here, of course, he had struggled. But not enough. And always under assault from that infernal trinity: doubt, fear and solitude.

Now he was near his cross. So near he could smell the alloy of the nails, hear the sap oozing from the freshly cut wood. Now, life eternal was on offer, and his skin was alive and fit for sacrifice.

The question was: would he dare arrive at his cross? Or would he run, at the next step, to that other wilderness – the lush one that mocked Jesus' desert – where the earthly life postured as the only gift from God.

31
The jasmine of the wasted human spring

'How did it go?'

'Kempin's dead.'

Rice negotiated his way towards the drinks table. It was not midday yet but he looked drunk. 'That much I know.'

'How...?'

'Big news splash. The government's taking all the credit. Nazi war-criminal killed resisting arrest. Proof that the country is a justice-loving democracy. Want to tell me what really happened, Dan?'

Daniel stared past him at the bedroom door. 'What's this about getting ready? I've seen her in all her states!'

Rice rummaged through the whisky bottles until he found one that was not empty. 'She's been mourning. She didn't think you'd make it.'

'When I rang – didn't you tell her?'

'She wouldn't believe me.'

Daniel shouted. 'Beatriz! I'm here! I'm back!' The bedroom door remained closed. 'This is ridiculous!'

'Will you have a drink?'

'All right.' Daniel lit a cigarette, then looked around the room. Boxes packed with books; a desk where the typewriter and telephone were submerged by newspapers, magazines and sheets of copy. The kitchen counter piled with shoes, jars, pots and groceries; the sink full of dirty dishes. Clothes hooked on the pictures on the walls; laundered items strewn on the four armchairs; and an untidy sleeping-bag fighting for space on the floor.

Rice handed him his drink. 'Looks like a tornado hit the joint, huh? I insisted she had the bedroom.'

'She stayed here all the time?'

'We played father and daughter. Did us both good.'

'I got worried.'

'*You* got worried? You disappeared for three days!'

Daniel swirled his drink. The lie had popped out easily. He had not been worried. He had not known how to face Beatriz. How could the heart, the eyes, speech and touch be the same after Kempin? He had taken a long time, upon his return last evening, to make his way from the airport to her villa. Not finding her, he been relieved. He had taken just as long to go to the atelier and had been equally relieved to find it empty. He had wondered, briefly, where she might be. Then, he had gone to sleep. This morning, he had contacted Rice. But he had not rushed over.

Rice, pushing aside some underwear, sat in an armchair. 'I'd like to know what happened, Dan. Off the record.'

'Another time.'

'That bad?'

Daniel pointed at the packed books. 'Moving out?'

'Sending them to the States. To my sister.' He smiled, self-deprecatingly. 'I've never been able to throw away a book.'

Daniel gulped down his drink, uninterested. He cast an impatient look at the bedroom door, then picked up the whisky bottle. 'Mind if I have another?'

'Help yourself. It's been rough here, too. They've got Guillermo.'

Daniel looked up sharply. 'Guillermo!'

'I was at the other end of the phone when they took him. He'd rung, I guess, to warn us. I could hear Angelito in the background.'

'Fuego said nothing to me.'

'Maybe he's biding his time.'

'He told me about Huaman. He knew about us getting him out.'

'I've warned Huaman.'

'Why Guillermo? Why – after all this time?'

'I'll give you what Beatriz and I managed to piece together. Guillermo was at the airport when you left with Fuego. We think he saw you – thought you were under arrest – and decided to run. We know, from one of my contacts that he filed a flight plan for somewhere in the Amazon. We think the airport alerted the SES. They have lists of people who mustn't leave the country.'

'Are you suggesting – if I hadn't gone with Fuego...'

'Who can say? But I think that's what Beatriz thinks. She is shattered. Not only the loss of a friend. It was she who involved Guillermo. And, naturally, she thought you'd disappeared, too.'

'What will you do – if Fuego comes after you?'

'Fight my balls off. I've sent my account to the paper. They won't publish it – not now. But they sure will if one of us disappears. I've also alerted some of the watch-dog institutions – via the International Telephone Exchange which SES monitors. So they know – if they touch us, there'll be a hell of a stink. *You* fight, too, Dan! You've also got clout!'

Daniel nodded vaguely and stubbed out his cigarette.

The bedroom door opened. Beatriz emerged. A crescent moon of a smile, wide, beneath a face in shadow.

Daniel stood up, hesitantly. 'Hello... love...'

She was wearing the shift she had had on when he had left her – badly creased now and stained with perspiration. She was gaudily made up. A travesty of her normally subtle application of cosmetics.

She moved to him, trying to keep her smile together. But her lips sagged, her eyebrows protested, and her tears erupted. Then she started pounding him with her fists. 'Are you free now? Are you free now?'

He took the blows silently, nodding automatically.

Suddenly, she was spent. She clung to him and laid her head on his chest. He pressed her against himself.

She began to laugh. And still cried.

He thought of stroking her hair, but could not. 'It's all right. It's all over...' He wondered whether he was trying to comfort himself. For he could have been holding anybody. He felt nothing.

32
To impose their heaven on us all by wounds or pistol

Angelito watched the group of Indians waiting to undergo baptism in the creek. The wind, charging at the estuary from the sea, carried the chilled spray of the Humboldt Current. The village of Las Dunas, subsisting on fishing and sea-coal, cowered behind the shifting dunes that had given it its name. The coastal Indians, save for the purple cheeks of high altitude, looked the same as their Andean counterparts: spectral.

Dr Luke Williston flashed his beatific smile. 'Baptism, Angelito. From the Greek word for drowning. The good people here are identifying with Christ's death and resurrection. We immerse them three times. First to wash away their sins. Then to drown the person they were. Finally, to give them a new life.'

It was a sacred day for the Indians, the Feast of San Juan, celebrating Saint John's pronouncement, *Behold the Lamb of God*. It had become doubly sacred, with the absorption of an ancient ritual soliciting the fertility of the flocks, as the *Day of the Sheep*. Williston's missionaries had added a third celebration by organising mass baptisms.

'Yes, sir!' Williston, wading through the surf, might just as well have been walking on it. The effect was the same. He had come to judge the zeal of his missionaries. But he had not been able restrain himself from officiating in the baptisms. 'We are chosen to cure man of his malignant disease. And by golly, we're giving them the right medicine – *The Word as Antibiotic*!'

They were certainly giving medicine: assorted drugs – from a tent manned by missionary wives rudimentarily trained in nursing – to any Indio who complained of an ailment. But only after he or she had been baptised. They were also giving, again after baptism, the actual *Word*, copies of the Bible translated into Quechua, though none of the Indians could read. Later, they would give sheep – the rarest of luxuries – so that the community could make its fertility offerings and eat the rest. All told, this would be a memorable Feast of San Juan. But it would be the last for these people. Tomorrow, when the streamers and confetti were swept away, Moral Crusade would demand full conversion for continued beneficence. By next year, drinking would be forbidden; and any vestiges of Catholicism or syncretism would be declared an unforgivable sin.

'But make no mistake, Angelito. If we let the iron in our calling rust, we shall most certainly fail.'

Those baptised, though shivering in the cold, appeared to be on fire as they sang the missionaries' hymns. Those waiting to be baptised stared at the waters in terror as if a leviathan lurked there. Which it did. *Two* leviathans, Angelito thought: the white man and his religion. The first, still gold-hungry; the second, still the slayer of cultures.

'What do you think?' Williston was standing in the water with his back to the ocean, gazing at the wilderness before him. With his massive frame solid as armour, he looked like Pizarro stepping ashore.

'Very impressive.'

Williston faced Angelito, brimstone eyes turning soft as lamb's fleece. 'Never fails to turn me on, baptism.' He waded out of the water. 'Should give you an idea of *our* power.'

Angelito handed him a towel. 'I never underestimated your power.'

Williston began rubbing his head dry. 'You had your doubts. Nowadays, people hardly believe God-fearing men can also be warriors. They forget history. *Crusade*, Angelito. We don't use the word in vain – particularly those of us on the move in Washington's corridors of power.' He started walking briskly towards his station-wagon. 'Let me get changed before I catch my death of cold.'

Angelito, tidying up his uniform – it would need to be cleaned: the sand and the spray had marked it – followed him.

'Still – doubts are natural. Healthy. And when they're dispelled, you get a smile on your face. I had doubts about you, too…'

Angelito looked up, offended. 'You did?'

Williston beamed. 'Not any more. Not since I saw you in action in Monte Rico.'

Angelito was flattered. 'That was nothing.'

'A segment is all it takes to know an orange.'

Angelito smiled. The day had been highly enlightening. As he had escorted Williston to Las Dunas to see, as Williston had put it, what the Moral Crusade shop had to offer, he had revised his opinion of the man. A weirdo, certainly; but never a functionary. A fanatic. With a very sharp mind. Prepared to use anything that would further his cause – not unlike himself in that respect. Healing the world of its malignant disease, for instance. Inspirational. Straight out of Hitler.

'Take a look here, Angelito.' Williston had stopped near a missionary who was recounting the story of Salome and John the Baptist to a group of Indian youths. The latter were captivated. '*The Word as Antibiotic* – see how they're lapping it up.'

Angelito saw. So easy to seduce these so-called Children of the Sun. All they wanted was the lotus of myths and fantasies. Which explained why they were for ever condemned to lightless ages. Which also explained why political ideologies seldom appealed to the Indios.

'We save them today. And tomorrow they'll give us a society as orderly as that of the ants. Then we shall have Mammon, not as an unruly idol set up by Satan, but as the Lord's servant. I tell you, we can make this planet what the Lord made of America: the Coming Kingdom on earth!'

Angelito smiled. Such absurdity! But it would do – as long as it brainwashed the masses. In the final analysis, weren't all ideas absurd, weren't they all rooted in some myth? The Cross, in one guise or another, stood the best chance of mastering this retarded continent – he could see that now. Consequently, he could also see what a formidable force Moral Crusade was and how it would perfectly complement New Order's ambitions. That was the message for the *kamaraden*: if they thought the alliance was a marriage of convenience, they should think again.

Williston, feeling the chill, hurried towards the limousine. Angelito followed him.

'What were we talking about before I got carried away? Oh, yes. Kempin. Stroke of genius, getting Fuego to do it. Didn't resent it, did he? Wasn't fond of him or anything?'

Angelito swept his tongue over the crowns that had replaced the teeth he had lost during his fight with Fuego. 'Fuego doesn't lose sleep over anybody.'

'That's how it is with the damned. But rejoice! We did the smart thing about Kempin. We can now stop worrying about Brac and the Jew-boys. But more important, you should see the headlines back home. Victory against Fascism! Brave New South America!'

'Made quite an impact in Europe, too.'

'Dandy. But it's back home that counts, Angelito. We've got more human rights morons than the rest of the world put together. This'll shut them up! And give me and my buddies plenty of elbow room to exploit it. If an ageing war criminal can set up a stall here, just imagine what Commies in their prime can do – that sort of thing. Put the fear of the Lord into every good American!'

'It's a good line.'

'We're thrusting for Christ, conquering souls, defeating perdition. And there are times when we have to fight Satan with Satan's weapons. The Lord Himself has shown us how to confuse the enemy.'

They reached the car. Williston brought out his spare suit, as perfectly tailored as the one he had ruined. 'Stand in front of me, will you. Turn your back. Let's show these natives decency is next to Godliness.'

Angelito positioned himself as asked, disappointed that he would not see Williston undressed. Did he really wear nappies?

Williston started taking off his clothes. 'What about the *kamaraden?* How's their morale after Kempin?'

'There are some who are despondent – mainly the old horses. I'll see they're put out to pasture – their time is up anyway. I'll also suggest new measures. Like promoting our young technocrats; recruiting fresh blood, particularly from problem industries. I'm also going to blame Kempin's death on the Jewish conspiracy. That should get the adrenalin going.'

Williston, stark naked now and crouched behind Angelito, dried himself. 'Just what the doctor ordered. Mark you, putting down the old – that's not likely to be easy.'

'Easy enough. We're very skilled at surgery.'

Williston sprayed himself with his pine-oil deodorant. 'The Lord be with you, Angelito. You're now in Kempin's shoes – the guy your party will be looking to for inspiration. Show them you're destined for the very top. It's the likes of you who make history – not followers and back-room boys.'

Angelito beamed. 'I intend to.'

Williston started putting on his clean suit. 'One other thing – Huaman... People are saying he is Manku Yupanqui. You've got to deal with him before he becomes a pest.'

Angelito spat venomously. 'We're hampered by Fuego's whim. He wants to give Huaman rope – or so he says.'

'Hmm. Tricky fish, Fuego. The Lord, for reasons known only to Himself, has endowed him with too much power. So we've got an Indio who thinks he's better than us – and that's worse than a nigger or a Yid. We've got to push him. Stalk him like a coyote. Move where the wind doesn't carry our smell.' Williston, fully dressed, scrutinised himself in the car's window. 'Right. Let's get the hell of here.'

33
The general in whose hand sleep thirty denarii

The Inca Atahualpa recounts his dream to the attending princesses. The Sun, his father, was shrouded in black smoke. The sky and the mountains appeared to be aflame. And a sacred spirit warned with the voice of thunder that iron clothes would blot out the horizon.

These people who celebrated their Saint's Day in outlandish costumes and grotesque masks, who drank and danced to stupor for a few days, who plunged further into debt to nourish their faith, who offered the Church their meagre produce like eggs, potatoes and maize, who bequeathed pathetic heirlooms, coins, photographs in propitiation for sins not committed, who begged the Virgin for health, work, food and fertile spouses... Why had he come to rub shoulders with them?

Atahualpa summons his soothsayer and commissions him to interpret his dream.

Fuego ploughed through the spectators around the Plaza de Armas. He had come incognito, he mocked himself, in a tattered suit, like a king in disguise.

The soothsayer wails. The Sun's eclipse augurs the destruction of the Inca Empire and religion. There have been other bad omens: earthquakes; tidal waves; broken rainbows; meteors; condors falling dead from the skies. Viracocha's prophecy is upon them. Bearded white men will be coming from the sea.

He pushed to the front of the crowd. A boy, wearing a devil-mask and assigned to keep the acting area clear, prodded him with his trident to stop

248

him from moving further forward. Typical. Give an Indio a drop of power and he forgets he is a slave.

The Spaniards arrive on a blue sheet, then step on the earth. They wave their sabres and cudgels and fire their guns.

He scrutinised the boy's devil-mask: a plaster snake crowning the horse-hair mane; huge glass eyes like beacons; sharp, pointed ears; bayonet teeth. Not as good as the ones he used to make. Really evil, his were. He used to come out of the mines and pour all his hatred into them.

A runner announces the landing of the bearded men. The princesses are horrified by the description of the iron suits and horses, awed by the fact that the white chieftain's hair is the colour of blood.

He had forgotten how bizarre the actors looked. The Inca princesses in white dresses, gold-paper coronets, sun-glasses and umbrellas; Atahualpa in embroidered poncho, red-tasselled fringe, ornamental staff and an ancient pocket-watch. The soothsayer leading a dog; the other Incas, dragging a motley of animal skins. Those playing the Spaniards in modern army uniforms.

Atahualpa sends the soothsayer to make overtures to the white men.

What was he doing here? He had a country to rule.

He could say he was a lonely man. Kinless. Friendless. Loveless. Godless. And such destitution was unbearable at fiesta time. But that would be flippant. He ruled like a potentate. At this very moment, there were a hundred lackeys at his hacienda celebrating his power. As for loneliness, he actually preferred being alone. Like a toilet attendant, when he had a day off he wanted fresh air.

The soothsayer meets the enemy triumvirate: Francisco Pizarro; his partner, Diego de Almagro; the Dominican friar, Vicente de Valverde. He asks: what brings them here?

Why had he come here? To Ciudad Esmeralda?

Because the masque here was the best in the country. Centuries old. It changed every year to reveal the Indio's vision. The Spaniards' goose-steps, for instance. That was how the campesino saw the army – like Daniel's Nazis.

Almagro moves his lips without saying anything. The Spaniards' interpreter translates the movements of Almagro's lips: they have come to eat gold.

Why not admit it? He came here because he had a soft spot for Ciudad Esmeralda. He was stationed here – when he was a captain. When he could still remember his Indio name, Cayllahua; when the alias, Fuego, was still a pretence of the fire it connoted. When there were so many generals fighting for power, he didn't know which arse to lick and had decided, in case he licked a loser's arse, not to lick any. So he had swung a posting here. Guarding the emerald mines. Chasing the poachers who, like his *guiñero* father, dug tunnels in the hills. The happiest two years of his life. No danger. Hardly any killing. A string of women. And especially Blandina with whom he had set up house. Lovely, she was, worthy of the saint's name she had been christened with – not much older than Teresa.

Friar Valverde clothes Almagro's bluntness with fanatical piety. They have come to save the Incas' souls.

When Kempin had discharged the abomination of desolation, Teresa had smiled.

People have three hearts, Blandina used to say. With the first they love; with the second they hate; with the third they breathe.

Pizarro, hidden behind a genial face, gives the soothsayer a letter for Atahualpa.

That youth playing Pizarro. That's my son. One of my sons.

How many sons did he have? How many daughters! Who knew? A soldier's life. He had moved around. Picked up temporary wives. Who cared?

But he had kept track of this one. Because he had seen him born? No. Out of curiosity.

Pizarro's letter mystifies Atahualpa and his dignitaries. They think it is a maize leaf. But since they have been told it contains a message, they place it on their ears. It emits no sound. Atahualpa then examines the writing. Seen from one side, the letters look like a colony of ants. Seen from another, they resemble the imprints of birds' feet on river banks. Seen from a third side, they appear to represent dead animals with their feet in the air. And seen from a fourth side, they seem to depict a herd of llamas who have grown antlers. Impossible to understand what they mean.

Why had he abandoned his children? Did he think they would end up hating him? As he had hated his father?

But his father had surrendered earth and sky to the white man. They had told him to live under their heel; he had done so. They had told him go chew up the mountain and give us the cud; he had done so. They had told him, let the mountains eat you as our offering; he had done so. He had died like the rubble he had mined – not even metal.

Atahualpa sends his envoy to Pizarro. The bearded men must take to their ships and leave.

Anyway, fathers were always hated – even the strongest. That's why Daniel couldn't kill Kempin. Daniel hated his father, so much so he even betrayed the God he loved. Renounced the hero's strength he craved.

Pizarro responds to the envoy by moving his lips silently. The interpreter translates. The white men are here to stay.

All Daniel's talk about God meaning forgiveness – pious farts! Daniel's heart of hate triumphed over his other hearts. That's how it was with most people. Daniel was simply a late developer.

When the envoy reports Pizarro's words, Atahualpa orders his generals to mobilise for war.

The first heart, Blandina had said, is formed by mother's milk; the second, by the poison the world eats which hardens to a stone. The third is a spark from the Sun and we are all born with it.

Pizarro pre-empts Atahualpa and storms the Inca's palace.

The first lives with you until death. The second can be shat out like a tapeworm. The third never dies; it becomes earth and makes the maize grow.

As his bodyguards lie slaughtered, Atahualpa confronts Pizarro and orders him to withdraw.

You were wrong there, Blandina. You can shit out the first and the third as well. You can shit them out and just keep the heart of hate. That's what Kempin did.

Am I like Kempin?

Pizarro moves his lips. The interpreter translates: Atahualpa is prisoner. His generals will cease fighting for fear he might be executed.

No. He was not like Kempin. He had shat out the heart of love and was using the heart of hate, but the third heart was still inside him – unfound, but inside him.

Was it?

Atahualpa offers to ransom himself with as much gold as can be piled within the radius of a sling-shot.

That was why he came here. To look at himself in the pool of his people. To see in the reflection whether he could ever make the maize grow.

Pizarro finds Atahualpa's offer insufficient. He wants as much gold as will fill the plains. Atahualpa agrees.

When Teresa said 'Shabbath shalom' on that video, Daniel burst into tears. Not ordinary tears. But tears which showed that Daniel had touched his third heart.

It made me envious.

Gold covers the plains of the four corners of the world.

The heart that breathes. My father had it. When that weak man died, he continued breathing. Daniel, another weak man, will do the same. Whereas I, stronger than the puma...

Pizarro reveals his perfidy. The gold is delicious and will be eaten. But he must also have booty for the King of Spain. Atahualpa's head will serve.

My son there. He, too, will breathe after he dies.

Atahualpa prepares to die. He bids his people to retreat to the wilderness.

He promises them: one day, the Son of the Sun will return to chase away the gold-eaters.

My son does not know me.

This morning we crossed paths. Blandina, who could touch all her three hearts, looked ancient. They did not recognise me. Shouldn't blood tell?

If a man shits out his third heart, no one recognises him.

Friar Valverde hands Atahualpa the Bible. Before he dies, the Inca must be baptised and confess his sins. Atahualpa throws down the Bible angrily. Valverde rages at the blasphemy.

His son! An emerald miner! White man's serf! In Pizarro's uniform! What does he think he is doing?

Pizarro garrottes Atahualpa then cuts off the head.

His son was parodying him. Laughing at him. Laughing at this Indio who had become the white man's clone. Accusing him of crushing his third heart with his foot.

The Inca princesses weep and wail. Without their god how can they know which way to turn? Without their god, what else remains but death?

His son was shouting. You, Oseas Fuego, dish out the white man's tyranny! You whip the Indio's face! You betray father, son and self, the mother who died giving you birth, the women who nurtured trees from your seed!

Pizarro, back in Spain, presents the King with Atahualpa's head.

This is where the masque degenerates into a fairy-tale. Time to leave.

Atahualpa's severed head, speaking to the King as one sovereign to another, accuses Pizarro of foul murder.

I have looked at myself. I can see what I am. Tragic that a man like me should be a traitor.

The King judges in Atahualpa's favour and sentences Pizarro to death.

His son shouting again: you can change. You can be what you should be! Just touch your third heart.

The King's musketeers execute Pizarro.

That would take spirit. That would mean crawling back to God.

Atahualpa's head is ceremoniously buried.

Do it!

I'd rather shit it out! Stop the maize growing for all time!

Why?

Because I am afraid of the third heart!

The Inca princesses sing the finale: Atahualpa's body will become whole again. And one day he will return to liberate his people.

Fuego laughed with his second heart.

The spectators rushed on to the square to join the actors. Beating the ground with multi-ribboned staves, ringing bells and waving gaudily painted crosses, they danced, chanted and ululated.

'Atahualpa is back!'

'He is already here!'

'With the name of his forefathers!'

'Manku Yupanqui! Manku Yupanqui! Manku Yupanqui!'

Fuego watched them. They seemed to be calling him.

He pushed his way out of the Plaza de Armas.

Someone – his son? – shouted. Stay with me!

No. You have your hell. I have mine.

34
Where the air is born

It was here that Manku came upon the Sun's missing ray, Teresa had told them. Here he would marry her. Can you see what a grand cathedral we have? Look, the valleys are the nave; the escarpments, the pews; and the summit, the altar.

The people took their places.

Teresa blessed them and proceeded towards the mountain.

The eyes of the people followed her. She was the most radiant bride.

The mountain, rising in a perfect triangle up to the hands of the sky, blossomed with exotic plants wherever she stepped. The Sun stood still at the summit, turning the snow garland into a bonfire that would be seen in the four corners of the world.

The Sun, Teresa had told them, would be officiating; he would marry them as he had married Manku Capac and Cura Occlo, the begetters of the Incas.

When they heard the words, *man and wife*, the people would know that the world had begun to change.

35

The nocturnal hand cuts its fingers one by one until it is no more, until man is born

'What are you looking for, Daniel?'

'The digestives.'

'You must have eaten them.'

'Not all of them! I bought some the other day.'

'Have these – almond ones. They're nice.'

'I've started work. I need digestives.'

'Daniel! You're superstitious! How wonderful! Do you have a ritual? What do you do?'

'I... dunk them in my coffee. Sharpens me up. Helps me to immerse myself...'

'How sweet! I'll go and get you some!'

Beatriz breezed out, blowing a kiss.

Daniel lit a cigarette. He had definitely bought the digestives. At a corner shop, together with some cotton wool. He had been anxious to buy both items before everything closed down for the fiesta. He had intended to start cleaning the third part of the polyptych and could not have done so without the cotton wool. Nor without the digestives which, as Beatriz had observed, had become a superstition.

He started rummaging again. He was anxious to start. He had hardly stopped sleeping since his return from Kempin's castle. Not even the fiesta had managed to drag him out of bed. Reaction, Beatriz had reassured him, normal.

Keep calm! She's gone to get some. It's not a matter of life or death. Not like in the dream.

He stopped rummaging. The old dream. But last night there had been something new in it.

He is searching for carob beans – frantically. Carob beans enable a person to change colour at will and thus survive. He needs them because he is on the run. So far, crossing temperate lands, he has had no difficulty finding them. But now he is on snowy wastes. Though the last batch had blanched him to merge with the scenery, the icy wind is peeling off the whiteness, exposing his real colour. Red the red of the blood that soaks his clothing, that has caked on his hands and face. Unless he finds some beans immediately, he will be spotted. Miraculously, he comes across an open-air tavern standing like an oasis. In its gardens, there is a carob tree. Reaching for the beans, he sees a shepherd, sitting at a table, dunking bread into a large cup of coffee, staring at him accusingly. Suddenly, the shepherd shouts: carob beans erase a man; eat crusts instead; crusts dunked into coffee is *keyf*...

On previous occasions, the dream had always ended with the shepherd's accusatory look. Now, a sequel. *Keyf*, which the Turks had bequeathed to the Balkans, meant bliss. A word much loved by his father.

A memory erupted.

His father, pacing up and down the veranda, drinking coffee from a *finjan*.

Why a *finjan* when Joseph Perera hated small cups and normally used a French *tasse*? Because it was wartime; there were shortages; it was the last of the coffee; no, coffee had become unobtainable; it was pulverised carob beans – from the trees in the garden – which mother served as a substitute; Joseph Perera hated carob, but drank it to please his wife...

His father; pacing up and down; drinking from a *finjan*; picking up a biscuit from a dish on the table; dunking it to make the carob more palatable; eating it distractedly; hands shaking; trying not to cry in front of his family: Sapphira and the children will stay together, hide in a farm; he was joining the partisans; he would visit them often. Dunking another biscuit; *this is not the end but a beginning.* Then weeping: *I don't know how to fight and I am so afraid.*

Daniel sank into the monk's seat. How had he exhumed that memory?

He would admit – albeit not very often – that much as he carried the past with him, that vast span of time was, at best, an impression. Like the memory of a severe winter, a sweeping image of endless frozen days with barely a recollection of how cold it had been, how long the ice had stayed on the ground, how frequently or infrequently the sky had cleared to show that the sun had not departed for good.

He would also admit – but only on those occasions when he could loathe himself without rancour – that the few episodes he did remember – a family occasion or two, odd incidents at the Brač monastery, and, of course, the massacre in the forest – he remembered them only because he had mercilessly branded them on to his mind. He had come to believe, he did not know how, that these memories contained his very identity, that should he forfeit them, he would also forfeit his soul.

He understood – though this he would always deny – that the desperation with which he had imprinted those memories was a defence against some greater horror. How else could he have discounted the conviction that those events were merely figments of his imagination? Or worse, that they had been – particularly his father's execution – his own evil work.

But now, this new memory. Undistorted by time. Dovetailing with the old dream.

The shepherd, he had long ago decided, was his father; the caked blood, his survivor's guilt; the carob beans, his will to live.

A beginning, Joseph Perera had said, dunking a biscuit. Now the son dunked biscuits before starting work. Carob beans erase a man, the shepherd had said. Did that mean that by living his life of flight, he had erased his identity? And not just his, but also that of his father, since the only life Joseph Perera now had was in his son's person?

And *keyf*... Was that Joseph Perera exhorting his son to fight? Instructing him that fighting evil was blessed because it gave meaning to life? Or was the murdered father cursing the boy – caked with paternal blood – for his cowardice, for his refusal to avenge?

Listen, listen. Kempin is dead. I am free of the past.

No. You were free of it until now. Hereafter, the past will possess you. Did you really think you could escape from it by propitiating a few demons?

I suffered!

By wearing the past on your sleeve – like you wear God on your sleeve? By disappearing behind a blindfold all these years trying to forget Kempin?

I pursued Kempin. I got to him.

You couldn't kill him.

If I had, I would have become like him. I am not a murderer.

You've been playing a charade, Daniel. But careful now. With Kempin gone, you're exposed.

How can I – or anyone – touch memories... It's impossible to imagine, let alone feel, the horrors of extermination. If I touch a crucifixion, I would be nailed myself. I would be a Jew. I would never survive.

Your soul would.

If I begin to understand why my people have been insanely erased, if I see that what happened to them was not just an aberration of history but the way of the world, the deed of man – any man, every man – then I would also see there is no design to existence, that every abomination, including the non-existence of God, is possible. How can the soul survive in nothingness?

By going beyond nothingness.

What can there be beyond nothingness?

God? Perhaps the very function of nothingness is to make you seek beyond, to lead you to God.

I want God here – with me. As the promise of life.

But it is life itself that frightens you. Even your work negates life. Restoring the dead. Ignoring the living. Abstaining from creating. Like your metachromatic carob beans, your work camouflages your existence.

What can one create after the gas chambers?

There is life after the gas chambers. There has to be. Or the Kempins will have won. Death would become unmysterious, meaningless; it would cease to be the vortex of life.

Hidden behind a blindfold. One could survive like that.

But there's no escaping life. Ultimately, it catches up with you. Your father… on the veranda… There's something about that incident that stopped you living. Something that stunted you even more than your father's execution. What is it?

My… my father's tears… His pathetic wail: so afraid… How could he? How dared he – that hero? Not that you'd ever have thought he had the makings of a hero. I used to be ashamed of him. Little man, balding, surrendering to a belly, colourless, offering *keyf* and the Talmud to all and sundry, with bird-like movements, fey, looking like an overgrown child. I could never understand why so many people loved him, listened to him, drank and ate with him, would do anything for him. He had a lot of friends among the farmers and the Gypsies, tough people like hewn rock, and there he was, half their size, with no biceps or pectorals, barely a shadow. I could never understand why my mother loved him, touched him all the time, purred when he kissed her, disappeared with him for afternoon naps. I could never understand why my sisters competed for his attention, insisted on sitting on his knees. I used to be ashamed of him and I remember how pleased I was when he told us he was going away to fight. How fervently I wished his visits would be infrequent. I remember I even thought maybe… Oh, God… maybe he might… die… Leave my mother and sisters to me… Me – as I would grow up to be…

Somebody colourful, made of granite, wide as a mountain…?

Is that why I couldn't kill Kempin? Because I didn't want to avenge my father? There was a moment when I wanted to kill him. Not for what he had done to Teresa, but because I saw him as myself. He calls himself Joseph Perera; I said if only for that, he should die. Did I want to kill him then because I saw him as my father? And the next moment, when I told myself this is Heinrich Kempin, soul-snatcher of Jews, my father's executioner, I could no longer kill him. Does that mean I spared him because he had killed my father for me? Did I hate my father?

You hated his cowardice.

But he made himself a hero!

He cried in front of you. You heard him confess his fear. He should never have done that! Everything else is bearable – not that!

But he conquered his fear! He made himself a hero!

And he made you – you, twice his size and strength – a coward! That's unforgivable!

'Here you are, Daniel.'

He jumped out of the seat. Beatriz was waving a packet of biscuits with that summer-day smile of those born brave. He avoided her eyes and crabbed towards the cooker. 'I'll put the kettle on.'

She followed him. 'Can you hold me – while it boils?'

He filled up the kettle, put it on, then faced her. 'With pleasure.' He held her, standing rigid. He gazed out of the window at the campesinos, still keeping vigil in the square.

She pushed him away angrily. 'You insult me – holding me like this.'

He forced a laugh. 'What should I do – crush you?'

'Yes!

'I don't want to harm the baby...'

'Liar! We've hardly touched since you've been back. There are suddenly walls between us...'

'I was drained. I had to sleep...'

'I was drained, too. I still am. I still have nightmares about Guillermo. You hardly knew him. And you've forgotten him, even though...'

'What? What? If I hadn't gone after Kempin, he'd still be alive?'

'I'm not saying that.'

'You're thinking it!'

'Yes. It's wrong of me. I apologise. You couldn't have known. Nevertheless, my guilt – not easy to live with. He was a good person. A sweet lover... Does that make you jealous?'

Daniel was surprised that it did not. 'No.'

'You see – even that's changed!'

'Beatriz, love – I've had a very rough time…'

'I understand. That's what I'm trying to tell you. But not touching – that's not us.'

He spooned out the coffee into cups. He thought of Teresa, contorting for Kempin, offering cunt, mouth and arse for any degradation. He had been aroused – not by the sadism, but by the fact that he had – had had – the gift of expurgating sadism, the vision to see a naked woman as the Holy of Holies, the belief that cunt, mouth and arse suckled the soul as much as God. In fact, he had looked at Teresa with eyes tempered by Beatriz's flesh.

But making a woman a sacred Object had its dangers. When the worshipper witnessed a desecration, he drifted away from his sacred object, taking the sin upon himself.

'Bear with me, Beatriz. Please.'

She nodded, struggled with herself, then snuggled up to him. 'I so missed you. I was so afraid. I was dead.'

He held her – not so rigid now, but muscles still functioning mechanically, spirit still severed from the flesh. It was true that the desecrated could be reconsecrated, but the grace for that was as elusive as courage. 'Poor love.'

'Poor you, darling, poor you.'

'The water's boiling.'

She disengaged passively, made the coffee.

He tore open the packet of dry biscuits and put the contents on a plate. He noticed his hands were shaking.

She sat on the monk's seat and stared at the polyptych. 'Daniel – what colour do you get when you mix blue and pink!'

'Purple – of sorts. Why?'

'Purple it will be.'

'What?'

'The baby's shawl. I've decided to knit something fantastic. I know we take it for granted it will be a boy – the New Man. But just in case it's a girl, purple is perfect. Part you and part me.'

'Sounds good. Purple signifies luxury and power.'

'Let's hope it might also come to mean sublime love.'

Daniel picked up his coffee and biscuits and moved towards the polyptych. 'I'm going to work.'

She moved to the counter and picked up her cup, then, brusquely, poured the contents into the sink.

She grabbed her pen and score sheets and stretched out on the hammock. She stared at the skylight, ready to garner the music that now ripened in her regularly and lushly.

The baby moved. As if to insist that he was more important a creation than her songs. And her immediate reaction to the movement, even after so many times, was of shock. The sudden disbelief that her body was recasting itself, altering metabolically as well as physically, that, in fact, it was no longer her body – not entirely – and that it would never again be because a child always took some of his mother's flesh with him.

Then she felt a smile rise. It told her that not only her body, but also her whole existence had changed. That now there was an added dimension where she and her baby were one and indissoluble. Where they touched. Where they would continue to touch for ever, even after they separated.

Bliss, Daniel. Which no man will ever know.

36

From our love, lives will be born. In our love they will drink water

The snow came down from the Sun, greeting her with showers of golden petals. The peaks, in white plumage and rainbow sashes, stood as sentinels. The condors, summoned from the coastal plains where they had been cleaning up the carrion, interlocked wings to form a canopy. The wind played a thousand sicus; the people sang Manku Yupanqui's song, and though they were far down on the slopes and looked as tiny as ants, their voices rose like church bells.

He is
the water that quenches the gods
the fire that cleanses the past

Teresa reached the summit. This was the highest point in all Tahuantinsuyo. From here, the Inca saw every foot-length of the four corners of his realm; breathed air that would leave the white man gasping; stood unsoiled by the waste that had grown around him for centuries. It was the perfect altar for the wedding that would beget the new world.

She gazed at the depths of the crater. The nuptial bed, woven from the Sun's reeds, blazed like the loins of her beloved. Incense fumed everywhere, smelling of almond – according to the wise old women, the fragrance of fresh sperm. The ice, which the Sun had laid as matrimonial sheets, swelled like the pain inside her.

He is
the earth where the spirit grows
the sky which shepherds the stars

She scanned the mountains encircling the crater. They rose, step by step, a causeway for giant spirits. At the very bottom, where the plains braided garlands, a constellation was rising. It was shaped like a glorious animal. She recognised the mane. Manku, climbing at a run, impatient to possess his bride.

She began to undress.

Dreams come true, Mother Superior! Look at me, Sister Columba!

The clouds, majestic in sombre vestments, laid out the shards of thunder which would chronicle the wedding.

He is
the eagle who husbands the sun
the puma which hurls rainbows

She stood naked.

He was rising rapidly. Brighter than bright. Even more glorious than the last time when he had tested her. Then he had been garbed for ritual and had remained a man; now he was unclothed, in the stature of a man-god as all men would be hereafter.

She lifted her breasts, so heavy with her love for him. Her flesh glittered. Her womb shrieked with ecstasy and pulled open her gates.

He is
the pure milk of a man's eruption
the kiss that opens a woman's legs

He reached the top of the causeway. Next to the Sun he looked like a second sun.

Farewell, Mother Superior. Faith never fails.

His manhood swayed like a eucalyptus tree. He called out with fragrant breath. 'Teresa, my love, my dove, my bride. How beautiful you are, how beautiful…'

Fond farewell to you, Sister Columba.

She cried out. 'Manku!' Her voice echoed across the universe.

He leaped to her side.

She ran to him.

Farewell, everybody!
They embraced.

He is
the hope born today
the stone that will build tomorrow

And they got married.

PART SEVEN

37

Your truth was the truth of the earth, sandy dough, stable as bread, fresh sheet of clay and grain, pure pampa

Beatriz kicked off her sandals and strummed her guitar. Then, wistfully looking out of the window at the people still keeping vigil in the square, she sang.

Come on to the beach
velvet skin
and I'll take you through time

Daniel concentrated on the Inca Dynasty.

The Incas had not developed an alphabet. But they had invented the *quipu*, a system of knotted and multi-coloured strings, to record both their history and day-to-day matters. The Spanish chroniclers, eager to document the past of the people they had so brutally conquered, but failing to unravel the *quipus* – still a mystery today – had had to be content with writing down oral tradition. The royal line was one of the many uncertainties. Fourteen monarchs was the number accepted by most historians.

I'll show you the reign
of the rose and the nightingale
limbs of lovers that rhyme

The iconography of the Inca Dynasty had been a popular theme in colonial art. This trend, in a ruling class rabidly contemptuous of the Indians, was a phenomenon that still challenged the experts. Daniel had wondered whether the romantic image of the Inca as the Noble Savage had advanced the continent's aspirations for independence by inspiring an equally romantic collective identity.

Come on to the beach
velvet skin
come and lie on my purple and fine linen

Fuego, in the days when he used to visit the atelier, had advanced his own theory. The Inca Dynasty had represented for the colonials the spoils of conquest. Like shrunken heads, the portraits of the vanquished paid tribute to the white man: to his Catholicism without Christ standing as the only authority for life on earth; and to his delusion of racial supremacy rooted in his power to enslave peoples, to destroy civilisations and to eat gold.

Beatriz, Daniel suspected, agreed with Fuego.

I know so many love games
we won't know where to begin

'Do you like my new song?'

Daniel peered down from the platform. 'Beautiful.'

'You weren't listening. It's about us. Want to hear it properly?'

'Yes. Please.'

'Hang on.' She pulled her loose-fitting slacks as high as she could. 'The elastic's killing me.' She breathed a couple of times. 'Now, it's pressing on my diaphragm.' She scratched her belly. 'The day this country produces decent maternity wear will be the day we achieve emancipation.' She took another deep breath, then steadied her guitar. 'Here we go.'

She sang the song again.

He listened, sipping his coffee. He had decided to give up biscuits.

She finished singing. 'Sad, isn't it?'

'Who is velvet skin?'

She put her guitar down and sat on the monk's seat. 'You.'

'Me – the rhino? Why not you?'

She stared into his eyes. 'I don't need an invitation to play love games.'

He looked away. 'That's not fair, Beatriz.'

'Not fair to me – I agree. I'm withering away.'

'You're pregnant!'

'You could let me roam over you. You could kiss my breasts. Caress me.'

'After the birth.'

She nodded without conviction and fiddled with her elastic again. Then she looked at her watch. 'Two o'clock...' She got up, trying to generate enthusiasm. 'Let's take the afternoon off! Let's do something... sensuous. Let's go to the cinema – sit in the back row.'

'I've got to work. You go.'

She pondered a moment. 'I won't give you the satisfaction.'

'Meaning?'

She shrugged and went to lie on the hammock.

He stared at her, irritated by her asperity. Then he went back to work.

The painter had ignored tradition in every respect.

In colonial art, the Inca pantheon was represented as portraits framed by medallions, sometimes positioned like individual paintings on rococo edifices looking like triumphal arches, at other times lined side by side in rows. In the polyptych, the Emperors were drawn full length and stood on different levels of a terraced Inca fortress.

In colonial art, the sizes of the portraits were invariably the same. In the polyptych, monarchs of historic stature were represented as giants.

According to Inca custom, the Emperor's attire had to be unique and uniform. In colonial art, the clothing was, in the main, hispanicised. The polyptych had modelled the accoutrements on Indian traditions. Thus, the Emperors were dressed in martial ceremonial regalia: a white tunic-poncho bordered with precious stones stretching down to the thighs; pad-like knee coverings of gold; a multi-coloured striped mantle hanging from the left shoulder; an embroidered woollen bag containing coca leaves in saltire from the right shoulder; a collar-necklace of emeralds; golden sandals with red feathers about the ankles; a crown of cords, ornamented on each side with golden spurs, with a silver clasp, over the forehead, bearing two white plumes of the alcamari vulture and the *borla* band, the scarlet fringe which was the insignia of royalty. In his right hand, the Emperor held a *tumi*; in the other, a rectangular shield with bright geometric designs.

In colonial art, the Emperors were invariably identified by inscriptions blazoning their names and the dates of their reigns. The polyptych identified them only by their names and these were scrawled, with the vehemence of a child's handwriting, across the shields.

Two evocative Inca symbols, the Sun-God and its messenger, the Condor, dominated the background.

The first was an idealised representation of the Punchao. This, the Incas' most sacred effigy, vaguely described by oral tradition as 'a majestic image of the Sun', was the one treasure which the Conquistadores had failed to seize. Reputedly hidden where only Inkarri, on his advent, would find it, the effigy had become a source for legends like the sun's missing ray in the Manku Yupanqui myth. The polyptych's painter, inspired by the Punchao's other connotation, 'dawn', had painted it, on the right-hand side of the sky, in cadmium orange, as a vast effusion of light emanating from an Intihuatana, a gigantic rock where, in Inca worship, the Sun was fastened to the earth.

The second, the Condor, its slate-grey feathers reflecting the Punchao in a pointillistic spectrum of red and yellow, occupied the left-hand side of the sky. Wings outstretched in full flight, it augured the return of freedom.

The most notable difference was in the figures of the Emperors. In colonial art, these were stylised: the bodies, where drawn, were almost identical and statuesquely rigid; the faces, often in profile, had the inanimate expressions of busts on coinage; the colorations of the flesh were invariably in monochromes. The polyptych, however, had been painted with a realism that was all the more enhanced by touches of expressionism; thus, limbs, features and objects, subtly distorted, created an intense emotional dimension reminiscent of Goya. The monarchs, including those depicted as giants, were singular personalities; their complexions were Andean and ranged from ferruginous red to magenta; their physiques varied; the faces, ravaged or scarred or wrinkled, but sensual and always arresting, were pure Indian. Daniel had rubbed shoulders with their doubles on the journey to Pintoyaku.

If he could be objective, the Inca Dynasty was a superior section even to that of Pachamama.

But he hated it. The Incas reminded him of Fuego.

Daniel threw his swab away. He had been cleaning Mayta Capac, the fourth Emperor, child prodigy and the Incas' Hercules. Aiming his *tumi* as Fuego had aimed the gun at Kempin. 'Christ! All I see is Fuego!'

'The offer still stands. Let's go to the cinema.'

Beatriz was gently swinging on the hammock. Her tranquillity, Daniel sensed, was shammed.

'Why Fuego? These are noble faces! Fuego is evil personified!'

'So are you – for him.'

Daniel glared at her. 'What?'

'Not killing Kempin. He'd see that as the ultimate evil.'

'He said that, did he?'

'I haven't spoken to him. But he's an Indian. Right and wrong are clear cut. Revenge. Manhood...'

'What's manhood go to do with it?'

'It's primal.'

'So is compassion!'

'He can't understand your sort of compassion. That's something one acquires. It can only revolt him. Threaten him.'

'And you? Do you feel threatened, too?'

'I don't know.'

Daniel jumped down from the platform. 'Answer me!'

Beatriz stopped swinging, offered a lame smile. 'We could go swimming if you prefer...'

He towered over her. 'You think so, too, don't you? You think I should have killed Kempin!'

She braved his eyes. 'I think there is something dangerous in your passivity...'

He grabbed her shoulders. 'It's not passivity. It's compassion! Forgiveness!'

Her voice turned icy. 'Call it what you like, Daniel. But what's more Christian? Forgiveness or betraying the good people in your life?'

He bellowed. 'Forgiveness! It erases – heals – betrayal!'

'That's frightening.'

His anger drained away. He let go of her. 'It should be reassuring.'

'If you really believe that, you can betray again. If you're just saying it, you're a hypocrite...'

He turned his back to her. 'Is this your revenge?'

'For what?'

'For Guillermo ending up in the death-pit!'

'I told you – I don't hold you responsible for that – not any more. *I* am responsible. *I* asked him for help.'

'All right then. Revenge for what you might call my manhood – or the lack of it!'

Beatriz, incensed, launched herself out of the hammock. 'What do you take me for?'

He spun round to face her. 'On the war-path, aren't you? Sharpening scalpels! Ready to cut my balls off.'

'Cut your balls off? You bastard! I'm trying to put life back into you! At least, the life your cock had! I'm offering you the Garden of Eden! A body worthy of the New Man! I'm still the woman you made me!'

'No. You've changed.'

'Not yet. But I will – if you keep rejecting me.'

He sneered. 'I'm talking about love – not coital gymnastics.'

She slapped him fiercely. 'You're blighted! You know that? Blighted!'

He outshouted her. 'Stop persecuting me!'

'You bastard!' She stormed out, slamming the door.

Daniel lit a cigarette. To his surprise, he felt calm. The quarrel had soothed him. Had freed him. Or rather – and this was more heartening – he had seized the freedom to be himself.

He could admit it now: he had been disturbed – to the point of despair – by his lack of desire for Beatriz. For someone so absorbed in sex, he had dreaded, there was nowhere else to go, nowhere he could feel alive.

But he had not panicked. Now, he knew why. He had rejected Beatriz because he had sensed her contempt. She condemned his values – all that had made him a tender lover, a giver of joy; and the most grateful receiver. How could he have desired and imbibed, inundated and surrendered to a woman who disapproved of him? He had not lost his virility. He had had erections – countless. If a woman came along now and recognised the love in him, gave him the freedom he needed, he would function as well as ever.

The freedom to be meek – that was imperative.

He climbed back on to the platform.

All this was a passing phase. Pregnancy had a different life-force. Expectant mothers always saw the world in absolutes. Beatriz would become herself again. After the baby came.

He made another swab and resumed work.

Mayta Capac. Thick animal thighs rippling like the walls of a waterfall. Mountainous shoulders. Arms forested with muscles and veins like roots. Brows jagged as thunderbolts. Eyes sharpened to claws. Nose bearing the imprints of stone missiles. Cheeks scored with hard labour. Ears unfolded, listening to the world. Mouth sagging with the weight of wisdom. Standing like the wrath of God, aiming a golden *tumi*.

As Fuego had stood and fired the gun. Satan as God's instrument.

Killing also words. And all the soul-searching and inaction that words spawned.

Had fired the gun. And had permitted Teresa to live. Had saved many innocents Kempin would have tormented.

Had fired the gun. And killed my past. Cut my umbilical cord. Buried my father, mother, sisters. Buried all the dead Jews. And this dead Jew, me.

Had fired the gun. And had killed my Christianity. And the future.

38

I am digging further than the human eyes, further than the claws of the tiger; what my arms bring up is for distribution beyond the glacial days

Gaspar Huaman scanned the clearing by the river bank. There were twenty men, all dressed as campesinos. Most were sitting around the camp-fire, seeking respite from the mosquitoes. Some had curled up and appeared to be asleep. A few were at the edge of the water searching for crabs.

If they were soldiers, they were unseasoned. They had picked the most vulnerable spot to bivouac. Here, the Rio Chiririnka – named aptly after the blue fly which the Indios believed was the harbinger of death – burst out of the deep defile, thundered through a stretch of rapids towards the giant waterfalls, and offered no chance of escape. The group was just as exposed on its flanks and rear. To its right stood the heights of the defile, presenting Huaman and his slingers a perfect vantage position. To its left and back lay the rain forest, thick and teeming with the rest of the guerrilleros, not to mention the nocturnal predators. Moonlight and the camp-fire provided good visibility, and the roar of the rapids drowned every sound.

'What do you think, Chauca?'

'Highlanders. You can tell from the ponchos.'

'They could be Bridegrooms in disguise.'

'Why disguise in heavy clothes in this heat? More sensible as jungle Indios.'

'Maybe they're bait. Maybe the main force is lying back. Waiting for us to make a move...'

Chauca surveyed the jungle. A liquid altiplano, like the sea he had once seen. Deep-chested, breathing sprays of humidity. But different from the altiplano because it was always surly, always rumbling, and it hid, wherever the feet touched the ground, the vicious tentacles of slimy *apus*.

'If there was a main force, *Comandante*, lookouts give signal by now.'

'Maybe helicopters lurking somewhere...'

'Where?'

Huaman scanned the sky. The heights of the defile were above the forest and offered a clear view of the horizon. Nothing except murky wisps collecting rain beneath the moon. Would Fuego have pilots capable of flying invisibly on the backs of young clouds?

'All right, Chauca. Move in. If they resist, no mercy. Don't use guns – in case there is a main force.'

Chauca slithered away.

Huaman tried to fight off tension by concentrating on the *daylongs* crawling up his legs. It was still a great effort not to attack them. The tribesmen used these giant ants for initiation ceremonies. They had powerful pincers and a venomous sting which produced a day-long fever, hence their name. Numerous stings could prove fatal. If left alone, they were relatively harmless; if disturbed, they dug into the skin and stung.

The jungle was horrific. Everything in it lived to kill or to be killed. Where there was blossom and scent, there was also decay and stench; trees fought each other to climb towards the sun; birds infested the foliage like insects and insects swarmed to displace the air or the rain. The humus on the ground competed with quicksands to devour a man; and the constant shrieks of birds and monkeys proclaimed, second by second, the roll-call of all that had ceased to live.

A place where fighting offered the only relief from living. Which was why he hoped the intruders were Bridegrooms.

Huaman checked his slingers. They were keeping alert: one eye on the camp, the other waiting for his signal.

He felt proud of them. Most were wasting away. Shitting and pissing blood – menstruating men, like the bilharzia-stricken Egyptians who had confronted Napoleon. No bilharzia here. But malaria, dengue, yellow fever. And tetanus, typhoid, dysentery, hepatitis. And a host of fungal infections which he could not diagnose because all he had as reference was the old, badly translated copy of *Price*'s medical textbook which, since his move to the backlands, had accompanied him everywhere.

Medication was already a major problem. No fatalities yet. But only because Father Quintana had had a supply of vaccines which he had shared out between the men in the hope that even reduced dosages might provide some immunity. Also, luckily, there was an abundance of cinchona trees; its bark provided rough quinine which was beneficial for a number of ailments besides malaria. Moreover, they had learned a trick or two from the tribesmen like smearing ash on the body to repel the mosquitoes. Indeed, the tribesmen had all sorts of strange remedies, but he tried those only as a last resort. The fewer dealings they had with aborigines, the better.

The tribesmen, in fact, might prove the most dangerous element in this God-forsaken place. Though, having some contact with civilisation, they were tamer than those living in the darkest reaches of the Amazon, it was best to remember that savagery, in these parts, was only relative. Some experts saw them as innocents; others conceded that, dying out from the white man's diseases and greed, they would be prone to free-floating hatred and go berserk without warning. The truth, as he saw it, was that these natives had had contact mainly with exploiters: land prospectors and cocaine smugglers. From them they had learned theft, treachery and murder for gain. Thus, if Fuego ever despaired of locating him and his men, all he needed to do was hire them as manhunters.

He caught sight of a movement near the river: foliage pushing forward as if carried by the wind: Chauca's group, closing in on the campers. It reminded him of an essay he had written at university, conflating the post-Che Guevara Latin America with medieval Scotland, and forewarning that the people would break their chains and march, like Birnam Wood towards Dunsinane, to topple the Macbeths ruling them. A laboured, youthful piece – but it had launched his career as a political giant.

A joke now – his career: lying sick, in danger of death. What a mistake to deploy to this hell. *Another* mistake! Trying to imitate Che Guevara? The eagle that imitates a duck gets drowned! You're an original in your own right! Will you never learn? Time is running out! Resurrect your career! You did it after Monte Rico! Do it again! Get out of the jungle! Out – before it kills you all!

Chauca's group sprang out of the trees, machetes flashing.

Huaman glanced at his slingers. They were standing up, waiting for his order.

Chauca's group had encircled the campers. The latter, caught completely by surprise, were offering no resistance.

Perfect planning! See – you're an original!

Chauca was waving his machete. The campers had surrendered.

Huaman signalled his slingers to hold fire.

He began to shake, reabsorbing the fear of the jungle. There would be no fight, no relief. Tomorrow, this nether world would swallow him up, spread dense foliage over his name.

'…We were there at the wedding. We saw Teresa climb to the summit…'

Huaman felt like screaming. Not even a small victory. Chauca had been right. The men were highlanders. Fools besotted with Manku Yupanqui and his so-called bride, Teresa.

'…We saw her up there, waiting…'

Pathetic men, rubbing their eyes with their sleeves to protect them from the ocular gnats. Only their spokesman, a sturdy *varayok*, had fire in him. He, at least, had taken the guerrilleros' advice and kept his eyes wide open to let the gnats suck the liquid and fly off.

'The clearest day we have ever seen. It had to be, didn't it – for such a wedding…'

The river, though far behind and laryngitic, still whispered threats. There was the infernal din of morning; vegetation groaning for the sun; shrieking macaws, parrots and the rest of the damned birds seething in malign rainbows.

'Then we saw him climb…'

Huaman turned round sharply. 'You *saw* Manku Yupanqui?'

The campesinos nodded excitedly. The *varayok* managed to smile with his wide open eyes. 'We saw his shadow. It moved up the mountain like the shade of a cloud moves across the land.'

'What makes you think it was not a cloud?'

'A clear day. No clouds.'

Chauca, Huaman observed, was holding his breath. Did he believe the man's drivel? 'Go on.'

'Then they got married.'

'They? Or just their shadows?'

'We saw the sun descend to the summit. There was such dazzle we had to lower our heads. We stood until the sun set. It set late that day in their honour. Then we waited for them to come down.'

Huaman watched his men. They had heard the story while bringing the campesinos to the base. But they were listening again, worshipful, oblivious of chores. Those hearing it for the first time – the sick who had stayed behind – were spellbound like natives at a ritual. And the men at the perimeter, lapsing completely in discipline, were repeating it to those manning the traps and tripwires at the approaches to the base. No doubt, those last were relaying it to the lookouts deep in the jungle.

'We waited for three days. Then we went looking for them. I and some *compañeros* – climbed to the summit. We saw they had left in a hurry.'

'How? Just flew off?'

'Obviously. Otherwise we would have seen them.'

'What makes you think they had been in a hurry?'

'We read the signs. There were no scraps – so they had not eaten. The snow was undisturbed – so they had not lain down to enjoy each other. And we found Teresa's clothes. She would have collected them if she had not been in a hurry. Clothes cost money.'

'She might have died. Did you think of that?'

'Yes. We did not find her body.'

'Maybe she fell into the crater.'

'We had a shaman with us. He questioned the volcano. The answer was no. How could she have fallen with Manku Yupanqui at her side? So... We are still looking...'

Indios! Born deaf to reason!

'Why look here?'

'People say Manku Yupanqui is here.' The *varayok* faced Huaman with his totem eyes. 'They say you are he. Some of your men also say you are he.'

There was that temptation again, offering the powers of the earth which Jesus, so stupidly, had rejected in another wilderness. Gaspar Huaman as Manku Yupanqui. Not Machiavellian any more. Not dishonourable. Not after burial in the jungle. 'And if I am?'

'Declare yourself. We will follow you.'

The temptation. Numbing the brain – like hunger. 'Declaration is easy. Don't you need proof?'

'Your wife will be proof.'

Huaman nearly burst with derision. Wife! Wife meant Kollur! Flabby Indio woman who wanted to fuck and breed like a rabbit. Wife meant children: dumb twin girls with runny noses and an ugly baby. Ghosts from the past. What had happened to them? He had not seen them since leaving for Monte Rico. Nor would he ever. Not very commendable. But how could he make history – with them in tow? Still, they, too, would benefit from the revolution. Until then, they should manage. The fug of Kollur on heat should attract any man.

'And if she's not here?'

The *varayok* was confounded. 'She must be.'

Huaman remembered Teresa from the necropolis. Hardly better than Kollur. Deranged young girl playing at womanhood and hoodwinking the countryside. Throwback to the epileptics who were revered as prophets. Imagine taking her to the presidential palace.

'We are preparing for war here, *compañeros*. Not a place for a woman.

Besides, there are your wives and children. They need care, too. She must visit them all.'

The *varayok* nodded humbly. 'We didn't think of that.'

Huaman smiled. The devil was in him. It was intoxicating. 'Ask for more proof.'

The *varayok* glanced at the campesinos. Tormented by the gnats, they could offer no suggestions. He asked hesitantly. 'The sun's missing ray. Can you show it to us?'

Huaman shook his head solemnly. 'If I did, you would be charred to cinders.'

The *varayok* pondered a moment, then nodded. 'Your word will be enough.'

Huaman rose, luciferous. 'Let me provide you with proof. The reason we rushed away after the wedding was because I had to be here with my men.' Maybe I've got malaria... that's why I'm ranting. But the *varayok* and the campesinos are listening as if I'm an oracle. 'So I did everything between one blink of the eye and the other. I married Teresa, escorted her to the highlands and returned. Only Manku Yupanqui can distort time. Ask my men. They didn't miss me for a second.' Original – you are original!

The *varayok* and the campesinos stared at Huaman's men. The guerrilleros stood mesmerised, drinking in the revelation. They would believe it because it was sweetly stunning, like all miracles. Only Chauca's eyes chided him.

Somewhere in the jungle a tree groaned and fell. The trees in its path wailed as they broke under the impact. Birds and monkeys intensified their litany.

Don't worry about Chauca. 'That's not all! Look at me. One arm missing. You believed Manku Yupanqui was a whole man. I am not. Have you asked yourselves why?'

They stared at him, confused, not daring to look at his stump.

Now, the *coup de grâce*! 'I'll tell you. The enemy was closing in to cut out my heart. So I grabbed Death by his collar. I told him my life belongs to the people. But I understand, I said, you can't leave empty-handed. So let's bargain. That's what we did. I beat him down to one arm.'

Chauca was staring at him, enraged.

Can you betray your *Comandante*, Chauca? 'Ask Chauca. He was there.'

Chauca began to shake.

The *varayok* and the campesinos gaped at him.

Chauca staggered towards Huaman. His lips, pounded by weird guttural sounds, twisted and turned as if possessed by the *ech*. '*Comandante*!' Then he slumped over and passed out.

Loyal Chauca. He could not betray. Primordial forces. 'You see how the memory affects him?'

The *varayok* scrambled across and kissed his hand. 'We need no other proof.'

Huaman felt the sun on his head. He was taller than the tallest tree.

Is this not yet another mistake?

This was preordained.

The new Trotsky – you're talking like an Indio!

This is power! They will take me out of this hellhole! Fight with me! Carry me to victory!

The *varayok* held out a delicately woven *borla*, the band with the scarlet fringe of the Inca monarch. 'We made a crown. Put it on. Declare yourself.'

Huaman donned the *borla*. 'I am Manku Yupanqui!'

39

The truth is that evil is the secret

This year the Independence Day Parade was truly splendid. Its venue, the Avenida de la Republica, had been widened to a magnificent, pink-asphalted mall stretching from the Presidential Palace to the Parliament.

The whole capital had come out to celebrate. Crowds, spuming and spraying flags, streamers and confetti, billowed like two halves of a divided sea. Portraits of the Junta, twinned with those of the liberators, San Martin, Sucre and Bolivar, sailed on the human waves in the spirit of a regatta.

The Junta took the salute at the Plaza de los Héroes, midway on the Avenida, from the balcony of the cupola of the Tomb of the Unknown Soldier. Stands erected on both sides of the Tomb accommodated the Establishment, foreign VIPs, the diplomatic corps and the press.

The march-past, well into its second hour, was triumphal. All formations, most noticeably the Sinchis' armoured and motorised units, were equipped with the latest US weaponry.

In the main stand, Fuego felt in harmony with himself; felt, indeed, a patriot in the mould of the liberator-generals.

This was 9 December. The anniversary of the final victory of the Army of the Andes over the Spanish forces in 1824. The day when every child swore to protect the future. The day when, since childhood, he had lived history as if it were the present, as if he was personally partaking in the rout of the colonial powers.

His day also because it had been during Independence celebrations, twenty-four years ago, that he had joined the Army. A runaway miner, penniless, crushed limbs barely healed, emaciated from a diet of wild berries, staggering into the capital, getting enmeshed with the crowds, dragging himself, hardly conscious, to the recruiting office and then no memory until waking up to shouts in a dusty compound which the rancorous Sergeant had called 'Mother' because it would breastfeed the dregs, turn them into proper sons.

Sweet patriotism! Land, as every man knew in his bones, was the only heaven. A country was that heaven writ large.

He hoped the mood would last, or, at least, compensate for having Angelito and Williston as company, compensate for occasionally ruffling the heads of Angelito's sons – carbon copies – Victor, Justiano and Teodoro, sitting next to him – fortunately without their mother who had stayed at home to endure bravely the morning, noon, afternoon, evening and night sicknesses of her pregnancy – compensate for watching Daniel, watching Beatriz – so robustly with child – both sitting, hand in hand, in the front row, as guests of the Ministry of Culture.

Williston, who had been whispering with Angelito, raised his voice. 'Adopted by Cuba, the *foco* was, Angelito. Became dogma through Castro and Guevara. Revolutionary nuclei. Mobile, versatile fleas at war. You're telling me Huaman is setting up *focos* all over the country?'

'According to our intelligence reports.'

Fuego, trying to preserve his mood, ignored them. They were baiting him.

His day! Did he still believe that? Forgetting that a new strain of colonialism had invaded Latin America and that he, in his determination to survive, was aiding and abetting it?

Put under the microscope, what were the Willistons, the Angelitos and all those backing them? Spineless and bloodless men who wished to reduce the world to blank, shrivelled protozoa in their own image.

The soldiers on parade, for example. Marching in goose-steps, wearing Third Reich uniforms, they were Kempin's legacy! Indio soldiers, for fuck's sake! As different from Nazis as tears were from spit.

Another example. The Tomb of the Unknown Soldier. A scaled-down version of the Invalides in Paris where Napoleon was buried; with the cupola modified to look like that of El Escorial, King Philip II's palace near Madrid; with a Latin inscription on the pediment, *Fides et Patria* – Faith and Country – as homage to the exemplary spirit of ancient Rome! European shit over the remains of an Indio soldier!

Don't forget the irony. Why was the unknown soldier a despicable native and not a superior Creole? Because no white family had agreed to surrender its fallen son to anonymity. So they had snatched the first Indio from the lake of the nameless dead.

Yet another example. The Junta. Standing on the cupola balcony. Taking the salute like Russian leaders on Lenin's Mausoleum! White man's mummery wherever you looked.

'To put together an act like *focos* – there's obviously more to Huaman than meets the eye.'

'Luck, that's all it is. Huaman was at the right place at the right time, Luke. The Manku Yupanqui craze – compounded by a mad girl declaring herself his bride and disappearing! Mass hysteria! Everything just fell into his lap.'

Williston and Angelito droning.

The day was in danger of being scuttled.

Teresa had smiled right through her ordeal. With her third heart. She had smiled and given Kempin love. Kempin had smiled and given her the abomination of desolation. And throughout it all, he, Oseas Fuego, had loved her, had wanted to protect her, spread balm over her abused flesh, enter her body and bathe in her soul. When he had been a boy, he had been obsessed with Mary Magdalen. She had been a loose woman, the priests had said, perhaps a harlot, but so pure beneath her skin that Jesus had loved her. As Teresa's smile had glowed, he had seen her as Mary Magdalen, had marvelled at her faith which, like the best of madness, had generated unimaginable strength. Up there on the volcano – she must still have been smiling. He could almost believe in her apotheosis.

Which was why, though he was aider and abetter, he was not like the Willistons and Angelitos – not a new man. He was in the old image – with blood and spine and three hearts; of the stock of his victims, Indio to the core.

And like all men in the old image, he, too, had glimpsed, before despair, the sun fully repaired and his land and people vested in light. The vision was still beneath his eyelid, wasting away. Waiting for him to kill it – as an act of mercy, or, failing that, in anger.

'I'll tell you what Huaman is, Angelito. Chaos seeking order. The people, sinners without hope, find that irresistible.'

'You mean, the lure of evil?'

Baiting him with a double act.

'You miss the point. Chaos is not evil. There is no evil. Isn't that so, Mr Brac?'

Williston, bending forward, had surprised Daniel as much by placing a hand on his shoulder as by his question.

'What...? Why ask me?'

'I see you as a God-fearing man. Someone who would know.'

Daniel grinned sardonically. 'Open your eyes. Evil is all around us.'

Williston withdrew his hand. 'You disappoint me. What do you think, Beatriz?'

Beatriz ignored him with a hostile look.

Fuego's eyes played with Beatriz's hair.

Williston shook his brimstone head. 'Oh, Lord, such misguided souls! What you people choose to call evil is merely an aspect of good. A manifestation, like fever in a body, which exposes our malady – the sin we're born with – so that it can be treated.'

Angelito nodded as if enlightened. 'I think I know what you mean.'

Fuego grimaced. This was more than baiting. This was Angelito announcing he had found gold whilst escorting Williston on the baptismal rounds. Not the gold of rebirth, but the gold which would secure Kempin's place for him.

He turned to Angelito's sons, drooling over the weapons on parade, and wondered how long it would take them to covet their father's shoes. Then he directed his attention to Daniel and Beatriz.

The way colours spread, Daniel had said on the way back from Kempin, reflects the life of a soul. Some colours run, carving paths like rivers; others provide light or shade; surrender or possess identity; highlight or conceal; not one is unassailable; all can be transmuted. What dimension the transmutation achieves is determined by the painter. We are the painters; God provides the colours. Some of us paint ourselves as Teresa and become sanctified; others as Kempin and end up damned. How do you paint yourself, Oseas?

As a man, as a puma, as an Indio, as a general, as Satan, he had replied, wondering why he had bothered.

It was the truth and not the truth. His colour was fear. Fear of mercy and fear of revolt. Fear of making the maize grow. Which was why he had allied himself with the maggots, the new forces of creation.

'Let me put it this way. History, which is a tool of the liberals, condemns the inquisitors. But the inquisitors were merely doing the Lord's work, striving to redeem mankind. Every torture, each burning at the stake, forced the victim to confess his faith and save his soul. In other words, evil produces good. Therefore, evil does not exist. Satan exists only as the instrument of God's goodness. I'm sure that makes sense to you, Oseas.'

The march-past had ended. The people were flooding the avenue to hold their own parade.

Fuego rose, eager to get away. He winked at Angelito's sons. They stared at him vacuously, young supermen embroiled in dreams of glory.

Williston blocked Fuego's way. 'Speaking of sense, Oseas. Shouldn't you be taking a decision on Huaman?'

Daniel, Fuego observed, was running away, carving a path for Beatriz with his huge bulk. 'Is that an official request?'

What colour did Daniel paint himself? The colourless colour of a vacuum? Or ditchwater grey, the colour of the blindfolded?

Angelito, full of swagger, was gathering his brood. 'The highlands are in ferment, General. We should act before things get out of hand.'

Fuego felt like roaring. He could no longer bear the other pain – that blank, pious maggot of Daniel's that was swelling Beatriz's belly.

Williston checked the creases of his immaculate trousers. 'My friends in Washington are wondering whether you're getting soft, Oseas.'

Fuego tried to walk past them. 'Tell them what you've been preaching, Luke. Good will come out of evil. I will sort out Huaman when I find him.'

Williston nodded, but did not yield ground.

'Guillermo told us where he was, General. That church in the Yungas. If we'd moved in time, we'd have had him!'

Fuego hissed, outraged that he was defending himself against Angelito. 'We would have had to chase him into the jungle. We'd have lost men. Made Huaman more of a hero.'

'Perhaps my missionaries can help, Oseas. They're all over the place. They could easily ferret about.'

Fuego smiled mockingly. Williston's missionaries were already ferreting about. 'They have enough on their plates trying to save souls, Luke.'

Angelito circled his arms around his sons. 'General, let me hit Father Quintana's church! That's the centre for base communities! That's where Huaman is co-ordinating his recruiting! They'll tell us where he is!'

'Makes good sense that, Oseas.'

Unceremoniously, Fuego pushed Williston out of his way.

The Junta had vacated their balcony. The stand was clearing. The crowds were flowing down the avenue.

Fuego envied them. They would get drunk in *chicherias* whereas he would be attending the official reception and listening to Angelito and Williston all over again.

Why did he hesitate over the order? What did he care about Father Quintana's church or the people there? True, the tactics were crude. Stupid to send a tank to chase a flea, particularly when this flea, Huaman, was doing everything he could to shorten his life. Manku Yupanqui! Teresa's husband! What next? The campesinos would soon unmask him and bury him alive in a glacier.

Williston and Angelito had followed him.

How could he stop the new men tainting him? How could he stop Daniel and Beatriz hurting him? And that *thing* in her belly diminishing him?

He turned to Angelito and Williston and smiled. 'All right, *compadres*. Let's hit the church!'

As if that would stop anything.

What would stop the hurt, stop it from spreading like rot, would be a deed of absolute mercy or absolute rage.

Rage – since he functioned best in the dark.

Therefore, a deed so evil that it would kill the colour of the sun!

40

It is written where it is never read that love, extinguished, is not death but a bitter kind of birth

Jerry Rice paid the bartender and left the promenade café. He trundled back to the beach, looking right and left for a kid to kick a ball at him. But kids in this country had no time for sun, sea and sand. They were trying to eke out a living in the streets. The same applied to the adults. No Adonises and Venuses doing exercises here. The few bathers he could see – the rich had their private beaches – were night people: hookers, pimps, petty criminals. Here was the Pacific bringing mystic messages from Asia and only a handful were present to decipher them.

He reached his deck chair, sat down and drank from his flask.

Beatriz waded out of the sea. Opulent, burnished flesh; proud, pregnant belly emphasised by her bikini; pearls of water on her skin; luminous long hair mapping her shoulders like coal seams. Almost as beautiful as Debbie. Debbie had been... Debbie *is*...

Tall and slim; small-breasted. She has the partly over-developed, hence somewhat distorted figure of an athlete. She was one: a sprinter. Had she trained seriously instead of running from one horrific assignment to another, she could have made the Olympics. She is unbelievably beautiful when we make love, when she lifts her muscular thighs to have me deep in her, rubs her calves, bulging like easter eggs, on my back, demands my hands on her supple buttocks spreading out like a tale from Scheherazade. And at her most beautiful when she yelps and comes and her nipples rise and her eyes turn to fireflies. She is so beautiful she can mock the disease that gnaws her to a skeleton. You've never answered this, God: if you fell in love with her – which I can understand – and were determined to abduct her – which I can also understand – why did you not take her whole?

'Won't you go in, Jerry?' Beatriz ran up, shaking off the water like a dog.

'I'm a Gulf Stream man. Not sturdy enough for your cold Humboldt. I'm happy just to sit and soak the sun.'

She knelt on the sand. Slightly out of breath. Her belly, a small globe. 'Soak the whisky, you mean. I saw you go to the café.'

'Sharp eyes you mermaids have.'

'Why do you drink so much?'

'Do I?'

She shook her head sadly. 'Shall we eat?' She opened the picnic basket. 'We've got all sorts of sandwiches. Ham, cheese, eggs, tuna, pâté. I think we should start with fish. OK?'

'Definitely.' On an impulse, he caressed her hair.

She looked up, suddenly tearful.

He smiled. 'I was thinking how lovely your child will be.'

'Thank you for saying that.' She dabbed at her eyes, then offered him a sandwich. 'Tuna.'

He bit into the sandwich as if very hungry.

She began to eat, too. 'Couldn't you have children?'

'Sure, we could. And we thought about it a lot. We just never got round to it.'

'Sometimes I think it's more sensible not to have any.'

'You're wrong!'

She was right, of course. But the cost... Debbie had died dispossessed of symbolic survival. And he, having left his seed to rot, had disdained the future.

She stared unhappily at her belly. 'I'm thinking of leaving Daniel.'

Rice nodded sadly. 'Thinking or decided?'

'I need your advice, Jerry. We were so in love. We only had to look at each other... and we were one... Now, we hardly talk... He – he can't even touch me.'

'Poor Daniel.'

She looked up angrily. 'Poor Daniel? What about me?'

'I take it you can still touch – at least, want to. That's a less terrible despair than his.'

'What has he to despair about? He's got me! We're going to have a baby! He's got his work! He's finished with all that stupidity with Kempin! What more does he want?'

'To be what he would like to be, I should think.'

'Jerry, you're supposed to be helping me! Don't take his side! Look, I know things aren't as simple as I make them. But he's like someone who's bleeding – and won't do anything to stop it! Won't let anyone treat him! He'll bleed until he's drained of life!'

'Maybe he needs to be – drained of what has been his life. Drained of his past.'

'What about the present? The future? Our baby?'

'Maybe he's trying to make space for you... I don't know. But let me tell you: it takes strength to drain yourself. Where does he get that strength? The answer might be you – and the baby.'

She thought for a moment. 'Or cowardice.'

'He was brave enough when we rescued Huaman. And he pursued Kempin to the end. So what cowardice are we talking about?'

'Fear of commitment. Inertia. You've seen it in him. All his life, he never fought to go where he wanted to go. He helped Huaman because we dragged him in. Same with Kempin – he went because Fuego summoned him. Even with me – had I not taken him to my bed, he'd still be waiting.'

'But he did commit himself after that.'

'Did he? We had something – yes. I believed we could become one – we were one. Now, I think, I wanted to believe that. That it was my need. I mean, I think I made it all up...'

'You couldn't make it all up. Some of it, no doubt. And no doubt Daniel did the same, too.'

'All right. But I'm not giving up! Why is he?'

How had it been with him and Debbie during that awful time when they had been estranged? Had it been the realisation that love, so-called consuming, healing, fusing, was a delusion? It was difficult to say even now. Somehow, despite that wonderful compatibility of the flesh and spirit, there had appeared a chasm. Two years in the wilderness. How had they survived them? Even more miraculously, how had they come back together? According to Debbie, they had matured, accepted the impossibility of achieving total union. That, she had said, demands the destruction of the self. Why should the world be deprived of the tulip and the rose in order to concoct something that diminished them both? Far better to remain two separate entities and give each other their individual gifts. Then we can create what can be created: a child combining your clay and mine. She had said all that. And he had accepted it. But had he believed it? The conviction remained: two bodies could create one soul and one soul could inhabit two bodies; remained so strongly, in fact, that all this time, thinking that Beatriz and Daniel had achieved oneness, he had envied them, had called for Debbie every evil night. Inevitably, he had drunk more and more.

'Self-hate, Beatriz. Producing fear that's unwieldy. Which, in turn, generates more self-hate. It's the most vicious circle there is.'

She shook her head defiantly. 'Circles can be broken.'

Yes. That was how it had been with him and Debbie. He had rebelled against self-hate and had run to find her where she sat surrounded by her gifts. He had not achieved union, but he had retrieved the joy of touching her, had even discovered that he, too, had gifts to give. It had been enough – a feast compared to the famine that was the fate of most.

'Tell me something. What made you fall in love with Daniel in the first place?'

'Why does one fall in love? It just happens.'

'It doesn't just happen. There's always a very good – or a very bad – reason. Take me and Debbie. I fell in love because she was very opinionated. She would argue yellow is pink until blue in the face. I loved that confidence. Loved her all the more when, those times she had been wrong, she eventually admitted it and turned all sweet and randy.'

Beatriz managed a smile. 'Do you know why she fell in love with you?'

Rice's eyes filled with tears. 'Yes. Because I cry easily. I tell you, she hated going to the movies with me. But afterwards, I was her baby – her strong, soft baby.'

Beatriz laughed.

'So. What do you love most about Daniel?'

She thought for a long time before answering. 'You won't believe me. His fear.'

'The very thing you hate in him?'

'It overrides my fears. Makes me strong and protective.'

'Then believe in that. Keep strong. Hopefully, one day, it will rub off on him. Then you can come together again. It won't be like before, but you'll still want to write home about it.'

Beatriz hugged him. 'Dear Jerry. Preaching resurrection. I'll buy it – even if it's another delusion.'

41

In you the light, like the darkness, is old, spent in devouring scars

Father Quintana raged at himself. He should be out there in the open, waving his fists, shouting his protests, calling God to swat those monsters out of the air. But terror had paralysed him. He remained flattened against the wall of his church.

Smoke and dust choked the breeze. A circle of fire consumed the outlying adobes. The relentless din of machines and cannon silenced nature.

There were old people lying broken in pools of the little blood they had; young mothers, trying to release the toddlers they had been carrying on their backs as they fell wounded; young men staring in shock at blown-off limbs; and children, mouths open in inaudible screams, tripping over crazed dogs, pigs and chickens.

And there were those who lay dead.

It had been market day, a social occasion offering some barter, laughter and gossip – the briefest of brief respites in a life of misery, Lord!

The helicopters were now suspended over the village. Spewing flames and earthquakes.

Was this real? Or was it one of those stories about the white man Indians told their children in the dark of the night so that it would filter into the child's sleep, transfuse his dreams and be a warning for ever.

The helicopters dropped on to the earth and disgorged men. Countless men.

Father Quintana recognised them by their uniforms: Bridegrooms – their arms extended with sub-machine-guns, flame-throwers, machetes.

As the helicopters' blades slumped and whistled shrilly, the din became noise and some hearing returned.

A tall, blond man directed the Bridegrooms to scour what had remained of the village. Such a handsome man. Father Quintana had never seen him before, but he recognised him: Colonel Angelito: 'Satan's Seraph', Jerry Rice had called him.

Father Quintana sank to his knees. Death was here. But he did not have the will to yield to it. Perhaps... If he reneged on his faith, took off his soutane, burned it, crawled on his belly and kissed their boots, confessed to anything they wanted, betrayed everybody he knew – whatever, whatever – perhaps they might spare him. Was that wrong? Had not Saint Peter denied Christ three times the night of His arrest? And later, had he not tried to flee Rome to escape martyrdom? Was it wrong to choose life and reject faith? Life once lost was lost whereas faith lost could be found again.

The Bridegrooms were running amok. They smashed a man's chest with a burst of fire. They crushed a child's head with the butt of a gun. They ripped open a woman's belly with a machete. They beheaded another man. They seized three girls and began raping them. They set alight a whole family with a flame-thrower. They gouged a boy's eyes, carved out his testicles and stuffed them into his mouth. They hacked an old man, then garrotted his wife. They cut off the breasts of the raped women and threw them at the dogs. They tossed babies into the air and shot them as they fell. When there was not a man or a woman or a child near them, they slaughtered the dogs, the pigs and the chickens. When they paused for breath, they turned the market place upside down, spat and pissed on the produce.

My God, my God, were these men?

Father Quintana found his legs. The altar – he should be safe there. The church was a sanctuary. He scrambled towards the door. Bullets screamed and ricocheted in front of him. Colonel Angelito was walking towards him, wagging a revolver like an index finger.

Suddenly, miraculously, Arana and Tinco, his ablest Delegates Of the Word, materialised God knew how and intercepted Colonel Angelito. Such defiance in their tears and screams; such priestly authority in their condemnations.

Father Quintana took advantage of their appearance and ran to the door. He heard two shots behind him, glanced back to see Arana and Tinco fall, then threw himself inside.

He ran to the altar and collapsed at the base of Christ's statue. 'Oh, Lord,

save me! Save me, sweet Jesus, save me! Please, save me. Please, Saviour...
Please, save me!'

'Sweet Jesus, save me...'

He could not tell how long he had lain at Christ's feet. His voice had
dwindled to a faint croak. Also, the sun's ray which had illuminated the Face
had shifted. The Sacred Blood dripping from the crown of thorns, matting
the Sacred Hair, running down the Sacred Cheeks on to the Sacred Beard had
transferred its sparkle to the Sacred Blood gushing from the Sacred Right
Palm.

Colonel Angelito was sitting on the Communion Table, dangling his feet,
smiling, watching. There were a number of Bridegrooms walking about like
visitors, sitting in the pews like members of the congregation, or standing
like men who had just received the Eucharist.

'Sweet Jesus, save me...'

'I doubt if he can. He has troubles of his own.'

Somehow, anger replaced terror. 'Get out! This place is consecrated! The
church is a sanctuary!'

That elicited a burst of laughter. What happened next shocked Father
Quintana more than the carnage he had witnessed.

Colonel Angelito jumped off the Communion Table. Immediately, six of
his men leaped on it, lowered their trousers and began defecating. This elicited
even greater laughter.

Another group of Bridegrooms came running out of the crypt, waving
Father Timothy O'Neill's sacred relics, beating them together like drummers
on parade, smashing them... The bones that had produced the golden blood!

My God, my God, were these men?

Father Quintana wailed. 'Why...?'

Colonel Angelito prodded him. 'Come along.'

'Why? Why? Why?'

'Gaspar Huaman – we want him. Come now!'

Father Quintana clasped the base of the statue, gripped the Sacred Feet.
'No!'

Colonel Angelito kicked him in the ribs. Some of the Bridegrooms seized
his arms and legs.

'No! Please, no! Please!' He clung to the Sacred Feet with all his strength.

They pulled him away viciously.

He felt his palms tear. He was being dragged up the aisle. He tried to
scream. But he had no voice left. He had a glimpse of his palms bleeding.
Momentarily, his fear dispersed. He had left his blood on the Sacred Blood
that was spurting from the Sacred Feet. He and Jesus had become of one

blood. *Happy is the man who shares in this first resurrection! Upon such the second death has no claim!*

The fear returned. He tried to scream again. In vain. But his body was articulate: it shook uncontrollably and it urinated. He smelled the smoke and dust. He was out of the church. No sanctuary now.

They dragged him through the square. He saw, upside down, some Bridegrooms interrogate briefly the few villagers who had survived and then shoot them. He urinated more and found some comfort in the warm liquid.

Then he was catapulted forwards. He landed inside a helicopter. He tried to get to his feet.

Colonel Angelito knocked him unconscious.

42
Closing that door which does not exist

'Are you happy – you two?'

Beatriz, having switched on all the lights, cast a glance over the sitting room. Untidy. So what? 'Very.'

'Then why isn't he here – gazing at your belly? It is past midnight.'

People in power are like serpents; the new skins often look benign, but they serve the same function as the old; they propel their owners to the prey – but faster. Aunt Luisa's famous argument.

Apart from the Independence Day Parade, when she had made a point of keeping her distance, she had not seen Fuego for weeks. Now she could note the change in him. His gait had acquired the disquiet of a deer. He had a brighter aspect, but its gloss suggested venom, ready to burst. Not a sudden change. Something to do with Kempin, too?

'He's working late. He has a tricky section to finish.'

'That is no excuse. I have ordered my men to quickmarch him back here.'

'Why?'

'So that he looks after you.'

Menacing jocularity.

She sat on an armchair, feeling constrained by the dress she had had to put on. She picked up the shawl she was knitting for the baby and tried to keep calm.

'Father Quintana has been arrested.'

She wailed in horror. 'Oh, no!'

'Alas.'

'Have you harmed him? Is he all right?'

'Perfectly. You can visit him if you like.'

Fear galloped; but she remained defiant. 'This sudden interest in us – is it to do with Father Quintana?'

Fuego moved to the window and stared out at the front garden. 'No. You are my friends.'

'I'm not.'

'Daniel is. And you are an old lover – same thing.'

'Why did you arrest Father Quintana?'

'For interrogation.' He grinned. 'Gaspar Huaman has declared himself Manku Yupanqui. Teresa Ayala has become his bride – though she is dead, by all accounts. Crazy, eh?' He moved back from the window and sat on the sofa. 'The maid's night off, is it?'

'I don't have a maid – you know that.'

'Oh, yes. You don't believe in exploitation. You use a daily. So who is in charge of hospitality?'

Beatriz put aside her knitting. 'Wine or pisco?'

'A fruit juice. I need a clear head.'

She moved cautiously to the kitchen.

'How is the pregnancy?'

'Fine.'

'Who would have thought it – you, soon to be a mother...'

She came back with a glass of mango juice, handed it to him and sat down again.

He sipped his drink. 'What do you want? Boy or girl?'

'I don't mind. As long as it's healthy.'

'Daniel wants a girl, I suppose!'

She was tempted to blurt it out: Daniel doesn't want the baby or me. She picked up her knitting again and forced a bright smile. 'A boy.'

'I thought sons of heroic fathers never wanted sons of their own. Can't meet the standards and all that.'

She felt piqued, compelled to defend Daniel. 'He is heroic in his own right.'

'You mean, your caper with Huaman! An aberration, that. The mountain giving birth to a mouse. Anyway, the effort has drained him. He has nothing left. He will abandon you. And the child.'

The cruelty of his words echoed her own qualms. 'Never! He sees the child as... No use telling you – only fathers would understand...'

'I am a father. I have several children, in fact.'

She faced him, surprised. 'Have you? Where are they?'

'I abandoned them – like Daniel will abandon his. We are alike in that respect – no disposition for brats.'

'You are poles apart. Daniel sees our child as the New Man.'

Fuego blanched. 'The New Man?' Daniel's blank, shrivelled maggot danced in his cornea – bloodless, spineless, heartless. 'You mean... a homunculus?'

Menace was filling the room. She clung to her courage. 'Like the New Adam. Jesus...'

His laughter became the snarl of a wounded animal.

'That's how normal parents see their children. Pure and loving.'

'I have a different vision of the new man.'

'Naturally.'

'Tell me – do you see yourself as the Virgin?'

'Sometimes.'

'A not so virgin Virgin. You poor bitch!'

Beatriz ignored his contempt. She herself had been surprised by her remark. She had not been aware that motherhood had engendered in her such mysticism. But, of course, there had been times when she had felt like the Blessed Mother; times when she had beguiling visions of Daniel standing as a god paternally ready to provide for her.

What about now – now that he could not even touch her?

Now – and this had kept her in harness – she felt blessed in a different way. Captive to another love. The primordial love that sequestered a woman and her child in a solitary realm far from the world – and, in compensation, sanctified them both. Now, in that domain which disbarred the spurning Daniel, which – the thought occurred to her – would have also disbarred the loving Daniel, she had become Mother of Earth, Mother of Man, Mother of God, Mother of Mothers, separately and all at once.

It further occurred to her that perhaps it had not been Daniel who had spurned her but she who had turned away from him. He was a sensitive man. He must have felt how unwanted he was in that realm of mother and child; and he must have run away from the seed – his own seed – which, by replacing him, would destroy him.

'Out of curiosity... How do pregnant women fuck?'

'What...?'

'Not the missionary position, surely. Sideways? Or female on top?'

She stared at him, chilled by his sanguine smile.

'Or do you just stop fucking?'

'You're sick, Oseas! You know that?'

'I do. But do you know how sick?'

She forced a smile, trying to banish the threat. 'Come on, Oseas... What's got into you?'

'Wait till Daniel comes.' He closed his eyes and pretended to sleep.

She stared at him, sickened by the enormity of her hatred. She thought of killing him – immediately, before he could perpetrate the evil that had brought him here. She had knitting needles. She should sink them into his eyes, then, as he groped about, fetch her gun. She could do it. Before Daniel came.

But her baby. Who would protect him afterwards?

She remembered other threats. Threats she had shared with Aunt Luisa. Why did she keep remembering Aunt Luisa now?

Aunt Luisa, as the sister of a political activist, Beatriz's father, had had her own dossier at the Security Headquarters. Thus, whenever there was a blood-letting, there they would be, Fuego's previous incarnations, invading her modest house, salivating as they smashed their truncheons on the furniture and, not infrequently, on Aunt Luisa herself.

And there had been that time, locked up in the attic – where Aunt Luisa had always hid her – when she had waited for days, when she had been convinced she would die there and be discovered as a skeleton hundreds of years later. Finally, a fat, middle-aged man, the country's greatest poet, had opened the trap-door and freed her, telling her they had taken Aunt Luisa to prison, but not to worry, he would have her released, until then, Beatriz would be in his care. True enough, a few months later, Aunt Luisa had been released; not as Aunt Luisa any more, not that plump, loving creature, but a shadow, balding, full of sores – with just enough wisdom left in her eyes to decide that she could no longer interlock limbs with the jovial, passionate poet. A few days later, she had taken the boat to the northern beach, and, according to witnesses, had leaned over to watch the propellers frothing the sea, and fallen overboard. Her body had never been found, and that had been her final victory, for she had always believed that good people should never leave their shit behind.

Beatriz, sixteen then, had stayed on with the poet to console him and to be consoled. Inevitably, in memory of Aunt Luisa, they had become lovers. On the first anniversary of Aunt Luisa's death, he had kissed her wings and sent her to fly, begging her to keep singing, out there in the jungle where the hyenas preyed, so that the people would hear her, take heart and hope.

Now, Fuego was here, acting out his uniform. The circle had been completed. The cretins who had killed her Indian mother, her Creole father, her Aphrodisian godmother, had finally come round to torment her. And her man.

How brave was she? How brave was Daniel? Ignoring her shaking fingers, she started knitting again.

She heard the key in the front door and then the footsteps. She rose as

Daniel walked in. There were two Bridegrooms with him, both armed with sub-machine-guns. Daniel, she could see, was primed with tension.

Fuego had opened his eyes. 'Ah. The prodigal returns.'

'What's going on?'

'Nothing – yet.'

'Beatriz – are you all right?'

'Yes.'

'Daniel edged further into the room. 'What *is* this? I get dragged away by your men...'

Fuego rose. 'You're so unwelcoming, you two. Sit down, Daniel. Be sociable.'

Beatriz touched Daniel's elbow. 'He has arrested Father Quintana...'

Daniel stared at her in fear.

Fuego waved his hands. 'Forget Father Quintana. He has nothing to do with you! Make yourself at home, Daniel.'

Daniel tried to sound reasonable. 'Oseas, I've been working since the crack of dawn. Do you mind if we go to bed?'

'You and me?'

'Very funny.'

Beatriz put out a warning hand on Daniel's arm. 'I'll make some coffee.'

Fuego intercepted her. 'Don't bother with the coffee. Go to the bedroom and undress. I will be with you in a minute.'

Beatriz, shocked, turned to Daniel.

Daniel took a tentative step towards her.

Fuego nodded at the Bridegrooms. Instantly, they pointed their sub-machine-guns at Daniel.

Daniel began to shake.

Fuego turned to Beatriz. 'Go on – into the bedroom.'

'I – I don't understand · · ·'

Fuego spoke whilst gauging Daniel. 'I am going to fuck you.'

Beatriz cast a desperate glance at Daniel.

Daniel, managing to look at Fuego, groaned. 'She's pregnant – for God's sake.'

Fuego's eyes blazed. 'I know, Daniel, I know. The New Man. I am very angry with you. You have hidden God – without telling anybody. Not even me, your best friend...'

Daniel, shaking all the more, began to cry. 'Please – go. Please – leave us alone...'

'But God is for everybody, Daniel. He must be shared. I need Him as much as you do.'

'Please…'

'Alternatively, if He insists on remaining exclusive, I must destroy Him. Drown Him in my sperm.'

Daniel, throwing his head from side to side, staggered towards Fuego. The Bridegrooms kept their guns trained on him. Fuego stood his ground, smiling.

Daniel raised his arms. Suspended over Fuego's head, they looked like quernstones, ready to pulverise. 'Don't do this!' Then the arms came down, but stripped of all their strength. 'Don't do this.' And they perched on Fuego's shoulders, weightless. 'Don't do this…'

Fuego grinned and pushed Daniel away.

Daniel's legs gave way and he collapsed.

Fuego turned to Beatriz. 'Your hero.'

Beatriz propelled herself towards Daniel.

Fuego bellowed. 'Go – and undress!'

Daniel moaned, unable to pull himself up. 'No… No…'

Beatriz looked down at him. Pitifully, at first. Then contemptuously. She moved towards the bedroom.

Daniel clutched at Fuego's legs. 'Please… I love her… Please, don't do this… I love her… Don't humiliate me in front of her…'

Fuego bent over and grabbed Daniel by his shirt. 'Stop me! Why don't you stop me?'

Daniel wailed. 'I… can't… Please, don't humiliate me…'

'Stop me! Stop me!'

Desperately, Daniel turned towards the bedroom. Beatriz was by the door, watching him – expressionless. 'Beatriz – don't let him… Fight him! Fight him!'

Tears formed in Beatriz's eyes. She went into the bedroom.

Daniel groaned.

Fuego spat on him, then moved to the bedroom.

The Bridegrooms, disdainful of Daniel, lowered their guns.

She stood in front of the bed, naked.

He undressed, watching her. He did not see her as a pregnant woman. On the contrary. She was a woman who had thinned out, whom Daniel had abraded, whose music he had stifled. Since she had let him do all that, she deserved everything!

She held her hands protectively over her belly. That was where fear screamed. Was this how those about to be executed felt? They always looked so calm in those photographs of firing squads…

The sound of Daniel's sobs soughed faintly.

Fuego had undressed. 'Time God shook hands with the Devil.'

His penis was limp. She looked at him with disdain. 'The Devil doesn't seem to be very keen.'

'Get on the bed.'

She lay down.

He stared at her. He would replenish her. Even in abomination, give her more than Daniel had given her.

She stared back. The baby – don't harm the baby! You bastard, Daniel, chicken-hearted shit, bloodless, spineless Judas! Kill Fuego, woman! Scratch his eyes out, then kill him, kill him, woman, because he's rabid, a maniac, a hyena!

'On your knees. We'll do it like dogs.'

She felt herself divide. One Beatriz repositioned herself as he had asked. The other stood as a stern witness. It was the latter who taunted Fuego. 'Afraid to look at me?'

He approached her. He was still limp. A deed so evil that it will kill the colour of the sun. He began to masturbate.

One Beatriz waited, listening to Daniel's sobs.

The other thought of Aunt Luisa. Rape was what Madrina had feared most. Not for herself – she had known good sex and forgotten the bad and could survive another brute or two or a whole gang. But she had feared for Beatriz. When her ward came of age, she had decided, she would be found to be healthy. Then she could enter, without fear, the labyrinth of sexuality and negotiate, equally fearlessly, the tunnels of false love and discover that the Minotaur was not a monster but a man desperate for love. Well, Madrina, I'm in the labyrinth. There is rape here, too, as you can see. But don't worry. I've also had good sex and bad and can survive a brute. In any case, Fuego is unlikely to be violent. He was a gentle and considerate lover.

Fuego had managed to arouse himself.

One Beatriz felt him probing between the cheeks of her buttocks. The other felt moist.

Then the two Beatrizes merged. She heaved and vomited. As he entered her, she screamed. 'Mind the baby!'

He saw himself in the mirror that served as the bed's headpiece. He shut his eyes. He tried to remember Beatriz as she had been. A woman he could have loved. Should have loved. Did love. 'I won't hurt you!' He moved gently, in and out. Come on, ejaculate and be done with it!

Beatriz, still dribbling bile, buried her head in the pillow. Let it be over, dear God, now, now! Oseas come and be done with it and I swear I won't hate you so much!

He continued moving in and out. But he had lost his erection. I can't do it! He managed a groan that sounded like an orgasm and withdrew.

She eased herself on to the bed. It's over! It's over! But he hadn't come…

He grabbed his clothes and brusquely walked out. I faked it, but it still counts as rape.

She curled up. It's over! Everything's over!

The Bridegrooms had left, dismissed.

Fuego was putting on his uniform jacket.

Daniel dragged himself off the floor. He had had a glimpse of Fuego's penis – handsome cock of a powerful male, savage uncircumcised cock wearing her perfume – and the pain of it had reanimated him. He could see Beatriz through the door, lying on her side on the futon, still naked, but belly intact. She was gazing. At what? Thinking! Of what?

It was over. She was unhurt. Just a fuck.

It was over. But it was the end of so much else also. Suddenly.

He staggered to Fuego. 'Why? Why pick on me?'

Wearily, Fuego buttoned up his jacket. 'I won the bet.'

'I loved her.'

'I imitated Kempin! With someone you love! Where was your God?'

'I loved her.'

'You did nothing!'

'I couldn't… But I loved her…'

'I would have died before letting another man touch her!'

'I loved her.'

Fuego shook his head pitifully. 'It is not just fear, Daniel, your curse. Something worse. Something that does not even have a name. You will not fight for anything! Die for anything! Not for God! Not for Beatriz! Not for your past! Not for your future! Not for anything!'

Daniel faced him. 'I could kill you.'

'My men have gone. You are stronger than me. Bare hands, that is all you need. Go on!'

Daniel tried to raise some strength. But it was over. The end of everything. He sank into a chair.

Disgustedly, Fuego moved to the door. 'The time I have wasted on you. Hating you. Seeing in you the man I could have been! Wanting to destroy you! You are not even a maggot! You are not even the man I am!' He pointed at the bedroom. '*I* would have died for her!' And he left.

How long had he sat on the chair? It had been a good time; a time of nothingness – neither thought nor awareness of self. Now the blood was back in his legs.

He rose and shuffled towards the bedroom. Beatriz was still on the bed, still naked, still in a trance.

'Beatriz...'

An age later, she looked at him.

'Are you all right?'

Another age later, she moved, dragged herself up to sit. 'You bastard!'

'I loved you.'

She hissed at him. 'Why didn't you protect me? Judas!'

'I loved you.'

'Any man! Any man would have protected me!'

'I loved you.'

'Were you listening? Did you hear me scream? Did it arouse you? Make you want to touch me again! Did you enjoy another man fucking me? Pervert!'

'I loved you!'

'You're vermin! I should kill you! Gouge out your eyes! Take out your heart! Quarter you! Burn you!'

Daniel shivered. 'You don't understand.' He began to weep. He should have been at Auschwitz. Not those innocents. 'No, you're right. There should be a limit to my disease. There often is... But not... in my case.'

She managed to stand up. Resenting her pity for him. Fighting the shock of the rape. Praying that the baby was unharmed. 'God, you make me sick!'

He edged away. 'My things – just send them on...'

She stared at him, defeated, confused. 'What?'

'I loved you – if you can remember that.' He tottered away.

She tried to winnow her thoughts, pick one that would still have a meaning. 'And now? Don't you love me now?'

'Nothing counts now.'

He lurched out.

PART EIGHT

43

I go singing in the middle of the night a song that no one has ever sung

The waiting enclosure extended from the reception block. With high walls on either side and a metal fence separating it from the prison's quadrangle, it looked like a cattle pen. They packed into it whilst the prisoners lined up in the quadrangle. A couple of guards manned the gate at the fence.

The visiting relatives directed Beatriz and Serafina, the student who, like Beatriz, was well into her pregnancy, to sit with the elderly on one of the two benches provided.

No one spoke. Everybody clutched their passes and the tattered shopping bags which contained food and cigarettes. Almost everything they had brought would be offered to the guards as bribes.

The tannoy began calling out the names. At each announcement, one of the prisoners in the quadrangle disengaged from his line; simultaneously, his visitors edged towards the gate, showed their passes, and went through. Out in the quadrangle, prisoner and visitors found a space where they could squat together, talk in whispers, and very occasionally brush hands or cheeks. They were allowed fifteen minutes. The children, Beatriz noticed, remained quiet, as they had been throughout the trip in the ferry.

Serafina was trying to compose herself. Daughter of a prosperous Creole family, she had fallen in love with a mestizo at the university. She had become pregnant around the time of the Monte Rico massacre. Ruiz, her boy-friend, had set out to collect money for the victims and had been promptly arrested.

Soon after that, Serafina's family, learning that she had sullied the family blood with a half-caste, had disowned her. Some friends had taken her in and there had been hand-outs from others, but how long could she live like that? Ruiz had another four years to serve; but he was already a wreck. Suicide, before the baby was born, was Serafina's idea of a solution.

Suicide certainly had become one of El Chulpa's traditions. The walls of the waiting enclosure were full of graffiti on the subject. *Husband of mine, I can't live without you! All the children are dead – why should I live? I have been with another man. I will satisfy your honour! I will never again see how they have tortured you!* And many more. Written tenderly like billets-doux, in shaky hands which, Beatriz felt, conveyed all the more poignantly the bold conviction that they would be read, by some miracle, by those to whom they had been addressed, even though the prisoners never set foot in the enclosure.

Serafina's name was called. She touched Beatriz's hand and shuffled away.

Serafina and Ruiz met silently, then sat down on the earth without looking at each other. Ruiz, Beatriz thought, was drained of his soul. Campbell, she remembered from the last time she had been here, had looked more alive as he had lain dead than Ruiz did now.

The last time she had been here... She had come in homage to Manku Yupanqui and to consolidate the reawakening she had experienced in the desert. Fuego had escorted her. Except for that commotion which had left Campbell dead, it had been a good day. She had sung defiantly and the prisoners had taken heart and sung with her. On her return to the mainland, she had met Daniel.

Daniel. The man whose touch had promised permanence. But who had stood by whilst she had been raped. Who then had vanished.

'Beatriz Santillan!'

Not the tannoy. A prison officer. All the visitors had been processed and were now inside the quadrangle. Those prisoners who had received no visitors were being taken back to their blocks. No Father Quintana.

She stood up. 'Yes?'

The officer indicated the reception block. 'This way.'

'But I've come to see a prisoner.'

'We've put him in a special cell for you.'

The special cell was in the infirmary – a crumbling box inside a derelict building. It had no windows. A single bulb of very low wattage provided the only light. The shattered frame of an examination table and two rickety chairs fought for space among broken bedpans, torn cartons, tattered sheets, old newspapers and years of dried excreta. The smell of decomposing flesh had replaced the air.

Father Quintana was slopped over one of the chairs – a pulped mass barely relating to the shape of a man. His face was the size of a large, amorphous boulder. If he still had eyes, they were peering from behind a range of contusions. Mouth, nose and ears seemed to be drifting, bereft. The glorious white hair had been shaved, leaving behind a pate scored with craters of dark lesions. Hands and feet, torn of nails, swung tuberously from arms and legs blistered by burns. An embroidered soutane – a gift from his flock, she had heard – torn and bloody, proclaimed that the rest of the body had been similarly laid waste. The only sign of life was an intermittent sibilation from vocal chords rubbing against each other like dry grass in the wind.

Nausea, barely controllable, possessed Beatriz. Her hands folded over her belly as if to protect her baby's eyes from horror. Simultaneously, she wanted to run home, to bed, to bury her head under the covers and never emerge again. She had come to seek counsel from the only saintly person she had known. Instead, she had found herself chosen to bear witness. Why her?

She found herself squatting by Father Quintana's feet.

The prison officer had not bothered to stay.

'Padrecito, Padrecito... What have they done to you?'

I hear you my child can't speak my Lady I washed my robes and made them white in the blood of the Lamb pain little Mother they broke me hot coals I choke on brimstone Hell must be this your sweet song my Lady I hear it I told them nothing they didn't know your song like no song I heard must be some good in me to hear it if I can see the sun once more

'Tears streamed down Beatriz's eyes. 'Oh, Padrecito... Padrecito...'

Little Teresa grateful for your tears can't speak my Lady they took my mouth my tongue great Mother questioned and questioned nothing I said of danger my Lady you found Manku Yupanqui now you are married happy are those who wash their clothes clean they will have the right to the tree of life remember little Teresa you ran away from the Sisters I helped you now you are Beatific when they took me I left my blood on His Sacred Blood

Beatriz stretched a tentative hand towards Father Quintana's face. 'Can I touch you...? Would I hurt you...?'

My blood on His Sacred Blood a Lamb with the marks of slaughter on him he had seven horns and seven eyes pain Teresa unbearable no escape you want to die but stay alive out of the smoke came locusts and they were given the powers earthly scorpions have I told them nothing my Lady they kill whales with harpoons over and over there are animals they club to death many times they quartered me can't be long death I told them nothing they didn't know.

Gently, Beatriz placed her hand on Father Quintana's cheeks. 'Oh, Padrecito, brave Padrecito... Saintly man... If only I could heal you...'

Thank you touching me sweet Teresa you are singing thank you such sweet song great Mother smells of the sea if I can see the sea once more when a child I loved the sea if I had not loved Jesus desperately I would be fisher of fish like Peter because loved Jesus I tried to be fisher of men like Peter not a good fisherman not for long time these last years I tried harder I stand knocking at the door if anyone hears my voice and opens I will sit down to supper with him and he with me

Beatriz could no longer smell, see, hear, taste and touch horror. She had absorbed all of it. Now, she had to purify it. Not knowing how she was doing it, but knowing that she was healing both herself and the holy Padre, she picked up Father Quintana. He weighed nothing, less than a baby. She sat on the chair and cradled him. The broken saint had not flinched. She began to weep with joy. 'We'll be all right, Padrecito... We'll be healed...'

I hear you my Lady thank you my child little Teresa the Beatific One your face upon my wounds your wounds upon my flesh I hear your song help me die pain little Mother unbearable but no more fear only fear of more pain fear of dying with sins in my heart be faithful till death and I will give you the crown of life may I confess Lady I love you I wish I were your husband the flesh still clinging to me I loved a woman before I was ordained older than me full of love warmth joy I had to choose her flesh or Jesus I never forgot her such pain great Mother I wish I were your son still remember her flesh her taste written upon him was a name known to none but himself and he was robed in a garment drenched in blood he was called the Word of God I still remember her flesh her taste

Beatriz rubbed her cheeks on Father Quintana's bloody soutane. 'We shall be all right... I need your strength. You need mine. I shall have your strength. You shall have mine. We will be all right...'

Little Teresa Beatific One great Mother give strength to die I didn't tell anything they didn't know to him who is victorious I will give the right to eat from the tree of life that stands in the Garden of God absolve me my Lady let me not betray Him strength to be victorious Mother of mine Consort of mine he who is victorious cannot be harmed by the second death sing your songs little Teresa my Lady great Mother touch my wounds give strength

'Time's up!'

Colonel Angelito was standing by the cell door, bright-skinned like an electric eel, his smile as casual as death.

Four guards marched in and snatched Father Quintana from Beatriz's lap.

Beatriz, trembling with rage, leaden-legged with sudden exhaustion, struggled off the chair. She wiped her tears. She found herself standing opposite Angelito. She mustered all her hatred and spat at him. 'Look what you've done to him! Murderers! Fascists!'

Angelito, having side-stepped to avoid her spit, smiled jovially. 'It's when we start chopping him into bits you should worry. No one mutilated leaves alive. Looks bad to the world, you see...'

'What sort of people are you?'

The guards were dragging Father Quintana out of the cell. Beatriz blocked their path. Devotionally, she kissed Father Quintana's cheeks and hands. She felt him tremble this time. And a whisper, so faint that it seemed to have come from the furthest innards of the world, acknowledged her love.

The guards left with Father Quintana's husk. She staggered after them, screaming. 'Murderers!'

Angelito chuckled. 'You'll injure your throat, Beatriz. Think of your singing.'

She spun round, screeching. 'You son of a whore! Arsehole!'

He seized her arm, no longer chuckling. 'Out of interest, who gave you permission to visit him?'

'Let go of me! Get out of my way!'

'General Fuego, was it? He should not have done it.'

'He owed me a favour. I let him rape me.'

She jerked her arm free and ran out.

44
They have neither mothers nor poets for their grief

Fuego had to admit it: the 'Sacred Valley' emanated divine essence. Hidden in the middle of the Cordilleras – a dimple in that vast stretch where the western and eastern chains ran close enough to be seen as conjoined – it was one of the few places in the world that had immunised itself against the white man. The mountains embossed the horizon; the peaks, with their helmets of ice, stood sentry, some 6,000 metres tall. Down in the valley, the Incas' river hurtled on its royal business in drapes of spume and tassels of rainbows, its majestic voice reverberating like distant thunder. In this valley, in the space of one swoop of the condor, the four seasons cohabited. By the river perpetual summer sat in tropical heat and lush green; above it, where the guanaco and the vicuña roamed, spring flowered forever; higher still, autumn combed the land to accommodate the alpaca; and up on this mountain pass where the two ranges briefly shook hands, eternal winter safeguarded its favourite creatures: the eagle, the llama and the Indio of the clouds.

Somewhere here Teresa had ascended to her throne as Manku Yupanqui's bride. He could almost believe that.

One of the men handed him a tin can of coca tea; another offered him a rolled cigarette; a third showed him a flower he had never seen, small with a red, tulip-like bulb; a fourth fed the fire with more *yareta* moss; the remaining two squinted into the distance, reading the past or the future.

Fuego glanced at the women, hardy shepherdesses, tending to a few llamas and alpacas. One rose from her haunches – she had been pissing, using her skirts as a screen – and immediately began to sing. How naturally the highlanders glided from one function to another.

Mother
graze the earth
fill your breasts
I need milk

The song was Beatriz's, an early composition, the one that had brought her international fame. Though it now stood as an ode to the Universal Mother, it had been inspired by a Quechua song about the alpaca, the Indio's *mamacita*, who provided everything he needed to survive. The fact that, after years in the white man's wilderness, it had returned to its source pleased Fuego.

Mother
bathe me in the light of the moon
clothe me with the Sun
anoint me with life

He, too, had returned to the source. He had found it still clinging bravely to the roof of the world, still asking the Sun why it had turned its face away from the Indio, when would it correct history?

Deadness chewed more of his innards. How could he have subjected Beatriz to abomination? How – just to win a stupid bet, just to crush a charlatan?

Mother
stand in front of me
hide me between your legs
protect me from the oldest darkness

Why had he returned – no, not returned: he was going back to the capital, back to his uniform, back to the hacienda he had bought with blood, back to absolute power – why had he come to visit the source? Why was he sitting here, as near to the heavens as he could get, in torn poncho, breeches and sandals, basking in the presence of toothless, emaciated members of a dying *ayllu*, feeling at peace, sensing mother, father, brothers and sisters around him? Why?

Mother
winnow the maize planters and the potato pickers
sift the weavers and the artisans
find me a sturdy spouse

Could he ever atone for contaminating Beatriz? Could he ever decontaminate himself of Daniel?

The men resumed their discussion. He, as a campesino passing through, would arbitrate. The issue was a forthcoming saint's day. Such a sacramental occasion required food, drink, musicians, dancers, new clothes and masks, banners, bunting and decorations. Though tradition specified that the expenses for these should be undertaken by individuals in rotation, the *ayllu*, perennially poor, had shared out the obligation equally. This year, however, the llamas and the alpacas had not been very fertile; consequently, even a collective undertaking would prove impossible. Overjoyed by this situation, the local landowner had offered to incur the expenses himself. The *ayllu* was loath to accept. Not only would it bestow honour and prestige on a white man who had stolen vast tracts of land from the campesinos, but it would also profane the saint's day which was one of the few occasions when the Indio could take sustenance from the times the Incas had ruled supreme, pretend that no *misti* breathed upon him with authority, mocked the wisdom of his ancient ways, ordered him to talk Spanish, forced him to elevate the Crucifix far above his many *apus*. The saint's day had to be worshipped. But how could it be worshipped without food, drink and music? What should we do, *compadre*?

Mother
raise the sap in the male
put growing greenness in the female
give me children

Starve, he wanted to tell them, let your children die rather than honour the white man. See the *misti*'s feet – there's slime on them instead of dust. That is because they are born in quagmires. Not like us Indios, born in rivers, mountains, grass, snow, thunder. Their bodies are diseased from feeding on gold, what we call godshit. Not like us who suckled on women who have bathed in the waters of the moon, whose breasts vie with one another for greater fullness. And the worst about the *misti* is his cock. It is like his weapon. It spews poison instead of sperm; it contaminates for generations to come. I know! I entered a woman who had been sullied by one. And look at me, my life drowns in a viscous pool. I was a puma; now I am fit only for the company of rats, worms and maggots. I will die without a sheaf of spirit in my sack. No maize will grow from my heart.

Mother
straighten my back
replenish my strength
your child is your child for ever

Instead, he told them to accept the white man's offer. Don't starve, don't let your children die. Sooner or later the *misti* will cease to rule. The Indio must survive – for he will replant sanity and harmony on earth. Take sustenance from your saint's day. Don't worry about the honour the *misti* will claim. Honour, in terms of the white man, is hollow. Eat and drink your fill, play and dance until you collapse, paint your village with bold colours. And all the while, secretly sharpen your knives.

Mother
close my eyes
open your flesh
take me in

They accepted his advice. They invited him to their village. He thanked them, but refused.

He began his journey back to the capital, back to his uniform, back to being the white man's fetch, back to where God did not exist, where he could laugh at Beatriz's rape, where he could pretend his penis had not been defiled by Daniel's putrid juices.

Back to what he was before: a traitor to his people.

45
Love, love, where does it go to die?

Doña Inez Claudia Isabel de Guzman had insisted on champagne cocktails. They were on their fifth and Daniel was quite drunk. The waiters, he thought, approved. The time was the magical hour before sunset, but the colonnaded balcony harbouring the hotel's salon was empty. Pilgrims to La Recoleta were determinedly abstemious.

'Madam, I feel wonderful!'

'You may call me Inez.'

Daniel raised his glass. Eccentric old lady. When she had inveigled an invitation to his table, she had insisted, regally, on being called by her full name. Now, she had the air of a courtesan. 'I feel wonderful, Inez.'

'I told you: nothing like champagne cocktails after penance. How are the legs?'

Daniel looked up at Huayna Santo, the young hill which rose 1,200 metres over La Recoleta and held at its summit the monolithic statue of Christ the Redeemer. To reach it, the petitioner had to clamber a torturous snake-path marked out by the Fourteen Stations of the Cross.

'Still trembling.'

Earlier, in the blistering heat, he had pathetically performed the ritual. There had been three Indian women climbing at the same time. He had paused with them at each Station, marvelling at the immaculate simplicity of their prayers. When they had reached the statue, its arms fully open to embrace the world, the women, burning offerings, had asked Jesus to watch over their men who had gone to the Sierra to join Huaman.

'Such a nice feeling – trembling legs. I loved it in my heyday. Now, on the few occasions it happens, I am more than grateful. That's trembling for different reasons, of course, but the sensation is the same.'

'It will be easier tomorrow.'

'You're climbing again tomorrow?' Doña Inez put her hand to her mouth in a coy gesture of incredulity. 'So much penance? What could you have done to need all that absolution?'

'I kept fooling myself.'

'That's not being sinful. That's defiance. Which is admirable. You should talk to the Tree.'

Daniel turned to look at the majestic cedar rustling in the square. It rustled even on leaden days, Doña Inez had told him, for it was Jesus' spokesman. Those who had ears to hear were told how they should live the present which bore the errors of the past, and how they should save the future by redeeming the present.

The giant cedar had been discovered early in the seventeenth century, by the Franciscans – the most gifted diviners of holiness, in Doña's Inez's estimation. They had named it the Tree of the Millennium. Naturally, the town that grew around it became unique. It contained two architectural wonders: the convent of La Recoleta which gave the town its name, 'the retreat', and the Cabildo, the palatial baroque town hall – now a luxury hotel – on the balcony of which they were having their cocktails. The buildings stood at either end of an even greater wonder: the grassy Parque del Arbol – the only main square in the country exempt from the martial nomenclature, Plaza de Armas – where the Tree stood as a solitary monument. Inevitably, it was to this town that Simón Bolivar had retired whenever the business of liberating a continent had allowed him respite. Indeed, it was whilst communing with the Tree that he had written his sad prophecies on South America's new-born states: that, given the colonial heritage, the only cadres available to assume power were the armed forces and that, if the people failed to enfranchise themselves quickly, the future would be ransom to a succession of military dictators.

Above all, Doña Inez had stressed, La Recoleta was a sacred city. The fact that Jesus had chosen the Tree of the Millennium as His spokesman had become apparent soon after its discovery. The number of desperados who had found their road to Damascus beneath its shade was astronomical. Rome, of course, had chosen to treat these miracles as native fantasies. But then how could Rome, ensconced in an old world which had forgotten the ways of Nature, understand the young world where people had retained the gift of penetrating the mysteries of leaves, branches, buds and roots?

'I've spoken to the Tree.'

'And?'

Daniel smiled at the thought of his foolishness. He had gone to the Tree, telling himself that his interest was purely professional, that the Tree of the Millennium had often been described as the Tree of Life and, as such, might have served as a prototype for the Tree in the polyptych's fourth section. But he had soon admitted he had been goaded by that peculiar compulsion people manifest towards wishing wells. He had gone in the hope that somehow – magically – he would receive a new soul.

'What did it say – the Tree?'

'It just susurrated.'

'That's wonderful! That means there's a new path for you.'

He smiled bitterly. Damnation, that was the new path. Could he claim that his stoic acceptance of it was a virtue? And the acceptance of death – for he had died, all but in the flesh – was that also a virtue?

'Don't look so solemn, young man. There's a clear message there. Think.'

He was fooling himself again. He had not accepted death or damnation. He still puked every day as his guts regurgitated Fuego's naked cock, damp with Beatriz. That anger was real, basic and primitive: the agony of the cuckold, the contamination of a man's flesh and spirit by another man's penis.

'Think, young man. What did you *actually* hear?'

He pretended to think. 'It sounded like "Pharisee". Repeatedly. Pharisee. Pharisee.'

'There you are. An excellent word.'

He attempted a joke. 'Or maybe it said, "far is he" – he being Jesus…'

'Impossible. Jesus is never very far. What does Pharisee mean to you?'

Pharisees, Papa had often disputed, were not the vipers the New Testament declared they were. But men vested with the Torah, humanitarians who had transmuted God's commandments into principles of compassionate behaviour; the mentors of the Sermon on the Mount, the sages who had inspired that other great book, the Talmud – Jesus' teachers, in fact. Why had the Evangelists calumnied them? Because, as they had spread out into a pagan world, they had thought it best to sever Christianity from its Jewish roots. Standard practice for every new regime to create scapegoats. Put another way, the Pharisees were the first victims of Matthew's time-honoured licence for anti-Semitism: *His blood be on us, and on our children!*

Daniel froze. 'My God!'

'What?'

He stared at Doña Inez. Who was she, what was she, this painted old bird? Why had she waylaid him? Why did she keep talking about the Tree? Was this how madness started! 'The Tree did speak!'

She smiled. 'So celebrate! Order another round!'

Daniel signalled to the waiter.

What the Tree had said was...

'Round', Doña Inez had proudly informed him, was a term she had acquired from Herbert, the Englishman who had rescued her from her fourth widowhood and with whom, in the romantic mode of the times, she had lived out of wedlock. It had been Herbert who had converted her to champagne cocktails. This indulgence, coupled with the wanderlust she had shared with him, had consumed the fortunes they had both inherited from their previous spouses. Herbert, God bless his soul, had timed his death perfectly: when there was just enough money left to pay for the grand funeral he had richly deserved.

What the Tree had said was...

The waiter served the drinks.

'Are you staying here long, Doña Inez?'

She pretended to be shocked. 'Dear me! You don't think *I* am a sinner, do you? I live here, my dear boy! On the outskirts. But I spend most of my time in this hotel. Pilgrims need a lot of comforting.'

What the Tree had said was...

'Bottoms up, Daniel.'

Herbert's famous toast. Daniel raised his glass. 'I think you'll drink me under the table, Inez.'

'It wouldn't be very comfortable under the table.'

'What?'

'Whatever you have in mind.'

She had actually fluttered her eyelids. To his surprise, he stammered. 'Nothing in mind.'

'Wise boy. That way you're pleasantly surprised when life throws you a bouquet.'

'One of Herbert's sayings?'

What the Tree had said was...

She was not trying to seduce him, was she? She was, according to the information she had volunteered, seventy-three. Probably nearer eighty.

'One of *my* sayings. I'm not just a body, you know. I also have an excellent mind.'

He was either too drunk or going mad fast or this was becoming obscene. She *was* trying to seduce him!

He could not resist assessing her. Well-dressed: bright-coloured taffeta, lace wherever possible and big imitation jewellery. Medium height. Slim and small-breasted. Very pale white skin and freckled. Arms and legs still shapely, but some varicose veins. She must have been a red-head: the auburn dye of her hair blended naturally with her complexion; her pubic hair, he guessed, would still be ginger. She wore heavy make-up – except around her eyes which were beautiful: large, black olives and still bright.

She had been watching him. 'Do you like giving presents?'

'Pardon?'

'I love getting presents. Nowadays I insist on money. At my age one loses interest in frills…'

Was she soliciting?

What the Tree had said was…

He began to cry.

What the Tree had said was… Become a Pharisee! Go back to your roots! Be what you were born to be!

Doña Inez was stroking his hand. 'Oh, poor you. Have I stirred memories?'

'No…' He could not stop weeping.

Become a Pharisee! Embrace the Torah! He who rejects his roots becomes an empty shell. Reconsider what is meant by 'the new man'. He is not someone we can manufacture; for whatever we manufacture is imperfect and, at its extreme, an abomination, like Hitler's Aryan race. We are man, created in God's image. The image is perfect. What is imperfect is our unwillingness to accept this image. The new man will be he who will accept the image, dispense love instead of hate, courage instead of fear.

Doña Inez was stroking his cheek. 'Poor boy. So full of suffering. What have they done to you? Such a lovely boy. You don't deserve tears. You deserve houris.'

He tried to stop crying. 'What?'

'Beautiful houris. To give you a bath. To rub your back. Caress your chest. Kiss you everywhere…'

Papa often told you: the purpose of the Torah is to guide man towards human perfection; then he can approach God in awe, love and joy. The Torah was given with three formidable elements: fire, water and wilderness. Man must journey through each in order to acquire wisdom and sanctity.

So become a Jew again! Put yourself in the firing line as is incumbent on every Jew!

Doña Inez was still caressing him. 'Alas, there are no houris here. There is only me. A bit worn, but still very gifted. The way I wash a man, the many ways I bring him to pleasure – pure vintage. That's what Herbert used to say. And Herbert was a connoisseur.'

He managed to stop crying. 'Are you – serious?'

She ran her fingers along his hand. 'And because you're such a hunk, I'll only ask ten thousand *reales*…'

Daniel felt shocked: he was erect.

Why not? What did it matter if she was old? What could he lose? At worst, further fragmentation inside a dusty vagina – but what did that mean for someone already in pieces! On the other hand, a chance perhaps to paste some pieces together, to reclaim a thimbleful of sexuality, the only substance he had ever had.

Doña Inez tweaked his nose. 'Life is throwing you a bouquet – grab it!'

Perhaps, a miracle: rebirth. From an ancient womb.

Daniel rose. 'I'd like that very much.'

Winsomely, Doña Inez waited for him to pull away her chair. 'Ask them to send up a dozen champagne cocktails.'

46

The throne of bloodstained gold, the whore freedom, the land with no overcoat

They had moved up to where only the snow grew and where even those with condor's lungs fought for air.

Here they were safe. Up here they could touch freedom, feel it stick to the skin like packed ice. From these mountain ramparts, they could mock the struggling armies and piss down on the wheezing helicopters.

The people had found a boulder, the largest and smoothest on the summits and had designated it, after the ancient royal podium, the Inca seat.

Huaman, wearing his scarlet-fringed *borla* and draped in the regal poncho the women had woven, climbed on to the boulder and sat down. Chauca sat to his right as his general – the only rank, the people had insisted, that befitted Manku Yupanqui's adjutant. He wore the title as uncomfortably as the lordly poncho he, too, had been given.

It was one of those fabled Andean days: the sky so clear that an eagle could scan the grass growing on the Morning Star; the ranges shifted perspectives like chessmen on a titanic board; the glaciers turned green with envy of the sky's blue; the snow acquired the reverse of total darkness; and the rocks recounted how, before petrification, they had been manna from Heaven.

The aged, the women and the children had spread out in concentric circles from the Inca seat. Though he had limited their visits to once a week, Huaman barely tolerated these camp-followers. His objective was to create a liberation

320

army superior to anything the world had seen; trailing a horde of civilians was not the way to achieve that. But, for the time being, they had their uses. They brought in supplies; maintained communications between the *focos*; provided intelligence on the movements of the security forces; and, above all, spread the word about Manku Yupanqui.

'Can you see the men, *Comandante?*'

Huaman surveyed the landscape. Frozen earth, rock, snow – nothing else. 'Are they in position?'

Chauca nodded and fired his rifle.

The slopes rippled as guerrilleros, waving machetes, surged out of their hiding places.

Chauca fired another shot.

Instantly, the guerrilleros disappeared from sight.

Chauca fired again.

The guerrilleros reappeared – this time, in a different formation.

'See, *Comandante*. No man in the same place twice.'

To the continued cheers of the camp-followers, the guerrilleros repeated the exercise, each time disappearing and reappearing from new positions.

Huaman was impressed. 'You've trained them well.'

'In the jungle, *Comandante*. It taught us what we forgot: how to be one with the land.' He fired two shots.

The guerrilleros brought the exercise to an end. They dispersed and, leaving lookouts at vantage points, ran down to join their folk.

Huaman rubbed his stump. It was aching today. A warning that the weather would change and that when the snow came it would throb mercilessly. He leaned on his good arm to let the sun warm the stump. He had to sit on the Inca seat until the camp-followers left that afternoon. As Manku Yupanqui, he had to perform the symbolic act of being tied to a rock as the Incas had tied the Sun to an altar.

He had come to enjoy the ritual. Adulation was seductive even if the purveyors were simple-minded Indios.

He had nothing else to do up here. Chauca, indefatigable, was in charge of the training. A number of able men, promoted to lieutenancy, executed the rest of the duties. A revolutionary leader, Huaman had decided, was like a poet: much of the time, he sat and mused, sifting the dirt and the air for the intangible; occasionally, he picked up gun or pen and did battle with self and the world.

The guerrilleros had joined their folk. Some were playing with their children, others catching up on news from their *ayllus*. Some of the old people had brought coca leaves and *aguardiente*, but the guerrilleros were refusing to partake. He had forbidden them their neolithic traditions. He still had problems, however, with their sexual needs. It was scandalous the number of times they took their women behind the rocks. Such indulgences eroded martial spirit. Masturbation was the answer. You start by doing it every day, then gradually you get bored with it and finally you lay off because it's too much of an effort. Or once in a blue moon, when you can't sleep because of the cold or rain or fever or frustration, you think of some voluptuous woman like Beatriz Santillan, and you jerk off for all you're worth. But, alas, masturbation was not a normal practice with the Indio. How to convert him to it?

Huaman noticed some women squatting near the Inca seat. They could not be waiting for him. That time the people had suggested he should exercise his rights, like the Inca Emperors, with any woman that pleased him, he had severely rebuked them. Having married Teresa, he had told them, he had no need of other women; Manku Yupanqui was better and purer than an Inca Emperor.

Chauca noticed Huaman's antagonism towards the women. 'They are on offer to me, *Comandante*.' He waved the women off. Then, hesitating a moment, he braced himself for an argument. 'The *compañeros* ask me to talk, *Comandante*.'

Huaman's mood changed. Asking was not a prerogative of the guerrilleros. 'Another time, Chauca. Go, have a woman.'

'It's about Father Quintana. The *compañeros* ask what we will do.'

Huaman became terse. 'Nothing we can do.'

'We believe Father Quintana is a saint...'

Chauca's identification with the people always cancelled that cartload of admirable qualities he otherwise had. 'Hardly that, Chauca. He's a nice old priest who dreamed about martyrdom – and will probably get it.'

'Some *compañeros* say he is Old Judge from Manku Yupanqui legend. They are surprised you do not save him.'

'What do they want me to do? Invade El Chulpa?'

'They expect you use sun's missing ray.'

That tone of censure – it was making him hate Chauca. Since that day when the people's representatives had crowned him Manku Yupanqui, Chauca's disapproval had hung around like pestilence. True, forever loyal, Chauca had not denounced him. But he had never once addressed him as Manku Yupanqui. Always *Comandante*, *Comandante*.

'You tell the people, Chauca... Just tell them to forget Quintana! He's not much use to us any more!'

'*Comandante*, you must do something.'

'Must? Since when do you have a say in strategy?'

Chauca remained unruffled. 'The men are becoming impatient. They want to fight.'

'When we're strong enough.'

'With the twenty *compañeros* who joined today, we are five hundred and seventeen men. Of those sick from the jungle, only nine are still ill – and they will be well soon. We are strong enough.'

Chauca might be a born commando, but here was proof of his ineptitude in the art of war. Five hundred men – and he saw that as a conquering army; not even considering that three hundred and fifteen of them were strewn all over the highlands manning and consolidating, in nuclei of fifteen, the twenty-one *focos*. 'And what do I do with the *focos*? I sweated blood establishing them! Are you suggesting I risk them?'

'Not more than necessary.'

'The *focos* will be our fifth column until we raise a popular army large enough to trample the government forces. That means they have to burrow within easy reach of strategic targets. And whilst they lie low, they have also to expand, politicise the locals, recruit some, ensure support from the rest. Above all, they have to achieve utmost mobility, prepare to operate separately or concertedly with other *focos*. I've already instructed you on these principles, Chauca! It would be madness to touch the *focos* now! That leaves us with barely two hundred men! You think that's enough to start fighting?'

'What is the measure for enough, *Comandante*? The *naturale*'s mug or the *misti*'s barrel?'

'Don't be clever with me! Have you forgotten what happened at Monte Rico?'

'*Comandante*, the men want blood on their hands. We can spill a few drops. We are enough to show the people your strength – so they can believe their strength.'

'Are you telling me they have doubts about me?'

'When people hear only talk and see no action, *Comandante*, they find some questions have bad answers.'

Insolent Indio. He should cut him down to size. Except that Chauca's tone now contained a warning.

Huaman had not been complacent about the people's adulation. Messianic faith had different dynamics from political ideology. Idols were worshipped until they exposed their clay feet; then, they were smashed. Disregarding Chauca – who would rather die than point a finger – the only factor that might challenge his Manku Yupanqui identity was his so-called marriage to Teresa. Questions about her whereabouts, activities and state of health had been incessant.

But Chauca was implying that the people were now demanding something more tangible. They were asking him to prove himself. 'A few drops of blood, you said...'

'One attack, *Comandante*. We kill some Sinchis. Take some prisoners. We ask to exchange them for Father Quintana. We smile a little.'

That was possible, of course. A variation on the strikes he had planned on Sinchi outposts to secure arms. Feasible with two hundred men. 'I'll think about it.'

'Thank you, *Comandante*.' Chauca saluted smartly and sauntered off.

Huaman shifted position. He was getting stiff. And cold. And the stump still ached. And now he had to generate the will for action. He *did* want action. He *craved* for blood on his hands. He had not been prevaricating. He had been assessing strategies. One never tasted defeat whilst one planned; whereas action was immutable. That was another thing common to the revolutionary and the poet: action became part of history like a poet in print.

Prevaricating, indeed! No one had forced him to take to the wilderness. He had done it by choice. If truth be known, he could have seized power the easy way, dismantled the Junta from the inside by staying in La Merced, using the family connections, infiltrating the luxurious mansions and the boardrooms – like the Americans did, wherever they went.

Oh, yes, he could have had an easy revolution. Gone to a soft bed every night after a hot shower, with decent food in his belly and intelligent conversations humming in his head. Instead of this misery!

Prevaricating, indeed!

47

The old smell of semen like a bindweed of ashen flour slides into your mouth

'A stone-mason expects the rock to be hard, Daniel. If it shatters like mica, he feels defeated.'

Daniel gazed at Fuego's bonfire. Pleasure, if it ever took on substance, would rise in flames and sing with orange and blue tongues. Pleasure, as Doña Inez had proved, was a good antidote for penitence. What could be more pleasurable than revenge?

'You gave me an easy victory, Daniel... I thought maybe salvation did flow through your veins... I thought, well, monks and nuns preserve their genitals for the divine fuck, so maybe I am blind, maybe God exists, maybe we recreate Him daily – make Him like we make babies...

Fuego stopped nursing the bonfire and stared at the night sky. The hillock where he had fought with Angelito had become his favourite retreat. Here he could sit as an Indio, chew coca solemnly, purify himself and be aware of the stars blossoming like daisies. But, alas, tonight, Daniel had returned from the white man's ossuary to spoil the heavens with his deadness. 'What brings you here?'

Daniel kept his eyes on the bonfire. He had to blot out the vision of Fuego standing stark naked with his handsome cock, stark naked as if he had anchored himself to that moment, two months now, when he had raped Beatriz. He lit a cigarette, trying to control the trembling in his hands.

God knows what Fuego is up to, Rice had told him on the telephone.

There are rumours that he drowns himself in wild parties; other rumours that he has gone native and obsessively performs purificatory rites.

Both rumours had been true. There was an orgy in full swing at the hacienda and here was Fuego riding into the occult on a bonfire.

'When I entered Beatriz, I was terrified. I thought I would find God where you had hidden Him. But all I found was a cunt you had contaminated. A cunt which, when I used to know it, used to transform winter to spring. But which had dried up, smothered by your poisoned desert.'

Only a thin barrier separated man from the occult – a thinner one when the man was an Indian. Cunning, the coward's artillery, could blow up that barrier.

'I wanted to quarter God before your eyes! Prove He was something man made in his image! I wanted to make you say who needs a deity that shits out his heart, how can anything man creates make the maize grow?'

That cock! Hiding its assassin's face in the sparse foliage of pubic hair! Oh, to seize it by its veins and bleed it dry!

Fuego faced Daniel. 'Don't you have anything to say?'

That cock! Hanging quiescent, bloodless, pastoral. Was it the ritual of purification that had given it its mask of innocence?

'The irony is, I did you a favour – though that was not my intention. I showed you the truth.'

That cock! Will you make me as evil? So that I can destroy you! You owe me that! My pound of flesh!

'I will tell you something else! There was a part of me that wanted you to prove God was what He ought to be: wise, just, compassionate, father to us all, tender as the breast. If you could have proved that, Daniel, my defeat would have been my greatest victory.'

I witnessed the ritual! I was hiding with all things evil. When I heard you'd gone native, I knew this was my chance! I've brushed up on Indian lore!

'But you never believed in God! That's why He was not in Beatriz's cunt! You did not have Him to put Him there!'

You started by chewing coca. Then you took your pulse from your wrists and fingertips. Then you shed your clothes: a threadbare poncho, patched breeches, tattered sandals. You burned them one by one. You continued taking your pulse – from your biceps, under your armpits, from your throat, temple, diaphragm, groins, toes and, finally, from that cock!

'He exists much more for me, Daniel!'

Then you chewed more coca. And you sucked those parts you could reach: wrists, fingertips, biceps. And those parts you couldn't suck – you blew your breath at them: diaphragm, armpits, groins, toes, that cock!

'At least, I treated Him as my greatest enemy!'

After the sucking and the blowing, you smeared your body with llama fat – several layers on that cock!

'I fought Him! Tried to push Him off the summits!'

You waited until the fat congealed. Then you scraped it all off, transferred it into a clay pot, sealed it.

'Drown Him in the rivers! Burn the forests He roamed!'

What you were doing was casting out the *susto*: that state of trauma which is the Earth's curse on those who trespass Nature.

'What good is my victory, eh, Daniel, if my enemy proves to be a mollusc?'

The sucking and blowing on pulse points draws out the *susto*; the llama fat absorbs it. You then either bury the fat or use it against an enemy. You chose to bury it.

'I'm still your enemy.'

Fuego spun round and faced Daniel. 'Found your tongue, have you?' To his surprise, he wanted to embrace Daniel, greet him like a brother – this man who had contaminated him. 'Where have you been?'

Daniel drew on his cigarette. 'I went searching for a hole.'

Fuego squatted on his haunches and guffawed. Daniel would for ever pursue meaninglessness. Why did I miss him? Why do I bother with him? That reflection of myself – I have destroyed that. What primitive need still attaches me to him? At the same time demands to be free of him, compels me into purificatory rites? 'What sort of hole? A hole-hole? A safe-hole? A black-hole? An arsehole? Or a spunk-hole?'

Daniel grinned. 'An ancient hole.'

Fuego smiled derisively. 'Did you find it?'

'Yes. Several, in fact.'

Fuego scrutinised Daniel. On the night of the rape, that massive frame had splintered on to the carpet; and he had savoured the moment as if it were history's revenge on the *misti*. Now, though the thousand cracks still showed, Daniel appeared to have glued his bulk together. What glue was capable of that?

'The hole of madness. And the hole of sanity. For a start.'

'We are in for some of your counterfeit talk, are we?'

'Not this time. Can you fight my madness and sanity?'

Fuego rediscovered his hatred; it pleased him. 'I can fight you whatever you are.'

'I'm counting on that.'

Fuego laughed. 'Don't count too much. The moment I move you are likely to run away.'

'I won't.'

Fuego became wary. 'Ready when you are, then.'

Daniel threw his cigarette in the bonfire. 'Be a Pharisee, Jesus' tree said. So I also found the hole of Judaism. I heard the commandment: throw yourself into fire, water and the wilderness!'

'I have lost the scent, Daniel.'

That cock! It was retreating into the depths of Fuego's body. Into invisibility.

Daniel grinned. 'I don't know whether I'll ever get to the water or the wilderness. But first things first. Fire. That's you.'

'That's me, no question. Come on, then.'

Daniel began to undress.

Fuego shouted hoarsely. 'At last! We're going to fight? And naked? Like the primitive men we are? Perfect!'

Daniel kicked off his shoes. 'Your enemy, God! He's still here!'

'To the death – shall we?'

Daniel shouted. 'He's still here! Still inside Beatriz! I've lost Him. You've never had Him. But Beatriz still has Him! And she will save Him!'

Fuego coiled up.' Come on! I am ready!'

Frenziedly, Daniel tore off the rest of his clothes. 'And listen to this! He is not outside any more – where you can see Him! He has penetrated you! Entered you like you entered me! Through your cock! From Beatriz's cunt!'

Fuego outshouted him. 'Poisoned sand! That's what you filled her with! That's what entered me!'

Daniel stood naked. 'Afraid?'

Fuego spat contemptuously. 'Of you?'

'Of what I'll become!'

'And what is that!'

'You. Fire.'

Fuego snarled. 'How?'

Daniel walked over to the spot where Fuego had buried the llama fat. He began to dig. 'Here's another hole, Oseas! The hole I've most wanted.'

Fuego became transfixed. 'Get away from there! Come and fight! Man to man!'

Daniel went on digging. 'Go ahead – hit me!'

Fuego took a step forward, then stopped.

Daniel laughed. 'You can't, can you? It would annul the ritual. Once you've buried the *susto*, you can't stop anybody exhuming it!'

'Stop that!'

'Tell me honestly – did you really think you could cast God out by siphoning Him off on to some fat?'

Fuego bellowed. 'It's not God I have been siphoning off! It's you! The contamination you left in her!'

Daniel pulled the pot with the llama fat out of its hole. 'Casting out evil — that's what you've done!'

'Your evil!'

Daniel broke open the pot's seal. 'Which of my evils? Cowardice? Hypocrisy? Godlessness?'

'Cover that! Put it back!'

Daniel began to smear the llama fat over his penis. 'Godlessness — let's say, godlessness!'

Fuego roared. 'Don't do that!'

Daniel gazed at the fat on his penis, then turned to Fuego. 'On second thoughts, I'll eat it. Should be more effective.' He crammed the congealed fat into his mouth.

Fuego watched him, transfixed.

Daniel guzzled the llama fat. 'On the other hand, maybe I'm eating God Himself- God whom you received from Beatriz! Something else you should think about.'

Fuego gesticulated wildly. 'This is Indio mumbo-jumbo, Daniel! Doesn't work on a white man!'

Daniel licked the last dregs of the llama fat and threw the pot at Fuego. 'We shall see.'

Fuego caught the pot and smashed it against a rock. 'Will you fight me now?'

Daniel walked off.

'You are running away again!'

Daniel waved at him. 'I'm going back to the hacienda. There's an orgy in full swing. I can't miss that.'

Fuego bellowed. 'Fight me, you bastard!'

Daniel disappeared into the darkness.

48

And what has become of it, where is that onetime love? Now it is the grave of a bird, a drop of black quartz, a chunk of wood eroded by the rain

'Dr Torres, please.'

'I'm sorry, Dr Torres is not on duty.'

'Can I reach him at his home?

'I wouldn't know.'

'I'll try him there. Can I leave a message – in case he rings in? This is Beatriz Santillan. I'm not due yet – not even eight months gone – so he isn't expecting me to be in labour, but I am...'

'I'll give him the message when he comes in.'

'Thank you.'

Beatriz dialled Dr Torres's home number. As it rang, she examined her panties again, then examined the bedsheet where she had been sitting. Blood.

No reason to panic. It's the show.

But normally the show is a little blood. So little that some women don't even notice it.

'Hello.'

'Dr Torres please.'

'He's not available.'

'Are you his wife?'

'Yes.'

'This is Beatriz Santillan. I'm sorry to trouble you, but I've already started. It's premature and...'

'*Abort it!*'

'What?'

'*This is not a world for children.*'

'Look, just tell me where Dr Torres is...'

'*Try the place where the cadavers appear...*'

The woman's controlled voice disintegrated in a wail. She disconnected. Beatriz stared in horror at the telephone. Dr Torres? Disappeared? No – not him! Why him?

She doubled up as the contractions started again.

Oh, Mother of God, did you suffer as much when the Lord asked to be born? Were you kicked in the back by a thousand mules? Did you feel your insides tearing? I need help!

Mustn't panic. Sing! Sing something!

Last night
I saw a vision
a new vision
as old as time

My new song. A psalm for the New Man. Ideally to be sung by an extraterrestrial voice – a child soprano, at the very least. Not in my nasal drone which the world loves but I hate. Jerry! Why didn't I think of him?

She dialled.

'*Yeah?*'

'Jerry... It's started and...'

'*Take it easy, now. I'll be right over.*'

Dear Jerry, dear Jerry, dear Jerry. Oh, the pain! Dear baby, sweet baby, you're breaking my back! Sing!

a vision
without knives
without guns

I'm bleeding again. It's not just the show. It's something more... The waters... That's it – the waters have broken. But it's viscous! It should be fluid... Maybe I burst a vein. It can happen – not very serious... If so, shouldn't the blood gush? And what about the waters – shouldn't they gush, too?

No. Waters can burst either as a slow trickle or they can gush. With me it's trickling, that's all there is to it. And that means I shall be delivering soon. My baby, my New Man, why are you so impatient to be born?

a vision
conquering famine
conquering drought

This is like a period – getting rid of what the body doesn't want, what my baby doesn't want. Expelling Fuego's evil. Daniel's betrayal…

a vision
healing wounds
healing sickness

The pain! I can bear it! Go on, my baby, don't worry about me, fight your way out! Come, flesh of my flesh, Mama wants you, Mama loves you! Just let me catch my breath, let me get some strength back! Listen, listen to my song.

a vision
untouched by barbed wire, prisons, windowless cells
untouched by disappearances

Dr Torres! How could they? He treated the poor also – was that why? Who'll look after me now? Who'll deliver my baby?

a vision
beyond treacherous couplings
beyond rejections

Jerry. He'll find a doctor. It will be all right. My baby, we'll be all right. How can Mama let anything happen to you when she loves you so much?

a vision
liberated from separations
liberated from the death of love

I can't sing any more. I need breath – to fight the pain. You understand that, don't you? And you heard what Jerry said – take it easy. I'm still bleeding! All right, the last stanza – it's my favourite, too…

I saw a vision
last night
when the world was
you and I and our child

Daniel, you bastard! Why aren't you here? Why aren't you helping me? Never mind, my baby, never mind! I'll be mother and father... Stop it, you beast! You're hurting me! You're hurting your mother! Don't you have any pity?

49

A son who will be stronger, stronger, much stronger than we

Daniel grabbed a bottle of champagne from one of the ice-buckets and moved into the ballroom.

The dancing was still serious. But at the periphery of the floor a few guests were already copulating. Rather then being cheered for their ardour, they were being ridiculed as philistines. Surrendering to impatience definitely showed lack of breeding; an orgy, the junoesque *bossa-nova* queen kept shouting, was like *haute cuisine*: it should be prepared and cooked painstakingly, not flung on a barbecue as if it were a hamburger.

Daniel drank half his bottle, then began to undress. He ignored the shakes. He was not often sober these days. For a moment, he stared at his fancy-dress – the black kaftan of a Talmudic scholar. It would serve him right if his penis flopped out as limp as a sodden biscuit.

Mercifully, it emerged erect. Good old slave, clinging to life long after its master had died.

Fuego was on the bandstand, leaning against a backboard. Since the night of the purificatory ritual, he had replaced the musicians with piped music and had made the bandstand his exclusive spot. To see, hear, touch, taste and smell everything, he had told Daniel, not entirely in jest.

Daniel was still unsure whether Fuego had taken his challenge seriously. He could not even convince himself that he had actually challenged Fuego. He remembered eating the llama fat, but that could have been an alcohol-induced hallucination. One fact was irrefutable, though: the Fuego who had gone native out on a hillock had rushed back to the white man's quagmire. Why? – if not because of the challenge!

Fuego was dressed as Bacchus – in woven beads of plastic grapes. He was again sporting some of his larger medals on a silk band around his neck. They were not meant to proclaim his exalted status, he had confided to Daniel at the last orgy, but to show he had a sense of humour. People were always at a disadvantage when dealing with someone who had a sense of humour. This orgy itself was pure whimsy. It would go on throughout Easter.

Four girls in their teens, new recruits to the circus, were fluttering around Fuego, flicking their tongues all over his body.

Daniel scanned the guests. A new record in numbers. Except for the Junta, whom Fuego had classified eunuchs, and for Angelito, whom he considered useful only for minding the security shop – but who, in any case, could not have come since his wife had presented him with another son on this Good Friday – everybody who was somebody in the State machinery was present. The sight of the nation's élite with their trousers down, Fuego had declared, always thrilled him. It confirmed the inviolability of his power. If the disgruntled populace could not stuff piles of Andean stones into these overfed, pampered, sick, withering cunts and arseholes, it could do nothing to shift him from the top of the mountain.

Daniel caught two smiles dressed as balloons. He approached the women and poured champagne over the first. 'I christen you Maria.' He emptied the bottle on the second. 'And you, I christen Dolores.'

The women clapped their hands in delight. One of them cooed. 'Like the song?'

Carefully putting the bottle on to the buffet, Daniel grabbed their hands and placed them on his penis. 'Come and lie on my purple and fine linen. I know so many love games, we won't know where to begin.'

The women shrieked delightedly. Maria licked his ear. 'That's from a song, too.'

'Composed by Beatriz Santillan. I knew her well.' Desperately, he looked at his penis. Shackled by the women s hands, but still erect – thank God. 'Shall we, ladies?'

Giggling, Maria and Dolores let their balloons fly off.

Daniel's eyes cleared as he stared at what they displayed. Maria was, if not the fattest woman in the world, the second fattest. Dolores, divested of her balloons, was skeletal, a toothpick with some pubic hair. 'The seven years of plenty and the seven years of famine!'

Maria shrieked with laughter. Dolores, looking insulted, pushed her scaffold forward, unfolded the lips of her vagina and ran his penis over it. 'Plenty here, too.'

That bony abyss was squelching wet. Miracle of miracles. Courteously, Daniel kissed her, then tweaked one of Maria's colossal breasts. 'All right! I'm the prize! Fight for me!'

Maria and Dolores, laughing frenziedly, grappled each other in mock combat.

Daniel, cheering them on, lost his balance and fell. As if this were their cue, Maria and Dolores abandoned their wrestling and tumbled over him. As their limbs entwined him, Daniel's impulse was to rear up and run! He forced himself to lie still.

'Get up, you goddam turd – get up!'

Daniel looked up, saw Rice and giggled. 'Hello, Jerry.'

'Get up! You're making an ass of yourself!'

Daniel wished he could kill him. 'Yes. But it's not helping, Jerry.'

Rice pushed Maria and Dolores off him. 'Get up!'

'Watch it, Jerry.'

Rice hauled him up. 'Come on!'

Daniel grabbed Rice by the shirt collar. 'You come on, Jerry! Join in! Which do you want – Fats or Slim?'

'I'm taking you home!'

Daniel shrieked with mirth. 'Home?'

'Beatriz needs you!'

Daniel screamed in fury. 'Get him! Somebody get him!'

The dancers stopped dancing; the orgiasts interrupted their copulation; Maria and Dolores, who had dragged themselves up to reclaim Daniel, edged back.

Daniel squared up to Rice. Miserable old man in a printed Florida shirt coming here to judge him. He should be dead and buried, tombless and forgotten.

Fuego intercepted with a mellow voice. 'Mr Rice – nice of you to gatecrash...'

'Sorry, General.'

'You are most welcome.' Fuego clapped his hands to summon the girls who had been attending to him.

The girls waded into the crowd and carved their way towards Rice. Rice watched spellbound.

Daniel giggled, waving at the air as if wanting to clear the bad breath left by Rice.

The girls pounced on Rice. Flicking their tongues like snakes, they started undoing Rice's shirt and trousers.

Rice gaped at them. 'Stop it – let go! Daniel – tell them to lay off!'

Daniel tittered. 'No mercy, girls!'

Rice, mustering all his strength, pushed them away. 'Beatriz is in labour! She needs help!'

Daniel grabbed Maria and Dolores by their arms and dragged them away. His voice screeched. 'You have both won!'

The young girls, pouting, reconverged on Rice.

Fuego flung them aside and grabbed hold of Rice. 'You said home! Why isn't she in hospital?'

Rice adjusted his clothes, glaring at Fuego. 'Her doctor has disappeared. The hospital's playing safe – they said there were no beds.'

'I will get her in.'

'No sense in moving her now. I found a midwife.'

'Let's go.'

As they hurried away, Rice glanced at Daniel. Standing vacuously by the French doors to the swimming pool, framed by his conquests.

Beatriz fought for breath.

Fuego wiped the sweat off her brow.

How come Fuego was standing by her side, draped in his General's overcoat, gripping her hands, conferring with the midwife.

The next contraction came as painfully as the one before. She screamed, bit her lips – already torn and bloody – and pushed, pushed, pushed.

'That is good – good girl!'

Not the midwife talking, but Fuego. Where had he learned all that? She began to weep. 'Why isn't Daniel here? It's his baby!'

'Hush.'

'Why are you here?'

'Don't talk. Save your breath.'

The next contraction. And the next scream – hoarse and as exhausted as the body.

'Push! Push!'

I need breath. 'Have you come to kill the baby?'

'No.'

'Why then?'

'I want to see what hope looks like.'

Another contraction. Mother of God! You're killing me! Push! I'm pushing! Push! I can't push any more!

'The head – it's coming through.'

That was the midwife.

'Ease it out.'

That was Fuego.

And another contraction. My heart will stop! And that will be it! Deliverance! Push! Push! Push! Ahhhhhhhh!

'I've got the head.'

The midwife.

'Gently now.'

Fuego.

'You want the baby? For you? To love?'

She. Shouting as she held precariously on to the world – to Fuego of all people because there was no one else!

'The head's out!'

The midwife.

'Oh, *Madre de Dios*!'

Jerry Rice kept his eyes on the whisky bottle. Soon now, very soon. The first glass to celebrate, the subsequent ones to get drunk – for once for a good reason. But until then, nothing. He had to be sober for that first encounter with the New Man.

The bedroom door opened. Fuego came out. A Napoleonic figure in his military overcoat.

Rice stood up. 'What's happening?'

'The midwife's dealing with the placenta.'

'It's finished then? He's born?'

Fuego, without responding to Rice's smile, moved towards the front door.

Rice edge forward. 'Can I go in? Gosh, I didn't even hear it cry!'

Fuego, shivering suddenly, wrapped his overcoat tightly around himself and walked out.

Rice shouted at him. 'Everything's all right, isn't it?'

The Penitent, in sackcloth and veil and smeared with ash, carried a bundle.

Daniel, pinned down by Fuego's four nymphs, stared at the figure.

Stepping over the exhausted bodies, skirting round those still copulating, the Penitent progressed slowly across the ballroom. The shoulders could now be seen to have collapsed – the crushing weight of a terrible past.

The writing on the Penitent's bundle, '*El Nuevo Hombre – The New Man*', fell like spikes on Daniel's eyes.

He turned towards Fuego, wanting to shout: send her away. But Fuego, leaning against his backboard, appeared to be asleep.

At some point during these last days, Fuego had vanished. At least a day, perhaps more. And since his return, he had not moved, had not claimed a single woman, had just stood on the bandstand, wrapped up in his overcoat, eyes tightly shut...

The Penitent was close now. Progressing inexorably.

Daniel extricated himself from the girls and stood up. He wanted to run, but could not.

'Daniel Brac. This is yours.' A nasal voice – could be female.

Daniel stared at the bundle, read and reread the tag. He felt his hands stretch out and take the bundle, automatically, as if accustomed to receiving such things.

The softness within the bundle revolted him. He stammered hoarsely, trying to give it back. 'I don't want it!'

The Penitent walked away, same slow steps.

Daniel staggered forward. 'Take it back!'

Fuego materialised. 'What's that, Daniel?'

'I don't know.' He made another effort to run after the Penitent, but with Fuego standing in front of him, he lost the momentum. 'Hey, come here, you! Take it back!'

Gently, Fuego took the bundle. 'It says "The New Man".'

Daniel mumbled as he watched the Penitent walk away. 'Beatriz...'

Delicately, Fuego unfolded the bundle.

First a wrinkled leg, no bigger than a thumb, then another, caked in uterine blood. Daniel felt he was going blind like Saul who became Paul. But he knew that when he saw again, there would be no Holy Spirit to fill him.

Fuego whispered reverently. 'The New Man.'

Daniel stared at the baby. Its umbilical cord was wound around its throat. 'Oh, God!'

'But dead, Daniel. Born dead. Which means he has never lived – except in the womb.'

'Oh, God!'

'The womb does not count. Everything must live outside, survive outside – in the world, in our Kingdom!'

'Oh, God!'

'There is no God – you know that...'

'Why did you kill the baby?'

'I did not. He died when his father stopped loving him.' Fuego placed the baby in Daniel's hands. 'Here, take it.'

Daniel retched and staggered backwards. He was floating now, swaying. His hands abandoned the baby. Aeons later, he heard it hit the floor. He yelled.

He kept on yelling, hoarsely, not knowing whether it was he who was screaming or his son.

Finally, he opened his eyes and wiped the sweat and vomit off his face. He was no longer drunk. He made himself look at the tiny creature he and Beatriz had created in love.

He heard the laughter of the guests. Rumbling, echoing. A thousand eyes were watching his penis. He was urinating uncontrollably.

He started laughing, too, pointing at the way his water splashed off his dead son.

He caught sight of Maria and Dolores. He beckoned them.

Fuego sat naked on his hillock and watched the sunset.

He had washed the New Man. He had buried it in a doll's-house that had once belonged to one of Vargas's daughters so that he would have a home in the other world.

And into the grave, he had put a nest containing a llama foetus, some llama fat, incense and aromatic herbs, a variety of sweetmeats, a few coca leaves and a piece of melted tin – all in homage to Pachamama so that the New Man would have peace under his nether roof.

He had done all that unthinkingly.

Now he was asking the dying sun: why?

Eventually the sun answered: because now you are afraid that you might be right: that God does not exist.

Then the sun buried itself.

PART NINE

50

Earth kept breaking all he had: the horse, the bullet, the bull, the stone, the snow, the luck

Rice was not going to ask him in. He was blocking the door to his flat with his concave chest and defying Daniel's bulk by holding his never-empty glass like a weapon. He smelled of stale perspiration and was unsteady on his feet.

'I stopped fornicating, Jerry... Stopped drinking, too...'

Rice gulped down some whisky.

Daniel, unable to look Rice in the face, ran his eyes over the door frame. In his childhood home the front door had a *mezuzah* – made of olive wood. Every time his father had left for work, he had kissed it. There had been a *mezuzah*, too, by his parents' bedroom door. Had they kissed it every time they had retired? And when they went for siestas and ended up laughing? Laughing, a colleague had once told him, was how the Chinese referred to orgasm.

'I've only got the last section left... I'll finish that... I'll work day and night – nothing else to do... Then I'll be gone.'

'Uh-huh.'

'But... before I shut myself in, I want to see Beatriz... Apologise...'

'Apologise?' Rice grabbed the door to slam it shut.

Daniel wedged himself between the door and the frame. 'What do you want me to say? What would have any meaning?'

Rice glared at him, taking another mouthful of whisky.

With his powerful body slouched into an untidy heap, Daniel looked defeated. There was penitence, too: unshaven though he was, he was clean. Rice could smell his peculiar perfume: soap blended with paint and tobacco.

Rice shuffled away from the door. 'Have some coffee…'

'Thank you.' Daniel stepped into the room. It was in even worse disorder than when he had come to fetch Beatriz – after Kempin.

Rice heated up the coffee. 'She'll never forgive you.'

'She's not at home. It's closed up. Where is she?'

'No one will ever forgive you.'

'Where did she go?'

Rice handed him the coffee. 'I didn't ask.'

'Come on, Jerry. I'm going mad!'

'She didn't tell me.'

'Jerry, I'm desperate! I'm begging you.'

Rice gave him a contemptuous look then moved to his armchair and sank into it. 'She didn't tell me – I swear. She didn't want anybody to know.'

Daniel placed his coffee on the table. 'She's not likely to… do something stupid!'

'I keep telling myself she won't. She's got guts. That's my hope.'

Daniel perched on the edge of the desk. 'When she left – not too weak, was she?'

'No. But battered. In pain. She was also having trouble with her breasts – the milk. You can imagine how she felt: full breasts but no baby to suckle…'

Daniel moaned. He began to wheeze. He wheezed regularly now. Suddenly his breath would fail. And briefly, he would live his son's death.

Rice stretched for the whisky bottle. 'There are pills to stop the milk. She promised she'd go to a doctor…'

'It was a boy, Jerry.' He struggled for breath, tears streaming down his face. 'What actually happened? Was he really strangled by the umbilical cord?'

'Yes. It happens. I wasn't in the room. Fuego was.'

Daniel jerked to his feet. 'Fuego? He didn't tell me!'

'He was a great help – according to the midwife.'

Daniel bellowed. 'Fuego?'

'Some world we live in.'

Daniel wrapped his arms around his head and howled.

51
We demand a country for the humiliated!

In one of his early pamphlets, Huaman had stated that the colonists had brought two strains of smallpox to South America. The first, the disease, had decimated the Indians; the second, greed, had pockmarked the continent with prospectors' settlements.

Of those grotesque settlements most had dried up and died; those that had survived had been dealt with in the manner families deal with their maladjusted members: neglect and doses of basic medicine – the latter, in terms of Latin American, being a military presence.

Puerto Nuevo, 'new door', was one such forgotten settlement. It had come into existence less than a hundred years ago at the end of the rubber boom and the beginning of yet another gold rush. In the event, no rubber and little gold had crossed its threshold. But the village, standing by a tributary of the Amazon, had never ceased to believe that a region of rain forests and bald mountains capable of producing both yellow and black gold must have countless other treasures in its soil. This faith had remained, even though the cocaine boom of the present days, centralised by the Junta in the capital, had also bypassed it. But then, as Chauca had quipped, eternal hope was a treasure in itself.

Puerto Nuevo would soon have its dreams realised. By choosing it as the venue for his re-emergence, Huaman had presented it with a niche in history – as his Finland Station. It would become a place of pilgrimage.

His stump itched. There was a swirl in his genitals which seemed to defy fear. He waved Chauca forward, then took command position by the edge of the bush.

Flies swarmed.

The target was the largest dwelling in Puerto Nuevo, a log edifice situated where the main street ended and the jungle began. Built originally as a land registry office, it had been provided with a sizeable courtyard to accommodate the influx of families. Thereafter, it had housed those few government agencies that had briefly visited the village. Now it was the barracks for the token force of Sinchis.

It stood, in the light of the dawn, spiritless, as if resigned to death.

Chauca, having spread out his squad behind the courtyard wall, signalled readiness with a bird-cry.

Huaman scanned the terrain for the rest of the guerrilleros. No one was visible. Two hundred men had blended with the scenery like birds in dense foliage.

He directed his attention to the other end of the street where the church and its presbytery stood. The first housed a group of Moral Crusade missionaries; the second, a team of American scientists. As yet, no one had stirred in either place. They should make the most of their sleep – shortly, they would be his hostages.

From the time he had started planning this operation, the Americans had become his main objective. The missionaries were not here solely to enslave the Indio's soul; they also intended to destroy the Spanish spirit which gave the country its greatness. The way they had deconsecrated the church before consecrating it as their tabernacle had been symbolic of their aims. As for the team of scientists, rumour had it they were testing a new birth-control drug. And that was an insult. This country, more Latin than Indio, was no Third World dump to be used as a laboratory.

Inside the barracks reveille sounded.

Huaman kept watch on the windows. He could see the odd shadow move. No lights. Puerto Nuevo did not have electricity and the Sinchis, trained for hardship and brutality, disdained such luxuries as candles.

He checked his watch. In fifteen minutes the Sinchis would pile out into the courtyard. A minute later they would be dead. The swirl in his genitals recommenced with that promise of an erection.

There was half a platoon in there: twenty lives. They were not ordinary recruits; not dim-witted campesinos harnessed in uniforms so that obese generals could boast of an army, but Fuego's own myrmidons – on unofficial holiday. They served in the backlands on a rota basis, for three weeks. They were permitted everything – provided they daily raised and lowered the flag and kept their guns oiled. They performed the latter duty either with arbitrary acts of brutality or, more flamboyantly, by driving recalcitrant men into the bush then hunting them down.

He would enjoy killing them. Had he really, ever, believed in the proscription against killing – except as an affectation? Well, the wilderness had put matters in perspective.

Two Sinchis, a Lieutenant and a Sergeant-major, sauntered on to the courtyard. Then the other men emerged and fell in line.

Huaman checked his watch. They were punctual. He envied their discipline and collective power – real martial men, like the Foreign Legionnaires who had caught his imagination in his teens.

A bugler sounded the flag-raising ceremony. The Lieutenant and the Sergeant-major marched to the pole.

Huaman caught sight of some women at the windows. Local girls taken for sex. Yet they were watching the proceedings with admiration, smiling, looking happy, as if they belonged there, like army wives.

He raised his pistol. His would be the first shot. He fired.

Chauca's squad opened fire from the courtyard walls.

Eight Sinchis fell immediately in ungainly pirouettes.

The rest, well trained, sprinted, churning dust, searching for cover.

The women at the windows screamed and ducked. Two of them, hit by stray bullets, slumped over the sills, half-hanging out, spurting blood.

Three more Sinchis fell.

Huaman ran towards the wall, boring through the chaos, his voice a continuous growl, firing without taking aim.

The Lieutenant, howling orders, tripped over the flag.

The survivors zigzagged, trying to regain the barracks.

The rest of the guerrilleros broke cover, swung their slings, waved their machetes, shouted their war-cries and advanced to tighten the circle.

The dust steamed.

The Sergeant-major ran at Chauca. Chauca fired. The Sergeant-major, hit, still staggered forward. Chauca fired again. The Sergeant-major sank to his knees, flailed in slow motion, vomited blood.

Stones from the guerrilleros' slings swished through the air.

Four more Sinchis collapsed.

The guerrilleros poured over the wall.

Machetes scrawled death sentences.

The last three Sinchis were decapitated; their limbs writhed.

The Lieutenant disentangled himself from the flag. Seeing all his men dead, he backed against the pole.

Chauca's squad surrounded him.

The guerrilleros formed an outer ring.

Huaman carved his way through them. Grinning.

The Lieutenant raised his arms in surrender. The dust, spent of its frenzy, began to settle.

Huaman surveyed his men. They were yelping like monkeys set loose in a banana plantation; some were smudging blood on their hands and faces. The stooped men of yesterday were now standing with their shoulders above the clouds. He, Gaspar Huaman, was responsible for that.

The Lieutenant was mumbling. 'Who are you? Who are you?'

Huaman, shaking pleasurably, placed his pistol against the Lieutenant's temple. 'Manku Yupanqui.'

The Lieutenant blinked vacantly; either the name meant nothing to him or his mind had crumbled.

'Don't kill him! Don't kill him! Please!' A woman, dressed only in cotton pants, was running towards them.

Huaman scrutinised her bouncing breasts: sixteen, if that.

She squeezed through the ring of guerrilleros and threw herself at Huaman's feet. 'Don't kill him – please!'

Huaman judged her without hesitation. A scavenger who had imbedded her teeth into a prize morsel. Where else but in this mudbank would she have caught a Lieutenant? Shaking all the more, he pressed his pistol against the Lieutenant's head.

The girl wailed. 'No! No! No!'

Chauca pulled her away, gently muttering to her in Quechua.

Huaman fired.

The Lieutenant catapulted on to the flag.

The girl tore free of Chauca, flung herself at Huaman, and spat at him. 'Animal! Assassin!'

Huaman struck her with his pistol.

The girl collapsed. Weeping, she crawled towards the Lieutenant. 'Armando... Armando...' She cradled the corpse.

Chauca moved to help her.

Huaman bellowed. 'Leave her!'

Chauca looked at him, puzzled.

Huaman could not stop his shaking. That sweet thirst for killing was so compelling. He aimed his pistol at the girl's naked back. He was aware that he was smiling, aware that no force on earth could stop him.

He fired once. Then again. And again. He emptied the magazine. Quenched. But the glorious certainty that the thirst would return, seize him with mystic webs, levitate him as he was levitating now.

Chauca grabbed his arm. 'Why? Why?'

Huaman smiled. 'A lesson for all those who fraternise with the people's enemy.'

Chauca shook his head. 'A girl...'

Huaman extricated his arm and yelled at the guerrilleros. 'Open up the arsenal! Ransack the barracks! I want every single weapon! And the radio equipment – spare parts and manuals!' He turned to Chauca. 'Let's get the hostages!'

52

And then I shall return to growing until one day I am so small that the wind will carry me away and I won't know what I am called and when I awake I won't be

Fuego's office!

A large Hepplewhite mahogany desk, bare except for a battery of telephones. On a short pole by the door, the national flag: horizontal strips of red, yellow and blue – the central strip bearing the national emblem: a white star suspended over the Tree of Life. Six Louis XVI armchairs upholstered with Beauvais tapestry. Three Turin gilt wood console tables. An exquisite Nöstetangan chandelier – two bulbs missing. Embroidered Spanish curtains and valence in traditional sampler patterns. Three vast carpets: Turkish, Persian and Bokhara. The walls whitewashed in colonial style.

Hanging on the walls: the ubiquitous portraits of the Junta; a Sheraton tabernacle mirror; a Ministry of Tourism poster showing a collage of churches, Inca ruins, beaches, mountains, rain forests and happy Indians tending to llamas; a large-scale map of the country; and clustered together – criminally – eight glorious aquatints by Goya.

Except for the ivory-handled revolvers thrown casually on to one of the armchairs, nothing personal of Fuego's. It was as if Fuego wished to convey that, though he was the longest serving Chief of Security, he was still a temporary incumbent and, therefore, unaccountable for the killing that was the daily business of this office.

Fuego was staring at the map. Daniel sat in the armchair facing the desk and trawled through his exhaustion for a shred of energy. It had taken him ten days to raise the courage to come crawling to Fuego. Ten days of scouring the capital for a clue to Beatriz's whereabouts, of knocking on the doors of musicians and publishers, record companies, television and radio stations, disc jockeys and singers, discos and dives. Except for the Indians in the slums, who had been distrustful, people had tried to help. To no avail. Beatriz had disappeared – leaving in her wake all the dread that word generated.

Fuego spoke without turning round. 'Be quick, Daniel. There is an emergency. Your old friend, Huaman...'

Daniel looked up wearily. 'Huaman?'

Fuego pointed at the map. 'Puerto Nuevo – look at it! Waiting for the Amazon to drain it into the Atlantic! Hardly the place to start a revolution...'

Fear struck Daniel. Could Beatriz have joined Huaman? 'What happened?'

'Our outpost was attacked. We lost radio contact. But an Indian Affairs agent reported seeing a column of men – led by a one-armed *misti*. What can I do for you?'

'Was Beatriz involved?'

Fuego turned round, amused. 'Beatriz? With Huaman!'

'She has disappeared.'

'Has she?'

Daniel found himself standing, suddenly energised. 'You know she has. Not in a death-pit, is she?'

'Hardly. Are you growing a beard?'

'What?'

'You look a mess. Do you wash?'

'Of course I wash! I want you to find Beatriz for me!'

Fuego hissed in fury. 'You son of an arsehole!'

'Rice told me what you did at the birth...'

'And you think I have turned soft?'

'Compassionate.'

'You know me better than that. It was fear.'

Daniel hung on to the word. 'Fear! All the better...'

Fuego laughed at Daniel's expression. 'Not what you think – not fear of retribution! Fear of hope! Face the enemy always – that's me! I went to see what hope looked like... how to fight it!'

'I don't believe you!'

'I should have known: hope is always stillborn. Either that or I killed it when I raped Beatriz. Maybe that's why I raped her.'

Daniel began to wheeze. 'Please...' His son, struggling, suffocating, passed across his eyes. 'I'm begging you... I must see her – just once...'

'Find her yourself!' Fuego sat at his desk. 'I have work to do.'

Daniel staggered after him. 'You're my last chance, Oseas! Do this for me! You'll never see me again – I promise you...'

Fuego faced him, disconcerted – and surprised that he should still feel for this man who, far from proving himself an enemy of stature, had shamed him as an illness can shame a person. He forced a laugh. 'Your God forbids that sort of thing. And I can't see you using anything except sleeping pills.'

'I meant home. I'll be going home.'

'I see. I misunderstood.' Fuego seethed. Departure, he felt, would cause a greater loss than death. He could mourn death and be finished with it. But the knowledge of Daniel living, thousands of miles away, safe from him, as if they had never tangled with each other – that would ache for ever. 'You have no home, Daniel. It is the brave who have homes. You are that rare animal who does not make a lair for fear of being cornered. What about the polyptych?'

'The Tree of Life – that's all I've got left to do.'

'The Tree of Life – what an irony...'

'I must see her – just once...'

'You have other unfinished business! You swore to destroy me! You cannot go before you have achieved that!'

'You're already destroyed. Not the way I'd have wanted it. But you're not what you were. God has entered you.'

Fuego rose from his desk, chuckling unconvincingly. 'What nonsense, Daniel!'

'Look, I beg you... I'm crawling... Find Beatriz...'

Fuego spoke venomously. 'On second thoughts, I think you should leave! You should leave today!'

'I always honour my contract.'

'Honour! You certainly know how to choose your words! You can be released from your contract – I will arrange it!'

'It has to be finished – you said so yourself.'

'It is not important any more.'

'Why not?'

'Because you have touched it! Everything you touch dies!'

'I've also touched you.'

'Get out, Daniel!'

'Contaminated you – through Beatriz! You said so!'

Fuego strode over to Daniel. 'Out!'

Daniel stood his ground. 'And you still think you haven't changed? Look at you! Infected with God, you are! That's why you went to help Beatriz!'

Fuego punched him, catching him on the chin.

Daniel staggered backwards, but stayed on his feet.

Fuego closed in on him.

Daniel became aware of his arms straining, of his hands locking into each other, of his body moving independently, of his mind leaving his body, stepping to one side as if to observe it better. Thus when his interlocking hands flew and smashed upwards, he had no sense of having struck Fuego, only the sense of witnessing dispassionately his transformation.

And he glimpsed – no, entered – his former self, a short-lived former self, running riot after the war, hitting blindly at the world, searching the base of its neck for that one blow that would kill it and, in that sweet bitterness of joy and madness, feeling alive, smelling air fragrant like sea-spray, touching feelings untainted by fear.

Fuego had collapsed; there was blood trickling from his mouth.

Fear rushed back at Daniel. He flung it aside. Madness was in him; madness, beautiful like Beatriz – madness like salvation.

Fuego pulled himself up. 'This is magic, Daniel! Your testicles have descended!'

Breathing like an athlete. 'I warned you. The llama fat. Remember? I am you now!'

Fuego stared at him, gauging him. 'And if my men rush in now?'

Daniel kept his hands interlocked and let the strength run wild in his arms. Madness was in infinite supply. He was ready to fight – at last! 'Let them!'

Fuego leaned against his desk and wiped the blood with his sleeve. 'The fact is, they are used to hearing beatings in this room. And since I have never been at the receiving end, they won't be alarmed. I could call them – but what is the point?'

Daniel towered over him. 'You'll find Beatriz for me. Then I'll be gone.'

'What about the war between Good and Evil?'

'That's ended. Each has defeated a soul.'

53

Oh wound into which fall to their deaths the blue guitars

We were standing here. Daniel there. Me here. Fuego there. The others – I can't remember where. Way over there sat the families. The children huddled there. The corpses lay there. The mummies sat exactly where they're sitting now.

Beatriz squatted, clutched handfuls of sand and let them trickle through her fingers.

The desert was not this dry. It had soaked up too much blood. Nor was the wind so fierce. It tiptoed like an undertaker, professionally elegiac. The silence was unbreachable. Yet the spirits of the massacred must have been screaming, the mummies must have been keening on their behalf. But I couldn't hear them. Why was I so confident of life?

She stood up; then she ran between the mummies.

I still can't hear them. Now all I hear is your death-wail. Oh, my poor son, you were conceived to save God, but I let Satan into my womb and he suffocated you.

I carried hope that time. I imagined the old dead and the new would soon flower into life. I carried that hope as if it were you. I sang to it so that it could dance inside me like you used to when your father smiled at us. I loved its bulk pressing on me – it felt as good as Daniel's weight. It even had a taste – tart and gritty like strawberries.

She stopped running. She let herself fall.

But that's me, isn't it? I pretend there is life where there is no life. I suckle a man who is stillborn.

Did that shock you? It's true. Daniel is my first stillborn.

She stretched out on the ground, pummelled it with her head.

I can explain. I've been an orphan. Oh, there was Aunt Luisa, but how could she have been the same as my mother and father? Besides, she died, too, after a while. Orphans need someone immortal. Someone to paint them the sky, the seas and the mountains. Someone to hold their hands steady so that they can look at their palms and find north, west, south and east. I convinced myself Daniel was immortal.

When you're an orphan, the days are always cold, the nights always threatening. You ask yourself, how can a loving mother and father abandon a child to such terrors? So you begin to think the fault must be in you, that if you have been abandoned, there is evil in you. You observe how destructive the world is. You see how destructive you are also. You understand it is you who killed your parents.

Eventually you get your punishment. Your good body – what you thought was your good body – kills your baby. How can a mother kill her child?

She rolled over. There were cuts on her head and face. She stared at the sun, let her blood trickle into her eye.

But you are not entirely innocent.

Birth, I know, is a life-or-death matter. I know as you prepare to be born the womb becomes a tomb, you taste live burial, you hear earth being thrown on your coffin, you know you have one chance to push the lid open. Most babies seize that chance. You didn't. Why? Why – when you had the New Man's strength? You could have torn me open, erupted out of me!

Yes, it's your fault, too! You should have fought me.

You would have saved me! You would have given me back my illusions. I would have gone on thinking my body, my breath, my songs had a place in the future.

She pulled herself up and surveyed the necropolis.

So... you brought me here. At least, we are with our ancestors.

She arranged herself in a position identical to the mummies. Momentarily her eyes lingered on a dust trail in the distance.

Oh, Mama, Mama, Mama... Why are there children who have no mother? Mothers who cannot have children? Children who eat their mother? Mothers who eat their children?

She registered that the dust trail was a vehicle. She thought it odd there were still people in the world, travelling.

She, too, had travelled – on foot, by bus, carrying breasts full of milk and arms without a baby. But there was an end to every journey.

She closed her eyes. Oh, Mama, Mama, Mama... Cradle me... Let me sleep...

54
Brothers, God has been divided between us!

They had failed to locate the guerrilleros. The helicopters had returned from Puerto Nuevo with the corpses of the Sinchis, with the shocked but unharmed American scientists and with a message from Huaman written in blood on the outpost's flag. The Moral Crusade missionaries would be held hostage until the government exchanged them for Father Quintana; the scientists had been released as proof of goodwill for the negotiations.

Dr Williston's mood was ugly. The stench of the cadavers from the *barranco*, riding the hot wind from the tropics, had invaded even his penthouse suite in La Merced's tallest and most luxurious hotel.

Fuego enjoyed Williston's discomfort. Actually, the white smells of Williston and Angelito, sweaty miasmas blended with pungent colognes, were worse than the stink of the *barranco*.

Williston was pacing about, looking, in his immaculate suit, like a padded American footballer. 'Pacification is the name of the game. Take it as read, that's what the Lord wants.'

Angelito produced a cherubic smile. 'As it happens, New Order, too, wants action. Even a pathetic revolution, a few soldiers killed, can get a country infatuated with dialectics.'

'Right. So what we got to decide is how we pacify – without harming the hostages.'

Fuego gazed out of the window. The city was like a syphilitic sore. And yet a different pair of eyes, eyes that had retained wonder, would see the Divine Hand in the way the harbour sheltered the calm waters from the rolling sea, the way the river ran and the mountains rose, even the way the abominable skyscrapers played hopscotch with the sprawling slums. Above all, such a pair of eyes would remember that the ravine where the disappeared rotted, had once had a paradisaical beauty and was thought to be the gate to El Dorado.

There he was thinking of the Divine Hand again. Maybe Daniel was right. Maybe he had become infected by God…

'What do you think of my idea, Oseas?'

'What idea?'

'You haven't been listening.' Williston overrode his rancour. 'From where I'm standing Huaman doesn't look like your great idealist. Not a man of mercy. Don't be fooled by his leniency towards the scientists – that's eye-wash. He didn't spare any of the Sinchis. More to the point, there was that girl, the Lieutenant's whore. According to the other whores, he killed her himself – in cold blood.'

Angelito nodded as he stifled a yawn. His wife, he had told them, could not yet entrust their new son to the nanny, so he was getting little sleep.

Williston cooled his sweaty face with a cologne-wipe. 'My hunch is Huaman's got hooked on killing. The message he left – written in blood…'

Fuego grinned. 'I liked the message. The sort of thing I would do…'

'That's what I mean, Oseas. Huaman's become like you guys. Soldier and pragmatist. Knowing when to kill and when to spare. So, I've been thinking. He's an ambitious cur. You might be able to tempt him. Say you offered him a full pardon – and with it, a position in the government…'

Angelito livened up. 'It's worth a try.'

Fuego stared at Williston. 'Are you serious?'

'Nothing you need stick to, naturally, Oseas – not unless you thought it had advantages. But it would stay his hand as far as the hostages are concerned.'

'Huaman thinks he's Manku Yupanqui.'

Williston smirked. 'Well, he's not, is he?'

'How do we know?'

Williston humoured Fuego. 'We haven't seen any signs of that.'

'We might still. Daniel Brac hasn't finished the restoration yet.'

Williston looked puzzled. 'What are you talking about?'

'The polyptych – it is supposed to tell us who Manku Yupanqui is.'

Williston snapped angrily. 'Come on, Oseas. This is serious!'

Fuego, amused by Williston's disquiet, smiled. 'How do we tempt Huaman? Send Satan as our envoy?'

Williston readjusted his sleeves. 'He's got a radio now. We can devise a code – slip it in during the hostage negotiations. Then repeat it daily.'

Angelito nodded enthusiastically. 'That's a good idea!'

Williston turned to Angelito, pleased. 'And simple.'

Fuego stopped listening. Turning his back to Williston and Angelito, he gazed out of the window again.

Infected by God, am I? What nonsense!

But what about Beatriz? Since the death of her baby, you have not let her out of your sight. Good thing, too. Or she would have perished in the necropolis. Isn't your concern for her proof of God's infection?

I am not infected! I will prove it!

He turned back to Williston. 'These missionaries. Are they important?'

The question struck Williston as ridiculous. 'They are Americans!'

Fuego smiled. 'I know. But are they Moral Crusade's prize llamas – or just missionaries?'

'I don't know what you're getting at, Oseas. They are some of our best men and women...'

'But expendable.'

Williston glared at him. 'Now, wait a minute! These are the Lord's servants! Children of God!'

'Let's not fool ourselves, Luke. They may be children of God, but they are not the Lord's servants! They are pawns like everybody else. For the godless – for big business, big nations, big brass, big politicians! For little people like you and me and Angelito who gang up to look big. Right?'

Williston was enraged. 'How dare you...'

Infected by God, am I?

Fuego smirked. 'Now, these missionaries... Crusaders, they call themselves – meaning they are soldiers. Soldiers get killed. Death is part of their rations.'

Williston looked apoplectic. Impulsively, he touched the bowl of apples which was a fixture in his room as a reminder of man's fall. 'Sacrificing *American* lives...? That would be breaking the rules!'

'There are no rules, Luke. The Americans sacrifice lives all the time – including their own poor bastards. More to the point, as capitalists, they know everything has a price. They won't mind paying.'

Williston was barely audible. 'Let's get this straight. What you're suggesting is...'

Fuego's voice sizzled. 'I am not suggesting. I have decided. There will be no exchange – no deals with Huaman.'

55

Here comes the tree, the tree nourished by the naked dead!

'*Come on to the beach, velvet skin. Come and lie on my purple and fine linen.* She loved me lying on her lap. Loved my big bull's head. She called me her baby.'

Daniel jumped off the platform. The Tree of Life section had been extensively cracked and he had had to retouch all the stoppings. It had been a niggling job. Amazing that he had managed it. 'Nothing amazing about a professional. I bathe my hands in rainbows – even with so much earth above me.' He guffawed.

He was ready to start inpainting. He inspected the brushes on the work-bench, then picked up those he needed.

He climbed back on to the platform. 'God planted two unique trees in the Garden of Eden: the Tree of Life and the Tree of the Knowledge of Good and Evil. The fruit of the first imparted everlasting life. The soul of man, the Jews say, is God's spirit moving over the waters of chaos. Therefore, it was God's first creation. And as He wanted His foremost work to live for ever, He instructed Adam to eat the fruit of the Tree of Life.'

He was talking non-stop and too loudly. He began to wheeze. Meticulously, he lined up his brushes on the low table he had made for the platform. 'We were going to call our son Adam. Adam Joseph Perera. I was thinking of changing my name back.'

He jumped down from the platform again. *Daniel Brac, this is yours.* He staggered to the work-bench.

He put some paints on to his palette. 'The fruit of the second tree imparted lust. Lust is the comprehension of the mysteries of the flesh. It reveals the conjunction of life's transient goodness and death's permanent evil. It is a comprehension which makes God God. Consequently, God forbade Adam and Eve to eat that fruit.' He climbed back on to the platform. 'Not bad, eh? I know my stuff.' He placed the palette on the table and paused to catch his breath.

Coffee, I need coffee. And biscuits. He began to laugh. 'Coffee and biscuits. Here I am condemned to roam the bowels of the graveyards… Condemned to roam for ever and never to rest… and I still want coffee and biscuits.' He jumped down.

He put the kettle on, picked up the turpentine and the solvent, climbed on to the platform again, and placed the bottles by the table. He pummelled his chest, trying to clear the tightness.

Who is that naked infant? Why doesn't he have earth from the Mount of Olives on his penis? That's a tradition for Jews who can't be buried there; they bring the Mount of Olives to the deceased instead. The son puts the earth on the dead man's penis. Thus the covenant of circumcision is renewed.

The kettle had boiled. He scrambled down again. 'But the Serpent tempted Eve. Eve tempted Adam. They both ate the forbidden fruit.' He began to make the coffee. 'And God was angered. And He said: man has become like one of us, to know good and evil. And He drove out Adam and Eve in case they lived for ever. And He placed cherubim and a flaming-sword-which-turned-every-way to guard the Tree of Life.'

He took his coffee and some biscuits, shuffled to the monk's seat and sat down. He gazed at the Tree of Life. *I want to sleep with your cock in my mouth*. She said that – many times. I'm not this boy's son, I'm his father. Can a father put earth from the Mount of Olives on his son? 'Hello, Adam. Adam, look, I'm wheezing. I started wheezing after you died. I will suffocate with you.'

He dunked a biscuit into his coffee and ate it. Why did God say *one of us* when He is the Only God? Why shouldn't man know good and evil – how else can he recognise evil and turn against it? Why, if God originally wanted man to live for ever, did He plant the Tree of Knowledge? He must have known man wouldn't be able to resist its fruit. And what is a holier act, a better antidote to hate, than making love? Why did God make that state of grace the sin from which all other sins are born? Was it because He didn't have a lover? Did He become jealous of man?

He began to cry. 'Son, son. Can you forgive me? Would it help if I said, death is an untruth – that's what the Indians believe. Because we'll never stop being born.'

He intoned like a priest. 'The Fall is a foundation stone for both Judaism and Christianity. For Jews, it is the directive for man to mend his ways and strive for the advent of the Messiah and the Millennium. For Christians, it is the very event that led to the arrival of the Messiah Jesus who redeemed man by offering His earthly life. The fact that God sacrificed His own Son is proof that He loves man.'

He wailed. 'I sacrificed you, too, my son. But what did I redeem? Would it help if I told you the knowledge of the Ineffable Name can make you master over death?' *He died when his father stopped loving him.* 'It's not true, Adam. Don't believe him. That's Fuego twisting the knife.'

He wiped his tears, gulped down his coffee, got up to make himself another one. As he passed the window, he paused and peered into the night. There seemed to be thousands of candles burning in the square. Was it his imagination or were there more people keeping vigil? He declaimed, as if lecturing to them. 'When Christianity came to dominate Europe, the Church, determined to preserve and extend its power, made certain that the Fall became the lodestone of morality. You can see, such a theme – as opposed to immortality cruelly taken away by an unnerved God – was a most effective weapon to control man.' He moved to the kitchen counter. 'Thus, medieval art, whenever it depicted the Garden of Eden, favoured almost exclusively the Tree of Knowledge.'

He was out of breath. He decided he did not want more coffee. He should get to work. He moved to the dimmer switches and adjusted the lights. 'I must start, Adam. I'll see you again. I'm roaming the graveyards. For ever. That's my punishment.'

He found himself lingering by the window. Definitely more people. 'Enlightenment and Renaissance brought a reinterpretation of the Tree of Life's symbolism. On the one hand, as in some medieval stained-glass windows, it depicted it as the Tree of Salvation also known as the Tree of Jesse – basically a family tree which traces Jesus' lineage to Adam.' Oh, Adam! 'On the other, as in Ignacio de Ries's famous work, it depicted it as a Tree which Death is in the process of cutting down whilst man shelters in its branches. A tree of *mortality*, in other words.'

He saw a shadow on the window. Hello. Someone else. A severed head. Tupac Amaru. I'm glad you're in the same graveyard as my son. He, too, is a tragic figure. Watch over him. Please.

He moved to the scaffold. 'With the possible exception of Hieronymus Bosch's *The Garden of Earthly Delights* where the Tree of Life stands isolated in centre background as a gothic, tabernacle-shaped fountain, I can't think of any work in Western art that attributes to it its biblical designation. Only in Eastern art, in some Egyptian paintings, Moorish textiles, Hindu sculpture, does it appear as a symbol of immortality.'

He started crying again. When I sucked at her fount, I saw the New Man. *Where else except in there – where I am reborn?*

He leaned against the scaffold, thumping his chest to ease his breathlessness. 'The Tree of Life became a favourite subject in Latin American art. One reason was that popular legends had proclaimed the newly discovered Americas as the original location of the Garden of Eden. There were even maps which showed the Tree situated in the Amazon basin. For all that, Latin America followed the Renaissance tradition. Its most famous example, by Tadeo Escalante, is an almost identical copy of Ignacio de Ries. A sturdy tree. In its rich foliage, a group of people frolic at a well-laden table. They are oblivious of the fact that Jesus is tolling a bell hanging from a branch because Death, in the shape of a skeleton and aided by a demon, is chopping the tree down.'

Wheezing heavily, he stopped crying. 'Come on! Work!' He clambered on to the platform. 'I keep having this vision. God – or is it Beatriz? – picks me up by my feet and slaps my bottom.'

He wiped his hands on his dungarees as he gazed at the Tree of Life. 'The polyptych has shunned all the traditions. Here, the Tree extols immortality. Can you improve on that for a message of hope? The unknown painter was a subversive.'

He peeked at a shadow on the canvas. Another severed head. Ah, yes. José Gabriel Condorcanqui, Tupac Amaru the Second. José is my father's name, too. 'But you see, José Gabriel. For me, caught on the horns of good and evil, divested of woman and child, it's a message of eternal death. Of not having lived even briefly. Like my son. That's why I'm here under the earth. In tunnels deeper than the one I crawled through to save Huaman.'

He picked up the palette and a brush. 'This Tree of Life is stupendous. A cornucopia of styles. From classicism to primitivism. There are some touches of realism that remind me of the Tree of the Millennium in La Recoleta. But overall, it's a tree that can only exist in the unconscious. That can only be touched by the viscera.'

Hope is everybody's birthright.

Where can I find it, José Gabriel? In subversion? By following your example? And the painter's? 'I will confess I wanted to be subversive all my life. But every time I came near it, I ran away.' *Carob beans enable a person to change colour at will.*

'See with what difficulty I breathe.' Good.

'This Tree of Life is unlike any other. For a start, it's an inverted tree. Its roots, twelve of them, glowing in hues of orange and red, curling and twisting like streams of lava, disappear in billowing clouds. The clouds are depicted as female figures gloriously pregnant.' Oh, Beatriz, Beatriz. 'They're painted in every shade of Inca blue set in a sky of gamboge yellow which undulates like a peaceful sea. The trunk has fluted bark, and is as majestic as a Doric pillar. The branches and the thick foliage cover the entire foreground. Their extremities burrow into a field that's spread like a multi-coloured poncho – like Joseph's coat. Bounteous crops of potato and maize cover the field. The tree itself is the coca, the divine plant. It's a mark of the painter's genius that it strikes the eye both as a delicate bush – which the coca is – and as a tree grown to titanic proportions. The leaves are individually drawn with a boldness comparable only to Douanier Rousseau. Yet the ensemble has the density of a Constable. The fruit is the guava. It teems on the branches. A few, fallen on the piles of potatoes and maize, are split open and display countless seeds. The seeds of immortality.'

OK, let's start. He dabbed his brush into the orange paint on the palette. 'The roots first.' He tested the colour on a spare piece of canvas. Satisfied, he began inpainting.

Here's another man. Lying naked on a pile of corpses. And there – there's my mother. Just a mound of ash. And my sisters. Bloated, searching for their heads and limbs which have been hacked off. The man is my father. His penis, like my son's, has no earth from the Mount of Olives. He is crying – with open eyes. *I am so afraid.*

He stepped back, wheezing, and scrutinised the tiny area he had inpainted. 'Another original feature. The Tree is not one tree but two. A thick branch incorporates its trunk with the Tree of Knowledge. That stands upright – in the background. Smaller but equally luxuriant. Its roots, only just visible in palest magenta, and its foliage, in the subtlest verdigris, intertwine with the foliage and roots of the Tree of Life. The fruit of the Tree of Knowledge is mango. Indisputably, the fruit of the gods.'

He began inpainting another patch. Yes, Papa. When I finish the polyptych, I'll have completed the journey. Then judgement. Either my tomb will disappear without trace. Or it'll open. Yes, there is hope in that. 'I keep having another vision. God – or is it Beatriz – pushes me out of Her vagina. And I feel an endless depth both inside and outside me.'

He paused and examined the patch. He wiped his brush and dabbed some paint on it. 'Four streams, spurting out of the trunk, cascade down and form rivers and deltas around the Trees. They are the four rivers of Paradise. Water, milk, honey, wine.'

He inpainted again. Yes, Papa. There is something on my penis. No, it isn't earth from the Mount of Olives. It's blight. Don't look at me like that, Papa. You conquered your fear. I couldn't.

He paused, pressed his hands against his chest. Really rough today, my breathing. 'Jesus is crucified on the trunk of the Tree of Knowledge. The inscription above His head declares Him the Son of Man, the Son of God, the Son of the Sun. A god is always crucified on a tree. But the fact that Jesus is crucified on the Tree of Knowledge indicates He ate the forbidden fruit and thus became God. So: to attain immortality one must eat the forbidden fruit and be crucified. How's that for an idea?'

He mixed some orange and red for a special shade. 'That's the hope. That's what's subversive about this picture. The Kempins and the Fuegos exist simply to crucify men and turn them into gods.' *It is not just fear, Daniel, your curse. You will not fight for anything! Die for anything! Not for God! Not for Beatriz! Not for your past! Not for your future!* It's true, Papa.

He tested the colour mixture on the spare canvas. 'Yet another original feature is the inclusion of the cherubim and the flaming-sword-which-turned-every-way that God placed as guards. The cherubim are represented as groups of fierce grey eagles standing shoulder to shoulder to the right and the left of the Trees. The eagle is the Incas' other sacred bird. The sword, at the centre, is shaped like a *tumi* and appears to be in mid-revolution. Its hilt is covered in countless eyes and looks like a peacock's tail. Its shovel-blade glistens in ivory black. Tongues of fire burst from it.'

He inpainted. Yes, Papa. God resides in he who defies death. But why was I stillborn, like my son? Because you cried, Papa. You showed your fear. You crippled the life you gave me, strangled my breath. You're not without blame, Papa. Here I am with you. And we're both crying. Are you happy now? *Are you free now, are you free now?*

He paused, realising that he had been crying. He wiped his tears. 'The sword stands not to guard the Tree from man, but to guard man from his fear. You can see man there – in the persons of the Inca Adam and Eve. They're climbing through the roots towards Heaven. They're naked. They almost blend with the roots. Can you see? The twelve roots represent the Zodiac.'

He took deep breaths to stop wheezing. 'That's another subversive aspect of the picture. It gives the lie to the primary sin. It says God is not the stern, jealous, punishing deity we've come to think He is. He is as God should be. Fighting on our side. Urging us to be what He created us to be. His image. Not parodies.'

He mixed more paint. 'The Inca Adam and Eve are called Manku Capac and Cura Occlo.' *Mother stand in front of me. Hide me between your legs. Protect me from the oldest darkness.*

He started inpainting again. Are you trying to see what they look like, Papa? The faces aren't very clear. I haven't worked on them yet. *Trees – can we become like trees? Join our roots? Turn green? Flower?*

You can see it all, Papa? Tell me.

'This Tree of Life with its other half, the Tree of Knowledge, standing like the two great pillars at the entrance to Solomon's temple, is the Jew's tree. The tree which became the Torah. The cabbalists' inverted Sephirotic Tree which links the celestial with the terrestrial, which is the conduit for the sun which illuminates all, which shines in the day and in the night, which is the gate to the Holy of Holies, to the Tetragrammaton, the awesome Ineffable Name through which the Just will enter Paradise and be master over death. The Jew's Tree, Papa, yes!' *Live through winters? Green and flower again?*

'This Tree is the Heavenly Tree which brings the Sun down to earth! Therefore, it is also the Tree of the Children of the Sun! The Indian's Tree! Yes, Papa!' *You are light. Life.*

'This Tree is the Truth! Therefore, it is also Jesus' Tree! The Christian's Tree! Papa, yes!' *I want to be born.*

'And the Muslim's! And the Buddhist's! Everybody's Tree! Yes, Papa!' *I can see God. In there, my love! Inside you.*

He stepped back, straining to breathe. Don't go, Papa! Papa, don't go!

A spectre pulled him up.

'Who are you? I know you.' Tall. With the gaunt cheeks of a prophet. In a poncho like a prayer-shawl. Fearless, like Jesus. Strong like the two Tupac Amarus. Heroic like my father. Brandishing big hands – like my hands – caked and mottled with paint. 'I know you!'

Listen to the painting. What does it say?

'It says the Saviour will come. He and his woman, Pachamama, will lead the persecuted – all the Incas of this world – to immortality.'

Remember that.

'Who is the Saviour?'

Manku Yupanqui.

'Who are you? I know you!'

The painter.

'What's your name?'

Manku Yupanqui.

'You don't exist.'

Look at the Inca Adam. It's my face.

'Your face? No. More like my son's face! My father's face!'

Look again.

'Like Huaman's face, too! And Fuego's! And that yellow streak over there.

365

Like my hair! It's my face also! You're mocking me! Driving me insane!'

Now, look at the Inca Eve.

'My mother's face! My sisters' faces!'

Look again.

'And that poor girl's face – Teresa's! No, it's Beatriz's face. Definitely, Beatriz's face!'

'Daniel.'

He looked up, startled. He was stretched out on the floor. Had he fainted? Fallen off the platform? Had a fit?

'Daniel!'

He turned towards the voice. Fuego, in full uniform, shadowy under the arch of the door.

He pulled himself up. His chest almost too heavy to carry. He began to laugh. 'I just saw you.' He pointed to the polyptych. 'The Inca Adam – he is Manku Yupanqui. It's your face.'

'What?' Fuego, shaken, clambered on to the platform. He inspected the Tree of Life at length, then, angrily, jumped down. 'What are you talking about? You can't see the features! There's a lot of damage…'

Daniel's laughter turned into hysteria. 'You will see it – when I finish. I saw it. Last night. Your face.'

'Not funny!'

Daniel continued laughing. 'Even funnier. It was also my face. And Huaman's.'

'You've gone mad!'

'Yes.' Still laughing, Daniel staggered to the window. Peering at the square, he stopped laughing abruptly. 'They've gone!' He stared at Fuego. 'The people – keeping vigil. They were there last night. Hundreds of them. Now, they've gone.'

Fuego strode to the window in disbelief.

Daniel staggered towards the sink. 'Bloody nonsense! Absolute bloody nonsense!' About to wash his face, he turned round, suddenly seized by hope. 'You found Beatriz!'

Fuego moved away from the window. His voice limped heavily. 'Do you still think I am infected by God?'

Daniel held on to his hope. 'Oh, yes. We all are.'

'Come with me.'

56

The light of the earth comes from its eyelids not like the stroke of a bell but rather like tears

The day had all the ingredients to produce immortality. The wind exhaled the gentlest of breaths. The sea was uterine. The sun showered golden rays – even on the abomination that was El Chulpa. But the day had been stolen for an execution.

'Man is the only animal that feeds on guilt – as if that only ensures survival. I tell you, God is worse than opium! At least, with opium you get high as you die. With God, you get all the horrors of withdrawal!'

Fuego's voice droned relentlessly. Collectors of the dead in a plagued city, Daniel imagined, must have called out for corpses in the same cadence.

Jerry Rice, his hands on his hips, was staring at the sun as if determined to go blind. The flask which he had hurriedly drained, hung from one wrist and reflected the dazzle.

Angelito, immaculately turned out, stood by the firing squad. He had the same proud smile as when he had waved at his wife who had dropped him at the ferry terminal.

'We interrogated the good Padre, you know.' Fuego was grinning, but his eyes were vacant. 'What had turned him towards Liberation Theology? Was it the communists? Any of their mutants? Did Jesus appear before him on an Inca trail? The logic of penance, he said. Started with easy parishes, you see. Became guilty. This is not the path to God, he reasoned. Poverty, turning the other cheek, imitating Jesus, that is the path of God. So he went to shepherd the campesinos. Illogical logic, you must admit, when the country is in the jaws of wolves. So here, between my teeth, his pact with God ends.'

Daniel's eyes strayed to Father Quintana again.

They had tied him to a pole that had once been a goalpost. The compound, Fuego had told them, had been a recreation yard in the good old days when El Chulpa had been an ordinary penal establishment.

They had cleaned him up. They had washed and ironed his soutane which, over a body reduced to a skeleton, now hung like a massive shroud. Angelito had gleefully boasted that they had prepared Father Quintana as if for his wedding. The embroidered soutane, given by his flock, was his bridal gown.

But no amount of cosmetics could have hidden the devastation. The head, shorn of its glorious white mane and beard, glistened, waxen, like the face of a mummy. The eyes, shrunken to two desiccated grains, floated, lightless, in brindled pools. The only sign of life came from the lips which trembled, and Daniel could not determine whether they trembled because they could not anchor on gums whose teeth had been torn out or because Father Quintana was trying to intone the last rites that were being given to him by the obsequious prison chaplain.

'So what good is his allegiance to God? Does it stop the slavery in the mines, give land to the campesinos, reduce the disappearances, feed one – just one – hungry child? I tell you, he should have made his pact with the Devil, joined the Marxists or picked up a gun, like Huaman. At least then, he would have had a chance to kill me!'

Suddenly Rice wailed. 'I can't watch this! I won't!'

Fuego strode over to Rice and bellowed. 'You stay where you are! I gave you the choice – you decided to stand by his side! So stay! A man of God should not die alone!'

Rice, his eyes still seeking blindness from the sun, began to weep.

Rice, too, was going mad. Daniel had been concerned about him when they had met at the ferry terminal. Rice had been defiant, cursing Fuego and Angelito, gabbling that he had come because he loved Father Quintana, that he would kick up such a row about his death that the world would have to sit up and take notice. Poor Rice. Since Father Quintana's imprisonment, he had filed copy after copy excoriating Fuego and demanding the priest's release. But not one had been printed. He had confided that he suspected Williston had arranged for their suppression. These days, Williston and Angelito appeared to be inseparable. Moreover, Williston, regularly interviewed for American television, never failed to whitewash the 'troubles' as subversive propaganda. Williston, in fact, would have been present at this execution – to give his own prayers to a misguided soul, as Angelito had put it – but had had to stay at his office to await news of his hostage missionaries.

'Well, what do you say, Daniel?' Fuego had strode back and was pointing at Father Quintana. 'There is the man infected by God! Look at him! Then look at me! Can you see any similarities?'

Daniel, ignoring Fuego, put a comforting hand on Rice's shoulder.

The chaplain was now extending a crucifix towards Father Quintana's mouth.

Daniel shuddered. Death had arrived and had frozen the sun. He began to wheeze.

Something was still alive in Father Quintana. It could hear words. It could glimpse light and stars. It could hear wings flapping. And it could see the Bread and the Wine descending to touch his lips... *Take, eat; this is my body... This cup is the new testament in my blood... drink it...*

Father Quintana's trembling lips snatched the crucifix which the chaplain had offered him to kiss. The suddenness of the act, its furious hunger, gave it the quality of violence.

Fuego, Daniel could see, was shocked; Angelito, angry; some of the soldiers in the firing squad grinned as at a freak; the chaplain turned towards Fuego begging a directive.

Daniel screeched. 'Yes, Padre, yes, yes, yes!'

Rice wept all the more, his eyes glued to the crucifix in Father Quintana's mouth. The priest's lips, miraculously, were no longer trembling.

Fuego strode over to Father Quintana. He pushed aside the chaplain, then took out a blindfold from his pocket.

The chaplain, resuming his prayers, hurried deferentially to his designated place by the firing squad.

Fuego stooped over Father Quintana. 'Blindfold. Do you want a blindfold?'

Why should I need a blindfold when I have the Flesh and the Blood pouring into my mouth when Sweet Jesus on the Cross is shining His light into my soul healing this pathetic Quintana of his confusion when He is taking me to my death so that I can live

Blindfold blindfold blindfold

No no no don't take the Bread and the Wine out of my mouth

Answer answer answer

No... Blindfold... *You* need it... *You* need it...

What was that? Speak up?

Hear me... I have no tongue... No blindfold... No blindfold... I am shaking my face... No blindfold...

Very well, no blindfold!

Now give back... the crucifix... The Bread and the Wine... The Flesh and the Blood... give back...

Fuego stared at the crucifix which he had wrenched from Father Quintana. Then he rammed it back into the priest's mouth, hammering it in, twisting it and screwing it, churning the lips and the gums into a minced, bloody pulp. Finally, in a frenzy of frustration, he broke the crucifix in two.

Give back put Jesus back on my lips and all your sins might be forgiven give back let me die with Life in my mouth.

Fuego flung away the pieces of the crucifix and barked at Angelito. 'Get ready!' He stomped back, staring at the blindfold in his hand.

Angelito ordered the firing squad. 'Aim!'

Fuego took his place by Daniel and looked at him with demented eyes.

Daniel felt his head spin.

Brusquely, Fuego turned to Angelito. 'Kill him!'

Angelito bellowed the order. 'Fire!'

Fuego turned his back on Father Quintana.

A time of absolute silence.

The squad fired.

Another time of absolute silence.

Father Quintana's body buckled and reared against the pole, then concaved into a flaccid mass.

Fuego turned and smiled bitterly at Daniel. 'Infected by God, am I?'

Rice had collapsed. Daniel did not see it, but sensed it. He himself, he realised, was submerged in the sea of his own tears. Fuego, he could just observe, had dropped the blindfold and was walking away, dragging cloven feet.

Daniel plunged his hands into his tears, rummaging for the blindfold.

He straightened to get up, but found himself stretched out on the earth. He held on to the blindfold. He could see Father Quintana's figure slumped against the foot of the goalpost. Rivulets of blood ran on the cleaned, ironed soutane.

He was seeing, he realised, from his worm's-eye view, the Son of Man rising. The broken pieces of the crucifix glittering on the earth were stars. He was witnessing immortality.

A burst of sub-machine-gun fire dispersed the waters.

Daniel watched, one eye on the demented Fuego firing from afar, the other registering the holes bursting from Father Quintana's corpse. This, he decided, was a good time to end the world. He pressed the blindfold against his eyes.

PART TEN

57

The sun reaches my mouth like an old buried tear that becomes seed again

Fuego scanned the Plaza del Arbol: the park was peaceful and empty. The Tree of the Millennium rose from its centre like a hot spring imprinted on the night at the moment of its eruption. Beyond it, the convent's swarthy shadow stood watchful.

Beatriz was in that convent.

He scanned the rest of the square: the Cabildo, the old town hall that had been converted into a hotel, was sharing the dreams of its pilgrim patrons. The colonnaded promenades were deserted.

La Recoleta was asleep – it had been for hours. He had made sure of that by imposing a curfew.

He turned to the *curandero* sitting next to him. 'Now!'

The old healer momentarily stopped chewing coca and peered through the windscreen. 'There is still light.'

Fuego barked. 'Where? There is no moon. And I have had the street lights switched off.'

The *curandero* pointed ahead. 'Light – in the Tree.'

Fuego stared at the Tree of the Millennium. The giant cedar appeared to glow from the inside. 'You are imagining it.'

The *curandero* dug into his poncho to scratch himself, releasing a smell of sweat, urine and shit that was as old as his age. His needle-eyes declared that there was no difference between imagination and reality. The same message was etched on his geographical face: a sheer side of a mountain plunging from high cheeks that had been buffeted by the elements to a craggy chin; wrinkles carving channels through sparse facial hair and moustache. The only things human about him were his threadbare breeches and poncho. The other item of clothing, his fedora hat, sat on his head like a cock's comb. 'We go out of town. To the fields. Totally dark there.'

Fuego's impatience exploded. The old man might be the best healer in the land, but he, too, knew a thing or two about casting out infections. All that was needed was a darkness that would expose the malign spirits. This was as dark as it would get anywhere in the country. The Tree might have a glow, but so did stones and mountains, rivers and fields. 'We will do it here!' He pushed the car door open. 'Now!'

The *curandero*, wary of Fuego's sharp tone, sat up. 'Why must it be here?'

'Because I say so. Out!'

The old man pulled his hat down, picked up the rabbit sleeping on his lap by its ears, hauled himself out of the car and shuffled towards the Tree.

Fuego's annoyance turned against himself. He had a good reason to come to La Recoleta. It was not because of Beatriz, flirting with God in that convent. He himself had placed her there. She had nearly died in the necropolis. The nuns were special people – women who had repaired themselves. They would give her the right care.

It was because of Daniel. It was to La Recoleta that Daniel had come to be healed. Here, he had talked to the Tree of the Millennium, embraced madness and sanity. From here, he had brought enough cunning to possess his enemy, enough power to keep him infected by God. He had to break the magic the Tree had imparted to Daniel with some magic of his own.

He got out of the car. He inspected his uniform, tried to look at himself in the window, but there was not enough light to give a reflection. He probably looked as he felt: fragmented. He checked that all his medals were securely pinned.

Hesitantly, he picked up the plastic shopping bag in the back seat. It contained Father Quintana's soutane. When he had picked it up from the mortuary, it had burned his hands; he had barely managed to stuff it in the bag.

He slammed the car door shut. He strode across the road and went into the park.

The *curandero* was scrutinising the giant cedar with misgiving. Brusquely, he indicated that Fuego should sit at the base and lean against the trunk.

Fuego did so. Immediately, his back, where it touched the tree, lost all sense of feeling. He became aware of a luminosity and some heat.

The *curandero*, one hand still holding the rabbit by its ears, picked up Father Quintana's soutane from the shopping bag and laid it on the grass.

Fuego became absolutely still.

The *curandero*, holding the rabbit by its four legs, stooped over Fuego. First he rubbed the rabbit over Fuego's uniform and medals. Then, pulling off Fuego's jacket and trousers, he rubbed it over Fuego's arms, chest, abdomen, loins and legs. Throughout this, the rabbit squealed pitifully. Finally, the *curandero* rubbed the rabbit over Fuego's head and face. Then he moved back. He held the rabbit by its ears and watched.

The rabbit convulsed and died.

The *curandero* nodded to indicate that the way the animal had died augured well.

He laid the rabbit on Father Quintana's soutane. He took out a knife and slit the rabbit down the middle, from its head to its tail.

He laid open both halves so that all its organs were exposed. He sat down and contemplated them.

Mesmerised, Fuego lost all sense of time.

The *curandero*'s shriek broke Fuego's trance.

Gasping, mouth frothing, the healer was pointing at the rabbit's entrails. 'No cure – for this, no cure.'

Fuego tottered over to him. 'What is it? Say it!'

The curandero shrank back. 'Don't touch me!' As Fuego closed in, he screamed. 'I go! I go!' And staggering as fast as he could, he disappeared into the night.

Fuego stood transfixed, stunned by the miscarriage of the *curandero*'s magic, yet relieved because now he knew he would die of his infection. He moved to the soutane, squatted and examined the rabbit's entrails.

Occult ratios had matched the animal's gender, lifespan and colouring with his own. Rubbed on to his clothes and body, the rabbit was invoked to develop the malignancy that threatened him. Here, in the entrails, could be seen how extensively God's infection had spread, where it would attack next, when it would consume. Having established these facts, the *curandero* should have recited incantations and spread herbs over the diseased areas until the infection had drained back to its source, in this case, the soutane, the cloth which represented God. If all had gone well, both the rabbit's carcass and the soutane would have disintegrated.

No hope of a cure, the *curandero* had declared.

Time passed without passing.

Then Fuego saw what was happening. The rabbit's entrails were weaving themselves into the soutane, rethreading fabric into the bullet holes, putting breath and image on to the bloodstains. They formed a picture, a Trinity, like in the polyptych. Only here, the faces were not identical. There was the Father, tall and blond like Daniel. There was the Son, in the image of Manku Yupanqui as he appeared in the campesinos' icons. And there was the Holy Spirit bearing Father Quintana's face.

And no traces of the rabbit's carcass.

More time passed without passing.

The sun announced its imminent birth.

A rainbow appeared, carrying a gourd at each end. One gourd contained the sap of the Cross; the other the *chicha* of the ancestors.

Fuego took the gourds, poured the sap and the *chicha* on to the earth.

The earth produced a giant breast.

Fuego suckled the breast.

Its elixir was potent. It contained the pulp of the dead gods and the blood of the New One. This was the nectar every man, woman and child of every tribe, every race, every colour would drink hereafter.

Fuego rose. He felt whole, replete with soul, body and three hearts. He saw he was standing naked; his clothes had formed a bonfire; his bemedalled uniform sizzled as it burned.

The Tree of the Millennium, shaking its branches, sang the song of the dead gods. It confirmed that the Crucified One was alive – all the dead gods were alive.

Yet more time passed without passing.

Fuego saw he was no longer naked. He had been vested with Father Quintana's soutane. He felt fire consuming him. He began to shake.

Time accelerated.

A gale carried away his flailing body.

The sun rose.

The gale tossed him against a mountain; then propelled him towards the summit.

He hit rock fourteen times.

Thrice he saw Jesus fall under the weight of the Cross.

He saw the Virgin.

Simon the Cyrenian.

Saint Veronica.

He saw Jesus stripped of His garments. The Roman soldiers casting lots for them.

He saw the raising of the Cross and the Crucifixion.

He saw Jesus laid in the arms of His Mother.

He saw His entombment.

The gale abated.

His convulsions ceased. His burning ceased. His eyes opened and he perceived everything.

He was on top of a young, arrow-tipped mountain, lying at the feet of Jesus whose outstretched arms embraced the world.

He was still wearing Father Quintana's soutane. It had reverted to what it had been when he had picked it up from the mortuary – riddled with bullet holes and covered in bloodstains. Yet it had become part of his body, soft and taut like skin. And the Trinity it had borne had seeped down to his bones and was now implanted in his marrow.

He looked up at Jesus' eyes.

The Eyes reflected him.

He had been transfigured: his puma's body had changed to that of a lamb; his face, he could now see, was that of the Inca Adam in the polyptych. He was Manku Yupanqui.

The cloisters should have barred his way; the pillars should have sprouted spears; the sweetly singing birds should have thrown grenades; the rose garden should have turned into a forest of poisonous plants. Collectively, they should have destroyed this man of utmost evil.

As for her... She had hurried out and sat with him, holding her aching breasts, self-conscious of her bleeding, anxious that the simple white dress she wore might be stained if her sanitary towels became saturated, wondering whether he would react with pity or remorse seeing how much weight she had lost, how she had brutally cut most of her hair, how pale she still was.

And she was sitting calmly as if he were an old friend who had come to visit her. Listening to his every word.

This man who had raped her, who had destroyed the man she loved, who had murdered countless others, who, only yesterday, had executed Father Quintana, and because of whom, this morning, Huaman had announced the death sentences of his American hostages.

She was not just listening, but believing him. *I have wrestled with God. And I have lost*, the message he had given the nuns had said.

Did she believe him because this was also the man who had toiled as her midwife, who had sent men to snatch her from death, who, despite the call of evil, had not entirely squandered his soul?

He had been telling her about his seizure under the Tree of the Millennium, of his ascent of the Fourteen Stations of the Cross on Huayna Santo, of his conversion and his transfiguration. He had come to her, he had said, immediately after all that.

Now, he was silent. He was walking among the rose bushes, occasionally laying his face on a flower like a lover, seeking, she could see, something else to say, something that perhaps offered an explanation, convinced her, thawed her hatred.

He bore no signs of the transfiguration he had claimed he had experienced. He looked as if he had wrestled not with God but with death. There were bruises on his face and deep shadows between them. He still wore Father Quintana's soutane.

Beatriz took up her basket-weaving. She had set herself the task of making ten a day. They were popular with pilgrims to La Recoleta and the convent needed the money.

As if alarmed that he had lost her attention, Fuego strode across and sat down on the grass by her feet.

She studied him again. This time she saw him as he really was: an eater of the dead who had just emerged from a pit piled high with his victims.

She began to burn with hatred.

Simultaneously, she became aware that her bleeding had stopped and that her breasts, still stubbornly producing milk, ached less. Unaccountably, she was feeling stronger.

He braced himself to speak again, then changed his mind. Slowly, he ran his eyes over the convent's old plaster walls, the murals – each depicting the martyrdom of a saint – painted by anonymous nuns, the cool Moorish cloisters transposed from the Alhambra to the New World, and the garden with its central fountain simulating Eden.

He shook his head in wonder. 'This is a beautiful place. I am glad you are here.'

She tried to concentrate on her basket-work. 'God should have killed you!'

He held up the straws to facilitate her work. 'We know why a volcano erupts, what causes an earthquake. But there is no explanation for evil. It is there. It is not as we *naturales* believe, one half of Nature. Nor is it, as the Church believes, a force without which good cannot exist. I am not puzzling over a new question, I know – but I reject all the answers, because there is no explaining evil.'

'You personify it!'

'No longer. This is what I am trying to say. There is no explaining it because it can be spat out with one hefty cough – as I have done. If it's so insubstantial, how can it have such dominion?' Gently he placed a hand on her foot. 'Am I making sense?'

She recoiled from his touch.

He looked at her, miserably. 'I am sorry – that was an innocent gesture...

You are no longer a carnal person for me. This is another thing I want to say. You are my mother, my sister, my daughter. I have betrayed you. I won't ever again. Now, I want to care for you – come with me. Be my family.'

Beatriz swept the basket off her lap, got up, and moved away. 'I want you destroyed. I want your bones blanched and dead. I don't want you a penitent!'

He ran his hand over the grass, a blind man reading in Braille. 'Am I penitent? I can't believe it yet! I hope it is not the Devil playing tricks. But I swear I will care for you – wherever I am.'

She felt her hatred slipping out of her heart. 'Where will wherever be?'

Fuego stood up and wandered off to the rose bushes. 'Tomorrow, this country. The day after, this continent. The day after that, the world. How I will get there, I don't know.'

She strode to the bench and picked up the knife she had been using to cut the straw. 'I should have killed you, Oseas. The moment I saw you in this holy ground. Now that you're meek and crawling, I can't! Why can't I?'

Gently, Fuego seized her hand and took the knife from her. 'Until today, you could have killed me any time, *querida*. I would not have stopped you. But not now. Now there is much I have to do.'

She extricated her hand and ran towards the cloisters.

He shouted after her. 'I have one last thing to say! I now know: I had to try and destroy God. It was my way of finding Him. I knew: if I could not destroy Him, if He survived me – if He survived me then He must be real. He is! He is!'

Beatriz paused by a pillar. 'And if He destroys you?'

'Not if. *When*. Because He will.'

'*When* He destroys you?'

Fuego smiled. 'He will be all the more real.'

She could no longer contain her confusion. She disappeared behind a door.

58
The twilight comes weeping in the shape of dark poppies

Dr Williston was on the platform. A vertiginous elephant on a tightrope. He had arrived unexpectedly and demanded to see the polyptych. But he was giving it only a cursory look.

'So which of these doodles is supposed to be Manku Yupanqui?'

Daniel squatted on his haunches. 'Doodles? You won't see a greater masterpiece if you live to be Methuselah.'

Williston rasped. 'Which one?'

Daniel, taking pleasure in Williston's agitation, pointed at the Inca Adam. Williston studied the figure. 'How do we know?'

Daniel began to wheeze. 'We don't. But he's the likeliest candidate.'

'Rumour says it's Huaman. Doesn't look like him.'

'It did, I thought – briefly. Looks more like Fuego now.'

'Fuego? Nonsense!' Williston gave the figure a closer scrutiny. 'I'll tell you what he looks like. A Semite. Definitely more a Semite than an Indio.'

Daniel smiled. 'Strange you should say that. There is a theory – it was quite popular last century – that the Incas were descendants of the Hebrews. That they'd come across the Bering Straits. That they had racial and ritualistic parallels with the Jews. And some similar laws and legends.'

Williston sniggered. 'I can believe that.'

Daniel smiled. 'Maybe he looks like me. I sometimes think he does.'

'Hardly.'

'That's a relief. I thought I was distorting things – like all Jews.'

Williston ignored Daniel's sarcasm and carefully eased himself down from the platform.

Daniel leaned over the scaffold. 'Is that it? All you wanted to see?'

'Yes. Thank you.'

'Out of curiosity. What's your interest in Manku Yupanqui?'

Williston moved to the door. 'He's the enemy – Antichrist by another name.' He checked his watch. 'There's a special programme on the radio – in about an hour. Listen to it. He stars in it.' He paused at the door. 'Oh, just to put you straight. That rag you call a masterpiece is a pagan abomination – as sure as the Lord made green apples.' He left, banging the door behind him.

On the radio, Angelito exhorted the nation. The people would no longer tolerate atheistic dogmas. They now saw that the preservation of moral values was a sacred duty.

Daniel stepped back and studied the Tree of Life. Williston's interruption, irritating as it had been, had cleared his thoughts. And the open windows, though barely getting rid of the American's pine-oil odour, had helped his breathing.

He had not got some of the details right.

The flaming sword-which-turned-every-way... It looked like a comet with a dark, burning centre and fiery tails. A sword that could cut through the entire universe. But he was not recapturing that effect. His mixture of orpiment yellow and iodine scarlet was pathetic – a novice could have done better.

The people had accepted, Angelito pronounced, the need for sacrifice. They knew the salvation of the country was at stake. They were ready to fight until total victory.

Mixing pigments was his forte. Why was he having trouble now? Damn the Sword! It seemed to follow his every move, laugh at his efforts to cling to life, leer when he masturbated, five, six, eight times a day.

There was not the shadow of a doubt, Angelito declared, that the enemy were vermin afflicted with moral degeneracy. And like all vermin, they were determined to infect the healthy.

The leaves of the Tree of Knowledge... Mixing assorted greens to a base of light cadmium vert was producing the right colour but not the right texture. He needed a heavier foundation. He should try an arsenic-based pigment. Scheele's green might do it.

The identities of the vermin, Angelito stated, were known to the nation.

The Crucified Jesus... Here, the son of Man, the Son of God, the Son of the Sun had been painted as the literal representation of the Suffering Servant:

ugly, deformed, scourged, pierced and flayed of His very skin. But as majestic as Jacob wrestling with the Angel of God. Here, too, he was not conveying the artist's intentions. He needed shades where raw flesh smouldered like fire and nerve ends crystallised like salt pillars. He needed a red that radiated both death and rebirth.

Priests who opened their churches to communists, Angelito affirmed, were vermin. Peasants who terrorised landowners for a patch of earth, miners who downed tools, savages who impeded progress in the Amazonian humus, intellectuals who strove to destroy order with the object of defiling the people's mothers, sisters, wives and daughters were all vermin.

Daniel jumped down from the platform and put the coffee on.

The special programme Williston had mentioned had turned into the usual boring stuff. He debated whether he should change stations. No point. He would either get mindless music or even more mindless quiz games. There were the odd foreign stations of some quality, but these days anything of quality disturbed him. The other day, it had been a programme on Beatriz's compositions. *I saw a vision last night when the world was you and I and our child.*

In the unlikely event that the malignancy of the vermin needed proof, Angelito proclaimed, he was here to provide it. He had in his possession a tape...

The last statement engaged Daniel. He poured himself a cup of coffee and listened. Strange that it was Angelito broadcasting. Such pontifications were usually Fuego's prerogative.

The tape, Angelito announced, was sent by an Antichrist who masqueraded as the people's inquisitor, called himself Manku Yupanqui and led a pack of cretins whom he declared were revolutionaries. The tape recorded the last moments of the hostage American missionaries. Let the people hear how these vermin fed on brutal murder.

Daniel stretched out on the hammock, lit a cigarette and sipped his coffee.

The hostages' cacophony filled the atelier. Muttered prayers. Hysterical screams. Desperate pleas to be spared. In counterpoint, the rebels' tumult: angry voices bent on revenge. Mockery of Christians who could not embrace martyrdom bravely. And the shrill voice of reason, Huaman's: from now on, twenty eyes for the loss of one.

Daniel blew out smoke rings.

Sounds of fires blazing. Inconceivable screams of people being burned alive.

Somewhere in his mind, Daniel visualised the missionaries' death. Bodies that twisted like matchsticks, blood that steamed, flesh that turned into cinders.

He should be revolted. Huaman, kicking history back to barbarity, was dealing with innocents as Torquemada had dealt with the Jews during the Spanish Inquisition. As the Conquistadores had dealt with the Indians.

He sipped his coffee.

Angelito urged their prayers.

A tenor sang Gounod's *Ave Maria*.

A clear baritone with an American accent intoned: *To him that overcometh will I give to eat of the Tree of Life, which is in the midst of the Paradise of God.*

Daniel drained his coffee, stubbed out his cigarette in the mug. He had problems to solve. He placed the mug on the floor and closed his eyes to concentrate. He fell asleep instantly.

'Daniel!'

He woke up with a start.

Jerry Rice was staring at him. Damn the man!

'Sorry to startle you. I rang the bell a few times...'

Daniel clambered out of the hammock and glanced at his watch. He had been asleep for more than three hours. 'How did you get in?'

'The nightwatchman.'

Daniel grabbed a cigarette. 'You've got a constipated look, Jerry. What is it?'

'A message from Fuego – about Beatriz...'

Daniel's sleep-dry mouth turned acid. 'He's found her?'

'She's at Father Quintana's old church...'

Daniel faced him sharply. 'They've razed that place to the ground! What's she doing there?'

'She wants to see you. I've got hold of a Land-Rover. We can leave when you're ready.'

'We?'

'She asked to see me, too.'

59

I thrust the turbulent and sweet hand into the very genitals of the earth

Daniel jumped out of the Land-Rover.

Beatriz was standing by the church's door. She was in a white shift, coarse and shapeless, mapped with dirt and sweat – the sackcloth she had worn when she had brought him their dead baby.

He ran towards her.

She watched him impassively. As if he no longer had any flesh, heart or history.

Discouraged, he stopped running. The heat and the teeming insects repossessed him.

He told himself she looked radiant. She looked, in fact, like a statue, like clay that had conquered time and the elements at the expense of life.

She slipped back into the church. Her walk had not changed. Her body still rolled as gently as a summer sea.

Daniel glanced back at Rice. The old man, debilitated by the heat and saturated by whisky – he had drunk over ten bottles during their three days' drive – was struggling to resuscitate himself.

Daniel waited. He needed a token somebody who could serve as a crutch. Much as he had yearned to meet Beatriz, he had realised he did not have the courage to face her alone.

He struggled with the insects: his shirt and trousers, drenched by the humidity, had stuck to his flesh; and the mosquitoes were sipping his blood through the cloth.

There were some people about: Indian women and their children. Most of them squatted in the shade of the church; heads burrowed into laps, they looked like friezes on a stele. Some worked at the edges of the square, clearing the detritus of the burnt adobe huts.

There were no men.

No animals.

Since no one had survived Angelito's raid, these women and children could not have been of the region; sniffing death in the wind, they must have swooped down here to scavenge. The rags they wore were ruddled with bloodstains and must have been taken from corpses; their battered utensils and broken bric-à-brac had obviously been salvaged from what had been left of the market stalls.

They had buried the dead. The bones that lay scattered were the remains of animals.

Daniel shivered. The devastation of the village, though furred by the passage of months and the rainy season, still arrested the beholder. The screams of the murdered had fossilised in the thick dust; the earth bore the pallor of mummies. Only the church, with its golden blood coagulated, its massive walls barely pecked by bullets, defied the compulsion to return to an inorganic state.

Rice had dragged himself forward. Daniel tried to catch his eye, beg support. Rice walked on, still spurning any intimacy. Unforgiving bastard!

Daniel followed, nauseous, wheezing.

They entered the church.

Beatriz was sitting in the front pew, head down.

Rice pushed past him and shuffled to her side. He touched her hair. She looked up, clasped his hand and placed it against her cheek. Like father and daughter reunited. Finally, Rice disengaged, kissed her forehead and moved back slowly. Ignoring Daniel, he sat in the last pew and took out his hip-flask.

Beatriz, her hands now enfolded in her lap, had lowered her head again.

Daniel found the strength to move forward. He eased himself down alongside her.

She did not look at him. She began to cry.

Daniel stared at the wooden statue of the Crucified Jesus. It was smeared with flakes of excreta. Its eyes appeared to be fixed on the communion table – hacked to pieces and strewn with the remnants of Father Timothy O'Neill's relics. No one, it appeared, had dared clean up Angelito's desecration. But the statue's expression was not desolate. Everything temporal can be repaired, it seemed to say. You are a restorer, you should know that. What cannot be repaired is what we defer to the next life. The next life is only for judgement, not for reparation.

Hesitantly, Daniel placed his hand on hers. He felt her flinch, but she did not pull away.

If he could only say something simple and miraculous. He began to cry, too. His breath dwindled into drips. 'I have killed our son... I have killed our love... I may have killed you... Can I be forgiven...?'

She hissed. 'I want my baby! Give me back my baby!'

'If only I could... Maybe... If I can be healed... If you can help... forgive...'

She turned on him, her face distorted by hatred and fury. Wailing like a cornered animal, she spat at him.

Then she ran off to the corner of the transept aisle. She huddled there, her back turned, her face pushed against the wall.

Daniel sobbed in abandon.

A hand came to rest on his shoulder. A voice, raucous but mellow, whispered. 'Do not give up. She is full of pain. Let yourself be broken. Broken, you will be whole.'

Timorously, disbelievingly, hopefully, Daniel scanned the statue for a sign that it had spoken.

The hand on his shoulder edged forward. Behind the hand there was a soutane – embroidered, dirty, blood-spattered, riddled with bullet holes. And inside the soutane stood the compact figure bearing Satan's luminous face.

Daniel lurched to his feet. 'You!'

Incongruously, Fuego was carrying a plastic shopping bag. He smiled serenely. 'Thank you for coming, Daniel... Thank you, Mr Rice... Beatriz...'

Confused, Beatriz looked up, but remained pressed against the wall.

Rice craned forward angrily. 'You set this up?'

Fuego nodded apologetically. 'I had to get you here.' He looked around for somewhere to put his bag. 'Using you as pretexts for one another was the only way.' He placed his bag near Jesus' statue. 'You must be witnesses to my conversion.'

Daniel spluttered. 'Is this another one of your stunts? What do you think you're doing with that soutane! You've murdered Father Quintana! Isn't that enough?'

'Don't you understand, Daniel? You won the bet. God exists. I have found Him.'

Daniel fought for breath. He felt as if his chest had caved in. Jealousy – sudden and primeval – consumed him.

Beatriz slunk along the aisle where bold murals depicted the Stations of the Cross.

Rice remained seated, for once oblivious of his hip-flask, bewildered eyes darting between Daniel, Beatriz and Fuego.

Fuego shook his head in wonder. 'I have found God. It was so easy. All I did was put on this soutane. I meant to exorcise him. Instead, He reclaimed me.'

Daniel roared in anguish. 'Bastard! Bastard!'

Fuego caught Daniel's hand and rubbed it against the soutane. 'Look, He is here! In the cloth!'

Daniel punched him viciously. 'No!'

Fuego managed to hold his ground. 'Look! Touch the cloth! Feel Him!'

Daniel threw another punch. 'No!' And another. 'No!'

Fuego reeled. He shook his head to clear the pain and stupor. Then, his own fury erupting, he threw himself at Daniel.

They fought like the last of two species, both doomed.

Beatriz's hysterical screams, as she ran from one Station of the Cross to another, counterpointed their snarls and groans, the sounds of pounded flesh.

Rice had dragged himself up and was waving his hip-flask, shouting drunkenly. 'Bums! Bums! You goddam bums! Be damned – the both of you!' And pitying. 'You're gonna kill each other! It'll serve you right! But what for?'

Daniel and Fuego fell in a heap and grappled in the nave.

Daniel pinned Fuego down and kneed him in the ribs. He growled through torn mouth. 'Who am I fighting? You or God! You or God?'

Fuego heaved and butted him in the face.

Blood from his cut forehead flooded Daniel's already swollen eyes.

Fuego scrambled to his feet.

Daniel tore off his shirt, wiped the blood and sprang up. He staggered towards Fuego.

Fuego retreated to the altar. He stumbled over its wreckage. He grabbed one of the jagged pieces of timber and held it like a sword. 'Stop or I'll kill you!'

Daniel continued advancing.

Fuego prepared to strike.

Daniel closed in.

Fuego hesitated, then flung aside the timber.

Daniel struck him with every ounce of strength he could muster.

Fuego collapsed. Instinct urged him to get up. But his body failed. He fell flat on his back, bleeding and breathless.

Daniel, bent double with aching lungs, towered above him. 'You just like uniforms, don't you? Even a soutane... Well, not this time... Where's your God now, eh?'

Fuego muttered, barely able to enunciate. 'I had Him…'

Daniel dropped into a pew. He became aware of Beatriz's hysteria, of Rice's incoherent curses. Wearily, he waved his hands at them. 'It's all right… Nothing's happened…'

Beatriz's screams faded. She sank to the floor and buried her head in her lap.

Rice folded into his pew.

The sun, Daniel remembered, had been shining on Jesus' statue when Fuego had stolen into the church. Now, it was seeping away through the window. Evening was approaching.

Hours must have passed. Hours he had mercifully lost. Hours, though scored by coughs, groans, bruised movements and painful breathing, of silence, of unblemished refuge.

He turned towards Beatriz. She was still on the floor, in the aisle, her head buried in the crook of her arm.

He turned towards Rice. Still crumpled up in his pew. Snoring the oblivion of the drunk.

Finally, he dared look at Fuego. No longer sprawled on the nave, but rocking on his knees, watching an old woman lighting a wick in a small bowl of fat. When had she come in?

Daniel fumbled for his cigarettes. The box had been crushed; the cigarettes broken into bits. If only the silence would continue for ever…

The old woman was going out, muttering prayers. And Fuego was fidgeting… snorting like a bull… bucking like a horse…

Fuego charged towards Jesus' statue. He threw himself on the floor, spread out his arms and raged. 'Don't do this to me! I slaughtered my doubts! I have seen You! I have accepted You! Don't reject me now! Look! I stand before You naked – like Adam! Clad only in Your cloth!'

Daniel looked up at the statue, wondering whether it would respond to Fuego… or strike him dead.

Fuego beat his hands on the statue's feet. 'Don't reject me! Touch me! Breathe into me! Make me Your man! Accept me, damn You! Accept me now!'

Daniel saw Jesus' features transmute into a voluptuous woman: naked breasts round and full, silken muscular legs open to expose her wondrous mount. This was God! God was a woman as magnificent as Beatriz! And God was beckoning!

Daniel saw himself move towards Her. Instantly, seven rivers materialised before him.

Intrepidly, he kept going forward. The first engulfed him in a fiery storm, but he traversed it by clinging to a rider on a white horse. The second chased him with four creatures in human form; he escaped by clinging to a rider on a red horse. The third surrounded him with the creatures' faces – those of a man, a lion, an ox, an eagle; he broke through by clinging to a rider on a black horse. The fourth tried to seize him with the creatures' human hands; he evaded them by wresting from Death its sickly horse. The fifth charged at him with the sparkling wheels of the creatures; he flew clear by jumping on the souls of God's servants. The sixth barricaded his way with a wall of ice; he burst through it by riding a violent earthquake which moved mountains and islands from their places.

Finally, he reached the seventh river. There, God. Her nipples erect, Her legs open and inviting, smiled and lay down on Her sapphire throne. Seven angels, each with a trumpet, greeted his arrival.

He lay next to Her. As he clasped Her to consummate his love, a revolving sword flew out of Her vagina and cut him into countless pieces.

He wailed.

Fuego was also wailing. He was pounding the altar, striking at protruding nails and the pieces of splintered wood. 'Accept me now! Accept me now!'

Suddenly, he jumped to his feet and faced them. He held up his palms. Oozing blood. 'Look! Stigmata! Look! He has accepted me! Look! Stigmata!'

Daniel, still lying in fragments before God's nakedness, saw Fuego cross the seven rivers. Negotiating no hazards. Simply walking on the waters. He saw him reach God. He saw God spread Herself for Fuego. He saw them embrace and quicken in bliss. And he died in each one of his countless pieces.

Fuego was still shouting. 'Look! Stigmata! Look, He has accepted me!'

Beatriz crawled on the floor, her head rolling in disbelief, her strained voice protesting weakly. 'No! They're your doing! You wounded yourself!' She collapsed, curled up into herself and whimpered.

Daniel pushed himself off his pew and tottered towards the door.

Fuego ran after Daniel and seized him. 'Wait!'

Daniel pushed him away.

Fuego held on to him. 'I will give you more proof! Hit me!'

Daniel tried to extricate himself.

'Hit me! Hit me! Hit me, damn you, hit me!'

Daniel veered round and struck him across the face.

Fuego threw himself back, offering the other cheek. 'Again! Hit me again! Hard as you can!'

Daniel plunged into madness. He lashed out, brutally, dementedly. Hammer-blow after hammer-blow.

Fuego, having offered no resistance, finally keeled over. He muttered faintly through his pulped lips. 'I passed the test, Daniel.' Then he lost consciousness.

Daniel, drained, collapsed into a pew. He looked at Beatriz, then at Rice, then at Beatriz again... They returned his look with glazed eyes.

Regaining consciousness, Fuego put time back into motion. He rose from the floor. Ecstatic in his pain, reborn in the blood that covered him, he approached Daniel, touched him lovingly. 'Stay with me, Daniel.'

Daniel catapulted up and edged away.

Fuego careened after him. 'God wants you. I will find you a soutane. All you have to do is put it on.'

Daniel howled. 'Stop tormenting me!'

'You can take it off after God has possessed you. We don't all need a uniform. You can carry Him any way you want.' He pointed at Beatriz and Rice. 'She carries Him in her heart. He in his pen.'

Daniel backed away. 'Enough! Enough of this charade!' He ran to Beatriz, stretched a tentative hand. 'Come with me...'

Beatriz recoiled from his touch.

Fuego shuffled over to Beatriz. 'You will stay with me.'

Beatriz, recoiling from him, too, sprang up and ran to Rice.

Rice held her protectively. 'You guys should be put down! Deadly – both of you!'

Wearily, Fuego leaned against the aisle wall. 'You should all stay with me... Liberate God... Be liberated by Him.' He brandished his wounded palms. 'Can't you see? He is with me!'

A faint voice addressed him. 'Papacha...'

A young woman, holding a baby, stood in the shadows by the door.

Fuego, angry at the interruption, shouted impatiently. 'Later, *mamacita*!'

The young woman, though intimidated, edged forward. 'God – is He really with you, Papacha?'

Fuego's tone softened. 'Yes, compañera. He is.' He showed her his palms. 'Look!'

Rice, still holding Beatriz protectively, interjected. 'Don't be taken in by him, sister! He inflicted those on himself!'

The young woman, ignoring Rice, approached Fuego. 'Tell God – my baby...' Desperately, she bared her breast. 'Look – I have plenty milk... But my baby...'

Beatriz, agonised, peered at the mother and child.

The young woman pushed the baby to her breast. The baby, emaciated, remained insensible. 'Look... won't suckle... Tell Him – make the little one suckle...'

Beatriz buried her face in Rice's chest. 'Send her away! Send her away! Please – not a dead baby!'

Daniel, tormented that he could not offer any solace to Beatriz, sank to the floor.

Fuego, casting a pitiful look at Daniel, held out his arms to the woman. 'Give me the baby. Boy or girl?'

The woman handed him the baby. 'Girl.'

Fuego rocked her tenderly. 'She's pretty.'

Tears welled in the woman's eyes. 'My first. Make her suckle, Papacha.'

Fuego nodded.

Somehow Beatriz found another reserve of strength and disengaged from Rice.

Fuego carried the baby to Jesus' statue and laid her by its feet; then squatting by her side, began to sing. *'We will not stop until words can be spoken again, songs find the faith to be born, freedom is raised from its pit of cadavers.'*

Rice looked at Beatriz. The song was the anthem she had written for Huaman at the time of the miners' strike in Monte Rico.

But Beatriz did not appear to be hearing it. She was mesmerised by the baby.

Rice observed the others. The young woman had knelt down as if receiving benediction; the baby had started whimpering; even Daniel, who had been raked through his many hells, appeared peaceful.

'We will not stop until we reach the rainbowland we promised our children...' Fuego finished singing and picked up the baby.

The baby began to cry.

Fuego took her back to her mother. 'Give her the breast now.'

The campesina sat in a pew and directed the baby's mouth to her nipple.

Beatriz, Rice and Daniel watched in a trance.

The baby did not suckle; tossing her head from side to side, she cried in greater distress.

Angrily, Fuego ripped the woman's shirt and exposed her other breast. 'Try again!'

The campesina switched the baby to her other breast.

The baby, still crying and tossing, turned away. Fuego pushed her back. The baby hesitated. Her crying dissolved into whimpers. Hungrily, she began to suckle.

The campesina, awed, looked up at Fuego.

Fuego's eyes blazed. 'Give the first breast again.'

The campesina turned the baby round. The baby uttered a brief cry of protest then took the breast eagerly. The campesina clutched Fuego's hand. 'You are a saint, Papacha.'

'God is with me.'

The campesina nodded devotionally. 'He is, Papacha!'

Fuego, about to move away, turned to the campesina. 'You believe that, *mamacita*?'

The campesina clutched his hand again. 'Yes, Papacha. I can see Him in you.'

A cunning smile broke through Fuego's air of serenity. 'Then tell the people. Tell them what happened.'

'I will, Papacha.'

Daniel thundered. 'So that's it! That's your game! How much did you pay her, Oseas? What did she put on her breasts to stop the baby feeding?'

Fuego looked at him sorrowfully. 'Why won't you accept it? Look around you – everything is bathed in the supernatural! Look at me – the man I was, but also a new man. Desecrator, blasphemer, torturer, killer, Antichrist! Yet I am with God!'

Daniel fulminated. 'There can't be God *and* you!'

Fuego roared with equal passion. 'There can't be God *without* the likes of me! How else can evil men abandon their ways?'

Brusquely, Daniel turned to Beatriz. 'Come with me...'

Beatriz, ignoring him, moved hesitantly towards the campesina.

Fuego brought out a dirty blindfold from inside his soutane. 'Remember this, Daniel? The blindfold Father Quintana refused to wear! You picked it up – remember?'

Daniel blared at Beatriz. 'Are you staying with him?'

Beatriz sat next to the campesina. Weeping silently, she watched the suckling baby.

Fuego waved the blindfold. 'Why didn't you keep it? Did you think you didn't need it? Who were you trying to fool? Yourself? Or me?'

Daniel grabbed Beatriz by the arm. 'How can you? He raped you! Killed Father Quintana!'

Beatriz, without taking her eyes off the baby, jerked her arm free. 'Go away!'

Fuego grabbed Daniel and stuffed the blindfold into Daniel's trousers' pocket. 'Here! Take it! You can't live without it!'

Daniel shoved him aside. 'Let's go, Jerry!'

As Daniel moved up the aisle, Fuego shouted after him. 'And my strength! What did you do with my strength? What happened to the llama fat? What did you do with the strength you took from me?'

Daniel opened the church door.

Fuego bellowed. 'Daniel! *I am not afraid, any more!*'

Daniel faltered, then scurried out.

Fuego sat down wearily.

Rice moved to Beatriz. 'What will you do?'

Beatriz wiped her tears, took his hand and placed it against her cheek as she had done before. 'I need to think.'

'Shall I stay around?'

'No... No... If I decide to go back to the convent, I can make my own way...'

'Do you believe in all this?'

'I don't know. Do you?'

'I wish I could.' He let go of her hand. 'If you need anything... I'll always be there...'

Beatriz nodded. 'Dear Jerry. You'll be my father – for ever...'

Rice, tearful, walked away.

Fuego drew himself up. 'Mr Rice... Whether you believe me or not is immaterial. But you have a good story on your hands.'

Rice paused and smiled sarcastically. 'You reckon?'

Fuego picked up his plastic shopping bag and brought out an envelope. 'I want you to write it.' He handed the envelope to Rice. 'And I want you to include this.'

'What is it?'

'Call it my gospel.'

Rice looked at him mockingly. 'Your gospel, no less. Assuming I agree, who'd print it? Except for some innocuous pieces, my work is being censored.'

'You'll find my clearance and my authorisation for translation inside. I am still Head of Security. Just hand your copy to the official news agency. Don't let me down.' He grinned self-mockingly. 'I need the publicity.'

'Publicity?'

'You can't start a revolution without publicity.'

'What revolution?'

'The long-awaited one. God's. Manku Yupanqui's.'

'Let me get this straight. You're joining up with Huaman?'

'Huaman is a puffed-up frog. He can never succeed. I can.'

'You're the revolutionaries' greatest enemy. They'll kill you the moment they set eyes on you.'

'Not if they know about my conversion. Hence, my gospel.'

'And if you take over – what then?'

'Then we start changing the world.'

'If we're going to speak in clichés, General... the more it changes, the more it's the same.'

'Cynicism does not become you, Mr Rice. Unless we change the world, they will kill God.'

'*They?*'

'New Order and Moral Crusade. And all their camp-followers. They can't rule as long as God is alive. You know that as well as I. That's why I am counting on you. *Vaya con Dios.*'

Rice walked out of the church on unsteady feet.

Fuego turned his attention to Beatriz. She was still sitting with the campesina, watching the baby. The latter was now happily asleep on her mother's breast.

He squatted next to Beatriz. 'Tomorrow, I am going to the mountains... Will you come?'

She looked at him, trying to see into his heart. 'This revolution of yours – how many will it kill?'

'I don't know...'

'Daniel's right then. You're not changing profession – just your uniform...'

'I have finished with killing. I swear it! I will fight without guns.'

'How?'

'I will find a way.'

'When you do, I'll join you.'

'Until then?'

'I might stay here. There are many women with children. They might teach me how to have a baby without killing it.' She turned to the campesina and, hesitantly, touched the baby. 'May I hold her?'

Proudly, the campesina handed her the baby.

Beatriz began to sing. '*Mother, bathe me in the light of the moon, clothe me with the Sun, anoint me with life...*'

60

For my people life was not permitted and the tomb was denied

...This is the unholy alliance between MORAL CRUSADE and NEW ORDER as I, Jerry Rice, an ageing hack, see it. I have, alas, a reputation for jeremiads and a greater reputation for watching them fall on deaf ears. Consequently, I shall relinquish this platform in favour of a voice to which you might listen more readily.

This voice is General Oseas Fuego who, until his sudden conversion to the service of God, was the Security Chief of this country.

You may well doubt his credentials and ask yourselves, quite rightly, whether a person whose image, hitherto, has only reflected utmost inhumanity, can have any credibility. Judge him as you see fit.

This is what General Fuego has to say:

'I know the evils of NEW ORDER because I have used them as mercenaries. I have paid them with the blood of compatriots I have killed.

'I know the evils of MORAL CRUSADE because they have used me as their mercenary. They have paid me by washing the blood on my hands.

'These forces support our government as they support every tyrannical state in the world.

'These powers have two declared aims. One: to seize power everywhere. Two: to retain this power at all costs.

'To this effect, they seek to make us, the people, our own enemies. They feed us the big lie: that freedom resides in our slavery, happiness in our brutality, life in our death. They urge us to breathe in fear, to take the food from our children's mouths, to praise God by ignoring His commandment and kill in His name.

'We can stop them.

'We have a formidable weapon: God's love.

'For God is on the side of the poor, the oppressed the disenfranchised, the peons, the hungry, the suffering, the tortured, the murdered – all who crave for brotherhood, who believe in peace and tolerance, who seek further reflections of God in the very differences of man's colour, creed and soul.

'Remember, Jesus was on the side of the poor, the oppressed, the disenfranchised, the peons, the hungry, the suffering, the tortured, the murdered.

'So is Manku Yupanqui.

'Remember, Jesus was a revolutionary.

'So is Manku Yupanqui. .

'It is they we must follow.

'God's bosom awaits us!'

Dr Williston swept the newspaper off the desk. 'Damnation take him!' He leaned back in his chair and scrutinised Fuego's office with distaste.

Angelito, standing by the window, pushed the shutters half open.

Down on the Plaza de los Héroes, the crowd was gathering. More and more people were spilling out of their offices and shops, out of the cafés and restaurants. More and more people were being disgorged by the trams, buses and taxis. On the peripheral roads, they were abandoning cars, motorcycles and bicycles in a rush to get to the square. Traffic helicopters had reported that the people in the barrios were straining to join the demonstration; every truck and coach on the outskirts of the capital had been commandeered.

The demonstration itself was frustratingly peaceful. People were simply standing in silence and reading their newspapers, all of which carried the Fuego diatribe. The riot police and the Sinchis, pouring into the square, were having a miserable time: all their efforts to provoke the crowd into disorder were proving unfruitful.

Williston's manicured nails drummed the table. 'What I'd like to know is what happened to the censors in this God-fearing country? How come every newspaper, every agency carried those sonsofbitches' poison! You answer me that, Colonel!'

Angelito turned round and fixed his eyes on the Nöstetangen chandelier. He did not like Williston sitting at Fuego's desk as if he owned the country. As for being in this office... he, at least, had a right to it, he was Deputy Security Chief.

Williston prompted him sternly. 'I didn't catch what you said, Angelito?'

Angelito eyed Williston. But this man and his gang controlled his ambitions. 'It was released through this office – with Fuego's personal authorisation.'

'What?'

'No newspaper can ignore a communiqué from Security. If they do, they are closed down.'

Williston shook his head, not without admiration. 'You sap – he beat you at your own game. That explains why that garbage got syndicated in the US of A. Why our buddies couldn't kill it like they've been killing all of Rice's drivel.'

'I suppose it does.'

'Sure, it does. We've got a free press there. Except for the few we control, we can't gag them. What we can do is kill the copy at source – that's how we've been stopping Rice. But once that trash got printed here, nothing anyone could do.'

Angelito nodded.

Williston straightened the sleeves of his jacket, then rose from the desk. 'All right, he kicked us in the teeth. But the Lord will see we get even.'

Angelito tried to sound reassuring. 'I'll find Fuego if it's the last thing I do.'

Williston paused in front of Angelito, straightened the Bridegrooms armband on Angelito's resplendent uniform, then took his arm and forced him to walk alongside. 'What about the Junta? Any old loyalties there for Fuego?'

'They want him dead.'

'Does that mean they've appointed a successor?'

'Not yet.'

Williston made him pause in front of the Goya aquatints. 'I guess they're having a hard time deciding.' Gazing at the pictures, he shook his head ruefully. 'Imagine, some people call this art.' He smiled at Angelito. 'Wondering who they can trust...'

Angelito barely restrained himself from shouting his candidacy. He began to sweat. He was poised, he knew, between full power and more lost years. 'There are a few...'

'Tell me, Angelito – do you like Fuego's hacienda?'

'It's nice – yes.'

'Just what your wife would like, I bet. All those vast acres – ideal to turn children into fine men. And this office? You like this office?'

Angelito's sweat turned sweetly cold. He could feel it – power, teasing him with ice-hot promise. 'Fit for an emperor.'

Williston started walking again with Angelito. 'Well, if it's fit for an emperor, it's fit for you. And the hacienda goes with it.'

At last. 'But the decision is the Junta's.'

'I'll see to the Junta. They always accept my recommendations.'

Angelito could barely contain his exaltation. 'I – I will not fail!'

Williston patted him on the shoulder. 'Sure you won't.' He broke away abruptly, moved to the window and watched the crowd in the Plaza. 'Still gathering. Still peaceful.'

'My men will soon get them going.'

Williston sat in one of the Louis XVI armchairs and cooed. 'Sit down, Angelito. There's your desk calling you.'

Angelito marched to his desk. Awed, but confident.

Williston took out a cologne-wipe and started freshening up his face. 'Whilst I still have my Washington hat on, Angelito, let me give you a piece of advice. About the crowd down there. Pull out your men. Any violence now, in the wake of Fuego's filth, would be damning. Let the world see the people demonstrating freely this once, anyway. Next time, you can go to town. Patience has its limits as everybody knows.'

Angelito pondered solemnly. Williston was dictating terms before he could even call the desk his own. Fuego would never have stood for it. But Fuego had always been myopic. Fuego had never seen a horizon stretch to infinity. Power, albeit with strings attached, was not to be scorned. Power could be secretly strengthened. He nodded. 'Good thinking.' He picked up one of the telephones. 'Major Salinas – pull back the troops! Immediately!' Quietly, he replaced the receiver. 'Anything else?'

Williston looked in distaste at the dirt on the cologne-wipe then threw it into the bin under the desk. 'From what you gleaned from Rice and Beatriz, it seems certain Fuego will try to join up with Huaman. I'd like to think Huaman and his men will tear him to pieces. But Fuego has nine more lives than your ordinary cat. He might convince Huaman he is a good element to have. We don't want that. Now, if I read Huaman right, he would resent sharing his thunder – even for expediency. So we must really treacle our carrot and subvert him.'

Angelito produced a perfect smile. Power could be stealthily fed until it became supreme power. 'It's a sound proposition.'

'There you go then.' Williston rose magisterially. 'Just think how difficult the world finds it to achieve harmony, then take a look here – easy as pie.' He cast a final look at the office, then winked at Angelito. 'Oh, a minor point. I'd puke if I had to read anything else by that old fool, Rice. He should retire, take things easy.'

61

It is the voice of all those who did not speak, of those who did not sing and who sing today with this mouth that kisses you

There is one wind, Chauca's father used to tell him, which is so mighty that it forces the mountains to bend their heads, drives the glaciers to stampede and freezes the fires of the volcanoes as they erupt. This is the Inca wind and it comes once every generation, always on a day when the *naturales* assemble to assess the strength of their blood. Those who survive it carry the Sun's image to the next generation.

It was such a day and there was such a wind.

Because he had trained them, Chauca knew the guerrilleros would acquit themselves well. But, like an eagle watching over its young, he ran his eyes once again down the ranks. They stood in Inca formations, like clusters of boulders. Their staunch marrow, taut like the shields of illustrious ancestors, repulsed the swirling balls of snow. Their eyes, proudly marked with the knowledge of the past, looked unflinchingly at the face of tomorrow. They would all prove worthy sons of the Sun.

But he had reservations about the *Comandante* who sat on the Inca seat, more like a mummy with his countless layers of cloth, than a cacique bearing the august name of Manku Yupanqui.

It was a treacherous thought, and Chauca was shamed by it, but there seemed to be much more spirit in the people's arch-enemy than the one sitting on the rock throne. Inconceivably, the murderer exuded courage, faced those he had wronged not as one who would be vilified and killed, but as a brother. He defied the wind, bareheaded and barefooted, in a fraying, bullet-riddled priest's soutane. Blasphemous as it sounded, he looked like Viracocha, the Universal God, who wandered the earth in rags and was reviled like a beggar.

'I am who I was: General Oseas Fuego. I am also who I am: a lamb of God. And I am who I shall become: Manku Yupanqui.'

The arch-enemy's voice traversed through the snow without a shiver.

'You shall die!'

By contrast, Huaman's voice carried the rattle of chattering teeth.

Fuego, Chauca observed, received the pronouncement like a tree which, having planted its seed, knows that it cannot die. 'Who among you will kill me?'

He was very impressive, this Fuego. He had impressed from the moment the lookouts had spotted him.

To Chauca, the sight of Fuego scaling the mountain at a run, effortlessly, like a waterfall travelling upwards, had seemed like a vision induced by coca. His voice, clear as lighting, shouting: *I am coming, compañeros, I am coming*, had been so awe-inspiring that not one peak had refused to echo it. When he had finally reached the camp, the men had found themselves in ranks, as if ready for battle. When he had walked, barely out of breath, past the ranks, his head all-seeing like that of the Serpent in the Zodiac, no one had dared speak to him or touch him. And when, pausing before the Inca seat, this Fuego had simply declared: *Tomorrow, the Sun will be freed*, all, even the snow and the wind, had believed him.

No, not all. Huaman was more excited by the stake they had erected for the execution than the good news about the Sun.

'In true democratic procedure, we shall each have a hand in your death. You will be burned alive. Every man here will place a fire on your body.'

Fuego picked up a handful of snow and began eating it. 'That is how the *misti* kills – how they killed our ancestors. I am of Inca stock. To kill me, you must cut off my head and use my skull as a *chicha* cup. You must stretch my skin on war drums. You must string my teeth into a necklace. You must carve a flute out of my shin-bone.'

Fuego, Chauca saw, leaned against the wind. He had a massive shadow even in the furious snow. What majesty!

'You will die at the stake!'

The same wind, the same snow, Chauca saw, had shrunk Huaman to a rodent's size.

'I must be judged! That would be Manku Yupanqui's command.'

'I am Manku Yupanqui. You have no defence. Sentence will be carried out.'

Fuego climbed the wind and stood taller than all. 'The man I was, Oseas Fuego, has no defence – that is undeniable. But the man I am now, a lamb of God, has truth that is as real as the Southern Aurora.'

Huaman screeched like a rat. 'Take him away!'

Fuego made a platform out of the wind. 'I shall be heard!'

The guerrilleros, an evergreen forest blanketed in ice, ceased their rustling in order to hear him.

'When a man runs away from God, he is certain to collide with Him. Because God is everywhere and the fugitive, always looking behind him, cannot avoid what is ahead.'

Huaman, on his rodent's feet, became snow-bound.

'So when he collides with God, the man feels afraid – as before a miracle. He realises he has touched the power which contains both life and death. He asks God: why have You spared me when You have every reason to kill me? God ruffles his hair. Why should I kill you, He says. I am the One who loves you. The One who has waited for your return. Then the man understands God is his Papacito. He embraces Him. And his Papacito invests him with light which, as we all know, is love that has shed its clothes and stands naked in original beauty.'

Huaman, in his rodent's body, thrashed in the snow.

'Then the man runs to his compañeros to proclaim the Truth as I am doing now. At first, they doubt him. For they have been brutalised by a legion of Oseas Fuegos. They have had their hearts and minds cut to pieces. But the loving man perseveres. He provides proof. Sometimes, like Father Quintana, he ascends martyrdom. Other times, he engineers his evidence – as I have done. Look! I have put on signs so that you can recognise God's breath on me. This cloth I am wearing was Father Quintana's. These wounds on my hands belong to the Crucified Son. Look! Pierced only yesterday! More will come: a spear cut at my side, scars of thorns on my head, lines of scourging on my back, nail holes in my feet. I will produce them all for you.'

Huaman, Chauca observed, had pulled out his pistol. But he could not aim it. His eyes had turned blind, not by the snow, but by the fierce light cast by Fuego's stigmata. Even he, Chauca, a man familiar with radiance because he had seen planets hover above his head when blissfully chewing coca, stood dazed by them. So did the guerrilleros.

'I am here to lead you to our Papacito. He wants us to sow the wilderness with justice so that it can feed us all.'

The light, Chauca observed, was suffusing the swirling snow and transforming it into flakes of gold leaf. The pitiless wind had acquired the warm breath of a sage talking about fire, earth, water and air.

'The fruit, when we harvest it, will have the taste of maize-bread, the consistency of quince, the durability of coconut, the goodness of mother's milk. When we have eaten it, there will remain not one person who suffers injury from his fellow men, not one belly that rumbles in hunger, not one invalid who dies abandoned, not one family that lives homeless, not one child who is illiterate, not one soul that despairs because he has no tomorrow.'

Fuego descended from the wind and lay on the snow. He bared his chest so that they could cut out his heart should they so decide. 'Now, judge the man I am.'

Briefly, the guerrilleros warbled like birds returning from migration.

Then they fell silent.

Fuego stood up and faced them. 'Your silence proclaims your verdict. I thank your pure souls for seeing the purity in mine. Now, you have a further task. Now, you must judge me as the man I shall become.'

Huaman, Chauca observed, had shaken off his blindness. His rodent teeth were bared. He was aiming his pistol. Chauca wanted to yell, but it was too late.

The pistol fired. A full magazine.

It was the wind or the nightfall, Chauca thought, that unbalanced the mountainside. Fuego was sent floating like a star bathing in a passing cloud: some of the shots were seized by the dusk and thrown down the escarpments; the rest fell as dirty hail and were buried by the snow.

Huaman, frenzied for having missed his target, drew his other pistol.

This time, Chauca did not hesitate. He rushed up to the Inca seat and wrenched the gun from Huaman.

Fuego sat down on the snow, opened his bag and brought out some coca leaves. Inviting the guerrilleros to partake, he began chewing. He talked entrancingly with the combined voices of a shaman and a story-teller.

'For every chieftain our forefathers had a set of trials. These ranged from ordeals of strength and endurance to debates and the unveiling of the self. Those who were successful proved three things: that they were physically fit; that they had a good mind; and that they were the person they claimed to be. Such a trial must take place tonight to decide who stands tomorrow as Manku Yupanqui.'

It had stopped snowing. Ice, in the moon's silver-blue cloak, resumed its reign.

Huaman sat on the Inca seat. It would remain his seat. All he had to do was compose himself and unleash his intellect. He had had his moment of fury during Fuego's so-called trial, and it had been a mistake. He was seasoned enough to know that fate always played dirty tricks. If they had not been on a mountain-top where everything for the imbecilic Indio got enmeshed in supernatural dimensions, if the freak weather had not numbed the senses and the mind, they would still be warming themselves by Fuego's cinders.

What galled him was that he, Gaspar Huaman, who had crossed that divide which separates a political contender from the man of history, should have to prove himself to a band of peasants.

This contest was cretinous – an insult to a revolutionary. He had half a mind to leave these apes to their primitive ways and return to the capital. Tomorrow, if he so chose, he could, quite effortlessly, pick up the laurel destined for him. Even the fascists wanted him. Coded messages from Colonel Angelito deluged his radio. The ripe time for an alliance. Senior cabinet post. Knighthood of the Order of San Antonio. Each as tempting as a soft bed in a centrally heated room.

Damned pride which always chose the hardest path!

Of the three trials, he had reservations only about the first, that of strength – and only because Fuego had the reputation of being a hard fighter. But, to even the odds, Fuego had proposed to fight one-armed. The handicap would affect Fuego much more since he, Huaman, had got used to functioning with one arm. Furthermore, as the stirring in his genitals confirmed, he now enjoyed violence as some men enjoyed women. Finally, Fuego had been chewing coca with the men since nightfall: his mind was likely to be a morass.

He had no reservations about the other trials. Those involved reason and he would win hands down.

Chauca, having taken it upon himself to act as the master of ceremonies, had drawn a large circle to set out the arena. He was now sanctifying it with the usual mumbo-jumbo of offerings and libations.

Chauca was in line for demotion – even execution. The debt to Chauca for saving his life had been paid – and with interest. All those months, a year almost, of lieutenancy was an honour that should last an Indio several generations. Despite that, Chauca had become unconscionable. For instance, always calling him *comandante*, never Manku Yupanqui. Criticising the way he had killed that camp-follower at Puerto Nuevo. Giving Fuego the benefit of the doubt and digging up a guerrillero who could read the newspaper Fuego had brought so that all the men could hear that rubbish about his conversion. Snatching his gun when he was about to dispose of Fuego – that was the last straw. Decidedly, this charade would be Chauca's last duty.

'Comandante!'

Chauca had finished the preparations. The guerrilleros, besotted by coca, were scrambling to take their places around the ring. Fuego was already in the arena, one arm tied behind his back.

Huaman left the Inca seat and strode into the ring.

Chauca withdrew to the edge. 'This trial of strength will be decided by a single fall. You can wrestle, punch, butt and kick. Begin!'

Huaman drew his arm up like a boxer and danced on his feet.

Fuego stood still.

Huaman threw a punch and drew blood. Fuego shook his head then offered his other cheek. Smelling a quick victory, Huaman threw another punch – harder. Fuego reeled but stood his ground. Huaman slammed his elbow on Fuego's neck. Fuego staggered forward. Huaman launched himself to deal the *coup de grâce* with a kick. Fuego spun round and straightened up. Huaman, missing his kick, collided with Fuego. Unbalanced, he sprawled on to the snow.

Chauca proclaimed. 'Fall!'

The guerrilleros cheered and applauded.

Huaman, livid, scrambled up. 'I lost my balance! It doesn't count! He didn't hit me – not once!'

Fuego smiled. 'God did.'

Huaman rushed at him. 'I'll kill you and your God!'

Chauca intercepted him. 'The contest is over, *Comandante.*'

Huaman, failing to reach Fuego, grappled with Chauca. 'Don't stop me! Or I'll kill you, too!'

The guerrilleros jeered.

Chauca locked his arms around Huaman. 'Rest now, *Comandante.* There are two more!'

Huaman, shackled by Chauca's powerful arms, forced himself to calm down. Finally, he nodded ungraciously. Chauca released him. Festering with resentment, Huaman walked back to the Inca seat.

Fuego moved out of the ring to receive the guerrilleros' congratulations. Chauca caught up with him and untied his arm. Fuego wiped the blood on his face with the soutane's sleeve, then picked up his bag. He took out some coca leaves and settled down to chew with the guerrilleros. Someone started playing a *huayno* with a sicu.

When the moon was at its highest point, they started the second trial. Fuego and Huaman sat down, inside the circle, opposite each other. The guerrilleros stood around the ring in silence. The wind, as if equally eager to hear their debate, ceased blowing.

Huaman felt composed, no longer smarting from his defeat which was not, in fact, a defeat but a moral victory, since he had drawn blood and had received no blows. He knew he would win the disputation. After all, his strategy was one which the guerrilleros had already embraced. He merely had to repeat it. Clearly and simply, as always.

Chauca officiated. 'This trial is for wisdom. You will explain how you intend to lead the people to freedom. The guerrilleros will decide the winner. Who wishes to speak first?'

Huaman exclaimed impatiently. 'I will.'

Fuego nodded, fuzzy eyes saturated in coca.

Huaman cleared his throat. 'You know my strategy. It is the one which united us and gave us such victories as Monte Rico and Puerto Nuevo. We continue as we have started: a nucleus of men who know that right is on their side. We work day and night to convert the masses. We teach them constant vigilance, permanent revolutionary commitment and action. We instruct them that our enemies are capitalists and fascists who live off our lands and our enslavement. That the only way we can seize our rights is through armed struggle. And as we instruct them, we train them. We grow in numbers. Month by month. If need be, year after year. Time is unimportant. What is important is that we continue struggling and multiplying until the whole country is of one mind, one heart, one vision. Thereafter, we toil, in perpetuity to preserve our Utopia. That is all.'

The guerrilleros burst into applause. A sicu trilled in celebration. Other sicus joined in the fanfare.

Huaman acknowledged the tribute.

Fuego waited for the cheering to stop. Then, tracing a cross on the snow with his finger, he began to speak. 'I don't have a strategy as such. I will simply propose we follow the spirit that is in us all – God's spirit. Let me tell you a story. Once there was a landowner who had enough riches to gold plate twenty mountains. But he didn't think all that wealth was sufficient. One day, it occurred to him that if he staged an event which the whole world would pay to see, he could be the wealthiest man on earth. So he asked all the wise men: what would the world most want to see. An unnatural act, they all said. Have men mount dogs, the wisest suggested. The landowner ordered his peons to mount dogs. Poor peons: threatened by death, how could they refuse? So men mounted bitches, women crouched in front of male dogs. And people came from the four corners of the world to see them doing it. The landowner grew richer and richer. But one night, the peons heard God crying. They asked Him: why are You crying? God said: mounting dogs is for dogs. People mounting people is how I arranged matters, because when people mount people there is pleasure, they make children, the men spread rainbows on the women and the women help the men across the storms on to sunlight. So the peons told the landowner: we are not mounting dogs any more. The landowner, incensed, opened fire. The peons, wanting to reason with him, marched towards him. The landowner went on firing. Some of the peons fell; the others kept walking. Eventually, the landowner ran out of bullets. Those peons who had not been killed continued forwards. The landowner, afraid that they might trample him, ran off like a hare. Thereafter, not one person mounted a dog again. Men and women mounted each other. And before long, they were fruitful.'

The guerrilleros greeted the end of the story with laughter and cheers.

Fuego continued. 'We need a similar revolution. We know how we should live because we have Jesus' life as an example. I ask myself: what would have happened if the Incas had known about Jesus? I mean the real Jesus, not the one the missionaries brought. You know how at the time of the Incas nobody went without land, house, food, dignity and pride. What would have happened if they had heard Jesus' words, known about struggle without violence? I tell you: there would have been no war in this continent. Even with the Conquistadores. As they arrived with their horses and arquebuses, the Incas would have simply walked towards them with open arms. The Conquistadores, of course, would have fired their guns – lust for gold was what was in *their* hearts. And they would have killed many – though, perhaps, not as many as they eventually killed. But, in the end, they would have been trampled on by thousands upon thousands of Incas. And the land would have returned to its paradisal state.'

Again the guerrilleros cheered.

Fuego continued. 'So I want to go the way of the Lamb. If you feel like me, let us throw away our guns. Let us ask our people to join us. Let us march to today's Conquistadores and landowners. Let us ignore their bullets. Let us march until they run away. That is all.'

The guerrilleros cheered wildly. Sicus and quenas lilted jubilantly.

Chauca stepped forward. 'Raise your hands, those in favour of the *Comandante*'s strategy!'

The guerrilleros kept their hands down.

Huaman stared at them, aghast.

'Raise your hands, those in favour of the Lamb's strategy!'

The guerrilleros, to a man, raised their hands.

Huaman sprang to his feet. 'You are mad! What he is proposing is mass suicide!'

Chauca faced Huaman. 'For your strategy to succeed, how many will have to die?'

'Many! But his way, there'll be wholesale death!'

'What is the difference between many deaths, year after year, and wholesale death?'

'Don't be a fool, Chauca!'

'The second trial is finished, *Comandante*. He has won. You must prepare for the third – it is the most important.'

Muttering obscenities, Huaman walked to the Inca seat.

Fuego moved out of the ring to receive the guerrilleros' congratulations. He sat down with them to chew more coca. Sicus and quenas began to play Manku Yupanqui's song. Soon, all the men were singing, *'He is the water that quenches the gods…'*

The Morning Star shimmered behind the wind. It was time for the last trial. Huaman and Fuego entered the arena. The guerrilleros took their places around it. Chauca waited for the contestants to sit and face each other.

The cold plagued Huaman like the ague. But there was not long to go. And there was not the remotest chance he could lose this last test. He had been crowned Manku Yupanqui by the men themselves.

He glanced at Fuego. Almost a pitiful sight: the ragged soutane was like the skin of a leper. As for those narcoticised eyes – dead to the world. Some Manku Yupanqui!

He barked impatiently, 'Let's get on with it!'

Chauca officiated. 'The third test is proof of identity. You, *Comandante*, have declared yourself Manku Yupanqui. You, the challenger, have declared you are to become Manku Yupanqui. The men will judge the evidence.'

Huaman rose. 'The proof is yourselves. It is you, in your wisdom, who have proclaimed me Manku Yupanqui.' He pointed at the tunics he was wearing. 'Look, my royal vestments. Embroidered by your women – on your instructions!' He displayed his delicately woven *borla*. 'And look, the scarlet fringe of the Inca monarch. You crowned me with it as Manku Yupanqui. No further proof is necessary.'

Fuego remained seated. 'Clothes and insignia can fall into wrong hands. In the case of Manku Yupanqui, there can be only two indisputable proofs. The first is the sun's missing ray which he possesses. This, you must take my word for it, will be displayed when the people are united. The second is his bride, Teresa Ayala. She is the only person who can identify him.'

Huaman shifted on his seat uncomfortably. 'That is reasonable. But, alas, she is not here.'

Fuego smiled. 'Summon her.'

'She is far away – caring for the women and children.'

'If you are her husband, summon her. She will come.'

Huaman shouted angrily. 'I'm telling you, she can't!'

Fuego turned to the guerrilleros. 'I will summon her.'

Huaman smirked, confident that Fuego, in his madness, had finally defeated himself.

Fuego called softly to the east, the west, the north, and the south. 'Teresa… Teresa… Teresa… Teresa…'

The wind, the guerrilleros felt, divided itself into four and carried Fuego's call.

The silence of deep snow descended.

Huaman became agitated. The wind was no longer assaulting him, yet his blood was freezing.

Fuego repeated his call. 'Teresa… Teresa… Teresa… Teresa…'

The sky lightened in the east. Fuego turned in that direction. So did the guerrilleros.

The silence thickened, filled the six senses.

Fuego pointed at the eastern peaks. 'There she comes!'

The guerrilleros watched the spreading light.

Huaman watched, too. 'There is nothing there! Dawn – that's all it is!'

Fuego kept on pointing. 'Look! She is skipping over the peaks! See her beautiful smile! Her immaculate face! Her breasts and haunches, bountiful like the earth! Look at her belly – heavy with our child!'

A few guerrilleros began pointing and whispering. 'There! There! There!'

Then more and more of the guerrilleros, standing in awe, whispered. 'There she is! Look! Here she comes!'

Chauca began to weep.

What a vision this was! That child-woman he had first encountered at Salinas and then met again on a festive day of ritual battle. He had known on that second occasion that she would find Manku Yupanqui, that they were destined to marry. There she was now, a glorious woman – many women in one: young girl, mother, grandmother, Pachamama, ancestral spirit. Smiling in blissful wedlock, sad for having seen so much suffering, serene from carrying a child, wise for knowing all the answers, generous as God expected man to be, immortal like her guardian angel, the Morning Star… There she was…

Here she was…

Fuego stood up and held her hand.

Chauca looked at the guerrilleros. They, too, were weeping. He dropped to his knees. The guerrilleros followed suit.

Huaman was running, stumbling, churning snow. 'She is not here! Can't you see, it's a trick of the mind! There's nobody here!'

No one heard his voice or saw his crazed movements.

Fuego and Teresa, hands interlocked, faced the guerrilleros.

Fuego addressed them. 'You have the gift to see, compañeros. And the gift to hear. Ask her who her husband is.'

408

Chauca, still weeping, asked. 'Who is your husband, blessed woman?'

Teresa's voice rang with pride and laughter. 'Manku Yupanqui.'

'Is he here?'

Teresa sat at Fuego's feet. 'This is he. He has my flesh and soul. I have his.'

'Give us your blessing, gracious lady, so that we can follow him wherever he goes.'

Teresa stretched out her all-embracing hand. 'Be like my Manku – know no fear. Then the Sun will be ours again.'

Chauca and the guerrilleros shouted in unison. 'We shall not fear!'

Tenderly, Fuego caressed Teresa's hair. 'Go, wife. Prepare for our infant's birth.'

Teresa laughed like a child, then ran off towards the dawn.

Chauca and the guerrilleros rose from their knees and only then became aware of Huaman.

He was running from one to the other, pulling at their clothes, screaming. 'This is sorcery! It's the coca! Nobody came here! Teresa is dead! Fell into a volcano! Crazy, she was! You know that! She is dead! Turned to ashes!'

No one listened to him.

Chauca moved to the centre of the arena and picked up Huaman's *borla*. He placed it on Fuego's head. 'You are the man you said you would become.'

The guerrilleros thundered. 'Manku Yupanqui! Manku Yupanqui!'

Huaman collapsed. 'Witchcraft! You stupid savages! Don't you see – it's witchcraft!'

Fuego thundered at the men. 'Follow me!' He began to move down the mountain.

Chauca and the rest of the guerrilleros fell behind him.

Huaman, abandoned, shouted incoherently at the rising Sun.

BOOK THREE

PART ELEVEN

62

Through the streets the blood of the children ran simply, like children's blood

Grey, the grey of the long dead, of the past, of ancestral suffering, of lost opportunities, grey, in all its lacklustre shades, was the perennial colour of the Plaza de los Héroes.

But not today. Today, the people had brought their multi-coloured skins, clothes and hats, their striking posters, the brilliant hues of their hopes and faith.

Today, exactly a month after the spontaneous demonstration that had followed the publication of Fuego's gospel, the people were in the streets again. And they had declared that, hereafter, they would come out each month until their rights were handed back to them.

Jerry Rice rolled with the human avalanche.

Impressions — that would be the way to describe this demonstration. Scintilla of movement, mood, facial expressions, postures, tears, laughter, declamations, casual remarks. His readers would know how to multiply them a millionfold and see in full dimension how this city had risen to her feet.

A group of women in bright ponchos and beaded triangular hats — definitely from the same *ayllu* — holding a vast banner: THE PEOPLE UNITED WILL NEVER BE DEFEATED!

Their children clinging to their skirts. Two toddlers fitted into a cardboard box bearing the fading legend: BIOLOGICAL SOAP.

A group of men in miners' helmets standing around the flag of their union.

A coca vendor, carrying the leaves in a huge bundle on her back, weaving through the crowd. Her clients smile at her, speak pleasantries. But she is stern-faced: work is serious business.

A throng of campesinos – men, women and children – standing tightly together, sharing a few ears of corn. There is amazement in their faces – obviously elated that they had the courage to come. Also fear – perhaps they are thinking they should not have come.

Another coca vendor. An old man. Grinning with toothless gums. Not a good advertisement for what he is selling. But he is doing all right.

People are beckoning him.

A new lease of life! Who would have thought it? Jerry Rice has a new lease of life given to him by Fuego of all people. What's more, Jerry Rice isn't drinking so much now.

A prostitute – dressed to take any high-class pick-up joint by storm. Pampered, well fed, a survivor in a rotten society. But here like the rest of them. She has a dog on the leash – an Afghan hound. No half measures for her.

A ruck of students carrying effigies of the Junta. Horse-playing and laughing as students had forgotten how. Faces of intelligence, enthusiasm and courage.

There is one in the centre of the crowd who looks like my Debbie. Athlete's gait. Oh, Debbie!

An old couple: the man leaning on his wife. Conservatively and impeccably dressed. You can hear the bank notes rustling. Old liberals, you can tell. He, definitely an aristocrat. She also, but with a touch of mestizo.

A crowd from the barrios – a whole neighbourhood by the looks of it. That air of living in each other's pockets, sharing births, deaths, weddings, hunger, sewers, clothes, food, wages, football, baths, songs, even wives, husbands and children. In their Sunday best. Hard, polished faces that dare not hope yet.

Riot police in full regalia. Like automatons from a science fiction film.

Water-cannon trucks – parked at each corner. Some of the riot police pouring purple dye into the tanks.

They're going to use them. The dye is for identifying people after the demonstration!

Armoured cars. An endless snake of them. In olive green – a beautiful colour spoiled by steel.

Sinchis in each car. Also in olive green. Armed to the teeth.

A group of mothers, standing arm in arm. Hanging over their bosoms, on necklaces of string, enlarged snapshots of sons and daughters killed or disappeared. They have no tears left. Just the residue of life called grief. And a dogged defiance which they assume is the voice of their children protesting from unknown graves.

A cluster of wives. Also arm in arm. Also brandishing photographs. The husbands they have lost. They are crying because they are still young and not yet bled of tears.

More armoured cars. The Bridegrooms. Black, Gestapo-style fatigues. Armbands. Sub-machine-guns. Gas masks.

Exhaust fumes banding together. A suggestion of early morning mist until the fierce sun shows them up as clouds of pollution. There were days when petrol used to smell nice.

The command car. Driven personally by Angelito. In a uniform shining like a metal planet. *General* now. Chief of the SES. The new broom that will make people grieve for the old.

Imprint them on memory!

Nothing can stop you being published now. The Fuego scoop opened up new doors. Unearthed editors who will fight tooth and nail for the freedom of the press.

Plus a new lease of life. What more do you want?

The crowd swaying now, chanting: THE PEOPLE UNITED WILL NEVER BE DEFEATED!

Mass after mass brandishing an icon. Manku Yupanqui's face. The effect is that of a tidal wave!

Look – the icon! Portrait of Fuego! Christ-like! Haloed! Che Guevara's smile!

Everybody's got them! When did they make them? Where did they get them from?

They are singing. Beatriz's song:

He is
the water that quenches the gods
the fire that cleanses the past

The water-cannon trucks are raising their hoses.
The armoured cars are emptying.

He is
the earth where the spirit grows
the sky which shepherds the stars

Sinchis falling into formation.
Riot police falling into formation.

He is
the eagle who husbands the sun
the puma which hurls rainbows

People bunching closer.
The Bridegrooms jumping off their armoured cars. Sub-machine-guns held high. Gas masks taut like skin. You can see those are their real faces. The human features were mere disguises.
People waving their icons.

He is
the pure milk of a man's eruption
the kiss that opens a woman's legs

Angelito furiously driving the command car. Checking battle stations. Jesus! They mean business!
The people still waving their icons.

He is
the hope born today
the stone that will build tomorrow

The people thunder: 'Manku Yupanqui! Manku Yupanqui!'
The Sinchis are ready.
The riot police are ready.
The Bridegrooms are ready.
The people's thunder echoes: 'Manku Yupanqui! Manku Yupanqui!'
Angelito signals attack.
The water-cannons spew their purple liquid.
A brief silence. Collective shock.
Then screams. People hit by the jets are thrown off their feet, skid, slide, slither. More screams. A new burst of singing. Mixed with screams.
People rolling on the ground, falling over, crushing each other, running anywhere. Purple quagmire everywhere.
Some people regrouping, clinging to their song, marching towards the water-cannons.
More people trying to join the marching group.

A woman, one of the mothers of the disappeared, pulls him by his sleeve. 'Come!'

'You don't stand a chance!'

'If they can do it in the countryside, we can do it here!'

'What?'

'Manku Yupanqui! The people are marching with him! They won't be stopped!'

A girl, drenched in purple dye, staggers up and falls in front of them. The woman picks her up, repeats her nonsense about the marchers in the countryside.

The girl weeps. 'But that's just a rumour. Nobody has seen them marching.'

The woman has no time to argue. She runs into the fray.

He holds the girl. 'Are you hurt?'

The girl pulls free, runs off. Athletic gait. Was she the one who looked like Debbie?

Water-cannons spewing. Marchers knocked down – so many of them! Some are even knocked into the air, fall and lie writhing.

Help them! Help them!

The square is a Stygian lagoon now. Bodies everywhere. Bleeding whales stranded on a beach. Jesus! Jesus!

He realises he is running! Where?

He hears distant shots.

Puffs of smoke all over the place. Tear-gas!

Motherfuckers!

Puffs of smoke billowing, turning into a cloud.

People screaming, holding their eyes, groaning, crying, even the tearless mothers crying.

He is still running! Where? Eyes have stopped seeing. Lungs cannot breathe!

He hears the rattle of sub-machine-guns!

They're shooting! Goddam motherfuckers!

He bumps into a wall. Am I hit? Falls. Strikes his head.

He regains consciousness.

Throbbing head. Eyelids stuck with blood. Acrid stench of tear-gas. Rumble of heavy vehicles. He wipes his eyes. But what the eyes see should not be seen.

The square is a purple battlefield. So many bodies. Men. Women. Children. An Afghan dog.

The crowd has dispersed. The water-cannon trucks have disappeared. So have the armoured cars – except a few parked at Avenida de la Republica. No Sinchis. No riot police. Just the Bridegrooms.

Lorries. Five, eight, eleven.

Angelito's command car. Weaving round the square.

The Bridegrooms are picking up the bodies. Throwing them into the lorries. Not a protest from the bodies, not a movement or a sound. Dead bodies. DEAD BODIES!

My God!

He tries to get up. Unsteady on his feet. Flops down.

A child wails. 'Mama!'

Over there. At the edge of the square. Where the bodies are thickest. Where the crowd were trampling each other. Not one child, but two. Only one crying.

He crawls to them.

A woman lying between the children. A broken, twisted scarecrow. Hardly any purple on her. Judging by her Sunday best, a woman from the barrios. Originally from the countryside. Her smart, colourful Andean hat lies by her side.

Don't look! The silent child is dead! Four years old, could she be? Crushed to death! Don't look! The woman is dead, too. Somebody put a bullet through her head.

He turns to the wailing child. A boy. Maybe nine. But ancient. 'Are you hurt, son?'

The boy points towards the Tomb of the Unknown Soldier. 'I was hiding.'

'Do you have a father? Anybody?'

'They were here. They were chased.'

'We'll look for them.'

'Police and Sinchis everywhere.'

'I'm a gringo. They won't touch me.'

The boy hesitates.

He pulls himself up. Steadier now. 'Come on!'

The boy holds his hand.

What'll I do with this boy? What if all his folk are dead? He laughs. New lease of life! Hey, Debbie, listen to this! Here I am, holding a child's hand for two seconds and I'm thinking wouldn't it be nice to be a father? Crazy!

'I'll take you where you live, son. Some of your people should have made it home. And there'll be neighbours and such. Where do you live?'

'The barrio.'

'Lead on.'

The boy pulls him to the Avenida de la Republica. 'We cross – quickly.'

He hobbles. Out of the corner of his eye, he sees the command car. Speeding towards them. He pulls the boy back to the kerb.

The boy freezes, terrified.

The command car is still speeding towards them. He can see Angelito now. Driving. Not a hair out of place. One arm casually slung out of the window. Smiling. Motherfucker!

He raises his fist. Shouts. 'Murderer! Motherfucker!'

The command car drives towards the kerb.

'You can't frighten me, you turd! I'll see you hanged!'

The command car accelerates.

Jesus! He means to run me over! 'Run, boy, run, run!'

The boy runs.

The command car jumps the kerb.

Jesus!

63

I don't mind being one stone more, the dark stone, the pure stone that the river bears away

In the wake of the tragedy of Plaza de los Héroes, the Junta had declared a week of national mourning. In accordance with this edict, General Angelito wore a black ribbon on the lapel of his white, ceremonial uniform.

'He ran on to the road to save a youngster, you know.'

Angelito held his funereal expression. It made Daniel and Beatriz all the more hostile.

Dr Williston, Washington smart in his dark suit, sombrely stared at the grease-sodden tarmac. 'He was a good man.'

'When the car hit him, it went out of control – hit the child, too. Horrific!'

Beatriz was finally revolted by the hypocrisy. 'What about the driver? He gets a medal, I suppose?'

She had aged, Daniel thought. Or was it her stern black dress shading the light of her eyes?

Angelito creased his face as if insulted. 'That's malicious and uncalled for, Beatriz. There'll be an inquiry. I'll conduct it personally. In the meantime, the driver is suspended from duty.'

Daniel loosened his collar and tie. It did not improve his breathing. The heat was as unbearable as the new Chief of Security. 'Whilst you're at it – why don't you suspend the rest of your gangsters? How many people killed at the last count? A hundred and thirty-eight?'

Menace shadowed Angelito's tone. 'I resent that, Mr Brac. My men were facing a mob of madmen. If they hadn't pacified them, there would have been thousands dead!'

'*Pacified*? The word's back in fashion, is it?'

Diplomatically, Williston manoeuvred himself in between the two and pointed in the direction of the airport mortuary. 'Here it comes.'

They watched the hearse drive towards the plane.

Williston spoke with the voice of an undertaker. 'His sister, Emily, is taking care of the funeral. She didn't want us to hold a service here. We'll just see him aboard. Not how I'd have wanted to pay my last respects.'

Daniel loathed Williston's presence. Jerry's sister, in fact, was here – in the departure lounge. Embarkation had been delayed until this business was over. Emily was formidable. A few years younger than Rice, but just as sententious. It had been she who had forced Angelito to contact him and Beatriz. Jerry, apparently, had written to her about them. On meeting them, she had all but accused them of being responsible for his death. They should have kept an eye on him. He was getting old. Beatriz had not minded being blamed, so she had got on better with her. They had cleared up Jerry's flat, giving everything away except the books. The books, Emily had explained, commissioning Daniel to pack and post them, would go to her local library. All of Jerry's books had gone there – some forty thousand, over the years, enough to prompt the librarians to dedicate one of the reading rooms to him. Then, when the flat had been cleared, she had bid them a curt goodbye. She would not be at the loading of the coffin. The less she had to do with these God-forsaken people, the better. She would attend to any formalities, any expenses incurred, through the Embassy.

The hearse stopped by the plane.

Whilst the porters took charge of the coffin, the undertaker presented the clearance documents to a customs officer.

Daniel turned towards the airport terminal: compact, modern, oval-shaped, like that of an exotic resort. He wished desperately he were in there, about to fly back to England, already shaking the dust of this accursed country off his person.

It won't be long now.

The coffin was placed on the cargo loader. Angelito and the customs officer stood at respectful attention. Williston, eyes devotionally shut tight, intoned prayers. The porters crossed themselves.

Beatriz began to weep.

Daniel watched the coffin move up the rollers. Was that what life was? All that fear, heavier than the whole world, was it just to postpone this crude packaging that posted you to God?

Goodbye, Jerry. I won't forget you. But I'll try.

The coffin disappeared into the hold.

Beatriz leaned against Daniel.

Williston, finishing his prayers, put on his White House face. 'A great American.'

Beatriz turned on him. 'A *true* American. The *real* American. Not like those we normally get here!' She pulled Daniel away. 'Take me somewhere clean. We'll drink to Jerry.'

They sat on the beach, almost touching the sea.

Beatriz had taken her shoes off. She had refused to sit on Daniel's discarded jacket. She needed to keep in touch with the earth, she had said.

They had not forced themselves to speak.

Beatriz was thinking about that day when she and Jerry had picnicked on this beach. She had asked him what to do about Daniel. Would she ever dare get pregnant again? The sun had been just as glorious. There had been a few bathers. The cafés on the promenade had been open. Today no one was about, everything was shut. Who could want to enjoy the sea after the killings of the other day? Daniel had had to pay a fortune to persuade one of the café owners into selling him a bottle of pisco at the back door.

Daniel... Daniel... How was it possible to sit with him, to love him, to desire him – yes, desire him – and not want to touch him, to see him as external to her life? Strange. Or perhaps not so strange. Nuns did it. They loved Jesus and they became His brides. They sat with Him, communed with Him, dreamed of Him erotically, even caressed themselves. And they lived on happily, they in one world, He in another. Perhaps that was the secret. To accept love as unworldly yet natural. As one finally accepts death. Then you can live in peace. You love and mourn – as you love and mourn your son.

Daniel... Daniel... My other dead son.

She sipped from the bottle. '*Salud*, Jerry, my other father. May your dust be for ever blessed.' She passed the bottle to Daniel.

Daniel did not drink. The sea, as ever, had taken him back to his childhood, to the island monastery of Brač, to those interminable seasons of gazing at Split across the channel, pining for his family and dying. Now, those memories were no longer painful. Even when Beatriz had said 'father' – not a pang. Now, the only pain he endured was the rutted chest of an asthmatic.

How desolate it was to have finally discarded feeling.

Yet... He was not insensitive to Beatriz's presence. He felt inconsolable. This was, he had no doubt, the last time he would see her. Much as he had accepted the fact stoically, there was still that man inside howling for her flesh, begging to give her another baby, cursing him for having buried him alive in the deepest tomb there was. Even juggling insane delusions, like Fuego, was better than living without feeling!

'Fancy swimming, Daniel?'

'No. Do you?'

'Yes.'

'We haven't got swimsuits.'

'We could swim naked. There's nobody around.'

He faced her, stunned with sudden hope.

But there was nothing of the old abandon in her eyes. Only sadness.

'Go ahead, Beatriz – if you want to... I won't!' That was pain! That was feeling! The mere suggestion of seeing her naked had aroused him!

The last time he had seen her naked was when Fuego had raped her. The intense guilt of that! The pain! Didn't they count as feelings?

She let some sand trickle through her fingers. 'It just occurred to me. We never went out much, did we? It was either bed or work.'

He nodded. Every word hurt. Doesn't that count?

She faced him earnestly. 'The convent did me good. I think I've recovered.'

He stared at the sea. 'I'll never recover.'

'No.' She grabbed the pisco bottle. 'That's how it should be! Be damned for ever!'

He fumbled for his cigarettes. The sudden hope of reconciliation died. The pain remained. 'Can't you find any compassion for me?'

She took a swig. 'No! I loved you! I still do!'

Hope again. 'Do you mean... we...'

'Not a chance. I have made my peace with you.'

He lit a cigarette. 'You still want to swim?'

'It would be nice. But I won't risk going naked in front of you.'

'I can go for a walk.'

'It won't be the same then.'

'I don't understand.'

'You never did, Daniel.'

He took the bottle from her and drank a mouthful.

She took one of his cigarettes and lit it. 'What's after the polyptych – anything interesting?'

'I don't know.'

She nodded. 'Difficult, isn't it – talking?'

'No. Yes... Will you start composing again?'

'Maybe... If I get the time.'

'What will you be doing?'

She looked at him, trying to hide her uncertainty. 'I'm going marching... with Fuego.'

He stared at her, shocked. 'You don't mean it!'

'I believe in him now. I believe he had a revelation. Maybe he has really found God, I don't know. But if this country can be changed, he is the man to change it.'

'He is a charlatan, Beatriz!'

'They say he has deposed Huaman, convinced the guerrilleros he is Manku Yupanqui.'

'I don't believe it!'

'Everybody else does. That's why they were all at the Plaza de los Héroes.'

'And look what happened!'

'Daniel, there are masses marching with him.'

'Rumours! Nobody has seen this great march! The army's out looking, but they can't find them!'

'Armies can't see what's before their eyes! They look at a mountain and see only rock! Or maybe that's Manku Yupanqui's magic.'

'Beatriz! That's people's wishful thinking! Fantasies! It's a different world out there! Not fairyland!'

'They marched in China.'

'That was revolution!'

'So is this.'

'You're going off to fight, is that it? Well, let me tell you: you'd accomplish more writing your songs!'

'I'm not going to fight. The people are not going to fight. That's his declared strategy! We'll be the earth's feet – and march!'

'March where?'

'Here – eventually.'

'And the Junta will let you? The Angelitos will let you? All your foreign masters will let you? Come on, face reality!'

'They can't stop the people.'

'Beatriz, they've just killed one hundred and thirty-eight persons!'

'They can't kill all the people!'

'You won't get all the people marching!'

'Why not?'

'Because things don't happen that way!'

'They might this time. We have Manku Yupanqui!'

'You have Oseas Fuego! At best, a reformed sinner!'

'No. We have *faith* in Manku Yupanqui! *Faith* in a Saviour! They can't kill that!'

'Beatriz, love, listen to me... They'll shoot you like those poor bastards in the Plaza.'

She rose to her feet.

He rose, too. 'Beatriz, listen to me!'

She shook the sand off her shoes and put them on. 'Will you take me to the bus station? On second thoughts, no... I don't want long goodbyes. Stay here. I'll go.'

He pleaded, tears flooding his eyes, strong arms clawing the air for lack of courage to touch her. 'Beatriz... Love...'

She grabbed one of his hands, kissed it softly, then ran off *'Vaya con Dios!'*

She did not look back. He could see, long after she had disappeared beyond the promenade, the image of her black dress waving in the air. A flag already mourning the future.

64

He who buys letters and considers himself literate, who buys a sabre and believes he is a soldier, but who, unable to buy purity, spits like a viper

Huaman gathered the dressing-gown around his waist: pure silk. He sat at the table and surveyed the breakfast: fresh orange juice, cereals, steak, bacon, kidney, eggs, hash potatoes, mustard and tomato ketchup, toast, marmalade, honey, various jams, rolled butter, jugs of fresh milk and coffee. All the meat cut into squares to enable him to eat easily one-handed. Everything on silver platters. Silver cutlery and cruets, exquisitely laced napkins. Bone-china plates bearing the legend: EMBASSY OF THE UNITED STATES OF AMERICA. Except for the *nouveau riche* feel of the ensemble, a table laid for royalty. He would make a pig of himself.

'You slept well, I trust?'

He looked at Williston, sitting to his left. 'Wonderfully.'

'Makes a difference – a bed, I bet.'

'The sheets. That's what one craves most. Will you join me?'

Williston glanced at the apple on his plate. Talismanic; not for eating. He pushed the plate aside. 'I'll just have coffee.'

'Help yourself.' Huaman peered at Angelito at the other end of the table. 'You, General?'

Angelito smiled distantly. 'Coffee also.'

'Perhaps you could oblige the General, Luke.' Huaman unfolded his napkin. 'If you don't mind... I'm famished.' He drank two glasses of orange juice, then served himself a large bowl of cornflakes.

Williston poured Angelito a cup of coffee. 'I've briefed General Angelito about your offer, Gaspar.'

'Good.' Huaman rushed through the cereal, impatient to launch into the main course. It had been the thought of this, his first sit-down meal, that had carried him through the long and painful journey from the mountains, through the utter loneliness, the humiliation, through the fear of ambush on the deserted roads, of being recognised in the buses, of arrest at army checkpoints and, particularly, through the indelible memory of that cold night of betrayal. 'I take it your response is favourable, General!'

Angelito stirred some sugar into his coffee. 'I'm still considering it, Huaman. I must admit, the fact that you didn't approach me directly makes me doubt you.'

Huaman, unruffled, placed his empty bowl to the side of the table and served himself some steak and eggs. 'Doubts are in order, General. Necessary – at this stage. It was my doubt about you that compelled me to get in touch with Dr Williston. Luke has credentials. I had met him in his official capacity, when I started my movement, when, presumably on your behalf and his associates' in Washington, he posed as a potential sympathiser. I knew he would hear me out.'

'So would I have.'

'Until I reached this Embassy last night, you and I were enemies, General. We had fought face to face at Monte Rico. If I had contacted you, you might have shot me first, asked questions later.'

Williston interrupted them. 'Gentlemen, I'm sure you're sophisticated enough to dispense with matters of protocol. May I suggest you get down to business.'

Huaman spoke with a bulging mouth. 'By all means.'

Angelito smiled. Huaman was even more ridiculous than he had expected him to be: a pompous mouse. 'Very well. Luke told me you're prepared to help us defeat Fuego. But he didn't tell me – or rather, you didn't tell him – your price.'

Huaman dunked a piece of toast into an egg yolk. 'I'll be satisfied with what you've already offered.'

'I haven't offered anything yet.'

'Let me remind you, General. Senior cabinet post. Knighthood of the Order of San Antonio. You broadcast them daily over the radio.'

'That was yesterday. When you posed a threat...'

'I shall accept nothing less.'

Angelito forced a chuckle. 'You're missing my point, Huaman. Today you are not in a position to bargain.'

Huaman added some kidneys to his plate. 'I am inside the American Embassy, General. If we don't agree terms, I shall seek political asylum. That will unleash the sort of publicity you would rather not have.'

Angelito felt a stirring of respect. 'Are you threatening me?'

Huaman smiled. 'I haven't eaten kidneys like this since the world was young.'

Angelito pushed his cup away. 'Fuck the kidneys!' He rose and strode towards Huaman. 'I'm calling your bluff!'

Huaman stuffed more kidneys into his mouth. 'Before you do, ask yourself whether you have the mettle to defeat Manku Yupanqui!'

'I can defeat Fuego any time!'

'I didn't say Fuego. I said Manku Yupanqui. That's who he is now!'

'No difference!'

Huaman turned to Williston. 'Perhaps you can tell him the difference, Luke.' He helped himself to some bacon.

Williston freshened his face with a cologne-wipe. 'Well, I can only repeat what I've reported to… my associates. Since Fuego joined the fray, we have a different ball-game on our hands. I mean, no disrespect to Gaspar, but we're not facing a bunch of ill-fed, ill-trained, pitifully armed guerrillas. There's half the countryside on the march out there! Swarms of Indios, defying God's Will, dancing widdershins to Satan's tune, frothing at the mouth to snatch the soul of the country. That scares me.'

Huaman scooped up some egg with his bacon. 'And after this country, General, there is the whole continent. And after that, the world. In view of the alliance between Moral Crusade and New Order, how do you think those powers will feel about a world ruled by a host of Manku Yupanquis? Because, make no mistake, if we have our Manku Yupanqui, every other nation will find one of their own also. That's a horrendous prospect!'

Angelito revised his opinion of Huaman. Pompous he might be, but there was a sharp mind there. Certainly, with his assessment of New Order's fears, he was on target. Much as Kempin's cronies proclaimed that the trawl they had cast over the future would soon be ready for gathering, that was the wishful thinking of old men. There was still a lot of work to be done before that. The better strategists, the new blood, were aware of the need for caution. Trawls could be swept away by storms, was their evaluation. And a host of Manku Yupanquis was just the sort of storm they most feared. Moreover, the new blood had been much impressed by his proposals for closer ties with Moral Crusade; a skilful use of caution now would elevate him a few more rungs. Therefore, much as it would rankle to make a deal with Huaman, expediency must overrule scruples.

'Before we discuss the finer points, Huaman, tell me why you've come over to us?'

Huaman helped himself to another piece of steak. 'I have not come over to you.' He smiled magisterially. 'At least, not in so far as my objectives are concerned.'

'You've changed sides. How can your objectives be compatible with ours?'

'As my men used to say, you can climb a mountain from many directions.'

'That begs another question. What about your men? Aren't you concerned for their fate?'

Huaman's bulging mouth twisted in a grim smile. 'Quite unconcerned, General. Hell has no fury like a leader scorned.'

Against the grain, Angelito felt some sympathy for Huaman. 'I see. Tell me, what makes you think you can help me defeat Fuego – bearing in mind that strength lies with me, that I have the power to throw the whole of the armed forces at him!'

Huaman munched his morsel of steak with relish. 'I know their strategy.'

'Marching – that's their strategy.'

'Have you seen them marching?'

'We're looking for them.'

'But you can't find them. And you won't. They know how to remain concealed. Where to feed. Where to take on more followers. Which tracks to take. When to march. When to lie low. I am familiar with those strategies. I can uncover them for you.'

'They can't remain invisible for ever. We'll spot them sooner or later.'

'Wouldn't you rather it was sooner?'

Williston toyed with the apple on his plate. 'Sooner is my advice, Angelito. Or you'll have to kill them wholesale. The Lord wouldn't want that. Not even your most sympathetic supporters would be able to condone that. And I'll leave it to you to imagine the sort of condemnation you'd get from those liberals on Capitol Hill – not to mention the average US citizen.'

Angelito sat down and poured himself another coffee. 'Perhaps you're right, Luke. I'd like to clear up a few points, Huaman... If we accept your offer, will you renounce your ideology?'

'Let's say I shall modify it.'

'How do you modify Marxism!'

'The way you've modified fascism. By transmuting the reformist dimension into a patriarchal one.'

'A welfare state?'

'In so far as that is practicable – given the Indio's insularity, the geopolitics of the times, the economic realities...'

'You're hedging, Huaman.'

'Well, let me put it another way, General. Whatever the reforms, constitutional changes, future policies, you and I should always end up on the same side.'

Angelito smiled. 'And if we don't? That, too, can be transmuted?'

Huaman nodded magnanimously. 'Quite.'

'Very well. We're still left with some practical problems.'

'Such as?'

'Bringing you back into the Establishment. Which cabinet post...'

Huaman piled some marmalade on his toast. 'I thought we should create a new ministry. With an evocative name – like National Unity. As for bringing me back into the Establishment – all that needs is a handshake.'

'Not that simple. You're a notorious figure. A ruthless enemy. The whole country has heard of you.'

Huaman bit into his toast. 'If we reach agreement, Gaspar Huaman will cease to exist. The person who joins your government will be a new man: Gaspar de Villasante y Córdoba. A man of the cleanest blood. A scion of one of the oldest and most illustrious families – with vast estates along the coast. And that, for a change, will be the truth. As you well know, I was *born* de Villasante y Córdoba.'

Angelito, though impressed by the simplicity of the plan, felt resentful. He realised he was jealous of Huaman's pedigree. 'In our day, you can't just live off your name. You need ability, too.'

Huaman smiled. 'That goes without saying.'

Angelito was grudging. 'Well. You seem to have thought it all out.'

'I've even thought out how we should publicise my sudden emergence. We'll declare I've been working abroad. Perhaps, to explain the loss of my arm, somewhere where there's always a war – like the Middle East. In view of the crisis in our country, I've been summoned to join the government.'

Angelito pondered a moment, then smiled. 'It's vague and grand... I accept your terms.'

Williston, as pleased as a successful matchmaker, rose from the table. 'My congratulations, gentlemen!'

Angelito moved to Huaman. Huaman placed his toast on the plate and stood up. They shook hands.

Huaman produced a kingly smile. 'And an *abrazo*?'

Angelito nodded impassively. 'Of course.'

Williston, as if to cleanse himself of their embrace, took out another cologne-wipe.

65

And I saw how many we were, how many were with me, they were not anybody, they were all mankind, they did not have faces, they were the people, they were metal, they were roads

The *chicha* smelled of stale sweat; the *humintas* tasted of earth and grass. Beatriz decided it was the best meal she had ever eaten.

Wherever she looked, Fuego was there, negotiating the darkness like an owl. His tattered soutane appeared to be luminous, lighting up the people's faces. The shiniest face was Chauca's. Chauca followed him everywhere.

She had no idea how many people were spread out on this slope. Thousands, certainly. Reclaiming, like lush vegetation, the agricultural terraces the Incas had cut on the mountainside.

A campesina brought her a *maté*. Beatriz held on to her hand gratefully. The campesina nodded uncomfortably and withdrew. Like the other campesinas she had approached on her journey here. At each village where the bus had stopped, she had looked for those who might accept her as a sister returning home and tell her where to find Manku Yupanqui. They had responded politely, but with restraint, affected by her request, but suspicious of her intentions; and, on occasions, the smart black dress she had worn to say goodbye to Jerry had frightened them as if she were the harbinger of a great mourning. Only on the third overnight stop had she had the wit to discard the dress and buy herself a skirt, a blouse and a poncho. Those she had met subsequently had been more forthcoming, but on the question of Manku Yupanqui's whereabouts, they had all said the same thing: no one finds him, he comes when we are ready to go.

She sipped her *maté*. It had a mouldy taste. Delicious.

She hoped they would begin to accept her after tomorrow's march. They knew her music. And though they sang it as if it belonged to them, there seemed to be a subtle reservation in their singing, an unspoken criticism – the regret, she thought, that the songs had been composed in the city instead of the countryside.

She would march tirelessly tomorrow. They would see she had abandoned her *misti* ways.

The bus, on this eighth day of her journey, had stopped for the night at Pintoyaku, the village, she had sadly remembered Daniel telling her, where he had found the Inca blue and from where fate had diverted him to the desert necropolis. Treacherous fate! It had shown them how damaged a pair of vessels they had been; then it had given them a glimpse of how perfectly they could be repaired; and then, because they had dared look at the future, it had shattered them irreparably.

From the bus, she had gone to the hotel – where Daniel had stayed – half expecting to run into people he had talked about, like Pillpe, the boy who had asked to be adopted.

To her consternation, she had found the hotel closed for business. The owner had told the passengers that the village was going to be abandoned and that they could sleep free wherever they liked.

She had not needed to ask why the village would be abandoned, and where the villagers intended to go. And she had suckled her hopes.

Then, after nightfall, like sudden rain, campesinos had inundated Pintoyaku. By the time its people had started streaming away into the night with ecstatic pronouncements of Manku Yupanqui, she had already been running around, shouting fiercely: take me, too!

Before long, Chauca had materialised. She had embraced him joyfully. He had greeted her warmly, but only after he had laid his hands on her hair, her cleavage, the small of her back and her crutch, explaining politely that he was checking for weapons, that Manku Yupanqui had forbidden weapons.

Then Chauca had asked the passengers whether anyone wanted to join the march. Those unattached had jumped at the chance; the rest had chosen to proceed to their homes in order to gather their families and friends.

Thereafter, they had climbed, light as a spray of pollen, to this terraced slope.

Here, Manku Yupanqui had been waiting for them.

As he had embraced them, one by one, as she had stood waiting for her turn, she had felt like wheat, tumbling in the wind, shedding chaff.

Now, she was in the first hour of her new life. Was it childish to be so exalted? She looked at the people. Were they not as exhilarated as she?

No, they were not. Or rather, they displayed joy only when Fuego approached them, stroked their children, asked if they had had enough to eat, if they were tired, how the old were managing, how the pregnant fared, did the young have too much to carry, could the provisioners cope with the food and the livestock. The rest of the time, they remained temperate: contented but impassive, as if this was the life they had always known, a life so perfectly earthbound that it had no need of rapture.

Fuego came over to her.

He had changed since she had last seen him in Father Quintana's church. The madness had gone; so had the ferocity. He looked young and old, childlike and wise, meek and formidable, innocent and worldly, unknowing and omniscient.

He sat down next to her.

She smiled at him. 'I have come for good.'

He smiled also.

'And I will do anything asked of me. Everything – and more.'

'Everything means being with us, marching with us. You can't do more than that.'

'I *mean* everything... Even if you wanted me... as your woman. I can – now that you are not what you were.'

Gently, Fuego kissed her hand. 'Thank you. But I have my consort.'

She looked up, surprised. She felt a twinge of rejection, then great relief. 'Forgive me. I wanted you to know how much I believe in this movement.'

'Your belief sounds too desperate. Let go of your desperation. No one will be asked to do what is not right. Not in this new society.'

She nodded.

'To put matters straight. Much as I love you, my new self, remembering the old, cannot touch you. Also, you still love Daniel – you always will. Lastly, I truly do have a consort. I am with Teresa. She is my wife. I have taken her into my heart. She will take life there – blossom into someone very much like you.'

She tried to find her smile. 'To put matters straight also. Daniel and I... have said goodbye.'

He looked sad, but that did not eclipse his radiance. He stood up. 'There is one thing the people might like. A new song from you. To colour their march.'

The request was pure joy. She became as luminous as he. 'Can you find me a guitar?'

He slipped away, so lightly that he might have skipped. She heard his voice and it sounded as if it was dancing.

'Chauca! We need a guitar!'

They resumed the march at sunrise.

Beatriz felt as fresh as the sea. Except for a brief period when Daniel had husbanded her days and nights, she had never been a good sleeper. She had either been prey to the tremors of the past or to the vile erosions of her profession. But last night she had slept like an Inca boulder, a solid cube impenetrable to nightmares. And when she had woken up, she had found that she had changed into a person she could hold and feed, wash and clothe without enmity.

Chauca had brought an old guitar that had been lovingly stroked by generations. The moment she had held it new songs had begun to germinate.

There was no specific order to the march except that imposed by the terrain. Where they had to skirt the mountains on narrow tracks or ledges, people fell into single file. Where the slopes were wider, they fanned out. Where they had to cross rivers, they turned into bridges. Where they encountered woods, they became moving trees. On rocky descents, they hurtled like a landslide. In deep ichu grass, they rolled like the surf. When they passed through a village, they became engorged with its people and, moving on, they put the village into a magical sleep so that it could be reawakened on their return.

But there was nothing haphazard in this march. Nobody had to be told what to do. Everything was done when it needed to be done. Rations appeared when it was time to eat. Livestock were grazed, milked or slaughtered. They rested when they felt no danger. They spoke, laughed and touched when there was need to. They chewed coca when they had to stave off hunger or when it was time to tell stories about the past as parables for the future. And when they sensed menace in the air, they blended into the landscape. Even children and livestock regulated their voices to accord with the communal good.

And always, on a high ledge or a rock, Manku Yupanqui and Chauca stood clear like guiding stars, like the head and the foot of the Southern Cross.

Beatriz dwelled happily in this new world. She prepared food, carried children, milked the llamas, collected eggs from the chickens, supported the old, shared loads with the young, played her guitar, sang her old ballads, worked on a new song and felt she was as vital a particle as the next person.

So they marched on.

The upper highlands of the Eastern Cordilleras, Chauca had told her, were now deserted. Prior to her arrival, they had traversed the range from north to south. Ail the *naturales*, except for those who refused to become burdens – such as the infirm and the very old – had joined.

Henceforth, moving in the opposite direction, from south to north, they would march through the lower highlands. That would take two months.

Then they would move to the Altiplano. They should cover it in three months.

Then on to the Western Cordilleras. The upper highlands and the lower highlands. About six months.

Then down to the Yungas. Three months.

Then into the desert. One month.

Then on to the coastal plain. Five months.

And finally to the capital.

By the time they reached La Merced, they would have been truly tempered. All the people would have joined the march – mestizos and *mistis*, too. For those latter also yearned for the rule of the Sun's Son.

Nevertheless, Chauca had warned her, it will be a dangerous march. You can't expect false men of God and bloodthirsty generals and bandits from overseas to hand over their powers and privileges meekly. There will be armies out there. Planes, helicopters, tanks, cannons and machine-guns. There will even be, if the rumours are correct, Gaspar de Villasante y Córdoba, Minister for National Unity, known, until recently, as Gaspar Huaman.

But in the long run, what can they do, those maggots? Can they kill *all* the people?

Besides, how many of these false men of God and bloodthirsty generals and overseas bandits are there? Let's count the other worms, too: the Sinchis, the Bridegrooms of Death, the landowners! How many all told? One, three, five thousand? Ten thousand? The rest, the soldiers, the pilots, the tank corps, the gunners, the riflemen – they are people, our people, *naturales* and mestizos and, yes, *mistis*, too. How many can they kill before they drop their weapons, parachute out of their planes, ditch their tanks, spike their guns? How many can they kill before they stop for fear of losing their souls? A culture that eats gold – the people still don't understand that. They will not accept it for ever.

Even so, Chauca had assured her, they will not be taking chances. You can see, we are a young movement and strong, but we need to be stronger. So we shall march slowly. That will put steel in our bodies and iron in our resolve. Those who have not yet joined will hear more about us; they will get impatient for us to come and collect them; as they wait, they will work harder and stockpile food and livestock, for they will know that until we return to our lands, we will be dependent on them to feed themselves and us.

We shall march, whenever possible, beyond the range of the false men of God and the bloodthirsty generals and the bandits from overseas. Much of the time, they will not even see us. Sometimes, they will catch a glimpse of us above them, behind them or at their flanks, but always out of their reach, on terrain where their planes are likely to clip their wings, where their armoured cars and tanks cannot manoeuvre, where the altitude or the cold or the heat or the dust or the wind or the isolation wilt their bodies.

But that does not mean we shall always avoid them. No! Now and again, we shall meet them head on. We must monitor their strength, you see, as well as their weaknesses. We must gauge the range of their brutality. At the same time, we must infuse our mettle, show them they cannot win. Particularly, we must expose ourselves to our fears. Above all, in order to remind ourselves why we are marching, why we must not stop marching, we must bleed.

We shall have such a confrontation soon. As soon as the false men of God and the bloodthirsty generals and the bandits from overseas decide to get off their fat arses.

And so they marched on. And on.

66

We, Christian patriots, we, defenders of order, we, sons of the Spirit

Angelito and Gaspar showed every sign of spending the day arguing tactics. Williston, having had enough of their talk, left the station-master's office that passed as their command post.

He searched for a place to sit.

He decided against the river bank. Most of the 400-strong battalion were sprawled there, eating their rations.

There was the station-master's hut next to the office, but it had a sheet of corrugated iron as a dividing wall and that would not soundproof Angelito and Gaspar. One thing about those two: though they quarrelled constantly, they had become inseparable, like an old married couple.

He spotted a mound at a siding where their train stood. He moved to it and sat down.

His sweat offended him. He felt as unclean as when he strayed. Naturally, he wanted to stray now. He could do it, he supposed, behind some bush. But he would end up execrably unclean. Besides, he needed to ration his cologne-wipes. In any case, with all these people around, he could not, afterwards, chastise himself thoroughly. More importantly, he was here on the Lord's business – though it had been Caesar who had sent him.

He had to admit, he was not very happy about it. Discounting preaching and baptising which was a vocation, he was not, strictly speaking, a field man. He had realised that at Monte Rico. The corridors of power were his domain; he excelled in scheming, twisting arms and putting the fear of the Lord into the misguided.

But Dexter Leacock who, by virtue of his lofty position in the State Department, formulated the strategies for Moral Crusade and its allies, had forecast that the Manku Yupanqui phenomenon would fragment South America and that he who moved fastest would be in a position to pick up the pieces. Consequently, he had recommended a high profile from his associates. Particularly from Williston who had become mentor to Angelito and Gaspar.

Even so, was it wise to send a puppet master to the front? Apart from the dangers – and fear – could a man of God function as efficiently as a military adviser? Moreover, was it wise to alert the world, at this stage of the geopolitical situation, that Moral Crusade was picking up its sword?

He would have to put these issues on the table at the next conference. In the meantime, he was here. A crusader. Let them see his fortitude.

He scanned the region, bearing in mind Gaspar's briefing.

They were in the Incas' Sacred Valley, a geological fault in the lower Eastern Cordilleras, running south to north for some two hundred kilometres. To the east, the ground rose gradually towards the concertina of snow-capped mountains, some as high as 6,000 metres. To the west, the terrain was altogether different. There, too, the mountains were lined up, but they were neither exceptionally high – 2,500 metres maximum – nor piled upon each other. They rose, side by side, often sugarloafed, occasionally acutely pyramidal, like countless giant ice-cream cones. The base of the valley itself, about twenty kilometres at its widest, twisted and turned to accommodate the River Huaca, one of the tributaries of the Amazon. A narrow road ran along the river's western bank, contorting to match its undulations. On either side of the river there were lush fields of corn and wheat. The humidity was palpable and lay on the skin permanently as thick slime. Satan's weather. In the course of the four hours since their arrival, it had changed from the dense mist of low clouds to blistering sunshine to torrential rain and now to suffocating closeness. According to Gaspar, that was nothing; the freaks were what really amazed – like downpours in brilliant sunshine which the Indios called *quantu*, after the Inca flower, in the belief that only such a combination could produce the flower's delicate crimson hue.

The railway station was called Mamasara, 'Mother Corn'. Before the present crisis had suspended train services, it used to be the terminal for two famous Inca ruins: Napa and Huaca.

Napa, a fastness at the base of the valley, lay fifteen kilometres to the south. It was named, Gaspar had explained pedantically, after the white llama which, according to oral tradition, had first appeared there. Its greater claim to fame was the fact that its occupants had fought the Conquistadores to the last person.

Huaca, a vast citadel, lay seven kilometres to the north, and was situated on top of a sugarloaf mountain. Despite its proximity to Napa, the Conquistadores had never discovered it.

Because of these ruins – overpraised beyond belief by those hordes of liberals – the corridor between Napa and Huaca was, in effect, the heart of the Sacred Valley. Consequently, Gaspar had argued, it was the one stretch through which Fuego, so obsessed with the ways of the Inca, would march at all costs. Given the geography of the salient, right here, at Mamasara, he would have to march in the open.

Intelligence – what there was of it – supported Gaspar's theory. Aerial reconnaissance had established that on a south to north bearing, the villages and hamlets of the lower highlands were being deserted one by one and overnight – in a pattern that had evolved in the upper highlands in the preceding month.

Williston did not need to be a five-star general to confirm that once Fuego left Napa, he would have little cover. His people would spread across the valley like lemmings running towards a cliff.

It ought to be a simple engagement. But both Gaspar and Angelito were treating it as a major battle. Hence the endless argument on tactics.

Gaspar wanted a wholesale solution: a merciless attack on all fronts. He had even favoured the use of helicopter gunships, but had desisted when Williston had pointed out that damaging the ruins would give the humanists the perfect pretext to churn up international opprobrium.

Angelito proposed assassinating Fuego and thus cutting the head of the whole Manku Yupanqui movement. So-called wholesale solutions, he insisted, often proved counter-productive. The massacre of the demonstrators in La Merced, for instance, had pushed the people into messianic zeal instead of terrorising them into submission. If Fuego could be exposed as a mere mortal before the very eyes of the people, the whole movement would instantly collapse. All that was required was to commission the crack-shots, himself included, to target on Fuego before the engagement.

Williston was inclined to side with Gaspar. If the Lord had not wanted a fly killed by a sledge-hammer, He would not have invented the sledge-hammer. What did Angelito think Nemesis meant?

67

The people set out and arrived and married new land and water to grow their words again

They had spent the night at Napa.

They had imbibed its spirit.

After the murder of Atahualpa, Manku Yupanqui had told them, a community of Incas had retreated to this place in order to preserve their way of life. The Conquistadores, maddened by such fierce love of freedom, had given chase and set up a siege. The Inca community had put up a valiant resistance. They had kept the Spaniards at bay for months. They had pursued happiness even to the day when, depleted of all provisions, they had become prey to famine. Then, rather than surrender, they had committed mass suicide. From the escarpment which resembled the neck of the white llama, they had thrown themselves on to the rocks below, every man, woman and child.

The people knew the story of Napa only too well. Though it had never appeared in school texts, though successive governments had deliberately suppressed it in order to undermine the *naturale*'s pride in his history, culture, race and self, it had been handed down, generation after generation, from father to son, from mother to daughter.

Even so, it was good to hear it again! Hear it here in Napa itself. Here, where the stones were imprinted with the shadows of their ancestors. Where the shards of broken pots chronicled the famine that had struck them. Where the ruins of temples, dwellings and armouries spoke to them face to face. Where the Square of Feasts still echoed the voices of poets, musicians and singers. Here, where the past mirrored the present. Here, where they could understand that in terms of freedom and justice, welfare and wealth, nothing had changed since the fall of the Incas! Here, where they could see that the present was still the colonial past!

Here, then, Manku Yupanqui had instructed them, the Children of the Sun must reforge their spirit. This time, the situation was different. This time the preservation of freedom was not in the hands of a small community, but in the hands of the whole people. This time, mass suicide was not a last option. This time they had united to seize life!

This time, above all, Manku Yupanqui had the sun's missing ray.

Let them now ask! What was the sun's missing ray? Where was it? Did he carry it on his person? Was it sheathed inside his heart? Was he wearing it in the manner of a sling under his soutane? Or had he left it in safe-keeping with a mountain?

And let him now answer! *They*, the people, were the sun's missing ray! *They*, who now had one thought, one voice, one heart! *They*, who by seeking justice for all mankind, had attained sanctity, *they* were the sun's missing ray!

So onwards to seize life, Children of the Sun, Children of Lightness! Ahead lay the Children of the Conquistadores, the Children of Darkness!

Some would die, but not *all* would die. For as fire spilled some sparks, so would the sun's missing ray spill some of the people that constituted it. But sparks were also seeds. They ignited a new world, they reforested the earth!

So onwards to seize life! They could not be defeated! Ahead also lay Huaca where all the gods who formed the One God awaited to join them!

Angelito was driving back from the southern sector, signalling his satisfaction to the snipers. Williston had already confirmed that the men were well under cover and could not be detected from the road.

Ten snipers had been chosen. They had been spread, at various heights on the slopes, over a distance of half a kilometre from the railway station. Angelito, unable to resist the opportunity of killing Fuego personally, had designated himself as one of the snipers. He had taken the advance position and had ordered the rest to wait for his first shot and then to fire concertedly.

At the northern sector, Gaspar was inspecting the battalion's formation. The Bridegrooms, in half-tracks, would deploy immediately after the snipers. The Sinchis, entrenched behind the station, would deal with those marchers scattered by the motorised unit.

Williston sat on the mound by the siding and watched the activity. Angelito and Gaspar had compromised by combining tactics.

The previous afternoon, scouts sent to the Napa area had reported sighting the marchers. Tens of thousands of them – which Williston presumed meant a few thousand – had suddenly emerged, in the even more exaggerated terms of the scouts, out of the earth and the rocks, the bushes and the trees, even out of the very air itself. And they had proceeded to the ruins, there to spend the night.

This morning, the scouts had returned with the report that the march had recommenced, and that Fuego was taking the valley road, as Gaspar had predicted, towards Huaca. They were expected to reach Mamasara at about noon. No one, as far as the scouts could ascertain, carried arms. Fuego himself, the scouts had stated, would be a clear target, for though he seldom stayed in one position, he always remained separate from the throng, in the manner of a shepherd. There would be no difficulty spotting him in the ragged priest's soutane which had become his only clothing. His one escort was an Indio who fitted Chauca's description.

'Won't be long now.'

Williston looked up at Gaspar who had strode over to him, then checked his watch: 10.57. 'Another hour or so.'

With his one hand, Gaspar fiddled with the loose arm of his jacket, trying to push it further into his belt. 'We won't see them before they're upon us.' He pointed at the road. 'Not until they clear that sharp bend.'

Williston studied Gaspar's suit. What did it look like? Martial, definitely. Gaspar, envious of Angelito's general's uniform, had demanded his own battledress. A toady in his newly formed ministry had come up with this particular number: a cross between a safari suit and a Chinese tunic. 'We'll hear them, though. Any minute now.'

Gaspar rubbed his stump. 'You think so?'

The beads of sweat on Gaspar's face, Williston thought, were not spawned by the humidity. The man was on heat – another unclean animal. 'The scouts said they were singing.'

'That's true.' Gaspar sniggered. 'Their swan-song.' He pointed at Angelito who had just drawn up in the command car. 'I'll be with our great general – finalising plans.'

The Children of Darkness were lying in wait, as Manku Yupanqui had predicted. From a crag alongside the road, Chauca had spotted a mass of troops.

It was time for the people to expose themselves to their fears, to look death in the face, to consolidate their strength, to acquire further proof that they must not stop marching.

Beatriz felt the fear. She told herself it was doubt – doubt that even Jesus had felt. Manku Yupanqui had asked her whether she wanted him to walk with her. She had refused. She would have no privileges. The people were his charge – he should walk with all of them.

To conquer the fear, she moved to the front. She felt better. If she were to die, she would not die alone, but as one of many sparks in a great fire. But still fearful: were she to survive, others will have died.

She sang her new song.

Now that a man no longer feels the air
enfolding him
like his woman

Now that a woman no longer feels the earth
smiling in her womb
like a flower

Now that a child no longer feels the water
rocking him
like a lullaby

Now that the people no longer feel the fire
quickening their limbs
like love

We know
life has lost
its salt

And the people sang with her.

She yearned for Daniel – the hidden Daniel, the Daniel who was as much an Inca, as much a Christian as he was a Jew. That Daniel should have been here, at her side, proudly swaying his powerful body as he marched. Then he would have assuaged her stupid fear. He would have told her that life was beautiful when, as now, its beauty was shared – *only when* its beauty was shared. He would have told her that death, no matter how brutal its face, could be transmuted into beauty, into life; that, as Manku Yupanqui had said, the seed died in order to germinate.

That was why their child had died: to give them birth.

The birth Daniel had refused.

The birth she had accepted.

Her voice became the voice of the Sacred Valley.

We know, too,
dear God
You do not want us to die
unsalted

So here we are
spreading ourselves
on
the wind
the rock
the spring
the sun
when we rise again
tomorrow
we shall rise
as
breath
land
river
hearth

Angelito's finger trembled on the trigger. Another few hundred metres and Fuego would be in the direct line of fire.

He had nothing to be afraid of, the marchers were unarmed. This shaking, this feeling of defeat was irrational.

Six hundred and fifty metres!

The marchers were singing. That bitch, Beatriz, was conducting them from the front. The sound was deafening. It rose from the ground in earth-shaking decibels, then reverberated from the mountains, even louder, like peaks colliding with peaks.

Six hundred!

What was incomprehensible, what terrified, was their number. Not a few thousand, like those that had demonstrated at the Plaza de los Héroes. But tens of thousands!

Five hundred and fifty!

Tens of thousands! As the scouts had reported and he, Williston and Gaspar had refused to believe.

Five hundred metres!

446

Tens of thousands! They stretched as far as the eye could see, as far as the telescopic sight on his rifle could see. The valley road could take but a portion of them. The rest hugged the slopes, the railway tracks, the river bank. Some – thousands – marched through the river itself!

Four hundred and fifty!

Fuego! He looked a hundred years younger. And a million years older. He looked, in that filthy soutane of Father Quintana's, like one of those youthful saints in church paintings. He also looked like the timeless ancients the Indios described as *apus*. The bastard – he looked like a god of war turned into a prophet! But not for long!

Four hundred!

Tens of thousands! This is where both New Order and Moral Crusade miscalculated. The people were vermin, yes, but, collectively, they were a tidal wave, collectively, they had a face, features, muscles that could tear the world apart, a will that was impregnable. Beware, my supermen! Your ideologies, uniforms, guns, the worship of the glorious past, discipline, whip, power, idyllic death, purity, all those may be to no avail. Collectively, these vermin can crush us. They could crush us even if we really turned into titans. The mercy was they refused to carry arms.

Three hundred and fifty metres!

Tens of thousands! How could they have remained unseen? How could they have blended with the earth, the mountains, the rocks, the trees, the grass? If they could do that, what was to stop them from flowing underground, a current of magma the size of an ocean, as far as the capital, as far as all the capitals? And then erupting right underneath their masters' chairs, incinerating order, uniforms, guns!

Three hundred!

Tens of thousands! And only a fraction of the rest! If they only knew, they could be invincible. They could, with one stroke of their arm, send the masters to damnation!

Two hundred and fifty metres!

Which is why you must not fail to kill Fuego! Now, before the tens of thousands become hundreds of thousands! Before he realises what power he can unleash! Before the people realise what power they have! Now, before New Order and Moral Crusade are shown to be emperors without clothes!

Target dead centre!

Fuego's head! Haloed head of a saint! Majestic head of an Inca! Noble head of a man! In perfect focus in the telescopic sight! The hairlines zeroed between his saviour eyes!

Angelito fired.

I am saving you, New Order! I am saving you, Moral Crusade! The least you can do is make me Chief Executive!

The very moment he had fired, Fuego had turned round.

But he hit him all the same.

He saw Fuego fall.

He heard the other snipers fire.

He fired again and again. This was the best remedy for fear. But it did not shift it – not a single atom of it.

The front marchers were rounding the bend in the road. They were still singing.

Manku Yupanqui, Chauca and a number of the former guerrilleros had moved to the fore for the confrontation with the troops. Manku Yupanqui was the first to spot them. He turned round to point them out.

At that moment, the bullet hit him – just below the neck. The impact hurled him to the right. Thus, the following salvo also missed his head and hit various parts of his body.

After that, the snipers could not have had sight of him. For first Chauca, then some of the former guerrilleros threw themselves on top of him to shield him with their bodies.

The people did not panic. Instead of scattering, they simultaneously closed ranks and fanned out.

They continued marching. And singing.

And as they passed Manku Yupanqui and the men protecting him – some of whom had also been hit by the successive salvos – they picked them up and carried them.

They carried them at waist level to conceal them from the snipers.

Beatriz was one of those who carried Manku Yupanqui. She had reached him soon after the men. She was, as yet, unhurt.

Chauca was another. Miraculously, he, too, was unhurt.

Angelito, assuming that Fuego had been crushed by the people coming up from behind, signalled his snipers to withdraw and join the mobilised units.

When he himself tried to follow suit, he could not move. Fear had paralysed him. He had killed Fuego, but it had made no difference. The people were still marching, still singing. Did that mean they could not be stopped?

The snipers down the road, he saw, had been flushed out by the people marching on the slopes. They had abandoned their rifles. A moment later, they were engulfed.

This time fear provided Angelito with wings. He launched himself forward. Too late. A thick mass of people appeared before him. He pulled up his rifle to fire. Hands snatched it away from him. Other hands smashed it to pieces. Several voices spoke to him.

'Don't kill us – join us.'

'Don't fight us – march with us!'

He sank to his knees and held his head in his hands. He was about to die. Stupidly. Before his time! Before his glory! Die! Stupidly! His lovely flesh torn to bits!

But they did not touch him.

They walked on. Wave after wave.

He crawled through the feet to shelter by a mound.

They marched past him. All the tens of thousands.

At the station platform at Mamasara, Gaspar and Williston watched the marchers gushing round the bend. An endless procession. Still singing. No break in formation. On the contrary, they stood solid – just expanding and contracting like a massive chest.

Gaspar spluttered angrily. 'The snipers must have missed Fuego!'

Williston craned for a better look. 'Can you see him?'

Gaspar glanced at the road. The Bridegrooms were in their half-tracks, engines running. He raised his revolver. 'We'll find him when we count the corpses.' He fired his signal.

The mobilised unit hurtled forward.

Chauca was holding Manku Yupanqui by the waist, his hands awash with blood.

Beatriz was holding Manku Yupanqui's face. He was unconscious, seemingly peacefully asleep. He had the softest of smiles. The blood from his various wounds had soaked his soutane, sanctifying it all the more.

Chauca signalled to some men. They rushed over and relieved him from carrying.

Chauca touched Beatriz's shoulder, encouragingly. 'Take him to the river bank.'

Then he ploughed into the people, shouting his orders. 'All the dead and the injured – take them to the river bank. All those not carrying, you know what to do!'

The half-tracks, keeping abreast, raced down the road. When they came within range of the people, they opened fire.

Those hit, fell. The rest did not scatter. Instead, they ran forward. The firing continued. More and more people fell. And more and more people,

people who had been on the slopes, on the railway tracks, by the river bank, ran forward. The Bridegrooms continued firing.

Still people fell. But now they were falling in front of the half-tracks, around them, behind them. Those people who had not been shot were throwing themselves on top of each other, forming massive human barriers.

The half-tracks that were in the middle of the road steered to their right or to their left to avoid hitting the human wall. In so doing, they collided with the half-tracks at their sides. They, in turn, lost control.

Some piled into each other, others crashed on to the people, two overturned.

Some Bridegrooms lay injured. Others tried to scramble to safety through the forest of bodies and feet. Yet others were helped to their feet and were urged:

'Don't kill us – join us.'

'Don't fight us – march with us!'

And the people smashed the weapons.

And they continued to march. Still in their tens of thousands. Still singing. Still collecting their dead and injured.

Williston muttered in a state of shock, 'I don't believe it! They can't do this!'

Gaspar screeched, 'Come on, they're almost here.'

They ran to the northern sector where the Sinchis had taken position.

Gaspar fired his gun repeatedly and shrieked. 'Attack! Attack!'

The Sinchis surged forward.

The people reached the station just as the Sinchis, some firing, some charging with bayonets, attacked.

More people fell.

More people surged forward.

The Sinchis continued fighting, but lost their formation.

Soon the people engulfed them. They snatched their guns and bayonets.

'Don't kill us – join us.'

'Don't fight us – march with us!'

Some Sinchis, as if hypnotised, tore off their ammunition belts, tunics, trousers, took off their boots. They shouted, 'Yes! Yes!' They wept. 'We will! We will!'

And they joined the people and marched with them.

Williston trembled as he watched the people approach. He was reminded of the Incas, happily absorbing the Conquistadores' shots in their desperate attempt to save Atahualpa. They could have wiped out the Conquistadores, but they had not dared lay hands on them because Pizarro had tricked Atahualpa and had held him prisoner and would have killed him.

Here, however, the new Conquistadores did not have Manku Yupanqui as their prisoner. Here, he was with his people. If he were alive, they would continue marching. If Angelito had killed him, they would be merciless. 'Oh, Lord!'

Terrified, Gaspar pointed at the train that had brought them to Mamasara. 'Over there! Or they'll trample us to death!'

They ran to one of the wagons and hid inside.

The people, now joined by some of the Sinchis, marched on. They rolled like the tide; and like the tide, they bore no fissures.

Williston and Gaspar hid in the wagon, huddled together.

They remained in that position for what seemed an eternity – until they could no longer see the people.

Then, hesitantly, they emerged from the wagon.

They could hear the people, in the distance, marching towards Huaca. Their singing echoed from the mountains.

So here we are
spreading ourselves
on
the wind
the rock
the spring
the sun

Williston and Gaspar staggered on to the station platform.

Angelito, keeping crouched, was running towards them.

The three met. They scanned Mamasara.

What should have been a battlefield full of corpses had reverted to a peaceful backwater. The only disturbing sight was the remains of the battalion.

At a rough count of discarded uniforms, over a hundred Sinchis had deserted.

There were seven dead and eleven injured – all Bridegrooms, all from the overturned half-tracks.

The rest of the men sat or lay stretched out or stood leaning against something, frozen and expressionless, like well-preserved relics of a volcanic disaster.

Except for pools of blood, nothing – not one single body remained of the people.

But their voices still echoed

When we rise again
tomorrow
we shall rise
as
breath
land
river
hearth

PART TWELVE

68
Without feet for the earth, without eyes for the sea

The polyptych was finished.

It had been finished for over a fortnight. But he had pretended he could still improve the odd detail. Now, any further work would be an infringement.

Daniel took a long look at the atelier then moved to his work-bench. Except for his brushes, he was leaving everything behind. The custodians of the Museum would store the paints and the pigments; the caretakers would dispose of the solutions and other paraphernalia.

He wondered what to do with the piece of black fabric, the blindfold that Father Quintana had refused. He should not have let Fuego force it on him. Why hadn't he thrown it away? Or used it as a rag to clean his brushes? How stupid to believe it always stared at him defiantly. How stupid to imagine that the two circular stains at its centre were the imprints of the eyes of those who had been executed before Father Quintana. Did this faded piece of cloth have the ultimate wisdom, the complete knowledge of life in death and thereafter?

He picked up the blindfold. Or did it obliterate all knowledge of life, as Fuego had said?

He moved to the kitchenette and poured a hefty measure of brandy into his coffee cup. He was going through the bottle at speed. This was the sixth in three days. He should watch out or he would end up like Rice.

He took another look at the atelier.

The curator and the custodians had been crowing with triumph. Their praise would travel swiftly on the grapevine. His reputation would soar. He would be swamped with offers.

He would be able to raise his fees, too. Though what he would do with the extra money – or, indeed, with his already considerable savings – was another matter. He could, perhaps, turn collector. Except that things like books, stamps, coins did not impassion him. Only paintings did. But paintings also depressed him; they reaffirmed he was merely a handyman, not an artist.

He studied the hammock and the rug depicting the Inca calendar. They were his, bought in the excitement of the early days. He could not decide whether he should take them. He associated the hammock with Beatriz; and he would always associate anything Inca with Fuego. There was also the monk's seat. The curator had insisted he took it as a memento. But that, too, had associations with Beatriz and Fuego.

He sat on the monk's seat and tried to take deep breaths. He wondered whether he would ever breathe properly again. Not a worry. The wheezing had become an acceptable part of himself.

He sipped his drink.

He did not need to strike the platform; the caretakers would do that. He preferred to leave the canvas on its stretcher until the custodians were ready to frame it – they were moving in tomorrow.

Just his brushes, then. Oh, and the books. He had hardly touched them. He should have time now.

Was there anything in the apartment the Museum had provided? No. He had emptied the place when he had moved in with Beatriz. After the rape, she had sent all his stuff here. And he had sent her the sofa she had bought for making love.

At long last, he could leave.

He would miss the polyptych. It had come to inhabit him. He had imagined countless times that the figures had leaped out of the canvas to keep him company, watch his progress, point out an area he had overlooked. Incredibly, they had never judged him. Even the Virgin – Pachamama, who, latterly, had taken to appearing in Beatriz's guise – had refused to condemn him.

She was there now in the shadows, leaning against the door. Wearing Beatriz's ankle-length shift. God as Beatriz. The only vision that made any sense.

Ah, the doldrums – perfect waters for hallucinations. Or was it the brandy?

He took another sip. Tonight, he could cope with hallucinations. He noticed he was still holding the blindfold. Impulsively, he held it to his eyes. What would he see in its dark pool? A Gilded Man, El Dorado, thrown into a miasmic lake because, with all the gold at his disposal, he had not paid his tithes to his past, his God, his woman, his child, his future?

He saw nothing. Just the last shimmer of light turning into a white patch, depicting nothingness, blotting out a clearing in a forest under snow where good men vanished without trace, where a boy froze in fear for ever, where the killers survived all eternity...

He lowered the blindfold. Not altogether true, some of the killers did not survive.

He grinned. What irony! He had found Heinrich Kempin; he had been instrumental in his death.

Absent-mindedly, he tied the blindfold around his wrist.

Strange how he had almost forgotten Kempin. So much had happened outside Kempin, and so much more since Kempin's death. He could almost doubt Kempin had existed. Well, he had existed, but, in retrospect, he seemed arbitrary, a disaster which life suddenly encounters in its path and smashes to pieces against it.

He lit a cigarette. He savoured the blended smell of tobacco and turpentine. His smell. The only thing about him that had not putrefied.

He gazed at the polyptych.

This was his crowning achievement. The cardinal rule, in terms of his profession, was that the restoration should not be noticed, that the painting should re-emerge in all its original glory. This work was the perfect example of that rule. Truly gratifying, considering the innumerable challenges it had posed, the way he had overcome them all. Had overcome them creatively, he could even say.

There was that, at least. He had saved a great painting – as great as anything in existence.

He swirled the brandy in the cup.

Pachamama had gone back into the canvas. But Beatriz was still there, still leaning against the door, eyes closed. Would he see her image at every corner, for the rest of his life? Was that one of his punishments?

He should ring British Airways and book his flight.

And get on with his packing.

Tomorrow morning. After the custodians arrived. When he would officially sign off.

Tonight, he wanted to commune with the polyptych. Gradually, painfully, take leave. He must get drunk, well drunk. If he had any tears left, cry a little. A proper farewell.

He drank a good mouthful.

He must not forget to ask for copies of the slides. The curator had commissioned an excellent photographer. The slides would take pride of place in his portfolio. Then there were the film and the video, showing the various stages of the restoration, showing him at work and, in some instances, showing Beatriz present – and pregnant. He should have copies of those also.

He glanced at the door.

Yes, she was still there. But no longer leaning. Standing still. Eyes open, watching him.

He took refuge in the polyptych.

What a masterpiece!

Four masterpieces, in fact. The Trinity. The Virgin as Pachamama. The Inca Dynasty. The Tree of Life.

A summation of what existence should be: Religion; Nature; Lineage; Immortality.

But, applied to him, a summation of all that he had lost: God, faith, goodness, salvation. Love, grace, Beatriz, happiness. Family, identity, honour, courage. Creativity, Jewishness, righteousness, children.

And weaving in and out of those losses there was Fuego's spectre. The Antichrist, the rapist, the mass murderer. And dealing the *coup de grâce*, the latter Fuego: the penitent, Manku Yupanqui.

Sense counterbalanced by nonsense.

He stubbed out his cigarette.

The Trinity. The Virgin as Pachamama. The Inca Dynasty. The Tree of Life. In effect, four mothers who had fought to possess him. In the end, all four had abandoned him. Each had realised he could not be her child because there was no blood in his veins.

Unless it had been he who had abandoned them, he who had run away from them, knowing what he lacked.

Or worse. Maybe he had also destroyed his fathers, the men his mothers had embraced. Starved them all by giving nothing of himself, by choosing to be stillborn. Mothers and fathers were just as fragile. They also needed looking after! They did not need children who lived stillborn.

And Fuego who had envied him, who had howled in pain thinking this rubble of a man was whole, was a mountain. Fuego, who, in one leap, had acquired four mothers. And four fathers. And forefathers!

Fuego who had been his twin!

Daniel drained his mug. He should ring British Airways and reserve his seat. He should have left last week, even the week before. All that shit about retouching some details – pathetic excuses!

The truth of the matter was that, though he wanted to leave this God-forsaken country desperately, he could not. For this God-forsaken country was not, in fact, God-forsaken. On the contrary. God was walking here as if the rest of the world did not exist. He was everywhere, the Bastard! She! She! God was a woman! She was everywhere, the Bitch! How else could Fuego

458

have found Her? How else could all those thousands be marching with Her?

He wanted to find Her also! To touch Her once! Just once – as Fuego had touched Her! To lay his head on Her breasts! He could die then without looking back.

He still expected to find Her. He, a thousand Judases in one, still thought he *deserved* Her. He still thought She would seek him out, show herself in full splendour, stretch Her hand and say, come with Me, there is neither past nor future where you're going, the past and the future are in My loins, come on, there is nowhere you can run, no way you can live without life, come on, there is no fight left in you, you cannot *despise* Me any more, come on, there is not even any *fear* left in you! Come on, Daniel, come on, it is time you were born!

Daniel shot up from the monk's chair, bellowing. 'Come and take me then!' He lifted his mug for another sip; finding it empty, he staggered to the counter and kept shouting. 'Come and get me! Come and take me!'

He sensed a movement by the door. Beatriz's image. Let her hear him – why not? He was calling out for her, too. She was God incarnate.

He spun round and round, repeatedly shouting. 'Come and get me!'

Beatriz moved from the shadows into the light. 'I am here.'

He shut his eyes. Hallucinations must not get out of hand, must not move and take voice.

She touched him.

He recoiled from the touch, forced his eyes open. She was standing there. Not a vision. 'Beatriz...?'

She nodded.

He glanced at the door, shook his head in disbelief.

She smiled. 'I was trying to think... how best to approach you...'

She looked so drawn – so fragile. Like a bird buffeted by a storm. Yet so alive. Such serenity in her eyes. 'How? How did you...?'

'I still have my key...'

He managed a smile. 'I don't believe it...' He so wanted to hold her, press her against his chest, lie with her. But he had to be reborn to be able to do that.

He reached for the brandy, grimacing, as one who had narrowly escaped disaster. 'I might have been – *gone!*'

She pointed to the polyptych. 'You finished. Congratulations.'

'I should have gone... But I couldn't...'

As he was about to pour the brandy, she took his hand. 'Leave that. We have a long journey ahead.'

He put the bottle down, anxious to please her and seized by hope.

'It will be rough lanes mostly – to avoid the checkpoints and the patrols...'

He stared at her, confused.

'We're going to Huaca. Manku... Fuego wants to see you.'

He grabbed the bottle. 'To hell with him!'

Again, she restrained him. 'He is dying.'

'Not him! He's got more lives than the Devil!' He noticed her eyes. The serenity was still there, but refracted through a pool of tears. 'What's wrong with him?'

'We were attacked. At Mamasara...'

He looked at her distrustfully. 'There was no mention of it in the news.'

'They don't want the people to know. They didn't stop us. But we've had casualties. Fuego was badly wounded.'

Daniel jeered. 'Good! About time!'

She slapped him.

He glared at her, then, brusquely, moved away and sat on the monk's seat.

She shouted. 'He is a saint now! Doesn't that mean anything to you?'

'He's been fooling you – all of you!' As he stared angrily in front of him, he noticed the blindfold, still entwined on his wrist. He untied it. 'You see this? Father Quintana's blindfold. Well, not exactly – because he refused to wear it. Now *he* was a saint! Do you know who killed him?'

'Why did Father Quintana refuse the blindfold?'

'I didn't ask him.'

'Why do you think he refused?'

'So that he could look immortality in the face.'

'How come you have it now?'

'Because...' He looked away, sensing the rush of tears. 'I don't know.' He broke down. 'To cover my eyes – according to your saint...'

Beatriz approached him, full of compassion. 'But you don't need it. You want to *see*.'

Daniel nodded, sobbing. 'Yes. And I can see... I did! When I was shouting, when you came... I was seeing things... You... Truths...'

Gently, Beatriz took the blindfold from him. 'Then we can throw it away.'

'I can accept everything... anything... except Fuego.'

Beatriz threw the blindfold into the rubbish bin. 'Come and see him.'

'I can't! Don't you understand? He has become everything I wanted to be... Found everything I sought... Has everything I crave...'

'Yet you are so like him.'

He turned to her sharply, thinking she was mocking him.

She suppressed her tears by smiling. 'That's what he said. Like two peach trees. He has fruited. You are still waiting.'

'He said that?'

'He also said you would come. If only to see him die.'

'No!'

'Because when he dies, you will flower.'

'No!'

'When you were shouting, weren't you shouting at him?'

'I was shouting at God!'

'Then come. He will show you God.'

'You stupid bitch! God doesn't do Fuego's bidding! Who do you think Fuego is? Just a man – stricken with God-mania, like me!'

Beatriz took hold of his hand. 'Come.'

He held on to her hand desperately. 'I'll go anywhere with you! But not to him!'

She pulled him. 'Come.'

He protested. 'Why won't you understand?'

She continued pulling him. 'I understand. Come.'

He could not fight her. Desperately, as if seeking a force or an ally that could help him, his eyes scurried around the atelier. 'No!'

Beatriz put her arm around his waist and tried to drag him along. 'Come. The polyptych is finished. There is nothing left here for you.'

'There's nothing left anywhere.'

Beatriz led him to the door. 'There is God. Come.'

Daniel cried out. 'I don't want to see Fuego die!'

Beatriz opened the door. 'That's not important. It's God who must not die. Come!'

Daniel grabbed her shoulders and forced her to face him. They stared at each other. Defiantly, at first; then tenderly.

Then he sighed, drained. 'Let me put out the lights.'

69
Ascend to be born with me, brother!

The Army had been everywhere. The Junta, the campesinos had informed him, had ordered general mobilisation.

They had circumvented the troops, the road-blocks and the patrols by taking disused Inca trails and mountain passes. Quispe Pacca, a paternal but dogged former guerrillero who had been delegated to accompany Beatriz, had guided them unerringly through the harsh wilderness.

Throughout the journey, Daniel had felt that he was both a moving force and driftwood.

There had been moments of simple communion. The sight of billowing valleys from a mountain ledge; oracular sunsets on the peaks; sunrise when the dew produced fields of pearls; skies as blue as seraph's eyes; the low clouds of high altitude where llamas appeared etched on the grass; and the flowers changing colour and identity, though never their beauty, as the land rose and fell.

Whenever they had had to negotiate dangerous terrain, Daniel had felt earthed to invincible powers, a protective force around Beatriz.

On the plains and desolate stretches, he had sauntered alone, listening to Beatriz's singing. Often he had found his father, mother and sisters, Adam, his stillborn son, Teresa, Father Quintana, Jerry Rice – even Kempin – walking beside him. He had felt mournful, but pleasantly. He had understood that they had come to re-enter his life, to occupy their rightful places after their long exile. And he had taken heart; he could re-establish them only when he had found God; the fact that they were patiently following meant they had sensed forces in the air preparing to alchemise him.

Once he had actually felt his substance flaking. An earth tremor had caught them on a slope; they had barely scrambled into a cave; as he had watched the rocks hurtling past, he had felt they were layers of skin being torn off him. And he had had a glimpse of himself pared down to essence: a light from the Jewish hearth, bearing the belief that the knowledge of God was the knowledge of the sacredness of life, the knowledge that revealed God's femininity. Hence, he had understood that he had abandoned his people because he had lacked the courage to celebrate his maternal nature; that he had sublimated his love into his worship of Jesus; that, indeed, he had converted to Christianity simply to preserve, secretly, his Jewishness.

Thus, in the grace of his Jewish essence, he had also discovered his Indian identity. In a continent maddened by ethnocide and genocide, the Indians had preserved the creative imperative.

Thereafter, he had discovered other sibling identities: every faith, every race, every colour.

And, like an astronomer who predicts the existence of a planet from the position of others, he had foreseen the greater grace of the new man. Whole: the male, co-partner of God's womb; the female, co-partner of God's virility.

Naturally, he and Beatriz had bathed in love – not the old love, though there had been many echoes of that; nor love that had resurrected – since it had not died; but love that had returned from an odyssey and was counting the wounds, appraising its chances of recovery, preparing to be healed. Consequently, there had been the consummation of naked souls, particularly at nights when eating a frugal meal or sitting around a small fire or listening to the stars. They had even lain together, side by side, sleeping-bags touching.

He had had no trouble breathing.

He had not felt fear – not once!

It had taken them six days to reach Huaca.

Daniel had not expected Fuego to survive that long. Beatriz had clung to her faith.

Daniel was not unfamiliar with Huaca. He had visited it on that first journey in search of the Inca blue.

Judged by its network of lanes, stairways, plazas and fountains, Huaca had been one of the largest of the Inca cities. But what made it extraordinary was its enigmatic history. It had been a hidden city, built, in the depths of the Sacred Valley, on the summit of an old table mountain, as a centre for worship and retreat. Young, towering sugarloaf peaks encircled it like the walls of a fortress whilst their narrow canyons formed a formidable inner moat. A craggy tor, rising sharply like a unicorn from the northern face, stood as a watch-tower over the four corners of the Inca world.

Having read extensively about its wonders, having been intrigued, along with countless scholars, by its inexplicable abandonment, having vicariously rejoiced at its fabled discovery, he had longed actually to be there.

But on his earlier visit, he had felt disillusioned; so familiar with all its details, he had failed to be astonished by any of its aspects.

This time, however, he felt awed. This time he was seeing it not as the ruins of a mysterious city, but as a settlement throbbing with life, as a reincarnation of the vital metropolis it had been during its halcyon days. For this time it was full of people – tens of thousands of people. Tens of thousands of people of such harmony that Huaca's name, 'holy', had become meaningful.

Though it had been barely two weeks that the people had occupied Huaca, they had begun to restore some of the buildings with stones from the Quarter of Quarries.

The ruins of the Urban and Common Sectors, the Industrial and Intellectual Districts had been refurbished as homes for the extended families.

The huts of the Caretakers of the Terraces had been turned into domiciles for those in charge of the victuals. Mostly young and single, these campesinos had repaired all the ducts in the Irrigation Station. And, in the unflinching belief that hereafter Huaca would always be inhabited as the cradle of Manku Yupanqui's new world, they had proceeded to plough the terraces of the Agricultural Area. They had also cleared the gaols, converting them into granaries and store-rooms.

The Royal Enclave and the Palaces of the Nobles had been allocated to those in charge of the livestock. The Principal Plaza, around which these dwellings stood, alternated as milking parlour and abattoir.

The Sacred Enclave had been delegated to the artisans. These people, mainly women, manufactured all the essentials from cooking utensils to clothes.

The Temple of Illapa, the god of rain and thunder, and the Temple of the Condor had been transformed into the kitchens and the refectory.

The Temple of the Sun and the Temple of Viracocha had been renovated as infirmaries. Men and women, proficient in the healing arts, nursed all those who had been wounded at Mamasara.

The General Cemetery and the Royal Tombs had been reconsecrated for the dead.

The enclosure of the majestic Intihuatana, the post on to which, in Inca ritual, the Sun had been fastened, had been preserved as hallowed ground and appointed as Manku Yupanqui's quarters.

Daniel had spent the night of his arrival alone, on the summit of the tor which stood sentinel over Huaca.

He had taken some coca leaves to induce visions. But he had not needed to chew. So close to the moon and the stars, so frequently touched by passing clouds, he had sprouted eyes that could see.

He had seen that the moon had ingathered the countless breasts of the Divine, like light ingathers colour, and had large aureoles and long pointed nipples dripping with milk; that the stars were the goosepimples of arousal on Her Body; that the dark firmament was the Vagina, inverted like the roots of the Tree of Life, which he had to penetrate in order to be reborn; that the billowing clouds were his own testicles; that their spray was his own semen.

He had seen that his semen was virile and soft, tempestuous and tender. Because it was also so plentiful, he had felt confident that it contained the one intrepid seed he needed to impregnate God so that he could be born.

The confidence had remained with him throughout the night and, consequently, he had felt he was bearing witness to his Lover. And a premonition, as powerful as the force that had made him climb the tor, had directed his soul to the Intihuatana, always a visible presence below. There, he would shed the penis of the stillborn and find the penis that would give him life.

He had come down from the tor at sunrise.

Beatriz had been waiting for him to escort him to Fuego.

He had followed her to the Intihuatana knowing that he had only one destination left.

Carved out of a single rock the length and breadth of twelve pumas, the Intihuatana rose, in wide steps, to an immense altar. The base of the altar had been smoothed out as a ceremonial platform and was rounded up with a seat. From the altar itself rose another platform, large enough for a person to lie down. At its side, a stubby, rectangular column, its four angles facing the cardinal points, stood raised towards the sky.

From the beginning of the march, Beatriz had told Daniel, Fuego had designated the Intihuatana as the Holy of Holies. The altar was one of the very few to survive the Spanish missionaries' assaults on the Incas' faith. It would serve as the Indians' bridge between the past and the future. Here the Sun and the Christ would assume their Single Identity.

Fuego had invented a myth.

The rock of the Intihuatana was the very stone which had sealed Jesus' tomb. When, on that miraculous Sunday, Mary of Magdala had found the stone moved and had been told by the angels that the Master had ascended to Heaven, she had rushed to tell the news to Joseph of Arimathea, the man who had owned the tomb. As he had listened to Mary of Magdala, Joseph of

Arimathea had heard himself summoned to the wilderness. There, he had found Viracocha, the Creator, who had instructed him to put the stone on a ship and let the ship drift, without captain or crew, so that it could find new people to honour Jesus. The ship with the stone had sailed all the oceans before finally reaching the land of the Incas. There, Viracocha had set the stone in Huaca so that the Children of the Sun could have a place to receive their Father whenever He descended to earth.

Fuego was on the Intihuatana itself, reclining against the column as if he were the tethered sun.

Chauca, who had not left his side since their occupation of Huaca, sat on a step by his feet.

Fuego had been in a coma since Mamasara. But the previous afternoon, at the very moment when Daniel and Beatriz had reached Huaca, he had regained consciousness. Informed of their arrival, he had spent the night, as Chauca put it, nursing the few embers left to him.

Fuego was naked. The poultices covering his wounds made him look like an ancient tomb, honoured only by fallen leaves.

His soutane – Father Quintana's soutane – lay by his side, neatly folded.

He had been hit eleven times. The first bullet, according to Beatriz, had damaged the spine, paralysing him. Three of the subsequent bullets had touched, in various degrees of severity, the lungs and the liver. The rest of the wounds were less serious: four on the legs, and three on the arms. He had lost a lot of blood. Yet, in order to prevent gangrene, it was necessary to keep him bled, a procedure that required the regular application of leeches.

He had other wounds: deep scratches on the crown of the head, a hole in both feet and a deep gash on the right side of the chest. Wounds which, together with those on his palms, now formed a full set of stigmata. So that they remained fully visible, no poultices had been applied to these.

'Beautiful, aren't they – the stigmata!'

Daniel barely registered the words. From the moment he had entered the enclosure, the Intihuatana had been summoning him. But Fuego was lying there. How could he make him move? He would not share the Intihuatana with Fuego.

'Making sure they don't heal – that's the trick, Daniel.'

The words began to register. Daniel became aware of Fuego's familiar mischievous smile.

'I have had to use some very nasty herbs.'

Daniel did not know which offended him most: the levity or the smile. Paralysed or not, Fuego's body had been torn by bullets and must hurt. Why wasn't he in agony? Moreover, up there on the Intihuatana, he was impaled by the sun's first rays. Why wasn't he burning?

'Aren't you in pain? Don't saints hurt?' Daniel heard the harshness of his tone.

Beatriz, he noticed, had lowered her eyes. Displeased with him. Chauca was impassive. No doubt also displeased. 'I mean… should you be up there… exposed?'

Fuego's smile remained. 'There's no remedy to my pain. There is for yours.'

The hoarse voice was also mellifluous. Its softness reflected the softness of the body. Probably because of the way he was reclining against the Intihuatana's column, legs parted, that rapist's cock shrunken to a thin cartilage and looking more like the vaginal divide, Fuego had the appearance of a woman. Perhaps that was what he had become. Transfigured into God. Maybe he had delivered his own existence. Become father, mother, midwife, newborn all in one. He had proficiency in matters of birth. He had tried to save Beatriz's baby. He had failed only because what had been stillborn had been the baby's father.

I want my birth!

Fuego beckoned him with his head. 'Come – near me.'

Daniel could have flown. Instead, he edged forward.

'Sit next to me. I can take a long time to die – but I can't chase you. My wings are broken.'

Daniel, trembling, sat on the seat of the ceremonial platform. Instantly, the Intihuatana invaded him, making him as much a part of it as its erect, imperious column. Making him feel the column was his own penis. His trembling turned into the tremors of arousal.

'Beatriz tells me you have finished the polyptych.'

'Yes.'

'I will look at it from up there. You get free admission to everything from up there.' Faintly, Fuego chuckled at his own joke.

Let me be born!

Fuego smelled of marigolds. Daniel remembered how putrid Huaman had smelled when he had pulled him out of the *guiñero* shaft. Huaman was alive. Fuego was dying.

'Finishing the polyptych – that is a message from God. Your turn to be restored.'

A gentle cloud passed by, caressing Daniel's face.

Restore me now! Please! I am ready! Show me how!

'I knew you would come, Daniel.'

'I didn't come to see you die.'

'Beatriz told me the state you were in. I knew you would be. Now, you will help me die. And I will help you live.'

The sun began to spread into the enclosure.

Daniel's trembling increased. A child escaped through his skin and ran to a pit in a clearing in a snow-heavy forest. There he found Fuego, talking from beneath the earth. Fuego was his father, Joseph Perera, rising from the grave because he still loved Daniel, still wanted him to be born.

'I need God to live, Papa. Can you give me God?'

'Why do you think I have kept alive all this time?' Suddenly, short of breath, Fuego began to wheeze heavily.

Chauca cradled him and massaged his chest.

Beatriz stooped down and breathed into him.

Daniel did not move. He was transfixed by God's reflection.

Beatriz was God's reflection. Bending before him, her buttocks pressed against her shift. There, where her moons joined, was the imprint of the lips that would give him *his* kiss of life.

To embrace those lips. To drink her. To enter her. To receive God. To die. To be reborn. To be the New Man. To eat of the fruit of the Tree of Life.

Fuego had found some breath.

Beatriz moved away.

Chauca remained, cradling Fuego.

'Time is defeating me, *hermano*. No more small talk. Prepare yourself for God.'

Daniel sprang to his feet and stood poised to jump on to the Intihuatana. He could not germinate whilst Fuego remained on it. He was ready to kick Fuego off. And Chauca with him.

Fuego must have read his mind. 'Chauca, take me down!'

Chauca lifted him up carefully, carried him down from the Intihuatana and propped him up against the enclosure wall.

The sun, Daniel noticed, filled the space that Fuego had occupied.

'Climb the Intihuatana, Daniel!'

Daniel climbed on to the altar. He stood possessed of the rock. The wind rose.

'He is coming, *hermano*. Feel His breath.'

Daniel focused on Beatriz. She appeared to have a million breasts. '*Her* breath.'

'What?'

'*Her* breath. God is female.'

Fuego saw how desperately Daniel's soul clung to Beatriz. 'Like Beatriz is She?'

Love had become Daniel's skin. 'They could be twins.'

'You want them both?'

Daniel saw two butterflies, blue-grey like the stones of Huaca. For a while, they fluttered salaciously over Beatriz's face. 'Yes. Both their Selves.'

'You want them as One?'

The butterflies alighted on Beatriz's head and fanned their wings to drink the rays of the sun. 'I want them as One.'

Fuego managed to draw some breath. 'Undress then!'

Daniel kicked off his shoes, tore off his socks and slipped out of his shirt, trousers and underwear.

Fuego fixed his eyes on him. 'Wanting God, *hermano*, is good. But it is not enough. To embrace Her, you have to become *more* of what you really are.'

Daniel lost sight of the sun. Nor could he see Beatriz. He was at one with the Intihuatana, naked and erect on it, but he had also been reduced to a pollen grain which a bee had carelessly dropped and which the wind had carried away to the desert. A lost seed.

He groaned. 'How? I am stillborn.'

'Be reborn. A new man. Fearless. *More* of what you really are. *More* of what you imagined you could be. Do you accept?'

The sun reappeared. Beatriz re-emerged with her million breasts. The butterflies still crowned her head.

'I accept!'

Fuego nodded at Chauca. Chauca lifted him up so that he could address Daniel directly.

'This is what you will do, *hermano*. The revolution can succeed. The people will keep marching. More and more will join. But only if Manku Yupanqui leads them. You will be the new Manku Yupanqui.'

Darkness descended again. The wind, Daniel felt, was plummeting the Intihuatana into the earth's deepest tomb.

'I don't understand!'

'You are the right person. A sinner hungry for God – the very dough for Manku Yupanqui!'

Daniel sifted the air in search of reason. 'I don't understand. Why not Chauca?'

'Chauca is not ready yet. He has abandoned his gun, but he still yearns for it. Maybe after you.'

Rats penetrated the darkness. 'After me?'

'If you die.'

The rats were dancing and grinning. 'If I die?'

'It is very likely.'

Daniel recognised the rats. Fuego. Beatriz. Chauca. His father. His mother.

His sisters. Adam, his stillborn son. Teresa. Father Quintana. Jerry Rice. 'You tricked me! All of you! You promised me God!'

'Become Manku Yupanqui! You will embrace God!'

Daniel collapsed on to the rock. He was not destined to have God.

He thought of his son. And, for the first time, felt that poor baby's agony. Stillborn, unwanted by his father. The stillborn father, unwanted by God.

'Are you afraid, Daniel?'

'No.'

'Then what is the problem?'

'Destiny.'

'No such thing.'

Daniel began to laugh. 'You don't understand! I have no fear. I have nothing to fear. Not even damnation – because that's been decided.'

'Take the soutane!'

Daniel burrowed into the darkness. 'Let me go, Oseas. I'm tired – finished. You've got your dying to do. Die!'

'Beatriz, give him the soutane!'

Beatriz climbed on to the Intihuatana and picked up the soutane. She stood in front of Daniel and held the soutane to him.

Daniel, prostrate on the rock, stared at her legs. Powerful legs! Legs that were deep in the folds of the sky. The legs of the Tree of Life. So real – yet so beyond reach.

Fuego's voice came on a ray of the sun. 'Put it on! God is in the soutane!'

Daniel began to shake. 'No!'

'Put it on! What have you got to lose?'

Daniel began to weep. 'It's a trick! You'll trick me again!'

Fuego's voice spilled over him in spurts. 'God is a woman! And She wants you! God is beautiful – like Beatriz! Motherly – like Pachamama! God wants you! Put it on!'

Fuego's commandments were echoing from every direction. Daniel clung to the Intihuatana's column and pulled himself to his feet. His erection was seeking life.

'Put it on!'

He stared at the soutane. There were moons on it. And stars. And a vast hole. And an endless stream of clouds.

'Put it on!'

He touched the soutane. It was warm and moist and it rippled like Beatriz's flesh.

'Put it on!'

He took the soutane from her.

God smiled with Her million eyes. Or was it Beatriz?

'Put it on!'

He unfolded the soutane.

He felt his blood rise, his body rise. He felt inverted, his feet planted in the firmament, his hair deep in the earth. He shouted. 'Here I am, God! Here I am, Beatriz!'

God took off Her shift. Or was it Beatriz?

'Put it on!'

Daniel lifted the soutane.

God touched him with Her million breasts, kissed him with Her million aureoles, fed him milk from Her million nipples. Or was it Beatriz?

'Put it on!'

Daniel lowered the soutane over his head.

God rubbed him with Her million bellies! Entwined him with Her million legs. Or was it Beatriz?

'Put it on! Let Her save you! Put it on! Save Her!'

Daniel gave out a primeval roar.

God kissed him with a million mouths. Or was it Beatriz?

'Put it on!'

Daniel entered the soutane.

God took him into Her million orifices.

But...

No birth!

His head could not pass through.

A noose... his arm or his leg or Her arm or Her leg was twisting round his throat.

He was suffocating before he could breathe.

He screamed. 'I will be stillborn!'

'Move your head!'

He moved his head. It cleared the noose. He felt the softness of the opening. But it remained closed. The darkness continued.

'I am stuck!'

'Open it up!'

He parted God's million legs. Or were they Beatriz's?

'Now push!'

He pushed against God. Or was it Beatriz?

'Push!'

He reached the opening. He felt the endless depth that was inside and outside.

'Be born!'

He felt his head emerge. He became a particle in a fountain. But it was his whole being that was flowing.

He roamed deep in God's garden and watered its soft earth and its beautiful flowers. He slithered through God's million vaginas. They watched his progress lovingly.

'Push!'

He crawled through God's legs. Or were they Beatriz's?

His feet bathed in Her fluids. His mouth suckled from Her nipples. His head rested on buttocks as soft as pillows.

'Push!'

And he was clear.

But he still could not breathe.

'I can't breathe!'

God – or was it Beatriz – slapped his buttocks.

It did not help.

'I am dying in my birth!'

God – or was it Beatriz – picked him up by his feet and swung him in a circle as if he were a new-born lamb with fluid in its lungs.

Fuego's voice, with the thunderous authority of a completed life summoning the new, commanded. 'Daniel, be born!'

God – or was it Beatriz – was still rotating him in the air.

Then finally...

Breath!

He erupted. Fully alive. Simultaneously draining all his life. In the throes of orgasm. Ejaculating oceans.

He roared.

He wept.

Snug between Beatriz's legs! Or was it God's?

Born! Finally born!

He was wearing the soutane.

Beatriz – or was it God – was holding his hand.

Flowers were growing from the bullet holes in the soutane.

And inside the soutane, his head lay on God's million breasts which were all Beatriz's.

Reborn!

He was the New Man.

He had given Beatriz a baby.

He was God's – and Beatriz's – baby.

He was Manku Yupanqui.

He was more, *much* more than he really was.

He was Beatriz's lover.

Together they would spread their roots in the air and their branches in the earth.

And they would fruit.

And the people would see they were of the Tree of Life.

And the people would eat them.

70
Every tear reaches its stream

Chauca was building a mound on the rim of the crater.

Daniel waited, holding Fuego in his arms. For ten days, he and Chauca had shared the carrying. He had conceived so much love for that weightless, child's body. His father had become his son.

Fuego's eyes, still meteor-bright, scanned the land. The summit of this volcano, he had told them, was the highest point in all Tahuantinsuyo; from here, an Inca could see every foot-length of the four corners of his realm; at this spot, Teresa and Manku Yupanqui had married. It was only right, therefore, that he should want to come here at the end of his earthly days.

Beatriz hummed one of her songs.

Chauca finished building the mound.

Daniel carried Fuego to the crater.

The lava sent up fresh smoke.

The sun began its descent.

The snow started to fall.

The winds rose.

Daniel set Fuego down, positioning him to sit with his back against the mound.

Fuego lifted his arms. The will that had kept him alive all this time had also, this morning, returned the use of his limbs.

Chauca went to him and they embraced.

Beatriz went to him and they embraced.

Daniel went to him. Fuego seized his hands.

After they had embraced, Fuego, still clinging to Daniel's hands, shouted. 'Chauca! Who is this man?'

Chauca looked at Daniel and saw a hero. 'Manku Yupanqui, *compadre.*'

'Beatriz! Who is this man?'

Beatriz looked at Daniel and saw a saviour. 'Manku Yupanqui, *compadre.*'

'Daniel! Who are you?'

'Manku Yupanqui, *hermano.*'

Fuego released Daniel. 'Look at your hands.'

Daniel stared at his palms. They were branded with the stigmata. He was not surprised. What else for a man who had conquered self and fear, who had found God, who had become more, much more than he really was?

And if that was the only belief left to him – that was as it should be.

'Leave me now.'

Solemnly they walked away.

Beatriz burst into the last stanza of the song she had been humming.

Mother
close my eyes
open your flesh
take me in

As they began their descent, they looked back.

Fuego had vanished.

Chauca pointed at the lava spluttering from the crater. 'He has become fire.'

Beatriz gazed at the snowflakes gathering on her hands. 'He has become water.'

Daniel stared at the last of the light on the horizon. 'He has flown to the sun.'

71

It will rain blood tomorrow, the tears will be capable of forming fog, vapour, rivers until the eyes melt

It will be the biggest slaughter since the gas chambers, General Angelito had predicted.

It will be like the Battle of Junín, Gaspar de Villasante y Córdoba had declared with amusement. But we won't get any glory because these damned Indios won't fight, he had added regretfully.

Williston had not been fooled by their bombast. Both Angelito and Gaspar were frightened. Witness how, in the deep of the night, only a few hours away from the battle that should be a straightforward massacre, they were cooped up in their tents, going over their maps with eyes that were too haunted to sleep.

Williston could not sleep either and sat at his tent – outside – also worrying – wondering what would happen tomorrow – today.

The Altiplano was quiet, seemingly dead. But he knew it was beating menacingly as one massive heart, and he could not hear it.

What was the power out there? It was – no question about it – mightier than Satan's. Indeed, it had the feel of the power of the Lord. But how could it be?

The engagement should be a wipe-out. Angelito and Gaspar had assembled a massive force: 20,000 men; 100 tanks; 30 pieces of artillery; and 10 helicopter gunships on stand-by. Moreover, they had an ideal battlefield: a vast plain where tanks could run riot and shells and bullets fly without having to turn corners.

And yet...

According to Military Intelligence, the marchers now numbered over three hundred thousand. At least a hundred thousand of those had joined up during the weeks the marchers had paused at Huaca after the engagement at Mamasara. They had simply arrived from all over the country, even from the cities. The rest had joined up in the past month when the people, resuming the march, had crossed, undetectably as ever, the lower highlands of the Eastern Cordilleras.

Now, they had appeared at the Altiplano and were camping at the boundaries of the plains like holiday-makers around a popular lake. And all the plains campesinos – at least two hundred thousand of them behind the Army's lines – waited to join them. Also waiting to join were the hundreds and thousands of campesinos of the Western Cordilleras where, Manku Yupanqui had announced, they would be marching next.

Thus, it was imperative they were stopped now. Here, the people had to come to their senses.

What power was out there that seemed to match the power of the Lord?

Manku Yupanqui, sure.

But who was Manku Yupanqui?

Not Fuego. Fuego had died.

One of the advantages – so far, the only advantage – that the Army had had over the marchers in this terrifying state of affairs had been the ease with which it had infiltrated agents into Huaca. They had gone in and out as they had pleased; no one had ever challenged them.

And they had confirmed, repeatedly, that Fuego, having been mortally wounded at Mamasara, had been nursed for some days and then had disappeared – presumed secretly buried.

Was Manku Yupanqui, then, the restorer, Daniel Brac?

The agents had reported that a day or so before Fuego's disappearance, Beatriz Santillan had brought a gringo to meet Fuego. The gringo's description had fitted Brac's, and his arrival in Huaca had corresponded with the time when Brac had mysteriously vanished. Circumstantial evidence pointing at the friendship that had existed between Fuego and Brac, and at the fact that Brac, having just finished restoring the polyptych, had not bothered either to acknowledge the acclaim he was getting, or collect the rest of his fee – a considerable sum – had further supported the possibility.

But how could Brac – a paint-pusher, a Jew, a nonentity – take on Manku Yupanqui's mantle? How could the Indios accept him?

Or were there many Manku Yupanquis? Did the people take turns at being Manku Yupanqui? For the agents had also reported that when the marchers had left Huaca, many of them were wearing a habit identical to the bullet-riddled soutane which Fuego had adopted as Manku Yupanqui's vestment.

But thousands of Manku Yupanquis – was that possible?

If it was, then there was every reason to be haunted.

It meant that here was a disease that threatened the Lord's immunity, that produced a Jesus-syndrome indistinguishable from true Christian devotion. Even more frightening, it meant that this disease could sweep all before it; destroy civilisation.

Indeed, there were already signs of it getting out of control.

There had been a number of soldiers, even officers, who, having caught sight of the marchers, had reversed their forage caps and attempted to desert. Naturally, they had been shot. But that had not deterred other conscripts from attempting to spike the mortars and howitzers. And though they, too, had been executed, might there not be other deserters and saboteurs?

One had to consider that most of the soldiers were campesinos themselves. One had also to bear in mind that it was virtually impossible to train a conscript to wade knee-deep in blood day after day. Indeed, one should remember that, at Mamasara, some of the recruits had failed to display that sort of crusaders' zeal and had joined the people. Finally, one should ask the question: what if, in the heat of the battle, some soldiers, sickened by the carnage, turned their guns against their officers?

Williston stared into the distance.

Fear, too, was contagious, and here he was biting his nails like Angelito and Gaspar.

And suppressing, suppressing that one heretical thought.

What if this Jesus-syndrome was not a disease, but the real thing?

And if it was what was he doing trying to destroy it? He loved Jesus! So much so, he even envied these damned Indios! So much so, part of him wanted to run to them, join them, be cleansed forever with them!

No! No! This was confusion! Confusion!

Tomorrow – today – as sure as the Lord made green apples, the Manku Yupanqui plague would be stamped out – for ever!

The world could not have changed overnight.

72
Everything swarmed behind the august chieftain, and when he advanced darkness, sands, forests, lands, unanimous bonfires, hurricanes, phosphoric apparitions of pumas advanced with him

The first ray of the sun appeared on the horizon.
  Manku Yupanqui, who was once known as Daniel Brac, sang.

Now that a man no longer feels the air
enfolding him
like his woman

His wife, Teresa Ayala, who was once known as Beatriz Santillan, sang.

Now that a woman no longer feels the earth
smiling in her womb
like a flower

A boy from Pintoyaku, Adam Joseph Eusebio Jerry Oseas, who was once known as Pillpe and whom Manku Yupanqui had adopted, sang.

Now that a child no longer feels the water
rocking him
like a lullaby

The ever loyal lieutenant, Chauca, who was always known as Chauca, sang.

Now that the people no longer feel the fire
quickening their limbs
like love

And the four sang together.

We know
life has lost
its salt

And the people joined in the singing.

We know, too,
dear God,
You do not want us to die
unsalted

The sun's arc crowned the eastern peaks that towered over the Altiplano.
Manku Yupanqui began to march.

Teresa, Chauca and Adam Joseph Eusebio Jerry Oseas took their positions by his side.

And the people followed, singing.

So here we are
spreading ourselves
on
the wind
the rock
the spring
the sun

Their voices engulfed the Altiplano.

The Army that was spread across the plains creaked at its seams like a city caught in an earthquake.

The people marched from every direction.

Manku Yupanqui felt prodigious; filled not just with the strength of the Jew, the Christian, the Indian, but with the strength of all men.

480

With the strength of the New Man.
The people sang louder.

when we rise again
tomorrow

The first shell exploded in their midst.
The people continued marching and singing.

we shall rise
as
breath
land
river
hearth

More shells exploded.

EPILOGUE

The slave with neither voice nor mouth, with endless suffering, became a name, called himself people

Dear Dexter,

You must have despaired of ever receiving this report. I've been meaning to file it for a long time. I couldn't. I don't know why. Maybe because shunting to so many places to get the full picture you wanted, I've lost track of time and place. How long is it? A month? two months? since you sent me here?

Anyway, I'm back in La Merced and more or less in harness. So to business.

First: Luke Williston. The event itself is quite clear. I found some footage of his 'charge' (as Gaspar de Villasante y Córdoba calls it) in a pile of confiscated newsreel – and this I enclose. As you will see, Williston broke rank suddenly, in the middle of an engagement in the Western Cordilleras, and ran towards the marching Indians. Note his state: like a rogue elephant. You can see him throwing away the toilet bag he always carried and tearing off his clothes. Note also that he is mouthing our Saviour's name. Those are the facts. But I find it impossible to evaluate whether Williston ran at the enemy in order to attack or whether he felt compelled to join them.

Nor can I determine what happened to him after that. I know for sure that General Angelito, thinking Williston was deserting, ordered his men to shoot him down. I have testimonies of a number of soldiers who saw him fall. But there are also some who claim they saw him get up and reach the Indians. One thing is certain. His body was not found. So, if Williston was killed, the Indians obviously picked him up as one of their dead. If he was not killed, he joined them. My guess is that he is now one of them – like so many Moral Crusade missionaries have become. I must confess, at times, I myself have been tempted to join them, too.

Now, for the rest.

The people are still marching. They are, in fact, approaching the capital.

They've been mowed down countless times. Yet, after each bloodbath, more have joined. The cities are practically empty. You can drive from one end of La Merced to the other without coming across another motorist.

There is still an army. But only of sorts. Most of the conscripts have dropped guns and joined the people. Fortunately, General Angelito and, particularly, Gaspar de Villasante y Córdoba, as acting President since the Junta decamped to the US, have been towers of strength. They do a fine job inducting the mercenaries you and New Order are recruiting into the Air Force and the Armoured Corps. These units strike as hard as improvisation permits. I say improvisation because virtually all fighter planes and helicopter gunships are either out of action or have become flying coffins – they've been damaged or sabotaged by ground personnel, most of whom have deserted. Ditto the tanks and the APCs. Fuel is scarce – most of the dumps have been flooded with impurities, invariably sewage. Ammunition is low, too – thousands of tons now lie at the bottom of the sea.

Manku Yupanqui is still around – though God only knows whether he is still that Jew, Daniel Brac. I've heard rumours that it's Chauca. Other rumours that it's Quispe or Antonio or Teofilo or Romero or Juan. It might be Luke Williston. Or Jesus Christ himself, for all we'll ever know.

This all sounds very bewildering. It is.

Conceivably the tide can be turned. My advice to you is to get Washington to send in the Marines. I realise the US will have a hell of a job justifying that to the world. And I'm damned if I know how you can convince your ordinary American and all those wet liberals in the Administration. But you've got to do it.

If you can do that, can you also find a bomb that defoliates an idea and kills the soul. That, basically, is what is needed.

Yours,

Bill

PS There is a new version of the Manku Yupanqui legend. Somebody has actually printed it. I enclose a copy.

Once there lived a man. His name was Manku Yupanqui, meaning 'rich in all virtues'. It was a fitting name. For Manku Yupanqui devoted his life to finding that ray of the sun which God had misplaced whilst creating the night.

He travelled far and wide. He crossed rivers and oceans, deserts and plains. He climbed to the roofs of the world and he burrowed into its bowels.

When he was forty times forty years old, he came upon a mountain in the Andes.

This mountain – which is called Huaca – shed from its summit an unearthly light.

Manku Yupanqui climbed the mountain.

The light, he discovered, was a revolving sword guarding the most beautiful woman in all Creation.

This woman was Pachamama.

'What are you doing here?' Pachamama asked.

'I am looking for the sun's missing ray,' replied Manku Yupanqui.

'Do you know what it looks like?' asked Pachamama.

'Yes. It is shaped like an egg,' replied Manku Yupanqui.

This surprised Pachamama, for it was the correct answer. 'How did you know?' she asked.

'I have always known it,' replied Manku Yupanqui.

Pachamama was even more impressed by this extraordinary man. 'I know where it is,' she said. 'I hid it.'

Manku Yupanqui was surprised. 'Why should you hide it?' he asked.

'Because I was angry with God. He should not have misplaced it,' Pachamama said.

'Where did you hide it?' asked Manku Yupanqui.

Pachamama opened her legs and bared her garden. 'In my womb,' she said, and looked at him uncertainly. 'Do you still want it?'

'Yes.'

'Know this then. To claim it you must answer three questions.'

Manku Yupanqui smiled. 'I am good at answering questions.'

'Only I must warn you. If you fail, you will die. The revolving sword will cut off your head.'

'Death is a lie,' declared Manku Yupanqui. 'Proceed.'

'What is love?' asked Pachamama.

'That which is contained in the missing ray,' answered Manku Yupanqui without hesitation.

'Correct!' shouted Pachamama. 'What is hate?'

'That which will be healed by the missing ray,' replied Manku Yupanqui, again without hesitation.

'Correct again!' shouted Pachamama. 'The third question is the most

· *difficult. Tell me not to ask it. Then you can go – with your head on your shoulders.'*

'Ask!' thundered Manku Yupanqui.

'What is fear?' asked Pachamama mournfully, certain that he would give the wrong answer and die.

Manku Yupanqui was perplexed.

'You have to answer,' said Pachamama, sadly.

Resignedly, Manku Yupanqui bared his neck to the burning sword. 'Alas, that is the one thing I have never known.'

'That's the answer!' shouted Pachamama, exultantly.

The burning sword disintegrated.

Pachamama held him to her breasts. 'You are the awaited one!'

They became man and wife.

Thus Manku Yupanqui fertilised the egg which was the sun's missing ray and which, as we all know now, was in reality the people.

And thus the New Man was born.

And the world was changed.

Sources

All chapter headings are quotations from the works of Pablo Neruda. The individual poems and the collections in which they appear are listed below in order of first Spanish publication.

'Viejo ciego, llorabas/Olld Blind Man, You Were Crying', 'Oración/Orison' and 'Agua dormida/Sleeping Water' from *Crepusculario/Crepuscular* (Editorial Seix Barral, SA, Barcelona, 1980)

'El amor perdido/The Lost Love' and 'Divinización/Glorification" from *El río invisible/The Invisible River* (Editorial Seix Barral, SA, Barcelona, 1980)

'Cuerpo de mujer/Body of Woman', 'Juegas todos los dias/ Every Day You Play' and 'En mi cielo al crepúsculo/In My Sky at Twilight' from *Veinte poemas de amor y una canción desesperada/ Twenty Love Poems and a Song of Despair* (Bilingual edition, English translation by W. S. Merwin, Jonathan Cape, 1981)

'Debil del alba/The Dawn's Debility', 'Fantasma/Phantom', 'Comunicaciones desmentidas/Refuted Communications', 'El joven monarca/The Young Monarch', 'Sólo la muerte/Only Death', 'La calle destruida/The Destroyed Street', 'El abandonado/The Abandoned', 'Naciendo En Los Bosques/Born in the Woods', 'Las furias y las penas/The Furies and the Sorrows' and 'España en el corazón/ Spain in the Heart' from *Residencia en la tierra (1), Residencia En la tierra (2), Tercera residencia/Residence on Earth (1), Residence on Earth (2), Residence on Earth (3)* (Bilingual edition, English translation by Donald D. Walsh, Souvenir Press (E&A) Ltd, 1976)

'Alturas de Macchu Picchu/Heights of Macchu Picchu', 'Cortésl Cortez', 'Cita de cuervos/Appointment with Crows', 'Llega al Pacifico/Arrives to the Pacific', 'Los Libertadores/The Liberators', 'La guerra patria/The War for the Country', 'El empalado/The Impaled', 'San Martin (1810)/San Martin (1810)', 'Mina (1817)/

Mina (1817)', 'Castro Alves del Brasil/Castro Alves of Brasil', 'Marti (1890)/Marti (1890)', 'A Emiliano Zapata con música de Tata Nacho/To Emiliano Zapata with Music from Tata Nacho', 'Recabarren (1921)/Recabarren (1921)', 'Los Verdugos/ The Executioners', 'Elección en Chimbarongo (1947)/Election in Chimbarongo' (1947), 'Los Siúticos/The Affected' and 'Las tierras y los hombres/The Lands and the Peoples' from *Canto General/General Song* (Editorial Seix Barral, SA, Barcelona, 1978)

'Las Vidas/Lives', 'El amor del soldado/The Soldier's Love', 'La Muerta/The Dead Woman', 'Epitalamio/Epithalamium' and 'La carta en el camino/The Letter on the Road' from *Los verses del capitán/The Captain's Verses* (Bilingual edition, English translation by Donald D. Walsh, New Directions Publishing Corporation, New York, 1972)

'Soliloquio en las tinieblas/Soliloquy at Twilight', 'No me pregunten/Don't Ask Me', 'Balada/Ballad', 'Sonata con algunos Piños/Sonata with Some Pine Trees' and 'Testamento de otoño/ Autumn Testament' from *Extravagario/Extravagaria* (Bilingual edition, English translation by Alastair Reid, Jonathan Cape, 1972)

'La Palabra/The Word', 'Adioses/Goodbyes' and 'A E.S.S./To E.S.S.' in *Plenos poderes/Fully Empowered* (Bilingual edition, English translation by Alastair Reid, Souvenir Press (E&A) Ltd, 1976)

'La tierra austral/The Land of the South', 'La Injusticia/The Injustice', 'Las Supersticiones/The Superstitions', 'Amores: Terusa (1)/Loves: Terusa (1)', 'Religión en el este/Religion in the East', 'Aquella Luz/That Light', 'Aquellas vidas/Those Lives', 'El fuego cruel/The Cruel Fire', 'Recuerdo el este/I Remember the East', 'La hermana Cordillera/The Sister Cordillera', 'Amores: Delia (2)/Loves: Delia (2)', 'Oh Tierra, espérame/Oh, Earth, Wait For Me', 'El Episodio/The Episode', 'La Bondad Escondida/Hidden Goodness' and 'El future es espacio/The Future Is Space' from *Memorial de Isla Negra/Isla Negra* (Bilingual edition, English translation by Alastair Reid, Souvenir Press (E&A) Ltd, 1982)

The majority of the quotations have been translated by myself (Moris Farhi). The rest are from the excellent translations by the authors listed above, namely, W. S. Merwin, Donald D. Walsh and Alastair Reid. With regards to these last, preferring, in some instances, a literal rendition, I have made minor changes.

The Inca masque in Chapter 33 is a free adaptation of *Tragedia del fin de Atawallpa*, translated from the Quechua with an Introduction by Jesus Lara and published in Cochabamba, 1957 (quoted in *The Vision of the Vanquished* by Nathan Wachtel, Harvester Press, 1977).